ML

ONE BLOOD

QWANTU AMARU

The Pantheon Collective (TPC)

www.pantheoncollective.com

The Pantheon Collective (TPC)
P.O. Box 799
Santa Cruz, CA 95061

ISBN: 978-0-9827193-6-7 (Paperback)
ISBN: 978-0-9827193-7-4 (Ebook)

Printed in United States of America

Cover: Designed by Cathi Stevenson, Book Cover Express
Interior: Designed by Stephanie Casher

To Mom.

You are my inspiration. Everything I am I owe to you.

PROLOGUE

1963
New Orleans, LA

During the day, New Orleans' most famous neighborhood was a tribute to architectural and cultural homogeneity. At night, the French Quarter's multicultural legacy blurred into an unrecognizable labyrinth; especially in the eyes of the drunk and desperate.

At the moment, Joseph Lafitte was both.

Joseph careened down the dark alley and absentmindedly brushed at the dried blood beneath his nose with his free hand. His tailor-made shirt and pants were drenched with sweat and felt sizes smaller. He was overcome with the sensation that he was running in place, even though he was moving forward at a brisk pace. Because he was paying more attention to what was behind him rather than what was in front of him, Joseph tripped over a carton some careless individual had placed in his path.

Upon impact with the concrete his cheek flayed open, but he barely felt the sting as his priceless nickel and gold plated antique Colt Navy Revolver clattered away into the darkness, out of reach. Even now, breathing as harshly as he was, he could hear someone behind him. Somehow they managed to stay just out of the range of his sight, but within earshot.

It was the ideal moment for them to pounce, but Joseph would not give in so easily. He pushed himself to his feet, his eyes like twin brooms sweeping the ground for his weapon. He located it near a dilapidated doorway. Clutching it once again, he felt some semblance of self-control return.

Until his dead wife called his name.

"Joseph? Joseph, where are you?"

That was all the motivation he needed. He broke into a full gallop but couldn't outrun what he'd seen back at the hotel, or what he'd just heard.

They are toying with me. Trying to make me doubt my own mind.

This *was* New Orleans after all. A place with a well-documented history of trickery and alchemic manipulation. He must have drank or eaten something laced with some devilish hallucinogen. For all he knew, his own son—Randy—had given it to him.

Randy still blamed Joseph for the car wreck that took his mother's life. Joseph had noted the murderous hue in Randy's eyes after Rita's funeral, and even though Joseph explained that it was an accident, he knew Randy would never forgive him.

Was this Randy trying to get some sort of revenge?

It didn't matter. Randy was weak—always had been and always would be. As an only child, he grew up to be softer than cotton—Rita's doing by babying and spoiling the boy.

Have I underestimated my son?

This thought, along with his first glimpse of light in quite some time, simultaneously assaulted him.

Where am I? And why haven't they caught up to me yet?

Maybe they want *me to go this way.*

Joseph glanced down at the revolver that had once been carried by the great Robert E. Lee. He'd show them who had the upper hand; if Randy was behind this, he would soon be joining his mother.

Rather than heading toward the light, Joseph turned left down another dark alleyway. The façade of the building was damp to the touch. Other than his troubled footfalls, there was no sound. Who knew a city nearly bursting at the seams with music could be this eerily silent?

Joseph used the quiet to collect his thoughts.

He'd spent that afternoon as he spent most Saturdays, sipping bourbon and talking shop with other New Orleans power brokers inside the private room in Commander's Palace. He knew something was wrong as soon as Randy appeared at the doorway, motioning to him.

"We have to leave New Orleans right now, Father," Randy said in a hushed tone as Joseph entered the hallway.

"What are you talking about, Boy, and why are you whispering?" Joseph replied, a little louder than he needed to.

Randy jerked Joseph's arm in the direction of the exit, his eyes pleading. "Something bad is going to happen if we don't leave here right away."

"No, Son," Joseph said. "Something bad is going to happen if you don't remove yourself from my sight this instant!"

And that had been the end of it. Randy left, looking back only once, as if to say, *Don't say I didn't try to warn you.*

Joseph returned to his drinks and colleagues. Afterward, he went downtown for a little afternoon rendezvous with a beautiful Creole whore. She came as a recommendation from his regular mistress, Claudette, who was on her cycle, and the girl certainly fit the bill.

He made it back to the hotel just as the sun set and settled down for a drink or three after taking a steaming hot shower. In the comfort of his armchair, in the privacy of his suite, his thoughts returned to Randy. It was Randy's eighteenth birthday and the boy had been acting oddly ever since he'd arrived in New Orleans two days earlier. In truth, he'd been acting strangely much longer than that.

Joseph would never forget the revulsion he'd experienced when the maid in their Lake City mansion had shown him the pile of bloody rags at the bottom of Randy's hamper. That disgust tripled once he found out the source of the blood. One night, Joseph waited until Randy exited the bath. The raw pink and black slashes across Randy's forearms, thighs, chest, and abdomen were all the evidence he needed. Apparently Randy had taken to cutting himself in the wake of his mother's death.

Randy was barely a teenager and there was only one thing Joseph could think to do to keep from locking the boy up in a sanitarium. He sent him away to a French boarding school and commissioned some distant relatives to keep an eye on him until he graduated. If he survived that long.

This weekend was supposed to be a celebration of sorts. Randy had returned from France a distinguished young man, and Joseph was ready to bury the hatchet.

But what if Randy doesn't want it buried? What if he wants my entombment and has been patiently waiting all these years to get his revenge?

Joseph grabbed hold of a lamppost to steady himself. A statue of a man on a horse loomed over him. His feet had brought him to Jackson Square.

Surely, nothing bad can get me here, right?

He'd believed the same to be true of his hotel room and that had definitely proven to be false.

Joseph had been cleaning his prized revolver before sleep overtook him. The sound of the door opening brought him back to consciousness. Even though all the lights were still on, his bleary eyes could barely make out the two figures—a young black male and white female—standing in his doorway.

Joseph sat up in his seat. "Who are you? And what the hell are you doing in my room?" His hand quickly found the revolver on the table next to him.

The man and woman looked at each other and Joseph heard a deep male voice in his head say, "Don't worry, Joseph. It will be ova' soon."

He felt the voice's vibrations in his teeth and jumped to his feet. The young woman reached out to him and he heard her voice in his mind as well. "Don't fight us, Joseph. It is so much better if you don't resist."

Joseph felt wetness below his nose and when his hand came up blood red, he bolted around the woman, out of his room, and out of the hotel.

Now he stood in the shadow of Andrew Jackson's immortal statue, exhausted and nearing the end of rationality. A sudden thought occurred to him.

Maybe this is all a nightmare. Maybe I'm still sitting in my chair snoring.

He latched onto the idea. Hadn't he heard recently that the best way to wake from a nightmare was to kill yourself?

Where did I hear that?

Ah yes, now he remembered. The Creole whore had mentioned her grandmother's secret to waking from a bad dream.

What an odd coincidence…

Joseph stared down at the revolver as if it were some magic talisman. If this were a dream, it was the most vivid of his life. He could feel the breeze from the Mississippi River, the cold bronze of the statue beneath his hand, his sweaty palm wrapped around the hilt of the gun. And he could hear footsteps nearing.

Rita's voice rang out across the square. "Joseph, I'm here to bring you home."

His mind showed him an image of what Rita must look like after six years underground. He hadn't cried at her funeral, but petrified tears streaked down his face as he gritted his teeth.

I have to wake from this dream!

The footsteps were getting louder and closer. He didn't have much time. To offset his fear and still his shaking hand, he thought of how good it would feel to wake up from this nightmare. He put the gun in his mouth, tasting the salty metallic flavor of the barrel as his mouth filled with saliva.

God, this feels real.

But he knew it wasn't. He attempted to gaze at the statue of Andrew Jackson riding high on his horse. The statue was gone. As was the rest of Jackson Square. It had been supplanted by that damnable live oak tree in front of his Lake City mansion. He should have chopped that thing down long ago.

Joseph let out an audible sigh of relief.

It is a dream after all.

"It's time, Joseph," Rita whispered in his ear.

Knowing what had to be done, Joseph squeezed the trigger.

PART I: REVENGE

"If you cannot get rid of the family skeleton, you may as well make it dance."

~George Bernard Shaw

CHAPTER ONE

September 27, 2002
Friday
Baton Rouge, LA

The Governor's workspace was modeled after the Oval Office. A brazen blue and gold state seal was embedded in the center of the wall, behind an ornate mahogany desk. The words UNION, JUSTICE, CONFIDENCE surrounded a spread-winged pelican looking down on three hungry chicks. Below it, on top of a mahogany credenza, prized pictures depicted Louisiana's fifty-third Governor, Randy A. Lafitte, holding court with the likes of sitting President George W. Bush and his own personal mentor and confidante, David Duke.

Randy sat behind his desk, hunched over two satellite images depicting the path of what he hoped was the last hurricane of the season. According to these snapshots, the storm would make landfall somewhere between Mississippi and Texas in the next three days. Having survived innumerable hurricanes during the past eight years in office, he knew the playbook well. Randy made a mental note to set up a meeting with the Federal Emergency Management Agency, and then buzzed his secretary.

"Robin, get me fifteen minutes with the President. If his people give you any flack, remind them that he still owes me dinner for losing that bet."

"Yes sir."

While hanging up, he caught his reflection in the window. Sometimes Randy didn't even recognize the elder statesman staring back at him. He smiled at the slightly distorted image. His hazel eyes brimmed with intellect and empathy. His laser-whitened teeth were attractive and reassuring. His square jaw and deep dimples, which his first campaign manager had often referred to as '*the lady-vote getters*,' were working their collective mojo.

And underneath the polish remained a hint of the young rabble-rouser he'd begrudgingly outgrown.

Underestimated from day one.

Randy was counting on that underestimation as his second and final term as governor drew to a close. He didn't possess his late father's intimidating persona, booming voice, or piercing blue eyes, but that didn't stop him from becoming the youngest man in the history of the state to hold a mayorship, and at fifty-seven he believed he had a strong chance of succeeding George W. Bush when he bowed out in 2008. The tragic events of September 11th would guarantee the need for strong, yet charismatic leadership in this country and Randy was just the man for the job.

But that was still six years away.

He checked the time. 4:20 p.m. His daughter, Karen, should be finishing up her birthday spa appointment and heading home, where a gleaming white Mercedes SLK roadster wrapped in a bright red bow sat in the driveway waiting. He wanted to make sure her eighteenth birthday was the best one yet—after all, you only turn eighteen once.

Randy did not have good luck when it came to eighteenth birthdays. Randy's father, Joseph, died just three days after Randy turned eighteen and then ten years ago, his son Kristopher was killed three days after his eighteenth birthday by a thug gangbanger named Lincoln Baker.

The papers sure had a field day with that one.

They called Randy the ultimate survivor, captioned under horrible headshots of his deceased mother, father, and son. They rehashed all the terrible memories Randy had tried so desperately to banish into the darkness. It was no wonder he became so sick.

Brain cancer was the diagnosis. It was 1994. His first term as governor was barely a month old when a team of neurological oncologists informed him that his odds of making it through the tumor-removal procedure were both "one in ten million" and his "only hope". Without surgery, he'd be dead in six months. Randy replied, "hope is not a strategy," and opted instead for an experimental radiation therapy. A year later, he was declared cancer free. But his hair never grew back; a small price to pay.

The Ultimate Survivor became his mantra and he rode it all the way to a landslide second gubernatorial term in 1998, only to nearly lose it all when a radical militant organization called the Black Mob placed bombs in the bowels of the Isle of Capri Riverboat where Randy was scheduled to deliver his acceptance speech. Ironically, he owed his life to his daughter. Karen had overdosed earlier that day on Coral's painkillers in a near-successful suicide attempt, so when the bombs went off, killing thirty-two people and injuring countless others, Randy was standing vigil at his daughter's bedside with his hysterical wife.

But the papers had it all wrong. Randy was no survivor. He was cursed. Cursed to watch his loved ones die. Cursed with tremendous success in his professional life and extreme incompetence in his personal life. And though they'd called his mother's death a tragic accident, his father's death a suicide, and his son's death a murder—Randy knew better.

The ringing of his cell phone rescued him from these thoughts. He brightened at seeing Lake City PD on the caller ID. There was only one man it could be, the Chief of Police himself.

"Billy Boy!" he greeted Bill Edwards. "What's up? How goes life in Pirate City?"

"Hey ya' Ran, you sitting down?"

"No, I'm ice skating. Of course I'm sitting down!" Randy could tell his oldest friend, the classic worrier, was perturbed. Randy furrowed his brow. The last time Bill called him out of the blue, it was with bad news.

"Ran, I really messed up this time. Paula's dead. Please help me."

"You're not in trouble again, are you? You know what? I don't even want to know. I've got enough drama to deal with 'round here. You seen the Weather Channel lately?"

"This is serious," Bill replied in a professional, measured tone with no trace of humor. "I just got a call from the Racquet Club. They say someone signed in trying to impersonate Karen. Did you or Coral order a massage for her today?"

Randy's good spirits vanished. "Coral did," he answered. "It's Karen's birthday. Who took her spa appointment?"

"Jessica Breaux," Bill replied. "They caught her going at it with one of the massage therapists." He paused. "I've got another call coming through, hold on."

Bill clicked over, leaving Randy to contemplate his daughter's disappearance as classical music played in the background. The first time Karen brought Jessica home from school, Coral warned him that the girl was nothing but trouble. Randy observed the teenager's coal black hair, dark eyeliner, nose and tongue rings, dragon tattoos snaking around her biceps, fishnet stockings, peeling black fingernail polish, and agreed. He recalled thinking that something was seriously wrong with his kids—they just insisted on associating themselves with the lowest common denominators, first Kristopher and now Karen.

Randy's calm was wavering. He was used to getting calls about his wild daughter's erratic behavior; it was something he had almost come to expect, much like high taxes or criticism from the press. But what Bill was alluding to was impossible. Coral and Karen had been assigned twenty-four hour security ever since Kristopher's death. How could she have shaken her guards?

Randy swallowed, tasting metal in the back of his throat.

Where are my Rolaids?

He jerked open the top left desk drawer, revealing his private pharmacy. Pulling too hard, the drawer flew out of its slot and clattered to the ground, scattering orange canisters, pill packs, and bottles filled with colorful elixirs around his feet. Before he could set things right, Bill clicked back over.

"Ran, you still there?" he asked.

"I'm right here, Bill. So what's this Jessica business again?"

Randy scanned the floor frantically and finally located the acid reducers buried beneath a pill pack of antibiotics. As he popped one, his heart-rate reducing beta-blockers called up to him, so he swallowed two of them as well.

"One of my guys just found a wrecked motor bike out on Freeman Road by Barton Coliseum. Somebody tried to hide it in the weeds off the side of the road, but they must have been in a rush because it wasn't hidden so good. He ran the plates and guess whose bike it is?"

"Jessica's, right?" Randy's palms had turned to blocks of ice, a telltale sign he was about to experience a panic attack. He regulated his breathing, sucking in air for a count of four and pushing it out for a count of eight until he felt his heart-rate begin to slow.

"My guy found two pairs of skid marks not far off," Bill continued, "one most likely made by the bike, and another from a much larger vehicle—one with four-wheel drive. There was a bloody trail leading from where the bike was ditched to the start of the skid marks. It looks like whoever was bleeding was dragged to the vehicle from the ditch."

"Thanks for the details, Bill, but Karen doesn't ride motorcycles," Randy replied, squelching the evil vision of his daughter crushed beneath a Harley.

"Ran, Jessica admitted to loaning her bike to Karen. Said it was a birthday gift. Do you get where I'm going with this? It looks like somebody knocked Karen off the motorcycle and into the ditch on purpose and then dragged her into the back of some sort of truck or S.U.V."

Clarity broke through Randy's natural coping mechanisms of denial and rationalization. His eyes narrowed as he mentally recited his personal mantra: *confront the brutal facts, focus on what you can control, be proactive.* He sucked in as much oxygen as his lungs could handle. "Okay," he said, after exhaling. "So you think someone took my Karen. But that can't be right, because if she was...kidnapped, there would be a ransom note, right? Where's the note, Bill?"

"That's what that call was about," Bill replied. "My guy found it in the bike's glove compartment. It's being delivered as we speak."

"Did he read it?"

Bill's hesitation told Randy all he needed to know.

"Who else knows about this?" Randy asked, praying that Bill had contained this thing.

"Come on, Ran. Let me do my job. If I don't follow procedure, the Feds will be living in my colon."

"So you turned it over to the FBI?"

"Not yet," Bill replied, sighing. "Only Officer Abshire, myself, and the Racquet Club manager know anything."

"And we're going to keep it that way, right?"

"Haven't I always been there for you? But please don't ask me to risk my job. These first few hours are crucial; especially first contact, and frankly I could use the extra resources the Feds bring to the table."

"Don't ask you to risk your job?" Randy repeated, seeing white spots before his eyes. "I believe smashing in your cheating wife's head with a brick did a pretty good job of that. You wouldn't have a job to lose if I hadn't gotten you off, remember that."

"That's not fair, Ran..."

"It's not about fairness," Randy replied. "One hand washes the other. Always has, always will."

He could almost hear Bill's brain working trying to come up with a suitable response. "But...but going public could help flush the kidnappers out—"

Randy cut him off. "Save it. There's more to this than you know. Meet me at the house in an hour and I'll fill you in. In the meantime, I need you to keep things quiet for me. I can trust you to do that, right?"

"Of...of course. I—"

"Good." Randy hung up. He suppressed his urge to drown four Xanax in alcohol. He needed a clear mind to think. Panic was paralysis. Not an option. He closed his eyes; his mind flooded with scenario after scenario.

Where are you, Karen?

An angry tear snaked down Randy's clenched face as he managed to slide the drug drawer into its slot.

"Everything alright in here, sir?"

Randy sat up quickly and saw his secretary standing in the doorway. "Yes, yes. Everything's fine." He turned and wiped away the moisture on his face. "I need you to cancel the rest of my appointments today. I have to get back home. Please call the chopper for me."

"Will do, sir."

Later, as he entered the helicopter cabin, Randy couldn't get the image of that old newspaper headline out of his head. ***The Ultimate Survivor***. He closed his eyes and saw his son's lifeless blue irises staring back at him. The bloody handprints on his cheeks. Randy shut his eyes as tightly as he could until a single ominous thought remained.

Maybe I really am cursed.

CHAPTER TWO

Randy struggled to compose himself prior to arriving at the Lafitte plantation—his weekend refuge from the Governor's mansion in Baton Rouge. His ancestor, Luc Lafitte, built the formidable waterfront estate in the early 1800's. After World War II, his father reclaimed the family's land and rebuilt the plantation. Upon inheriting the land, Randy erected what he thought of as his "American Chateau." The only trace of what stood before was the weathered live oak tree just off the driveway that Randy believed would outlive them all.

Randy stared at the tree, oddly named Melinda Weeps, still mulling over the best way to explain Karen's disappearance to Coral. He decided to cross that chasm when he came to it.

Bill pulled into the circular driveway in an unmarked car.

Randy felt a migraine brewing. He greeted Bill and invited him inside. He sounded calm enough, even though the compulsion to rip Bill's gun from his belt, shoot him, and then himself nearly overtook him. Instead, Randy opened the sealed envelope Bill handed him, unfolded the paper inside and read:

*THE ONLY WAY THREE PEOPLE CAN KEEP A SECRET
IS IF TWO OF THEM ARE DEAD BUT SOME SECRETS
ARE JUST TOO BIG TO BE CONTAINED IF YOU WANT TO
KEEP YOURS SAFE GO TO THE PAY PHONE ON AUGUST
STREET BEHIND THE 7 ELEVEN AT EXACTLY 11 PM
TONIGHT DO NOT BE LATE OR WE WILL KILL HER*

Randy looked up from the note and studied Bill as if he was a newly discovered species. "Did you or anyone else read this?"

Bill met his gaze. "No. I took it from Officer Abshire and brought it straight here. What does it say?"

Randy lowered his eyes. "Trust me, you don't want to know."

"That's not gonna work this time, Ran. It's my duty to know."

"Then arrest me for obstruction."

Bill stared at him incredulously and then looked away. After a moment he looked back. "I know a couple of good guys in the bureau who owe me favors. They know how to be discrete. Just say the word."

"Not a chance. Don't you remember how badly they fucked up with Kristopher? I've got my own guys on this one."

"The same guys who can't keep tabs on a teenage girl? I know this is a hard time for you, but you can't trust Karen's life to a bunch of hired guns."

"Bill," Randy replied, placing a firm hand on his shoulder. "If you want to help me out, make sure Officer Abshire forgets what he knows."

Bill opened his mouth but then nodded his head. "Okay, Ran. I want you to know I am making it my personal mission to find Karen. I won't sleep."

"Thanks. Let me know how things go back at the ranch—"

"Hey, honey, I didn't know you were home. Hi, Bill."

Randy and Bill turned to see Coral descending the grand spiral staircase behind them. Randy glanced over at Bill knowing they were both wondering the same thing—how long had she been listening to their conversation?

She reached the landing and Randy took in her form-fitting (but appropriate for company, thank the Lord) blue, floor-length house dress. At least she had done her hair and makeup, a sign she was having one of her "good" days.

"Hi, hon," Randy said, leaning down to give her a peck on the lips.

The fact that she was dressed gave another positive signal. At least three days a week, Coral would wake, decide getting up was too painful, and stay in bed the whole day. She'd been battling bipolar disorder since her first pregnancy ended in miscarriage, nearly three years before Kristopher had even been a thought.

But even when she was at her worst, Randy refused to see Coral as a damsel in distress. She would always be the beautiful, vibrant angel he met years ago at the Consolata Cemetery in Lake City where his mother lay at rest. He always considered it providence that Coral's grandmother's gravesite lay just a few feet away from the Lafitte family plot.

Two years after his father's death, Randy came to a crossroads in his life and went to the burial ground to confer with his mother. As he stared at Rita Lafitte's tombstone, he collapsed to his knees as shame and confusion overtook him. After a moment he looked up to find Coral standing beside him, sympathy and caring pouring out of her stunning blue-gray eyes like a beacon of hope. Everything fell into place.

Through Coral's influence, Randy found his purpose. Distraught over his parent's deaths, he threw himself into public service. Coral was the perfect wife for a politician-on-the-rise—graceful, classy, with just the right amount of sweet, southern charm. They were poised to conquer the world. But Kristopher's murder put his angel on an emotional rollercoaster where the valleys vastly outnumbered the peaks. Randy didn't dare think of what Coral might do if she found out someone had kidnapped Karen.

Coral regarded Bill with dismay. "What brings you to our neck of the woods, Bill? You haven't come by, well, since before Paula... I'm sorry, where are my manners? Can I get ya'll something to drink? Emmanuel can whip up some lemonade in a jif."

Bill gave Randy a quick look. "Thanks for the offer, Coral, that does sound delightful, but I've got to get back to the station. Ran, catch up with you later?"

"Right. Thanks, Bill. Keep me posted all right?"

As soon as Bill was outside, Coral punched Randy in the shoulder.

"Oww, hon."

"I thought I told you not to bring him into my house. What will the neighbors think?"

"He was acquitted, remember?"

"Thanks to your lawyer buddies. I never understood why you helped him get off. And don't give me that one hand washes the other crap."

Randy offered his softest look. "I just did what any friend would do, hon. You understand that right? Loyalty outweighs honesty."

"Well not in my book. If you ever did anything that terrible, I would hope you would tell *me* the truth." Coral frowned, putting a hand to her head. "See, now I'm getting a headache. I need to lie down before Karen gets home. I hope you don't mind, but I've planned a little surprise get-together for her."

"You did what?"

"Well, eighteen is a big deal. My sisters and I are going to take her out to celebrate her womanhood!"

Randy's mind churned as he led Coral upstairs to their bedroom and tucked her into their California king bed. He had to come up with an excuse for Karen's absence. After feeding her one of the more potent tranquilizers, he waited for the effects to manifest. "I have to tell you something, hon," he said. "But you have to promise not to get too upset."

"I will promise no such thing Randall Albert Lafitte," she whispered, already half asleep.

Normally Coral's use of his biblical name would have brought a smile, but he could manage little more than a thin grimace. "I sent Karen and a few of her friends to Cancun for the weekend. They should be touching down soon."

"Cancun?" Coral asked, eyes bursting open. "Randy, how could you?"

"I'm so sorry, hon. It was just...Christy, you know Bill's daughter, let it slip that they were planning to run away this weekend..."

Coral's face wrinkled in bewilderment. "Are you telling me that my husband, the most fiercely overprotective man I've ever known, just sent my daughter to Mexico unsupervised?"

Randy forced a smile and replied, "That's right, hon, this old dog learned a new trick this week. She was gonna go anyway. At least this way she goes with our blessing, clear expectations, and a small security detail…"

Coral closed her eyes again. After a moment she said, "Well you could have consulted me first. She's my daughter too, you know."

"I know, hon, there wasn't much lead time on this one."

"Don't let it happen again," she said, her voice fading. Then, "You did good, hon. I'm proud of you…"

Randy's resolve hardened as he looked into his wife's peaceful countenance. He waited until her eyelids twitched before retreating to his father's study. Sitting at the desk, gazing aimlessly at his father's enormous collection of rare books, Randy read the kidnapper's note until he memorized it. He had a feeling the author was bluffing.

Everyone had secrets, and obviously public figures had more to lose by exposing a clandestine fact than most. The genius of the term "secret" was that the kidnappers were betting on the fact that the recipient, in this case him, would automatically assume his most confidential revelation. Still, the reference to death bothered him and the last line, *WE WILL KILL HER,* could not have been any clearer.

Randy glanced at his watch. Three hours had passed since Bill's call. That left four to prepare for first contact with the kidnappers. This was getting him nowhere. He had to use his time wisely.

There was only one man Randy trusted to get his daughter back—Snake Roberts—a tracker, bounty hunter, mercenary, and

Randy's strong right hand. Snake's loyalty to Randy was inscribed in granite.

He grabbed the phone and dialed from memory. Voicemail picked up immediately.

"Snake, it's me. There's an urgent situation that needs your expert attention. Potential for big money. Call me back as soon as you get this."

CHAPTER THREE

Friday
Just outside Lake City

"Where are you holed up these days, Snake?" Randy Lafitte asked in his typical *"I'm the boss of you"* voice.

Snake Roberts stared at the traffic trickling past him as he sat on the roadside shoulder. "Yuh know me, Boss. If I can think, that means I need a drink." He took a generous gulp of Snapple fruit juice and forced a belch. "Now, what's this yuh say about a hefty payout? What's the job?"

Snake sensed Randy's hesitation, which was unexpected because Randy never hesitated when it came to his needs. It had always been that way. Even fifteen years back in that piece of shit bar in Cameron, where they'd met.

Snake had been sitting at his usual table in the quietest corner of the room, farthest from the door. A shot of Jamesons, one pint of Guinness, and one snifter of Bailey's Irish cream sat on the table before him, beside a weathered copy of Joyce's *Finnegans Wake*—what he thought of as his Irish quadruple mind fuck. The door opened, allowing enough sunlight inside to obliterate the bar's number one feature besides the cheap liquor—ambient dimness. Snake was not a fan of daylight; it gave him headaches and irritated his freckled white skin.

The bastard in the doorway clearly held sunlight in high regard; he had the nerve to keep the door open longer than necessary as he tried to penetrate the dim.

"Who you looking for, boy?" the barmaid, Gertrude, asked the intruder. "Think you might be in the wrong place..."

Snake doubted this because you had to go way out of your way down a less trodden tributary off the beaten path to find this hellhole. The visitor's eyes scanned the room as he ignored Gertrude's welcome, eventually coming to rest on Snake and his Irish posse. Blessedly, the man closed the door, then strode across the room to Snake's corner.

It took Snake's eyes a moment to adjust, but he finally got a look at the fellow when he sat down—directly across from him. Gertrude's description was on the money as usual. He had the height, build, and manner of a disciplined man, but at the same time he wore the face of a boy, and a privileged boy at that. But the eyes...the eyes were those of a man who'd seen a particular brand of darkness.

Those eyes reminded Snake of his fellow Vietnam vets—men whose innocence was scrubbed away so thoroughly that only the sinewy layer of skin between air and taut muscle remained. But Snake knew that was the toughest layer the same way he knew the man before him had never seen a real war. He was too cloaked in indignant self-righteousness for that.

"You're a hard man to track down, Mr. Roberts." The man-boy's voice was a brilliant instrument, relaying all the right pitches of assertiveness, pleasantry, humor, and grit.

If he wasn't a politician, Snake would eagerly gobble down his own shirt. Then it came to him in a flash of insight. He'd seen this man-boy before, as recently as a few weeks back, and much to the delight of his shirt-phobic stomach, he *was* a politician. Having placed the face, Snake reached for the name.

"To what do I owe the pleasure, Mr…"

"My name isn't important, but the work I'm offering you could be. I was told you were a man who could get tough jobs done, discretely. I've got such a job…"

Fifteen years later, Snake was still cleaning up Lafitte's messes.

"I need you to find someone for me, Snake," Lafitte said after a short pause.

"And what do I do once I find this upstanding gentleman?" Snake replied, taking another sip of juice. Reminiscing was thirsty work.

"It's a woman. Her name is Desiree Deveaux. She was once a fortune teller calling herself Madame Deveaux, last known to live in New Orleans. I need you to find her by no later than tomorrow night and bring her to me."

"That it?"

Another uncustomary pause. Maybe the instrument needed warming these days, the way an old car did. As if to confirm this, Lafitte cleared his throat. "Snake," he said. "Someone took my daughter today."

So it begins.

Snake had known this moment was rapidly approaching, but now that it was here, he almost felt bad…almost. "I'm sorry to hear that, Boss."

"I can't have the police or Feds involved in this."

"Of course not. Who needs 'em."

"I'm speaking to the kidnappers in about two and a half hours. Once I know their demands, I'll call you back so we can put together our game plan."

"What if they don't have any?"

"Excuse me?"

"Demands, I mean. What makes yuh think they've got demands?"

"Everyone wants something, Snake."

"But what if yuh don't have what they want or can't get it in time?"

"I'm paying you a lot of money to make sure that doesn't happen."

Lafitte hung up.

Snake placed the cell phone in the cup holder. The square green sign just beyond his windshield announced Lake City's municipal boundary. Snake had chosen his parking spot carefully, so he could remain within the city limits of Iowa (pronounced eye-a-way in Louisiana). He hated Lake City almost as much as he hated the sun.

Everything about the city bothered him. How drivers were forced to take the Interstate just to get anywhere; the billboards advertising casinos where all they did was take his money; the Super Walmarts on every corner. The whole city smelled like a chemistry experiment gone bad because of the throng of chemical plants down by Lake Francis, and it was downright insufferable. People couldn't even go to Prien Pines Beach anymore because of all the chemicals they dumped in the water. But most of all, he detested the fifty-five mile per hour speed limit.

Who the fuck could get anywhere driving fifty-five?

Snake dialed another number.

"Well, Jhonnette, the Governor went for it, just like you said he would," Snake said after his lover's greeting.

"Did you ever doubt me?" Jhonnette replied in that sexy, all-knowing way of hers.

Snake quelled the desire to proclaim his undying love. There would be plenty of time for that once this was finished. "Never that, my love. I'm putting everything in motion now. See you in a couple of days." Snake hung up and exhaled.

It was amazing how the world worked. A year ago he'd been lost. His gambling debts were sky high. Doctors had diagnosed him with chronic hepatitis and advanced cirrhosis. They told him that without a liver transplant, he'd be dead within a year.

Then he'd met Jhonnette Deveaux at an old Blues bar in the French Quarter. After six months with her, Snake's liver exams had returned to normal, he'd paid off his gambling debts, and had fallen madly in love. At first, Snake tried to manipulate Jhonnette as he did most women. But it was pointless. Jhonnette saw his every deception birthing. She saw everything—a gift from her mother. One night after lovemaking, she revealed his fortune.

"You will be a millionaire in one year's time."

He was now three days away from realizing Jhonnette's prophesy. Whenever Snake found himself doubting the course they'd laid out together, he remembered that everything Jhonnette predicted had come to pass. *Every* single thing. And though he'd never admit it to another soul, Snake knew when Jhonnette put her hands on him during those long gone days of sickness, she'd *healed* him.

Certain of his future for the first time in recent memory, Snake cranked up the stereo, rolled the windows down, and fed his rented Mustang some gas. It was going to be a historic weekend.

Lake City, here I come.

CHAPTER FOUR

Friday
Location Unknown

Karen Lafitte was lost in an unfamiliar forest. Fear drove her forward as she ran toward the light shimmering through the branches like a beacon.

Arriving at the forest's edge, she saw that the light was coming from a large house in the clearing. Less than twenty feet away, a man stood with his back to her wearing an orange fleece sweater and blue jeans. The man aimed a shotgun at something in the distance.

Instinct commanded Karen to stay put. She held her breath, afraid to make the slightest sound.

The hunter pulled the trigger on his shotgun. The backfire boomed like an explosion.

What is he shooting at?

The hunter prepared to fire again, then suddenly turned and glared in Karen's direction as if he'd heard her thoughts.

Karen ducked. She was shocked to discover that the hunter was her father. Her brother Kristopher was nailed to a post thirty feet away.

A large, bullet-riddled target was painted on Kristopher's chest, his face contorted in a twisted scream.

Karen's legs went numb and she crumpled to the ground.

"Get the fuck up, bitch, before you make me hurt you," her father growled. "Get up RIGHT NOW!"

Karen blinked her eyes open, the strange dream seared away by a bright white light assaulting her sensitive irises. She squeezed her watering eyelids shut to protect them. She heard a click and the light disappeared.

"'Bout goddamn time. You could sleep through fuckin' World War III. Been tryin' to wake your tired ass up for the past five minutes."

"Why's it so dark?" Karen asked, shivering. She felt an unnatural grogginess, similar to the waking effects of the sleeping pills she "borrowed" from her mother from time to time. "Where am I?"

The last thing she remembered, other than the fading dream, was speeding down Freeman Road on Jess's Honda Ninja. Karen had really gotten into the biker scene last year and had become a fairly capable rider. When she was on a bike, everything fell into place. She could usually outrun her worries—with the exception of her number one concern, her eighteenth birthday. Or "cursed-day" as Kristopher had christened it.

When Mom told her about the spa appointment, Karen saw it as another opportunity to do something *she* wanted to do today. It was her birthday after all, not theirs. Jess was happy to take her massage appointment; she could never afford such pampering on her own. All Jess had to do was sign in under Karen's name. No one would be the wiser.

"You betta stop axin' questions and start followin' directions, bitch, or somethin' bad gone happen to you." Big, abrasive hands pulled her into a sitting position.

"Don't touch me!"

She tried to squirm out of his grasp but was slammed against a rough wall that cut into the flesh of her back. Her arms were tied and left to rest in her lap. Frightened at the echo of her desperate cries, she sobbed uncontrollably. "Please let me go. Please! I'll do whatever you want!"

Flashlight Man chuckled. "You're damn skippy," he said. "I'm gone give you some ground rules now. Rule number one, keep your fuckin' mouth shut. Rule number two—"

"What do you want with me?" Karen wailed.

"It's not you we want," he whispered.

If not me, then who?

An internal alarm went off. Ever since Kristopher's death, Dad had warned Karen to be careful.

"People will try to hurt me by hurting those I love most. All it takes is one slip up."

Her father was convinced that Kristopher brought on his demise by making that ill-fated trip to Simmons Park that day. That's why he'd hired the extra security. Guards she became increasingly adept at duping and ducking over the years, and today was no exception.

A cold hand touched her thigh.

"Get away from me!" Karen twisted her head in all directions trying to see in the pitch black.

"See, there you go violatin' rule number one and it ain't even been an hour yet."

"You won't get away with this! My daddy—"

The slap came out of nowhere, like the darkness itself had assaulted her, snapping her head into the wall. Her teeth clamped down on her tongue, filling her mouth with the coppery taste of warm blood mixed with saliva.

"Which leads me to rule number two. *I'm* yo' daddy now. You do what I say, when I say, and you'll be aight. If not, I'll be forced to beat you like yo' daddy, you understand?"

Karen barely heard, much less understood. She swallowed some of her coppery flavored blood and her stomach quivered in near revolt.

"And rule number three: If you don't want to end up dead, don't try to escape. You take whatever I give you and don't give me any shit. I don't give a fuck if you're scared of the dark, needles, or if you don't like to swallow pills. You take that shit like a good little girl, and we'll be aight. Aight?"

She felt him tie a thick rubber band around her upper left arm.

The flashlight beam played on her arm as her oppressor pulled something out of his pocket. With the light out of her eyes she was able to make out a rotund black man of medium height. His face was not nearly as menacing as his voice, but his pitch black eyes held no trace of warmth.

"This gone sting for a second. Don't scream or make no sudden movements or I might miss the vein. We got to get you ready for the ceremony."

Ceremony?

Karen clenched her jaw in protest as the needle entered her flesh. She closed her eyes. She was usually the one giving the injections, not receiving them.

When Dad had fallen sick, the home care nurses taught her how to switch out his I.V.'s on nights when they weren't there.

Her nerves were so wracked the first time that she dropped four needles. Nevertheless, Dad calmed her down. He didn't yell even once, although she saw how he flinched each time she inserted a new needle.

Soon she could switch them out so swiftly Dad claimed not to notice. It had felt good being able to take care of him. Kristopher was gone and Mom was useless in her drug-induced fog. There was no way she was going to let Dad die and leave her alone with her mother.

Flashlight Man said something else.

Karen couldn't hear him over the bass drum pounding of her heartbeat.

Flashlight Man shook and then smacked her again.

Karen felt disconnected from reality. Hypnotized by the flashlight's beam—the sole source of illumination—the drug's effects took hold. The light became her sun and she bathed in its warmth as it melted the ropes that bound her physical self. Nothing could hold her now because she was flying.

CHAPTER FIVE

Friday
Lake City, LA

Randy picked up the pay phone on the first ring. One of the advantages of being a high-ranking public official proved to be a nuisance tonight, as he had to drive fifteen minutes out of his way to lose the state trooper escort. He answered the phone with as much attitude as he could muster. "Speak."

"Do you like puppets, Randy?" The kidnapper used some sort of modulator to disguise his voice.

"Puppets?" Randy's face wrinkled in confusion. "No, I don't. I just want my daughter back."

"I'm surprised to hear that, Governor," the kidnapper replied. "I thought you were a master puppeteer. But even a master puppeteer must sleep, right? Can't manipulate the strings all the time. Imagine what all those poor puppets do when they're alone in the shop…"

Randy's ears were suddenly filled with a roar of static, which he realized was laughter.

"Still waiting for the other shoe to drop, Randy?"

"I don't know what you're talking about. I just want to talk to my daughter."

"Well, everybody wants something, right?"

Randy's mind swam with déjà vu. He'd used those same words with Snake just hours ago.

"Randy, are you still with me?"

"Yes. I'm here. Now what do you want from me?"

"I'm going to *punish* you, Randy," the kidnapper replied. "But before we get to that, I need you to do some things. When I'm satisfied with your progress, then we can talk about you getting your daughter back. If I'm not satisfied, well, I'd think twice before getting into any moving vehicles, if you know what I mean."

Randy swallowed the obscenities forming in his throat. He took a few slow breaths.

Let him think he is in control. Eventually, he'll slip up and then you'll have him.

"I'm listening."

"In twenty-four hours, I expect to see a deposit of seven million dollars into my offshore account."

"You can't be serious. There's no way I can get that kind of money so fast."

Silence on the other end.

"Are you still there?" Randy asked. "Did you hear what I just said?"

"Don't..."

The menace in that single syllable petrified Randy's core.

"I don't know what you—"

"I can see how a man of your position and influence could begin to think of yourself as a master of the universe," the kidnapper interrupted. "But don't ever question my intelligence or my resolve again or I will put a knife through your daughter's gut and make you listen to her last screams."

Randy fought the urge to hang up the phone. An image of Kristopher, riddled with bullets, gave him pause. "Okay," he said. "Seven million dollars. When do I get the account information?"

"Did you think I would send you an e-mail?" the kidnapper replied through more static bursts. "It's on the back of the note. Apply a liberal dose of lemon juice and voilà."

Invisible ink. Very clever.

"Now listen carefully to this part, Randy. This money will purchase your daughter's life for the next seventy-two hours. Understood?"

"What happens after that?"

"That depends on how well you do with the rest of my list. Now, get out a pen. Write down this number: 6-7-5-4-3-9."

Randy scribbled the numbers on the back of an old business card.

"Read the number back to me."

Randy complied.

"Can you guess what the number is for?"

"Enlighten me."

"It's a prison ID. Specifically, the ID of a VIP—very important prisoner. He's a lifer at the Louisiana State Penitentiary. He is going to walk out of Angola at precisely eight o'clock Monday morning. If he doesn't...do I need to say the rest?"

Angola?

Randy wracked his brain to place the prison ID number. Why did it sound so familiar? "Listen, I want to help you, but what you're asking is impossible. Do you have any idea how long it takes to pardon someone? There's a process. Public hearings with witnesses and lawyers. Committees that have to meet and vote..."

"Not my problem. You've got the weekend to get it done. Also, don't involve the police any more than you already have and don't even think of calling the FBI or I will send your daughter's severed head to the Capitol. I don't think that would be very good PR, Governor."

Bill was right. I should have traced this call. I would have his location right now for sure...

"You still with me, Randy?"

"Yes. Yes, I'm still here."

"Good. I know what you must be thinking, but it wouldn't have done any good. I can't be traced or tracked. Technology is amazing, isn't it? For every scud missile, there's a patriot missile on the other side. For every police radar, a scrambler. And for every puppeteer, a very pissed off puppet. Let me reiterate, Randy, this isn't about the money—"

"Bullshit! It's always about the money with you people!" Randy yelled, immediately regretting his outburst.

"You should think of the money as a security deposit," the kidnapper replied calmly. "Let me be clear. This is NOT about money. That would be too easy for slime like you. *This* is punishment."

Randy's instincts kicked in. *Keep him talking. Make him give something away. Something you can use to cinch the noose around his fucking throat.*

"You keep saying that," Randy probed. "What am I being punished for? Why are you doing this?"

"That's for me to know and for you to agonize over. But I will leave you with this: From this moment forward, you are *my* puppet and I am pulling *your* strings. I am going to make you do things you never imagined. Think back to when you first started manipulating the strings in your favor. Take your motivations at that point in time, multiplied one hundred fold, and you might come close to my level of hatred toward you. Consider yourself exceptionally fortunate that unlike you, *my* beliefs will not allow me to spill blood without provocation. But do not try me. This is one election you can't steal. Get a good night's sleep, Governor. You're going to need it."

The line went dead.

Randy stared at the phone for a long moment, the conversation replaying over and over in his mind. Finally, he hung up and returned to his car.

He'd never smoked anything in his life but was overcome with a maddening desire to inhale cigarette after cigarette. And there wasn't enough alcohol in this entire god forsaken city to numb his pain. As he started the vehicle and headed home, he frantically combed through his memories for any clue as to who could be doing this.

Confront the brutal facts. Focus on what you can control. Be proactive.

The answer came just before he climbed into bed. He nearly collapsed under the weight of the memory. Suddenly, it all made sense.

"This is one election you can't steal."

Randy looked over at his sleeping wife in alarm, as if she might wake up from the enormity of his revelation. But she stayed asleep, oblivious to how the room had suddenly started spinning beneath them.

She has no idea who I really am. And she never will.

The kidnapper had given him a major clue to his identity, but Randy needed to confirm his suspicions. He texted the prison ID number to Snake and ordered him to get the prisoner's name as quickly as possible. Then he swallowed a couple of Coral's sleeping pills, trying unsuccessfully to close the portal to his past. He doubted that even the miracles of modern medicine could drag him into unconsciousness after a day like this; but soon he passed into a fitful sleep, where his demons eagerly embraced him.

CHAPTER SIX

39 Years Earlier
1963
New Orleans, LA

Randy stepped out of the air-conditioned womb of the hotel into the kaleidoscope of sights, sounds, and smells that made up his favorite street in his favorite city. He paused under the hotel awning, rubbing his hand through sandy blond hair, his clipped nails unconsciously brushing the still sensitive scar. His father had dropped him on his head as a baby—the first of many injuries. Randy wasn't a baby anymore, though, and the delights of Bourbon Street beckoned.

It was near dusk. The French Quarter was ablaze with the orange glow of electric lamps. The thick, sticky air hung suspended like spider webs of moisture, flavored by an eye-watering aromatic stew of magnolia, urine, cayenne pepper, and exhaust fumes. Randy's virgin ears buzzed with dusky jazz and blues melodies echoing down a street too narrow to contain the soulful yet sorrowful notes. The foot traffic of hundreds of thirsty, starving visitors—beckoned by the holy trinity of cheap booze, cheap (yet exotic) eats, and cheap thrills—replaced automobile traffic.

Randy was here for none of these, although a few drinks would probably help ease his self-consciousness. He stood out like an aristocrat among the groveling masses in his blue blazer, polo shirt, and khakis, but knew the uniform would please his father. After all, Randy's father was footing the bill for this little excursion, even though he was in the dark about Randy's real reason for wanting to come to New Orleans.

To keep up the façade of a celebratory party trip to the Big Easy, Randy had brought his partner in adolescent crime, Bill Edwards, along for the mission. Bill was a physical Adonis whose mental faculties were not much more advanced than a statue. His simple, go-with-the-flow attitude made him the perfect traveling companion.

After the four and a half hour train ride from the heel of their boot-shaped state, into the big toe, Randy and Bill checked into the luxurious suite Joseph had reserved for today's dual celebration of Randy's graduation from boarding school and his eighteenth birthday. Atop the dresser his father had left them a stack of cash and a note instructing the boys to explore the city. He'd try to meet them for a late dinner.

As the young men passed throngs of street musicians, hippy hustlers, and tourist shops, Randy considered New Orleans' deceptive nature, the gluttonous beast beneath the cultured veneer. The city reminded him of a decrepit venus fly trap, opening up her decaying petals to emit what was left of her allure. Randy could relate to that kind of deception and duality.

For an instant, Randy felt the presence of something dark, wet, hairy, and profoundly hungry stalking him. He looked over at Bill to see if any of this was registering.

His taller, bulkier buddy gestured excitedly at a sign advertising penny peep shows. "Check this out, Ran!" Bill whipped his head around and gaped at an attractive blonde who looked around their age. The girl glanced over her shoulder and gave Randy a look to which he'd grown quite accustomed. Southern girls played at being prim and proper but were easier to play than a pre-schooler's recorder.

"Forget those girls, Bill," Randy said. "We've got other plans."

"You serious?" Bill asked, following the blond and her buxom red-headed friend into a nondescript bar. The sign outside read: Jean Lafitte's Old Absinthe House.

Lafitte, hmm. Maybe it's a family-owned establishment.

"Come on, buddy, let's get some beers," Randy said, turning Bill away from the bar and pointing him in the opposite direction. Randy actually had no idea where he was going, but knew what he was looking for. He found it down a dark alleyway three blocks off Bourbon Street.

Explaining the essence of his plan to Bill, Randy got the response he anticipated.

"No way, Ran. I ain't goin' to no fortune teller."

"Who said you were?" Randy pushed Bill out of the way. His eyes were drawn to the sign on the worn door before them.

GOOD FORTUNES, it promised.

Bill interrupted his reverie. "Somethin' ain't right about this place. Can we please go?"

"Calm down, you big chicken," Randy replied. "Drink your beer and wait for me." Randy didn't anticipate much help from a mere fortune teller, but hoped she could at least point him in the right direction. He was searching for a place where spells, curses, and secrets were traded. Where blood sacrifice was the only currency that mattered. And later at dinner, Bill would corroborate Randy's story about how they'd spent their evening.

Randy winked at Bill and turned the knob.

"Now why you gotta go and do this, Ran. These places ain't safe!"

"Only one way to find out," Randy replied, pulling the door open. Lavender spice tickled his nostrils as he moved into the building. "See," he said, "what's so scary about this?"

Bill peered in briefly before Randy closed the door in his face.

Randy stared up a candle-lit stairway. "Hello! Anyone here?"

"Upstairs," a girlish voice sang.

Well, here goes nothing.

Randy's boldness was replaced with childlike fear and wonder. Swallowing his nerves, he slowly ascended the staircase, gazing cautiously at his surroundings. At the top, he was greeted by a golden light emanating from a room just off the landing. He looked around for the owner.

The space was empty, but for a myriad of plants and a small round table in the center of the room. Light radiated from a globe in the middle of the table. Randy sat in one of the two chairs and examined the sphere.

"You can touch it if you want," a voice whispered, an inch from Randy's right ear.

He jumped up and whirled around, his gaze falling upon a beautiful woman with curly, black hair. Her height and youthful bone structure surprised him even more than her sudden appearance.

He'd always pictured fortune tellers as older and gypsy-like, but this woman looked barely older than him.

"Did I scare you?" the woman asked, her green eyes glinting with mischief. Her near-white skin glowed from the light coat of sweat afflicting nearly everyone in this tropical town.

"A little," Randy admitted. "Why did you sneak up on me like that?" His eyes devoured the yellow summer dress clinging to her sultry Creole curves.

"I like to get a good look at my customers before we engage."

"Are you satisfied with what you see?" he asked. He noticed that her delicate hands were wrapped in looping henna script.

"Not quite. Come. Sit."

Randy sat before the beautiful prophetess. He felt an uncomfortable rigidness in his crotch.

Stay focused.

"What's your name?" he asked.

The woman smiled. "Madame Deveaux," she spoke softly.

Randy had to lean in to hear her. "You...you're not...what I expected." Their faces were inches apart.

"People rarely are. So, what brings you to me?"

Randy was losing himself in her eyes, forgetting his purpose. Willing himself from her hypnotic sway, he blurted, "I...I want to curse someone."

Her gaze sharpened. "I do not play games, young man. Nor should you."

"I'm very serious." Now that his dark request was out in the open, his heart pounded against the walls of his chest like a giant trapped behind a great steel door.

"We'll see about that. How much money do you have?"

"Money? I thought…"

"You thought you could pay me in pig's blood or some other foolishness?"

"Favors," Randy choked out, his cheeks burning with embarrassment. "I read…I mean, I thought you were paid in favors."

Madame Deveaux's face softened as she erupted in laughter.

"What's so funny?"

"You're just a boy," she replied. "Who could have possibly hurt you so deeply that you feel the need to hurt them in return?"

Randy stared at the impossibly young fortune teller, trying to decide how much to reveal. Either she would believe him, or she wouldn't. Either she could help, or she couldn't. "My father," he said finally.

She nodded. "Our families are often the cause of our deepest pain. What makes your case so special?"

Taking a deep breath, Randy began his story. It was amazing how easy it was to talk about this secret subject with a complete stranger.

"He killed my mother. In a car accident when I was twelve. Tried to say it was some kind of accident, but I know he's happy she's dead…"

After his mother's funeral, Randy was often dragged to meetings his father had with a group of men that Joseph referred to as his brethren. Even at the age of twelve, Randy was well aware of what his father and his friends did to pass the time. After getting drunk, they'd pull out their white robes and hoods and head into

North Lake City to "maintain the order of things," as Joseph liked to call it. Randy once asked his father why they had to patrol the area if that was the police's job.

Joseph snorted laughter and replied, "Look around the room, son. The police are right here. We just wear different uniforms at night."

One such night, the brethren were drinking heavily, their pores oozing the rotting oak aroma of Kentucky's finest bourbon. Joseph, three sheets to the wind, began recounting the accident that took his mother's life, looking Randy right in the eyes while doing so, as if daring his son to shut him up.

According to Joseph, he and Rita were returning to Lake City from Shreveport on US-151, just outside of Deridder, when a stupid black child chased a ball or something into the middle of the highway, right into their path.

"When I saw that niglet, I had a mind to do one thing and one thing only."

"What was that, Joe?" the brethren asked as one.

"To jam down on the gas and run 'im down!"

The brethren howled like hyenas before the kill.

"But then my stupid cunt of a wife grabbed the wheel and instead of hittin' that niglet we hit a ditch. Well…I hit the ditch. Poor Rita flew out the windshield like a witch on a broomstick! Ha! Good riddance, I say."

"It was supposed to be me," Randy whispered to Madame Deveaux. "It's my fault she's dead."

"How is it your fault?" Madame Deveaux asked.

"On trips, I was the navigator, so I always got to sit up front with my father. But I was sick this time and couldn't go, and she died because of it..."

Randy began two different lives in the wake of his mother's death.

In public, he played the part of the grieving only son of the affluent businessman. He attended school, studied hard, and hung out with friends. But he never shed a tear. That would have brought on a severe beating from Joseph for certain.

In private, he was in agony. He didn't sleep, eat, or pray. His brain was on a never-ending doom loop. Before long, he fell apart like a long buried skeleton.

One day, while desperately searching for some way, any way, to relieve himself of the crushing grief, guilt, fear, and shame, he took a steak knife in one unstable hand. Before he knew what he was doing, he slashed his upper forearm in a swift motion, reminiscent of a violinist with a bow. After nearly fainting from the sight of his own blood bubbling up to the surface of his pale skin like lava, the sensation of vertigo was quickly replaced by a surge of adrenaline and release.

Eventually, he graduated to butcher knives and long precise cuts to his upper thighs. He even grew accustomed to the additional sting from the sour-smelling vinegar he used to cauterize his self-inflicted wounds. Nothing compared to the merger of pain and exuberance he experienced whenever he plunged a knife into his flesh.

"So you wish to curse your father to punish him for killing your mother, correct?" Madame Deveaux recapped.

He nodded.

"Why a curse?" Madame Deveaux asked after a moment's reflection. "Are you afraid to get your hands bloody?"

Randy stared at her over the shimmering globe. "No. I'm not afraid. But there is a certain symmetry to doing it this way. You interrupted me before I could finish my story..."

One afternoon after the cutting started, Randy was wandering deep in the stacks of the Lake City Public Library, planning more self-inflicted incisions, when a book spine caught his attention. He pulled out the book called *The History of Magic* and cracked it open. Hope whispered to him from between the dusty pages.

He devoured the tome, chock-full of true stories about apparitions, divination, witchcraft, and spirit-rapping. Afterward, he became obsessed with all things occult, reading everything he could get his hands on. Most of the books dealt with the homegrown magic of Hoodoo and the religion of Voodoo. They described New Orleans as the epicenter of American magic.

Randy began daydreaming of one day possessing the power to bring his mother back from the dead. But those plans got derailed when their maid found his stash of bloody rags and damning books, prompting Joseph to ship him off to a boarding school in France.

While exiled, Randy had the opportunity to meet distant relatives and learn more about his origins. His father had always expressed extreme pride for their ancestor Luc Lafitte, a French buccaneer famous for many things, including the founding of their hometown, Lake City, in 1802. However, Randy quickly learned that his French kin didn't share the same affection for Luc. To them, Luc and his direct descendants were decayed branches that had thankfully rotted off the family tree.

After weeks of searching the library of his boarding school for the French version of Luc's story, Randy uncovered *Le Roi des Pirates, (The Pirate King)*, which described the beginnings of the Lafitte lineage in America. Apparently Luc had made his fortune hijacking Spanish ships in the Gulf of Mexico, eventually settling down in Lake City. The Lafitte's had always been an opportunistic clan, and Luc possessed the foresight to open a French trading outpost in Lake City that became a strategic center for French military operations. He married the daughter of a French aristocrat who eventually gave him a daughter and two sons.

Luc's life then became very unremarkable until his apparent suicide three days after his oldest child and only daughter, Melinda, threw herself from the roof of the Lafitte mansion on her eighteenth birthday. Randy combed through account after account of who was born to whom, who married who, and who died when. A dark trend emerged; Melinda's suicide had started something.

The more he read, the more he became convinced that fate put this knowledge into his hands at the precise moment when he could appreciate its significance. It was as if his mother were reaching out to him from behind death's curtain and pointing the way.

"Today is my eighteenth birthday," Randy concluded.

"And you want your father to die three days from now, just like Luc Lafitte, am I right?" Madame Deveaux asked.

Randy nodded.

"What if you're wrong? What if the curse doesn't work that way?"

Randy hadn't considered this, but couldn't let her know that. "Well…if it doesn't work…I expect a full refund."

Madame Deveaux laughed. "You really have no idea what you're getting yourself into, do you?"

Randy suppressed the urge to lunge across the table and choke her laughs quiet. "Look, there are a hundred so-called fortune tellers in this town. Are you going to help me or not?"

Madame Deveaux straightened. At once, she appeared taller and more present. Randy felt her essence envelop him from all sides, even though she never moved.

"I am no fortune teller, boy," she said. "I am *mambo*…ahh, I see you know this word, yes?"

He nodded slowly. "So…you are a voodoo priestess?"

"Yes. Now you know what and who you are dealing with. Do you still wish to proceed?"

"Yea-yes," he stammered.

"Very well, Randy," she replied after a moment. "Come back tomorrow afternoon and I will have everything you need."

Plodding down the stairs, Randy couldn't remember when he had told her his name.

"Oh man, am I glad to see you!" Bill exclaimed as Randy stepped out of the building. "What the hell took you so long?"

Randy's head buzzed. Madame Deveaux's incense had done a number on him. "What do you mean? How long was I gone?"

"Nearly two hours!"

That long?

"Well? What did she say?" Bill asked.

"She said that I should get rid of any and all chicken shit friends."

"Come on, man. What did she really say?"

In three days, Joseph is a dead man.

"Ran? You with me buddy?"

Randy looked over at Bill. "I need a drink. Then I'll tell you all about it." Randy stared back at the sign – GOOD FORTUNES.

Am I really going to go through with this?

He visualized his mother's kind face and felt his jaw muscles clench painfully. For the first time in years he felt the compulsion to bleed himself.

"Okay, no problem," Bill replied. "Hey, cheer up…it's still your day for another coupla' hours. Let's make the most of it."

Randy allowed Bill to wrap his arm around his shoulder and lead him back into the lights of the French Quarter.

Over the next three days, Randy followed Madame Deveaux's instructions without exception. She told him that sometime after midnight on the third day, Joseph would do something completely out of character. That would be Randy's cue that the curse was in effect. Just when he'd convinced himself that he'd been swindled, his father burst out of the front door of their hotel, a drunken, disheveled mess.

Randy suppressed his impulse to call the whole thing off and followed his father instead.

Joseph was clearly scared out of his mind. The stench of his fear hung in the air like a trail of breadcrumbs as Randy lagged behind him.

Before long, Joseph reached Jackson Square.

Randy found a spot where he could observe without being seen. He watched as his father knelt next to Andrew Jackson's statue and placed a revolver in his mouth.

It's working. He's really going to do it.

Joseph looked up as if in prayer and a tall, black man emerged from the shadows.

Randy stood. This wasn't part of the plan.

Joseph removed the revolver from his mouth at the sight of the black man and offered it to him.

Randy ran across the square.

Joseph sat in rapt attention as the black man spoke to him. Then the black man shoved the barrel of the weapon back into Joseph's mouth and pulled the trigger.

Randy watched the back of his father's head torn apart by the bullet. He stopped in the middle of the square like he was the one who'd been shot. Finally, he found his voice and screamed, "Stop right there!"

Randy broke into a run, but arrived at his father's side too late. The murderer was gone.

CHAPTER SEVEN

Saturday
Lake City, LA

Coral Lafitte shot straight up in the bed like she had a lever attached; Randy moaned loudly in his sleep beside her. Frightened and a bit peeved at having been awakened, Coral tried to shake Randy out of his nightmare—with no results. She hadn't seen her normally stoic husband in this condition since before Kristopher died.

Thoughts of Kristopher brought her daughter's image to the fore. Coral was desperate to speak to Karen. Karen was her baby, and she'd give anything to see her roll over and smile her father's brilliant smile as she tried to retract her feet from her mother's tickling. But her baby was in Cancun. *Cancun?* Coral was still amazed Randy actually permitted Karen to go so far away, on today of all days. Maybe he was learning some new tricks.

Randy was finally still. She reached for his cell phone and punched in Karen's number. Karen would answer Randy's call for sure.

Except she didn't. The line went directly to voicemail, just like it did with the thirty or so calls she'd made over the last twelve hours.

Coral glared at her husband's motionless form. Being married to Randy Lafitte was an exasperating existence. She was used to his controlling nature, but his behavior of late was just...strange. Not only had he refused to give her Karen's hotel information (explaining they needed to "respect her privacy"), but he'd also left the house at 10:30 p.m. to go God knows where. He'd returned sometime after midnight without a word about where he'd been, leaving her in the dark, tossing and turning, unable to shake the feeling that something was very, very wrong.

Now her anxiety was back and worse than ever. To rid herself of the *Girls Gone Wild* commercials playing on repeat in her mind, she went to the bathroom to take a Xanax. Then she headed down the hall to the spiral staircase.

Halfway down the stairs she tripped on the shift of her robe and almost tumbled the rest of the way down. Descending with more care, Coral was reminded of how much she loathed all ten thousand square feet of this residence, which she'd come to think of as "the fortress."

That home architecture critic had nailed it when he'd concluded, "The Lafitte Mansion is less of a home and more of an ill-devised plan of a young man with too much money and not enough taste." He'd rebuked their abode as "unnecessarily ostentatious" for the eighteen massive square columns, marble fountain, and antebellum staircase on the exterior, as well as the interior's six bedrooms, ten bathrooms, two libraries, den, movie theatre, bowling alley, and connected boathouse for Randy's yacht. All this space for three people orbiting each other like planets drowning in the ink of the cosmos.

Gazing upon Lake Francis through the large bay windows in the great room, Coral reminisced about the one-story, middle-class home in Iowa, LA that she grew up in. She almost missed the cracks in the walls and water damage that gave her parent's house so much character. This place was so immaculate it was practically sterile, with more than enough space to amplify the emptiness.

Coral endured years of merciless taunting at the hands of the rich girls at her high school because she was poor. But now that she had more money than she ever dreamed of, Coral understood what fueled the mean girls' spite. The more a person possessed, the greater the fear of losing it all. Nothing was promised.

Besides, all the money in the world couldn't prevent miscarriages or loved ones from being murdered. That's why she admired Randy so. If it wasn't for him and all he'd overcome, she might have given up after Kristopher's death. She'd fantasized more than once about ending it all. But she couldn't do that to him.

And she wouldn't do that to Karen.

Coral watched the moonlight dance across the deck, waltzing with the lazy current. A vision came to her of a tornado sweeping across the water, whisking their mansion away, like in the *Wizard of Oz*. Wiping the slate clean once and for all. The thought was rather appealing.

She wandered down a long expansive hallway adorned with portraits Randy commissioned of the Lafitte lineage. In classic bad taste, he placed his prized portrait of his father, Joseph, above the mantle in the great room. A breeze rippled through two shrouded paintings hanging at the end of the hall. Randy wanted to remove the portraits—one of Kristopher on his tenth birthday, and the other a family portrait—but Coral wouldn't allow it.

In the end, they compromised on the black silk shrouds.

Past the library was a hexagon shaped cul-de-sac with two closed doors opposite each other. Coral opened the door with a bright red STOP sign stuck to it and entered the freeze-frame world of an eighteen-year-old boy who would never reach manhood. The room was so full of Kristopher's essence, it often felt haunted.

Impervious to the eeriness, Coral went directly to the bed, running her hands over the LSU Tigers comforter and pillow on the full-size waterbed. She looked around the room at Kristopher's posters of Larry Bird, Pete Maravich, and John Stockton interspersed amongst others of Cindy Crawford, Pearl Jam, and Nirvana.

On the nightstand was a picture of the whole family taken at Kristopher's senior awards ceremony. Coral almost didn't recognize the pretty, middle-aged blond in the photograph. Her younger, smiling visage showed no trace of the crow's feet, wrinkles and dark circles plaguing her from the mirror these days. Whoever said "time healed all wounds" had never outlived their child.

Kristopher's death had devastated their family, plunging them into the suffocating darkness of grief and despair. Once Coral began her torturous crawl back toward the light, the overwhelming support from the public awed and humbled her into taking control of her grief. She harnessed her pain and poured it into *Catharsis in Crisis through Christ*, her bestselling book about dealing with child-loss-related trauma by fully surrendering to the will of their Lord and Savior.

As the book took up residence on the bestsellers list, Coral was thrust into the spotlight, the newly anointed expert on grief.

But in reality, she was ill-equipped to deal with the people who came to her for answers on how to handle the excruciating deaths of their children. She couldn't deal with the stories, each more tragic than the next. The pleading looks on their faces and the airy lifeless sound in their voices as they told their tales of woe were overwhelming. Coral became the opposite of the supposedly strong woman on the cover of that cursed book and retreated back into the darkness, taking Karen out of school in Baton Rouge and returning full-time to their home in Lake City.

The irony of it all was that even though she'd written the book, and believed what she'd been writing at the time, it had been years since she felt the presence of God watching over them. Why would God throw tragedy after tragedy her way—first Kristopher's death, then Randy's bout with brain cancer, and Karen's near suicide.

Coral sighed. Karen was so much like her father, it was frightening at times. Impossible to read, unfazed by the bumps life threw her, and filled with so much charisma that no one could deny her anything she wanted. As a licensed child psychologist, Coral knew her daughter better than she knew herself, but Karen's behavior of late left even her mother without answers. Coral did not like the fact that she couldn't get ahold of her daughter. Lord knows what shenanigans Karen might be up to. She decided to try calling again.

When she returned to their bedroom, Randy was awake. Coral could hear him rummaging through the medicine cabinet in the bathroom.

"Coral!"

She sat on the bed. "Yes."

"Where the hell are you hiding the rest of those damn sleeping pills?"

She yawned and stretched. "The same place I always keep them," she replied, unfazed by Randy's customary grouchiness. "In my overnight bag. It should be on top of the toilet right next—"

"Got'em."

She heard him turn on the sink and a few seconds later he clicked off the bathroom light.

"Nightmares," Randy said, as he climbed into bed.

"You were talking in your sleep," Coral said. "Who is Isaac?"

"Who?"

"You kept repeating that name, Isaac."

Randy frowned. "I have no idea what—"

Randy's cell phone rang, interrupting his train of thought. He looked around frantically for it.

Coral remembered her last call to Karen and picked it up off her nightstand.

"Karen?" she answered.

"Good evening, Missus Lafitte."

Coral recognized the deep country twang but couldn't place it. "You mean, good morning don't you, Mr.—"

"Snake. Snake Roberts. You remember me don't you ma'am? I was the one that found yuh son after he ran away."

"Yes…yes, of course I remember you. Do you know what time it is?"

Why in the world is Snake Roberts calling?

"Time to hand the phone over to yuh husband, don't you think? We got man business to discuss; it's best you don't axe too many questions." He gulped something and belched. "Aww…don't you worry your perty little head now…I'm gonna find your daughter. Hopefully she'll be better off than yuh boy ended up."

Find Karen? But I thought…

There was no oxygen in the room. Coral lost her equilibrium and collapsed.

CHAPTER EIGHT

Saturday
Lake City, LA

R andy stared down at Coral, passed out on their bed. "Goddamnit, Snake, you had to call in the middle of the fucking night, didn't you?"

"Well if yuh don't want to know where Madame Deveaux is holed up, I can always call back during nurmal bidness hours."

Randy heard the biting sarcasm in Snake Roberts' thick, country twang and knew the man was one beer from a blackout. He checked Coral's breathing and took the phone into the other room.

"You found her?" he whispered.

"A' course. But yuh won't be able to talk to her anytime soon."

"Why the hell not?"

"Because she's been dead for ten years. Heart failure."

"Dead?"

"As Elvis."

"Shit!"

"If it means anything to yuh, I did locate her daughter, Jhonnette."

"Her daughter? She can't help me," Randy replied. Then he thought of his father. "Wait. Maybe she can. Where is she, Snake?"

"She's in Nawlins. Do yuh want me to arrange a meeting?"

"You know me too well, Snake. Fetch."

"Okay, Boss. Oh, there's one more thing."

"What is it?"

"I got the name of the guy yer supposed to spring from Angola."

"Who is it?" Randy asked, fully expecting to hear Roberts say the name of some Irish mobster. When it finally registered what Snake was saying, he almost choked on the rage bubbling up from his gut.

"What did you just say?"

"I *said* it's Lincoln Baker. My source on the inside is a hunnert percent positive."

"But he killed Kristopher..."

"I know. Fucked up, ain't it, Boss?"

"I'll string Baker up by his balls. He wants to fuck with me."

"How you gonna manage that, Boss? Baker's on twenty-three-hour lockdown. Never leaves his cage."

Randy threw the phone across the bathroom.

Punishment.

CHAPTER NINE

"I'm coming!" Juanita Simmons said, hurrying toward the front door.

As she rushed through the opulent home she and Walter built after they won the election, she kept one hand between the heat of her thick dark hair and the nape of her neck. She hadn't thought to tie it back while undertaking the momentous project of organizing her husband's study, and now she was a sweaty mess, totally unprepared for company. Thankfully the cool hardwood floors beneath her petite bare feet provided brief relief from the heat.

Theirs was the largest residence in North Lake City. She and Walter had many spirited discussions over the location of their new home. He longed to infiltrate the exclusively white neighborhood of Oak Park.

"We have to break down these racial barriers, baby. If the first black mayor in the state of Louisiana can't live where he wants, then who can?"

It was a fair point. Juanita countered by reminding him racial tensions were higher than ever in the aftermath of the contentious

65

election between he and the hometown favorite, Randy Lafitte. Had Walter forgotten that a mere five years had passed since MLK's assassination? Change came slow in the South. Yes, his victory symbolized progress. But society still had a long way to go.

Truth be told, Juanita was not too keen on moving into a white neighborhood. While she was all for integrating the school system, when she walked around her neighborhood, she wanted to see her own people. It provided something Juanita had been searching for her whole life, the feeling of true security.

However, the tall dark-skinned man standing on her porch was an unfortunate reminder that Juanita had bigger things to worry about than the race of her neighbors.

Malcolm Wright, chief of Walter's security team, grimaced at her through the peephole. This, in and of itself, did not alarm her. Malcolm, a childhood friend, only possessed two expressions— anger, for intimidation, and dismay, for all other situations. Malcolm actually had a pleasant enough face, although she could never get used to the pirate-esque eye patch covering his missing left eye.

Though they dated briefly in High School, Juanita no longer trusted his wiry six-foot-four frame. He always seemed to be holding his coiled muscle back from some random act of violence. He was a living embodiment of the unfortunate misperception that the darker a person's skin, the darker their heart.

Juanita met Malcolm's grim countenance with a scowl of her own. These days she associated Malcolm's impromptu visits with agonizing pain. Opening the door, she silently prayed this wouldn't be a repeat of six weeks prior, when Malcolm had shown up at the house with an envelope containing pictures of Walter in a compromising situation with his white secretary.

Even with the evidence splayed out on the coffee table before her, Juanita refused to believe what she was seeing. Her anxiety multiplied as Malcolm explained that Randy Lafitte was trying to blackmail Walter with the information, but Malcolm intercepted the package before it got to Walter.

"So Walter doesn't know that I know?" she asked.

"No, but..."

"Good," she snapped. Before rationality could prevail, Juanita collected the envelope and its stinking entrails and bolted through the house until she reached the back deck. Standing upon solid wooden planks, she lit up a cigarette, ignoring her trembling hands, and set the envelope and its life-shattering contents ablaze.

Juanita tried desperately to purge her mind of the contents of that envelope, but she couldn't stop herself from drilling Walter about his whereabouts at every opportunity. One night, after finding lipstick stains on one of his dress shirts, she tore into him. Walter exploded in a cursing frenzy that reduced her to a tearful shambles, then left the house and didn't return.

Until last night.

After five nights away, he showed up with roses and spent hours filling her heart with hope and her ears with tearful apologies. Then he made love to her like he would never see her again. This morning as he got ready for work, he said, "Today marks a new beginning for us."

"Let me guess," Juanita said by way of greeting. "More bad news."

"Not exactly," Malcolm replied. "But it is time we speak about this, don't you think?"

She ushered him through the foyer, which was decorated with pictures of her and Walter in various phases of their relationship. Juanita privately lamented, as always, at the lack of smiling children in the portraits. The last photo, before the hall opened into the living room, was of Juanita and her mother in front of their old house in neighboring Fisherville.

"House," was a bit of an overstatement; it was really little more than a one-bedroom shack surrounded by shanties just like it. But her mother did the best she could after Juanita's father left them for another woman. She cleaned the homes of affluent white people and scraped together just enough money so Juanita could go away to college.

Over the past few weeks, Juanita often caught herself marveling at her mother's strength in the wake of her father's betrayal. She'd never seen her cry or heard her badmouth her father. It wasn't until her mother lay on her deathbed that she admitted the shame she felt over her inability to hold onto a man. At the time, Juanita's mind showed her the image of an enormous python with her father's head; her mother was desperately trying to hang onto the treacherous creature as it writhed in her tiny hands.

In recurring nightmares, Walter's face now supplanted her father's. Juanita was her mother's doomed understudy.

Malcolm sat on the leather sofa looking uncomfortable. Juanita saw him wince when she opted to sit across from him in one of the old-fashioned rocking chairs, instead of joining him on the couch. Prickly silence settled between them.

"Burning that envelope hasn't changed the facts, you know," Malcolm said finally, undoing the quiet. "Walter is risking everything. And for what? For some blond bimbo? Doesn't he realize what he stands to lose? Doesn't he see how Lafitte is playing him?"

"You know what I think?" Juanita asked, deciding not to indulge Malcolm's negativity any longer. "I think you're jealous. First you come out of nowhere during the campaign and offer help—which no one asked for, by the way—and now that he's in office, you're trying to ruin him. Is this how you treat your best friend?"

Malcolm's eye darted between hers in confusion. "Walter and I stopped being friends the moment I opened that envelope." He folded his arms across his chest. "Tell me, how many lies and excuses does a woman allow her philandering husband to feed her before she does something about it?"

"Fuck you, Malcolm!"

He recoiled, his jaws clenched. Finally, he replied, "You need to be directing that anger where it belongs."

Juanita's shoulders slumped, defeated. She was exhausted. "You're right, Malcolm," she said. "I'm just so confused. You have no idea how hard this has been for me. Walter came back last night. He told me it's over with her."

"And you believed him, right?"

It wasn't a question. She could tell from the incredulous look on Malcolm's face that he thought her a fool. Just some idiot woman too blind to see the truth in front of her. Juanita had suffered so much since discovering Walter's affair—the accusations, the denials, the fights, the hating and loving him at the same time.

Things between them had begun so differently.

Juanita and Walter met as undergraduate students at Dillard University. It was Malcolm who introduced her to Walter, his "best friend and future savior of the Afro-American race." Juanita was immediately drawn to Walter's strength, optimism, and chivalry. She was inspired by his bold vision to run for public office in a time when most black folks had been scared into silence by the Klu Klux Klan. His singing voice, a sonorous perfect tenor, had captivated her heart. They'd fallen in love during the March on Washington, standing side by side on the crowded steps of the Lincoln Memorial, accompanying Joan Baez as she sang "We Shall Overcome."

The two idealistic lovers married a year after Dr. King's *"I Have a Dream"* speech.

"What do you expect me to do, Malcolm? I still love him."

"And I still love you," Malcolm confessed. "I always have. Let me take you away from this place. I can remove all of your pain."

Juanita gazed upon Malcolm, sensing his sincerity. It was true that once upon a time, she considered Malcolm to be her ideal mate. But he'd returned from his tour in Vietnam a stranger, speaking of Voodoo and violence. Her Malcolm was gone, replaced by an adopted persona named Panama X.

Understanding dawned on her. "So that's what this is all about," she said, getting up. "You think I'm just going to leave this life I've scratched and clawed to build?" She paced before him like a lioness behind the zookeeper's fence. "You may have the rest of these black folks fooled Malcolm, but not me. You forget that

I *know* you. Save your medicine man routine for someone who cares. The protection of Jesus Christ presides over this household."

Malcolm smiled, but his eyes were devoid of humor. "Where was Jesus when Walter was fucking that bitch seven ways from Sunday?"

Juanita slapped him so hard her hand buzzed and blushed red for nearly a minute.

Malcolm's good eye darkened.

The telephone rang and Juanita jumped, startled.

"He-hello Miss Simmons." It was Carla Bean, Walter's secretary and lover. Juanita had thought she was impervious to surprises, but hearing that white whore's voice set her back.

"That's *Mrs.* Simmons," she replied. "What do *you* want?"

And what the hell are you still doing working there?

"Well, I hate to bother you, but Wally—I mean Walter—asked me to call and tell you he'll be working late again tonight."

Juanita swore she heard Walter chuckle in the background.

"Um, he said not to wait up. It's going to be a long night."

Juanita dropped the phone.

He's lost his goddamn mind. I'm gonna help him find it.

Walter and Carla's imaginary laughter echoed through the halls of Juanita's mind, consuming rational thought. She ran into the kitchen, opened the top drawer, and removed Walter's silver-plated revolver from its shelter of old dishrags.

Malcolm was hot on her heels. "I don't know what just happened, Juanita, but this is my burden. Not yours." He closed the distance between them and tried to extract the gun wedged between her palms.

71

"He's *my* husband," Juanita said, projecting her rage toward Malcolm as he twisted her left and right, trying to loosen her grip. In the struggle, Juanita's index finger found the trigger and she inadvertently squeezed.

The blast reverberated through her frame like a shockwave.

She stared in horror at the bullet hole in the tile floor between them, inches from Malcolm's feet. Juanita dropped the gun and the weapon clattered to the floor, coming to rest beneath the counter. From this vantage point, it was easy to pretend the revolver was just a harmless toy. Like, how before Carla Bean's phone call, it had been easy to pretend Walter was a good husband.

Oh God. What am I doing?

"I'm so sorry!" Juanita wailed.

Malcolm wrapped her up in his arms. His shirt was damp with musky perspiration. She heard the fear in his thudding heartbeat, but when he whispered to her, his voice was as calm as ever.

"I have seen your sacrifices firsthand, Juanita. You gave up everything for Walter. School, your career, even those five children you said you wanted. And what has he given you besides this big, empty house?"

Juanita collapsed against the cupboard, the layers of delusion starting to crack. "How could he do this to me?" she cried. "Oh God, I can't live like this anymore! I have to confront him, Malcolm."

"I know you do," Malcolm replied. "But you're not going alone." He stooped down and picked up the gun.

She looked at him with raised eyebrows.

"Just in case," he said.

They arrived downtown at the Lake City Fathers Building as the light began to wane. Parked in the nearly empty lot, Juanita commanded Malcolm to wait for her. Slamming the door in the middle of his protest, she raced up the five flights of stairs to Walter's office.

The small waiting area was vacant, the secretary nowhere in sight. The oppressive silence was unnerving. Juanita opened Walter's office door and surveyed the large space. Behind the desk, Walter's large leather chair faced the window overlooking Lake Francis and the Riverwalk.

A familiar scent tickled her nose. That bastard was wearing the cologne she'd bought him for their fifth wedding anniversary. She cringed at the visual of that homewrecking secretary smelling Walter's neck and then seducing him with her eyes.

He's probably daydreaming about which way to fuck her tonight.

A moan emanated from behind her. Against her better judgment, Juanita walked over to the closet.

They're in there!

Gripped by a sudden masochistic need to catch him in the act, she jerked the door open.

Walter was kneeling before the door, head bowed. He raised his face toward the light, recognition and fear filling his eyes. Duct tape covered his mouth. His hands were bound behind his back.

"Oh my God!" she screamed. "Walter! Who did this to you?"

He grunted something in reply.

As she struggled with the tape over his mouth, she heard a noise behind her. She whipped her head around just as a hard, jagged object smashed into her skull.

She awoke sometime later.

Her entire being was sore and bruised from rough treatment. She vaguely remembered her head being slammed repeatedly into the floor. She'd been hit with something else, too. The left side of her cranium was a sweaty, matted mess of hair, blood, and carpeting. Each breath was a scarlet torture.

Dark, tentacle-like tendrils of smoke smothered her sight.

Her arms were asleep. Above her head, her left wrist was handcuffed to one of the legs of Walter's desk. A wet, sticky substance trickled down her thigh as she tried desperately to remember.

Am I bleeding down there?

Juanita licked her swollen lips, tasting sweat and tears. Something crashed on the other side of the room. She managed to maneuver into a seated position. The desk obstructed her view.

Her throat threatened to close up on her. She lowered her head and covered her face from chin to nose with what was left of her blouse. Another crashing noise startled her back into action.

Gray-black smoke flooded the office. Juanita jerked violently at her restraint as blinding, stinging beads of sweat streamed into her eyes. She cried out in frustration. The handcuff bit into her skin like a stainless-steel vampire.

Using the blood as lubrication, she tried to free herself by yanking, jerking, and wriggling. Nearly delirious from the effort, Juanita tugged so hard she thought her veins would pop out of her arms. As the smoke tightened its death grip around her throat, she fought to remain conscious. Abruptly, the imprisoned hand pulled free. Juanita descended into a series of violent coughs as the office began to burn down all around her. Wincing in pain, she crawled through the oppressive cloud of smoke toward the door.

After four gasping crawls, she looked up to gauge how far she was from the exit. It seemed miles away. Then a voice spoke from a few feet in front of her. With the last of her strength dissipating, Juanita looked up.

A tall figure, wearing a gas mask, stared down at her.

"Help me," Juanita gasped. Her throat was a smoke-filled corridor.

The figure offered a muffled laugh. "Let's see how bad he wants you now."

CHAPTER TEN

Nine months later
1974
Houston, TX

J uanita lay on a lumpy mattress, legs spread wide. Harsh afternoon sunlight stabbed her through a small, barred window. Instead of giving birth in a hospital, Juanita was in the bedroom of a too small Frenchtown apartment, tucked inside the Fifth Ward ghetto. The one-bedroom safe house she refused to call home was now a prison.

Malcolm patted her sweat-soaked face with a once-cool rag gone warm.

Juanita took her eyes away from Malcolm's dark face. Staring at the scar tissue where his left eye used to be brought unhealthy visions of birthing a baby Cyclops. She knew she needed to focus on bringing this baby into the world, but her mind was stuck in a putrid whirlpool of negativity.

It wasn't supposed to happen this way.

"Almost time, baby," Malcolm said, grasping Juanita's hand in his large sandpaper paw.

"God, it's so hot!" she gasped.

"Everything is gonna be fine," Malcolm said, looking over at Velma Baker, the midwife. Velma was a short and stout woman, fair-skinned like Juanita, known as much for her sense of propriety as her competence. "Right, Velma?"

Velma responded by spreading Juanita's legs even wider. "This is it, Juanita," she said. "I need you to bear down now. Give us one last big push."

Heart-rate galloping, Juanita tightened her swollen abdomen until her vision burned and blurred from the sweat and strain. A scream escaped her lips. Despite her exertion, Juanita tried to visualize Walter's hands gently dabbing the rag against her feverish skin. When she opened her eyes and saw Malcolm hovering over her like a living, breathing nightmare, she remembered Walter was gone forever.

"I can see the head! Keep pushing, baby! Keep pushing!" Malcolm shouted.

He sounded far away, as if he were in the apartment downstairs. Juanita couldn't feel the mattress beneath her anymore. An all-encompassing bitterness about the life that had been stolen from her left no room for other sensations. She was coldly certain that whatever was inside her, struggling to get out, would not, could not, be human.

Babies were supposed to be born out of love, yet loathing enveloped her. Juanita squeezed her eyes shut and pushed like her very life depended on it. She needed to get rid of this hatred within her.

After collapsing on the floor of Walter's burning office, Juanita had resigned herself to perishing in the inferno. The next time she opened her bleary eyes, she found herself in the backseat of Malcolm's car, alive. Once she was coherent, Malcolm explained how he burst into the office, found her lying on the floor, nearly lifeless, and dragged her to safety. She asked him repeatedly about Walter, but his only reply was, "I didn't see him."

The newspaper helped Juanita fill in the blanks.

After the Lake City Fire Department put out the raging fire, they found Walter's barbecued body in the closet; a pair of bloody handcuffs connected to the desk; a twenty-two caliber pistol with rounds fired; and the body of Carla Bean—the secretary.

The headline declared, "Foul Play Expected Cause of Death for Mayor Walter Simmons and Secretary: Missing Wife is Lead Suspect." The police searched for weeks but were unsuccessful in identifying Juanita's whereabouts.

Meanwhile, Juanita and Malcolm took up residence in the ghetto safe house in Frenchtown. She tried to goad herself into leaving him and starting over on her own, but then the morning sickness started. That last night she and Walter spent together rendered more than a broken heart. It produced an embryo Juanita thought of as a curse from her dead husband.

As she entered her third trimester, she learned Walter's five million dollar life insurance policy and the bulk of his estate would be deferred to Lake City. To add insult to tremendous injury, Randy Lafitte, newly appointed mayor, vowed to the people of Lake City that Walter Simmons' legacy would "live on" through his deeds. He pledged to build a community center on the Simmons Estate, named in honor of the first black mayor of Lake City.

Watching Lafitte's pronouncements, Juanita became convinced that he was the man in the mask inside Walter's office. Lafitte had tried to blackmail Walter, and when that didn't work, he used his knowledge of the affair to set him up. He must have forced the secretary to call Juanita, knowing she would show up.

Juanita's survival was a happy accident. Had she perished in the fire alongside Walter and the secretary, there would have been many more questions to answer. With her gone, everything pointed solely in the direction of the jealous wife. Randy alone reaped the benefits. He got the money, the mayoral office, and a public mandate to make the changes he saw fit for Lake City.

Whenever Juanita closed her eyes she saw Walter's bloodied face staring up at her, pleading for her to save him. When Malcolm pledged that Lafitte would be justly punished for his crimes, she promised never to leave him.

"Something went wrong during labor," Malcolm said. "The baby is sick. Velma has to take him to the hospital."

Juanita wasn't surprised. She hadn't lit the fire that sealed Walter's fate, but she was as guilty as the papers described. Her breasts lactated, swollen with life-sustaining nourishment. But Juanita knew how putrid she was on the inside. Her milk was poison, her birth canal a watery grave. Nothing could come out of her unscathed.

Still, she needed to see for herself. "Bring it to me."

The infant was a helpless mass of wrinkled humanity squirming in the crook of Velma's arm.

"It's a boy," Velma declared.

"Let me hold him."

Malcolm intervened. "There's no time, baby. He's not breathing right."

Juanita glared at him.

"We've talked about this," Malcolm continued. "We have to let Velma take him. She will make sure they fix whatever is wrong and that he ends up in a good home. And when the time is right, I promise I will find him and bring him back to you."

Back in Walter's office, with everything burning around her, Juanita knew she was going to die; but then Malcolm pulled her from the burning tomb. Less than a month later, Juanita learned she was pregnant.

Juanita didn't believe in coincidences. It was no simple twist of fate that led her to Walter's side. No miracle that Walter's best friend saved her life and helped her pick up the shattered pieces of her porcelain existence. It was destiny.

Juanita felt her purpose returning. She gathered herself and replied, "Malcolm, no! If he goes to the hospital, we'll lose him."

"If we don't take him now, we're gonna lose him right here," Malcom said softly. "I'm not willing to take that chance." He motioned to Velma to get the baby.

Juanita tried to sit up, but her arms were too weak. "Velma," she admonished. "Don't you dare take my baby!"

"Wait," Velma said in a shaky tone, trying unsuccessfully to break the tension. "What are we going to call him?"

Juanita had considered only one name for a boy. The man Walter had patterned himself after. "Lincoln," she replied. "His name is Lincoln."

Velma put the baby in the bassinette and hurried out of the apartment with Malcolm. Lincoln started crying.

Each wail pierced Juanita to the core. Her body and instincts were on edge—she had to take action. In her mind, Velma Baker had morphed from a dedicated helper to dark schemer. Juanita clawed at the wall for leverage, screaming, "You can't take him, you bitch! You can't take him!"

The apartment door slammed, cutting off her baby's cries. Despite tremendous pain, Juanita made it out of bed, but collapsed on weak legs. She crawled toward the door, just as she had during the fire, screaming and stretching out her arms to welcome her child into the world. As his cries drifted away, her pain grew too intense to bear.

Curling her legs into her abdomen, she lay on the floor wishing for death. But not for herself. She passed into unconsciousness, fantasizing about how Lincoln would one day grow up to kill Randy Lafitte.

CHAPTER ELEVEN

24 years later
1998
Houston, TX

Amir Barber paused just outside of room 311 in the Houston Medical Center, preparing himself for what he would see when he pushed through the door. He rubbed his boot camp bald head compulsively. When he felt ready, he entered his mother's suite with a nervous smile.

Dear God.

Amir gazed down at his mother in the aftermath of her stroke. Always the picture of strength, Juanita had degenerated into a muddy puddle, waiting for the sun's rays to evaporate her into nothing. He whispered a silent oration to Ogou Balanjo, the Vodun spirit of healing, and set the flowers down on the nightstand.

Kissing her clammy forehead, he sat down in the chair next to the bed, clasping her hands in his own. Amir traced his fingers over the faded scar on her left wrist. He'd always wondered about how she'd gotten it and had sworn to himself he'd protect her against future harm. But he'd failed again.

I never should have left home.

Amir knew these thoughts were useless and unproductive. Still, he couldn't help but wonder what might have been if he'd stayed home after graduating from the University of Houston last year. Instead, he took his shiny new degree and enlisted in the Army as a Communication Operations Officer. He vividly recalled the look of betrayal in his mother's eyes when he told her of his plans. Dad's reaction had been predictably aloof.

"This is something I need to do for me, Dad," Amir said, as he and his father rested in the Kempo Dojo after their workout. Dad was still slightly out of breath. Amir realized for the first time his father was getting old.

They were seated in front of a large mirror. Amir compared his twenty-two-year-old frame to that of his father's. His father's skin was dark and course, Amir's fair and smooth. Amir's skin tone was the only physical trait he'd gotten from his mother. Other than that, he was the spitting image of his father. "You know I was in the service, right?" Dad asked.

Amir nodded. He knew all about his father's tour of duty in 'Nam. Anticipating his father's next words, he said, "Dad, I know you always tell me that the Army is no place for the black man, but just hear me out, okay? I'm not some dumb eighteen-year-old kid. I went to college, just like you asked me to." Amir swallowed his fear and continued the speech he'd been practicing for a week. "But if you hadn't joined the Army, you never would have discovered Vodun, right? So in a way, it was a positive experience for you. And you recruited your men over there in Vietnam, so had you not gone, the Black Mob probably wouldn't exist either. Shoot, you and Mom might never have gotten together." Knowing his father's one soft spot, Amir saved this point for last.

"That's not fair," Dad replied. "You know me and your mother are going through a rough time."

"Believe me, I know, Dad. But once I go away to boot camp she will be all alone and she'll need you. Ya'll can get back together."

"Don't change the subject. This is about you, not me. *You* want to join the white man's army. *You* want to die defending a country that does not give a damn about your people. *You* want to be a pawn...when I raised you to be a king."

"You don't understand, Dad. I read the book." Amir watched his father's good eye squint in anger as it usually did whenever anyone mentioned *Inside the Black Mob*, the unauthorized book written about his life and work. His father had maintained for years that one day he would write his own account and set the record straight.

Amir continued, "I need to learn what you learned, Dad. I know you think I'm too young, but I'm ready to do my part in the Liberation. You and I both know the other men in the Black Mob will never respect me or follow me if I don't do this."

His father's only reply was to stand up and walk out, leaving Amir alone to consider his future plans.

"Lincoln?"

His mother's voice startled Amir out of his memories. He looked down to see her gazing at him through pained eyes.

"Who's Lincoln?" Amir asked.

"No one. I'm so happy…to see you…my son." She tried to smile, but paralyzed muscles on the left side of her face turned her smile into a sneer.

"I brought you flowers, Moms."

"I…I saw. They're…beautiful."

"How are you feeling?"

She sneered again. "Looks worse…than it…feels."

Amir seriously doubted that. He brushed the hair off her forehead. "Is there anything I can do to make you more comfortable, Moms?"

"No…honey. I'm fine. Just…need to rest."

"Okay, Moms. Well, I'm here and I'm not going anywhere. The *loa* will watch over you and protect you."

The following days blurred together for Amir, as an endless procession of doctors, nurses, technicians, and counselors did their best to help his mother recover and dissuade his growing fears that things were far worse than they appeared. On the fifth day, he entered his mother's room to find her sitting up and crocheting. He felt a surge of hope at the sight of her.

"Hey, Moms! What are you working on?"

"Just keeping myself busy," she replied, sounding almost as good as she looked. "I've been waiting for you. We need to talk."

He took a seat. "What about?"

"Hand me my purse."

He passed the bag to her and watched her dig around inside with a look of pained concentration, finally pulling out two yellowing pieces of paper. She reluctantly handed them over to him.

Amir studied the faded newspaper articles. The headline of the first one read: "Gang Warfare Responsible for Simmons Park Massacre."

Amir recalled seeing the story on the news a few years ago. He'd forgotten how grim it was. Some high school basketball star, with gang affiliations, had shot up a bunch of gangbangers and cops in Louisiana. A group of first graders were caught in the crossfire, and a Louisiana state senator's son, Kristopher Lafitte, died there as well.

Amir winced as he read the gangbanger's name—Lincoln Baker.

"Moms, why are you carrying this old story around? And why did you call me by some murderer's name the other day?"

Juanita avoided his eyes. He asked her again.

"That...that murderer is your brother."

"What?" Amir yelled.

"Read the other article, Son. Please."

Amir wanted to challenge her, but decided to keep the peace for the moment. He unfolded the second article. This one was much older. Some of the type had worn away, but the headline told him everything he needed to know: "Foul Play Expected Cause of Death for Mayor Walter Simmons: Missing Wife is Lead Suspect."

"What the fuck?"

"Watch your mouth, Kareem." She coughed into her handkerchief. She only called him by his middle name when she was really upset. He *hated* his middle name.

"Naw, fuck that, Moms!" Amir glared at her. "You used to be married to the first black mayor in Louisiana?"

"He...Lincoln's father...was murdered."

Amir doubled over in the chair, choking back anger and confusion. The news hit him like opposing linebackers used to back in high school when Amir played running back. The thought of his mother with another man was inconceivable. If this was true, then everything he knew about his life was a lie. "This article says you're the lead suspect…"

"I know this is all very confusing, Son, but it's time you know the truth." She coughed violently again and wiped her mouth. "Amir, I waited too long to tell you all this and now it's almost too late. I didn't kill Walter Simmons, and Lincoln didn't kill those people." Her chest heaved from the effort it took to speak.

Amir choked back tears. "I don't understand. Just tell me what happened, Moms. Please?"

His mother's lips quivered as she said, "I've lost a lot in my life, Amir. But nothing has scarred me quite like the loss of your brother. If I tell you this, you have to promise me you will make things right with your father."

Amir didn't really believe that was in the cards, but nodded for his mother to continue.

A week after Amir learned that not only was Malcolm Wright not his mother's first husband, but that he had a half-brother named Lincoln Baker, Juanita Barber's chest rose and fell for the last time. But that chilly January day not only marked his mother's death, it also coincided with the beginning of Randy Lafitte's second term as Governor of Louisiana. A term nearly cut short by a bomb placed in the bowels of the Island of Capri Riverboat, where Lafitte was celebrating his re-election.

As Amir prepared to bury his mother, he learned his estranged father had confessed to the attempted assassination of Governor Lafitte.

CHAPTER TWELVE

1998
Angola, LA

Malcolm Wright exited the powder blue prison bus just inside the gates of the Louisiana State Penitentiary. The January air was brisk and cold. He took his first shuffling steps toward his cage, relishing the brisk wind after the stifling three-hour bus ride from the detainment center in New Orleans. The rattling of the steel chains binding his hands and feet brought on a memory of the creak of the rope around his lynched father's throat as his lifeless body twisted in the breeze.

His father had been killed because he was the most successful sharecropper in Lake City and had the audacity to try and renegotiate his share of the yield. Malcolm was only five at the time, but old enough to comprehend injustice, even if it took him much longer to put a name to the endless well of anger filling his heart. Thankfully, his oldest brother Frederick had been able to secure work as a day laborer and provide for the five of them left— Malcolm, the youngest, their mother, and his three older brothers Ralph, Duke, and Ronnie.

Frederick became an effective provider without turning into a stoic like their father. He married a woman, Abigail, blessed with the gift of balancing out their mother's alternating states of aggression, agitation, and depression. Ralph was the athlete of the family and a standout baseball player. But Ralph was playing ball in a pre- Jackie Robinson era, and his success had a direct correlation to the number of death threats he received. He eventually quit playing baseball for good and became a mechanic.

Duke was the family scholar. He introduced Malcolm to texts by Frederick Douglass, Marcus Garvey, and Richard Wright. Duke was murdered during a peaceful protest in Selma, Alabama in the early sixties. Ronnie and Malcolm, the youngest of the four brothers, were only sixteen months apart and enjoyed the closest bond. When Malcolm was eighteen he followed Ronnie into the Nation of Islam. Years later, Ronnie followed Malcolm into the Black Mob, and the Black Mob led Malcolm to the Louisiana State Penitentiary at Angola.

He sniffed at the air. Yes. This was the place. This was home.

He turned toward the snapping sound coming from his blind side and saw photographers capturing his picture from behind the gates. He was grateful he'd finally be out of the public's watchful eye.

The trial had gone smoothly. Except for his last conversation with Amir.

"Why did you do it, Dad?"

Amir's questions followed him all the way to his cell.

"Mom told me everything."

Malcolm sympathized with the boy's pain, but in time Amir would understand that, as always, Malcolm had done what needed to be done. Unfortunately, Amir didn't yet understand sacrifice, what it took to bring about real change.

Just like in chess, the trick is to learn to win from a position of perceived weakness.

Still, Malcolm was relieved his son finally knew some of the truth, even if the knowledge caused him great pain. Malcolm wondered if Amir would ever forgive him. He'd never wanted to lie to the boy, but Juanita had insisted they were protecting him. All Malcolm ever desired was to give Juanita the safety she craved and to provide their son, born two years after they lost Lincoln, with the benefit of their collective love and wisdom. And he'd been successful for a time.

In the eighties, as the AIDS epidemic and crack infestation destroyed black communities from coast to coast, the four-block community within Houston's Fifth Ward, known as Frenchtown, existed as a protected haven. Malcolm and his Black Mob created a veritable utopia for black businesses, schools, and families. Not even trickle-down Reaganomics could gain a foothold in Malcolm's sovereignty. His word was law and he ruled with a murderous regard for the criminal elements infecting nearly every other ghetto.

Malcolm made examples out of anyone who didn't adhere to the Black Mob's strict code of ethics. As a result, the community rallied around and insulated him from relentless attempts by the FBI and police to divide and conquer the Black Mob. Amir grew up healthy, intelligent, and conscious that his reality was different from many of his peers because his father had created a better world for him.

But it wasn't enough for Juanita. Despite his best efforts, every year that passed with no sign of Lincoln pushed them further and further apart. Eventually, Malcolm left Frenchtown, his wife, his son, and all that he'd built to find Lincoln. If he could do that, he could finally have his wife back.

But now it was too late.

"She's gone, Dad," Amir said, *tears streaking down his face like shooting stars.*

The woman he'd loved since they were adolescents, the only woman he'd ever loved, died the day of his ultimate act of vengeance. She ascended before he could accomplish the two tasks he promised to complete—kill Randy Lafitte and find Lincoln. But she would not die in vain.

Malcolm prioritized his next steps. He had been checked into the prison, strip-searched, clothed, and oriented on the ways of his new home. The guards kept asking him to state his government name. He answered, "Panama X" each time until the blows came and they dragged him to the hole.

Juanita was raised a devout Catholic and never understood Malcolm's conversion to the Nation of Islam. Then he returned from Vietnam claiming a new religion—Vodun. But it was his new first name—Panama—and the X connected to it, that upset her most, more than his foreign religious leanings. Juanita refused to call him anything but Malcolm.

He'd tried in vain to explain to her that Malcolm Wright was born poor and weak, a man who lived in fear of whites—until his brother Duke's murder transformed that fear to anger. That anger became focused power once he gave up his slave name and slave master's religion, and his power grew exponentially upon his indoctrination into Vodun.

Sitting in the dark, damp hole, he knew the last vestiges of Malcolm Wright had died with Juanita.

Panama X's mission was just beginning, however. After speaking with Amir, everything fell into place. He now knew he'd been sent to Angola to reconnect with Lincoln Baker—the man Juanita believed was she and Walter Simmons' long lost son.

It was ironic that Lincoln had been under his nose all this time. He'd grown up in Lake City, a mere two hours from his birth mother. Lincoln had also struck a far more significant blow against Randy Lafitte than Panama X had ever managed.

He killed the man's only son.

Panama X relished their first meeting. He could hardly wait to take the boy under his wing and begin working to bring his ultimate plan to fruition. Lincoln was the linchpin. Amidst all the evil he'd sown, Randy Lafitte had made one crucial mistake.

He should have killed Juanita when he had the chance.

CHAPTER THIRTEEN

Saturday
Angola, LA

Lincoln Baker twirled a homemade toothpick in his mouth, staring at the collage of newspaper and magazine cut-outs pasted all over his concrete home. The tattered remnants seemed to glow in the early daylight. Bold titles and stories worked in harmony—pieces of a jigsaw puzzle reflecting the man in front of them through a mirror of words. Lincoln had stopped reading the articles a long time ago. Now, he just looked at the headlines, captions, and pictures, allowing his mind to drift.

Crows just outside the block windows were engaged in an aerial clash over an insect. Finally, one crow cawed in victory and flew away with his prize. Lincoln's heart soared with the avian soldier, wishing him well.

Lincoln took a sip of lukewarm water from a chipped styrofoam cup imprinted with the letters LSP—Louisiana State Penitentiary. The oldest article, now barely legible, was entitled "Louisiana's Best Kept Secret." Another clipping from *Parade* magazine touted 1992's Parade High School All-Americans as the future of the NBA. Next to it was a ruffled cover of *Sports Illustrated*. It showed three young men standing under the golden arches of McDonalds, their smiles outshining the famous trademark. The headline read, "The Real Big Macs!"

But Lincoln barely saw these. His eyes always ended up on the headlines, "#1 Down the Drain: Angola Gets Top Draft Prospect," and "Gang Warfare Responsible for Simmons Park Massacre."

He touched the papers hanging on the wall. One article showed a picture of a smiling face, obviously a yearbook photo, posted next to a mug shot of the same face. Although the pictures were taken many years prior, Lincoln looked pretty much the same. He'd accumulated more tattoos on his fair skin since his incarceration, but by and large he was like a meat-filled refrigerator left off too long — same appearance on the outside, but utterly ruined within.

He stood up and approached the dented rusty piece of reflective glass — a joke of a mirror. Removing his sweatshirt, he applied shaving foam to his two-day stubble and took a slightly used bic razor to his face. As always, he contemplated taking the blade to his jugular, but it had been many years since he'd seriously considered suicide. Instead, after shaving, he examined the black skull with blood descending from both eyes inked on the muscled bulge of his right shoulder — the insignia of his gang, the Dirty Skulls.

Only two people in the world knew about the nasty scar beneath his first tattoo. The man who'd burned the five-year-old orphan in his charge with a soldering gun, and Lincoln. As he grew older, Lincoln covered many of his visible childhood scars this way. Fascinated with reptiles, especially snakes, he saw each tattoo as a piece of new skin. But the tattoo just below the skull that read R.I.P. K.L. #44 was a daily reminder that the deepest wounds could never be shed.

Lincoln thought about Kristopher Lafitte constantly. Even though he was ten years removed from the events that resulted in the death of his best friend, he couldn't erase the guilt he felt for what he did and what he failed to do. The left side of the wallpaper reminded him of a time before the death and sadness. Back when the media depicted Lincoln as a basketball god.

After his sentencing for the killings at Simmons Park, no one uttered a word about his bright future. Only words like gangbanger, juvenile delinquent, drug dealer, cop killer, and murderer were used to describe him now. The papers went from singing his praises to exposing his criminal past—starting with a convenience store robbery when he was eight. They described his upbringing, moving from the orphanage to foster home after foster home because no parents or blood relatives would claim him. They listed his many stints in juvenile detention centers. Their words damned him with the same question.

Why?

Lincoln had no answers for them. His adjudicators took his silence for guilt and condemned him to life behind bars. Infamy followed him from the streets into the cell, and Lincoln began to examine his life with the avid interest of a coroner probing a mutilated corpse for clues.

His morbid curiosity became so great he broke down the wall of silence between himself and Moses Mouton, the man who'd given him the only real break of his life. To the outside world, Moses was a civil rights activist and devoted preacher. To Lincoln, Moses was the father he never had. Ironically, Moses had spent twelve years locked up in this very prison.

Lincoln was looking at four years in juvenile detention for two counts of armed robbery when he learned a deal had been reached and he'd been sentenced to house arrest. Lincoln was sure the judge had made a mistake—how could he be on house arrest when he'd been living in the streets for the past two years?

The mystery was soon solved. The bailiff led him to a holding cell where a large, black man sat behind the table. He had the biggest hands Lincoln had ever seen and was reading a book called *Native Son*.

Lincoln thought it was some shit about Africa.

The man kept reading for a few moments, then lowered the book and looked at Lincoln like he'd just realized someone else was in the room.

"Good, you're here. Have a seat, Son," the man said.

"Who the fuck are you?" Lincoln replied, still standing.

The guard grabbed the tip of his billy club.

It's okay, Hardy," the man said to the guard. "Would you mind standing outside?" After the guard left the room, the man looked at Lincoln and said, "My name is Moses. Moses Mouton. I'm the reason you're here and not headed for juvenile detention."

"Yo' name Moses? Like in the Bible Moses?"

"Exactly…I see you know the Bible."

"Not really, Bruh, I saw that Charlton Heston movie. Whatcha mean you the reason I ain't goin' to juvie?"

"I told the judge I would make sure he never heard your name again in connection with gang activity. I'm here to make you an offer you can't refuse."

"Whateva man, I don't make no deals, already told the damn prosecutor that."

"This isn't a deal, Lincoln," Moses replied. "This is your last chance."

"Last chance for what, nigga? I'm a dead man. I walk outta here and the Skulls'll think I ratted 'em out. What kinda offer you got fo' a dead man?"

"Please don't use that n-word around me. In addition to protection from your gang, I'm offering you something that I never had. I was just like you, Son."

"Let's get one thing straight, Bruh, you ain't nuthin' like me," Lincoln interrupted, getting up from his seat. "I don't got time fo' dis shit."

"And that's exactly what I used to say," Moses said, standing up as well, the book gripped in his hand like a Bible. "I liked selling drugs, using drugs, and even robbing people. Unfortunately for me, I wasn't a minor when I got my last chance and they sent me up to Angola for twelve years. I was raised on these streets, just like you. My folks passed away when I was very young and my grandmother could never keep up with me—"

"Look man, what all this shit got to do wit' me?"

"I'm trying to tell you why I want to help you, Lincoln. I'm trying to tell you why that white judge is entrusting you into my care. Listen carefully to me, Lincoln, because I'm only going to say this once." Moses took a deep breath and sat back down.

Something in his eyes made Lincoln sit, too.

"Nobody has ever given a damn about you, Son. Nobody really gives a damn about any of our youth. You may not even give a damn about yourself, and that judge is more than willing to get one more thug off of the streets, so you're helping him out with your attitude. Now I told myself after I got released from prison that I would not and could not let my black brothers and sisters keep disappearing down the garbage disposal. I have a responsibility to you, and you have a responsibility to God not to squander the opportunities He's giving you to change your life. So here's the deal: you are going to be living with me from now on, you are going to obey your house arrest, you are going to go back to high school, and you are going to make something of yourself. And if you don't, that gang you run with will be the least of your troubles. I may be a man of the Lord, but I'll kill you myself..."

Moses did not mince words.

The terms of Lincoln's house arrest stated that he was only allowed to leave Moses' house to attend high school. The Dirty Skulls' rival gang, the Scorpions, took advantage of the opportunity, using Moses' home for target practice on several occasions. Each time, Moses locked Lincoln in the bathroom until he calmed down; but one night Lincoln snuck out of his bedroom window, looking to settle the score.

After cruising through the Scorpions' hood for a couple of hours, he returned to Moses' home to find the windows to his bedroom locked. With no other choice, Lincoln went around to the front door and boldly rang the doorbell. After a moment the door swung open.

Moses pulled Lincoln into the house by the front of his t-shirt and threw him down into a dining room chair. A rubber-gripped, silver-barreled .357 Magnum revolver lay on the kitchen table before him.

"Pick it up."

Lincoln stared at the gun and back up at Moses.

"I said, pick the gun up."

Lincoln reached for the weapon.

Moses grabbed his hand before he could grasp it. "When you pick it up, you either shoot me or shoot yourself, you hear?"

"I—," Lincoln started.

"I don't want to hear anything but you clicking back the safety and a gunshot. Make your choice." He released Lincoln's hand.

Lincoln reluctantly jerked the weapon up. He tried to speak, but nothing came. He held the weapon in front of him with shaking hands.

"You want to kill somebody so bad, pull the trigger."

Lincoln's senses were amplified. Moses' Brut cologne was as omnipresent as the stench of his own fear. The ceiling fan in the living room was as loud as helicopter blades. Every pore on Moses' livid face was apparent. Lincoln readjusted his grip.

"What are you waiting for? Pull the trigger, big man." Moses' words came in slow motion.

Suddenly Lincoln was nine years old again, with an older gang member holding his hand up while he pulled the trigger. The gun was so heavy in his tiny hand; the recoil almost knocked him over. In the distance, a kid not much older than himself lay twisted on the ground.

He blinked the memory away and slammed Moses' gun down on the table. "Fuck you, man! I don't gotta do nuthin' you say!" Lincoln screamed.

Moses picked up the firearm and walked around to Lincoln's side of the table. He pressed the barrel to Lincoln's temple.

Lincoln flinched.

Moses' lips brushed against his earlobe. "You've got a death wish, Son. I'll be doing you and everyone in this town a favor by putting a bullet in your head right now. You think you're invincible?"

Lincoln swallowed hard. "You ain't gonna shoot"

He was interrupted by the unmistakable click of the trigger being squeezed. It took Lincoln five seconds to realize he wasn't dead. He had collapsed.

Moses stood over him and whispered, "Boom. Lincoln Baker the gangbanger is dead."

The jingle-jangle of prison alarms dispersed Lincoln's memories.

It was 4:45 a.m. Most of the other inmates would be leaving their cells to work the eighteen thousand acres of farmland surrounding Angola. Before the Louisiana State Penitentiary became America's largest and most violent maximum-security prison, it was a plantation. The slaves that worked the land back then were from Angola in Africa.

Lincoln found it ironic that the ancestors of the slaves who originally toiled this land were still trying to get free. The statistics claimed that nearly ninety percent of Angola's five thousand inmates would die inside the prison walls. On day one, Lincoln vowed he would never die inside this cage.

Now, it was almost time to fulfill his prophecy. Nothing could take his hope away. He'd survived ten years of twenty-three hour lockdown and near total isolation and was done being a slave. Before sleep could claim him, Lincoln thought of the victorious crow and muttered, "It's my time to fly the coop."

CHAPTER FOURTEEN

Four years earlier
1998
Angola, LA

"Baker. You've got a visitor," the guard said, as he approached Lincoln and two fellow inmates shooting basketball in the yard.

Lincoln swished a three-pointer. "Wasn't expectin' nobody."

"Well, someone's expectin' you. Bring your ass."

Lincoln followed the guard through a succession of gates leading to the visitors camp. There was something oddly familiar about him. Just before they reached the visitors camp, the officer shoved Lincoln into a shadowy corridor between the buildings.

"What the fuck?"

"Shhh!" the guard hissed. "Shut the fuck up."

Lincoln debated whether or not to break the hand pinning him to the wall. "Nigga…"

A deep voice greeted him from the shadows. "Hello, Lincoln."

The guard released him and a moment later a tall, thin, dark-skinned man with short gray hair emerged from the darkness. He strolled toward Lincoln nonchalantly, as if he could walk out prison anytime he wanted.

Lincoln knew this man. Shit, everyone knew him. He was Angola's most recent and most infamous resident—Panama X.

Lincoln sized him up. They were both dressed in standard prison attire, but Panama X wore his as if they were vacation clothes. Appearing much younger than his years, Panama X exuded an aura of power and self-control. Awareness blazed from the man's one good eye; a patch covered the other.

Wonder how he got that?

Lincoln got an uneasy feeling as Panama X's good eye analyzed him. He'd heard stories that Panama X was some sort of voodoo priest and worshiped the devil. Supposedly he could possess a man just by uncovering the patch on his bad eye. Lincoln didn't know about all that, but kept a watchful eye on that patch, just in case.

Panama X looked over at the guard and smiled. "You were right, Amir, he does look just like his mother."

"What the fuck you just say?" Lincoln blurted.

Panama X continued to gaze at Lincoln in silence, as if he were seeing a ghost.

"I understand that you're new here," Lincoln warned through gritted teeth. "But you might want to watch yo' mu'fuckin' mouth."

The guard, Amir, planted a palm on Lincoln's chest, pushing him against the wall. "Easy, Lincoln."

As Lincoln prepared to snap the guard's wrist, Panama X intervened. "Let him go, Amir. He's not going to cause trouble. Right, Lincoln?"

Lincoln and Amir stared each other down for a moment, then Amir backed down.

"There's really no need to be rude, Brother Baker," Panama X said. "I meant no offense, believe me. It is truly an honor to meet you." Panama X extended his hand.

Lincoln stared at it like it was a loaded weapon, then reluctantly grasped the man's strong, smooth hand.

"You know, Brother Baker," Panama X whispered, "the handshake has destroyed more civilizations than any weapon."

"Brother Baker?" Lincoln asked, dropping his hand to his side. "There you go wit' that Moslem crap. I ain't got no brothers that don't wear the red and black."

"Well, you've got one more now," Amir interjected, staring at Lincoln intently. He pointed to the center of his chest. "But we wear the red on the inside, know what I mean?"

Lincoln's muscles tightened and twisted beneath his clothes as he prepared to give the guard an old-fashioned Dirty Skulls beat down just for daring to suggest what he was suggesting.

Panama X continued, "It truly is a shame that we all have to meet like this."

Lincoln's head was a mess. "What the fuck are ya'll talkin' 'bout?"

Panama X gave Amir a slight nod.

"We don't have much time," Amir said. "I took this job inside Angola to make sure my Pops—" he leaned in Panama X's direction, "—was taken care of."

Lincoln looked between the two of them and finally saw the resemblance.

"But that's not the only reason I'm here," Amir continued. "I'm also here to find my half-brother." He pressed a crumpled piece of paper into Lincoln's hand. "Take this."

"Keep an open mind, Lincoln," Panama X said. "When you're ready, you know how to find me."

With that, Amir and Panama X walked away, leaving Lincoln alone and more confused than ever.

Lincoln waited until he got back to his cell before unfolding the note. The spidery handwriting on the wrinkled paper was difficult to read but Lincoln's rage made it nearly impossible.

My Dearest Lincoln,

God, I never believed I would be writing a letter like this one. I never believed I would find you and have the opportunity to reach out to you in any way. I'm sure you must be confused by everything happening right now. The only thing I ask is that you read this whole letter before you decide to destroy it. Please.

My name is Juanita Barber and I am your mother. I used to go by Juanita Simmons, but that was a lifetime ago, back when I was married to your father, Walter Simmons.

I know I haven't been a mother to you and I'm sure you're asking yourself, why now? Why after all these years am I just now hearing from this woman?

Lincoln, baby, I knew the truth the moment I saw you on my television screen looking at me with my own lips and nose. At first I thought, how is this possible? How am I seeing someone that looks so much like he came from me, yet I don't even know him? But I knew, Lincoln. I suppose I've always known.

Lincoln, I've been looking for you your whole life. I lost you shortly after you were born, but I never gave up the hope of one day finding you…

It was too much for Lincoln. He covered his eyes with his hands as the letter drifted to the floor of his cell.

Lincoln had always wondered about his real mother and father. His entire life had been filled with strangers standing in as family. But now he held a letter given to him by a man claiming to be his half-brother, written by a woman claiming to be his biological mother. For some reason the name Simmons kept ringing in his ears, but the only Simmons he knew was…Simmons Park.

Goosebumps erupted all over his body and black stars descended over his vision. He couldn't breathe. Overcome by foreign emotions, he kicked at the stone walls of his cell, overturned his cot, and knocked his few material possessions off the sink before falling to the floor, gasping for air.

The next day, determined to get to the bottom of things, Lincoln called Moses.

"Hello?" a boyish voice greeted.

"Brandon?" Lincoln asked, a little choked up. He hadn't spoken to his adopted brother in what seemed like forever. "It's Lincoln."

"Hold on."

A moment later, Moses picked up the line. "Lincoln?"

"Hey. I can't believe that was Brandon."

"Yeah, he's getting bigger every day. I'll send you a picture."

Lincoln couldn't even imagine it. "That would be great. He's still not talking to me though."

"Give him time, Lincoln—he'll come around. I wasn't expecting to hear from you until Sunday. What's going on?"

Lincoln thought about nixing the whole conversation, but then forged ahead, telling Moses everything Panama X and Amir had said. He was certain Moses would write the whole thing off as fiction.

Instead, Moses said, "So they finally found you."

Lincoln tried to contain his anger, but it grew more difficult with each breath. "Wait a minute, you knew about all this?"

"I'm sorry for not telling you sooner, Son. I just thought...well it doesn't matter now."

"So, wait, this is real?"

"I can't tell you if this Amir is related to you or not, but yes, you *are* Juanita's son."

Lincoln couldn't believe what he was hearing. "And what does Panama X have to do with this?"

"I don't know, but Panama X is not to be trusted, you hear me? He only told you all this because he wants something from you."

"What? What could he possibly want from me?"

"That's what scares me, Son. Scares me to death. My advice: steer clear of him and this Amir character. I'll try to track down Juanita and clear this whole thing up. Can you hold on for me?"

"Well, what else am I gonna do? I've got nothing but time."

CHAPTER FIFTEEN

Saturday
Lake City, LA

Randy sat at his desk in the Governor's office. His face contorted as he re-read the passage from *The Pirate King*.

Overwhelmed with grief over his daughter Melinda's suicide, Luc Lafitte killed himself at the base of their live oak tree, just three days after her death. There was another prevailing theory as to what had overcome Luc, however. The slaves whispered about a voodoo curse...

He looked up, dazed, and stared at the framed photo of Kristopher and Karen, taken when Kristopher was fifteen and Karen was five. Nearly twenty-four hours had passed since Randy's last contact with Snake, and still no word.

The kidnappers had given Randy plenty to keep himself busy. The Pardon Board had convened earlier that morning in an emergency Saturday session and voted in favor of releasing Lincoln Baker. Not that it had been easy. Randy had been forced to proffer exorbitant favors—the currency of politics. This was after he'd lined their pockets, of course, and promised that Baker would never actually see the light of day.

Randy's thoughts turned to his wife's mental state. Coral had been practically catatonic since learning of Karen's disappearance. Episodes like this hadn't exactly been rare since Kristopher's death, but it did demand additional attention on Randy's part. Attention he did not have to spare.

"You really have no idea what you're getting yourself into, do you?"

Madame Deveaux's admonishment continued to torment him after all these years. But it had all been a ruse, hadn't it?

There is no curse. I was used by the fortune teller. She hired someone to kill my father.

Someone rapped on his office door. It was one of the mail boys. "Delivery, sir."

"Bring it on in, Chase." Randy prided himself on his ability to recall names. Randy signed the release form and tore open the envelope. It contained a single DVD. There was no note.

"Chase, do you mind setting this up in the DVD player for me?" Randy had never been good with technology.

Chase made it happen and left Randy's office as soon as the video started. At first there was nothing to see, just a pitch-black screen. Then Randy detected a faint bass drum pulsing in a rum-pum-pum-pum, rum-pum-pum-pum rhythm. Next, the screen filled with an extreme close-up of his daughter's face.

Randy leaped from his chair in shock.

Karen's hair was a dirty blond mop atop her head, her eyes half-open and rolled all the way back. Dried blood lay suspended between her nose and the top of her mouth, her lips curled into a lazy smirk as if she were in on a private joke.

A deep voice off camera began chanting.

"Say hey!
Seven stabs of the knife, seven stabs of the sword.
Hand me that basin, I'm going to vomit blood.
Seven stabs of the knife, seven stabs of the sword.
Hand me that basin, I'm going to vomit blood.
Hand me that basin, I'm going to vomit blood.
But the blood is marked for him.
I say hey! I'm going to vomit blood, it's true.
Seven stabs of the knife, seven stabs of the sword.
Hand me that basin, I'm going to vomit blood.
Hand me that basin, I'm going to vomit blood.
My blood is flowing, Dantò, I'm going to vomit blood.
My blood is flowing, Ezili, I'm going to vomit blood.
My blood is flowing, Karen, you're going to vomit blood."

Each time the speaker said, "I'm going to vomit blood," a dark, viscous substance that looked a lot like blood was liberally sprinkled over Karen's head and face. Throughout the dousing, Karen's facial expression never changed.

The speed and volume of the drums increased, becoming like a frantic tachycardia. Scattered shouts and moans punctuated pauses, creating a cacophony of chaos.

The drums abruptly stopped.

The speaker said, "Kristopher Lafitte, come forth. We welcome you back to the realm of the living."

Karen's head, which had been listing to the left, straightened. She started convulsing and frothing at the mouth, as if in the midst of a powerful seizure. Then, as suddenly as it began, the seizure stopped. Karen's chin dropped to her chest.

A conch shell rang out from the silence.

Karen raised her head in response. She stretched her neck in a circular motion and then stopped dead center. Her eyes opened.

Randy covered his mouth. Karen's hazel eyes were gone.

Randy stared into the piercing blue eyes of his long dead son, Kristopher. Any hope he'd reserved was replaced by a cold, murderous rage.

The voice continued, "Kristopher Lafitte, I permit you to leave the door of the spirit world. Look upon my enemy, Randy Lafitte, who deserves just punishment. Torture Randy Lafitte in the following nights with the worst dreams. Make him writhe in pain, fear, and illness. After fulfilling your task, you will return to your world and this door will close. Thank you for your services. Be it so!"

The screen went blank.

After a while, Randy got up and reluctantly replayed the video. But this time he looked for any signs of trickery or tampering. You could do anything with digital technology these days. He probably would have watched it the rest of the day if Snake hadn't called.

"Snake," Randy answered, trying to control the tremor in his voice. "For your sake you better have found her."

"Yup, Boss. I found Jhonnette Deveaux. What's the plan?"

Randy's mind returned to the image of those crazed blue eyes screaming out of his daughter's head.

"Boss? You okay?"

"Yes. Of course. Have Miss Deveaux meet me in New Orleans first thing in the morning. And make sure you have those other things I asked for."

"Sure thing, Boss. But I tell ya, this little chicky is a tough one. How you gonna get her to talk?"

Randy smiled grimly, seeing Madame Deveaux's face in his mind's eye. "That's not going to be a problem. Just make sure she shows up."

CHAPTER SIXTEEN

Sunday
New Orleans, LA

Jhonnette Deveaux entered the Presidential Suite at the New Orleans Sheraton. A large, burly bodyguard ushered her through the door into an expansive sitting room.

Randy Lafitte stood to greet her. "Glad you could make it on such short notice," he said, looking her up and down appreciatively. "I'm sure you hear this often, but you look just like your mother. My sincerest condolences for your loss. I imagine it hasn't been easy for you."

"Thank you," she replied demurely, ignoring his outstretched hand. As she took a seat across from him, her eyes were drawn to Lafitte's bald, freckled head. He used to have a movie star coif, but the brain malignancy had taken care of that. She wondered why he hadn't grown his hair back like so many other cancer survivors.

Still, he looked a whole lot better than the last time she'd seen him this close…

⁋

It was June 1994, and Jhonnette had just passed her six-month anniversary working as a nurse at the Oschner Cancer Center in New Orleans. One afternoon, she and her colleagues learned they would be receiving a VIP—the recently elected Governor of Louisiana. He was coming in for a series of tests to see if his brain cancer was spreading.

Curious, Jhonnette took a peek at the Governor's chart. It certainly looked like Lafitte's term was going to be cut drastically short. He had a malignant tumor the size of a plum in the pineal region at the base of his brain—one of the worst regions for a brain tumor. The pineal gland not only controls the body's hormonal systems, it also regulates the sleep-wake cycle. As the body's internal clock, its timer was rapidly counting down to zero for Randy Lafitte.

He was receiving a debilitating amount of pain medication for the vicious headaches associated with his condition, as well as meds to help him get some semblance of regular sleep. Jhonnette was covering for a fellow nurse the next evening when her curiosity got the best of her again. After all, Lafitte's story was famous. He'd lost both his parents as a young man and his only son had been killed the same year Jhonnette had buried her mother. Her heart ached for the suffering he'd endured, and since she knew she could make him more comfortable, she cautiously entered his room.

As a young girl, Jhonnette learned she was an amplifier, blessed with the ability to magnify the unconscious thoughts of others and manifest their deepest, darkest secrets. She could also boost the body's curative capabilities, a trick that always worked to endear her to whomever was blessed with her healing. Having the Governor as an ally could come in handy down the line.

She stood next to his bed, pretending to check the telemetry monitor. His eyelids twitched in the midst of R.E.M sleep. Gently, she placed her hands on his shaved head, sending energy through her palms to the diseased area. If she could just shrink the tumor a little bit, she might be able to alleviate some of his pain.

Beads of sweat broke out on the Governor's forehead from the increase in temperature. She was about to remove her hands when he forcefully grabbed her wrists. His eyes opened wide.

As she struggled to get free, she noticed that the white of one of his eyes was completely bloodshot.

"So you've come to finish me off, Madame Deveaux," he slurred.

Jhonnette froze. *How does he know my mother?*

"Do it. Finish it!"

In her panic to get away from him, Jhonnette felt a tremendous quantity of energy pour out of her.

Lafitte's hands dropped back to his sides, his tense neck relaxed, and his eyes closed again.

Jhonnette ran out of the room as fast as her feet would take her. Unfortunately, she couldn't outrun the memories she'd just lifted from Lafitte's subconscious mind.

One of the side effects of her ability was that she tended to receive trace information from the subjects of her healing. In her mind's eye, she had seen a much younger Randy Lafitte sitting across a table from her mother.

Her mother had said, *"You're just a boy. Who could have possibly hurt you so deeply you feel the need to hurt them in return?"* She heard Lafitte's reply.

"My father."

She'd quit her nursing job the next day. Every action she'd taken since had been leading up to this moment—her reunion with Randy Lafitte. Only this time, she felt no sympathy for the man whose life she'd unwittingly saved. If she'd known then what she knew now, she'd have slit his throat.

He doesn't remember me. But he will.

"The resemblance really *is* uncanny," Lafitte repeated.

Jhonnette smiled thinly. "Mother said you would say that."

"She knew we would meet?"

"Karen had to turn eighteen eventually."

Lafitte's eyes narrowed. "How do you know my daughter's name?"

Jhonnette met his gaze. "Mother kept tabs on you," she lied.

"What do you mean, 'Karen had to turn eighteen eventually'?" Lafitte pressed.

"You know exactly what it means."

Lafitte sighed. "So, I'm guessing it's no surprise to you then that she's been kidnapped." He stared at her intently. "I assume you know about the curse."

"Why else would I be here."

Lafitte leaned forward. "How do I save Karen's life?"

"You already know the answer to that question."

"I want to hear you say it," Lafitte demanded.

"You have to sacrifice yourself for your daughter. Or find a substitute that they will accept."

"What do you mean a substitute? And who's this 'they'?"

Jhonnette allowed herself to smile internally. She had him. "*They* are the spirits you invoked when you resurrected the curse to kill your father. And *they* demand the blood of a Lafitte, or else *they* will take you both."

"Bullshit," Lafitte spat.

"If you're so convinced it's bullshit, then why did you bring me here?" Jhonnette reached for her purse and stood up.

"Alright. Okay. Let's start over," Randy backpedaled, motioning for her to sit. "You know I met your mother on my eighteenth birthday, right?"

Jhonnette settled back into her seat. "I know you did your best to ruin her." After his father's death, Randy ran every fortune teller out of New Orleans. His own version of the Spanish Inquisition, minus the burning witches.

Lafitte fidgeted. "I regret that. I truly do. I was young and angry."

Jhonnette stared back at Lafitte and thought of her impoverished childhood. The multitude of men she laid beneath as a teenager to put food on the table after her mother's paltry fortune telling business dried up, along with her health. "That's no excuse," she said, her voice laced with bitterness.

"Well, now I'm in a position to make good," Randy grinned. "You have information I need and I'm willing to compensate you handsomely. What do you say?"

Jhonnette sighed. "I don't even know why I agreed to see you today."

"I'll tell you why," Lafitte replied. "Because you don't want to see an innocent girl die."

"Let's get one thing straight, Governor," Jhonnette said. "I don't give a shit about what happens to your daughter."

Lafitte flinched.

Jhonnette smiled slightly. "You should've thought of this day before you got your wife pregnant. But since you don't believe in the curse anyway, I'm sure you have nothing to worry about."

Jhonnette locked into Lafitte's hazel eyes and subtly pushed energy at him. Her palms tingled with the release.

Lafitte's face shifted. One second, he was a reasonably charismatic politician; the next, he was a man on the brink of collapse. His eyes lost their focus and he started grinding his teeth, only stopping to offer a savage grin. "You have no idea what I'm capable of," he spoke slowly. "Your mother was a far more reasonable woman. Smarter, too. She knew her place. Am I going to have to teach you yours?"

I'd like to see you try.

Still, Jhonnette knew in Lafitte's amplified state both his bite and bark would be bad news. She steadied herself. It was time to play her trump card.

"There is someone else carrying your blood. Someone who could be sacrificed."

"You're crazy," Lafitte said. "I am an only child and my son is dead."

"Maybe Kristopher and Karen weren't your only children."

He raised his eyebrows. "What are you talking about?"

"I inherited my mother's gift."

"Your mother was a scam artist. I've believed her lies for too long."

"Then why are we still talking?"

Lafitte held his breath, and then exhaled in a rush. "Go on."

"To save your daughter's life, and your own, you need to remember what you've done before it's too late. The timing of your daughter's kidnapping suggests her abductors know as much as I do about your family history. They are using that knowledge to their advantage. Narrow down the list of people who could possibly know about the curse and you'll find your daughter's kidnappers. But remember, finding them won't save Karen."

Lafitte smiled grimly. "Punishment, right?" He straightened in his seat. "Ms. Deveaux, why do you think I brought you here?"

Jhonnette went along. "Excuse me?"

"I needed to rule you out as a suspect, and there's only one way to do that." He paused and then yelled, "Come on in, boys!"

A moment later, three large men surrounded Jhonnette. She mock-struggled as they lifted her from the couch and tied her to a straight-backed chair. One thug wrapped a tourniquet around her forearm while another produced a large syringe filled with clear liquid.

"Psychic, huh?" Lafitte stood as the man handed him the syringe. "Bet you didn't see this coming."

Jhonnette squeezed her eyes shut as Lafitte plunged the needle deep into her arm. She hated needles.

Lafitte continued. "You see this Ms. Deveaux? This is sodium thiopental, otherwise known as truth serum. You're going to help me find my daughter, whether you want to or not."

Jhonnette looked deeply into Lafitte's eyes, projecting a final thought before the drugs took hold.

Believe.

CHAPTER SEVENTEEN

Sunday
New Orleans, LA

Randy positioned himself in front of Jhonnette Deveaux. With his guards gone, he could get started. He was desperate for answers he was certain this woman possessed.

Even though he'd removed the needle a long time ago, she still sat with her eyes clenched shut. He felt a familiarity with this woman that extended beyond the resemblance to her mother, but couldn't place where he might know her from. Slapping her face lightly, he said, "Open your eyes."

She complied.

"Where is my daughter? Where is Karen?" he asked.

"I don't know."

Already off to a bad start.

"Who has my daughter?"

She replied without hesitation. "Amir Barber."

"Who is he?"

"Panama X's son."

Randy suspected Panama X was behind this, but it was good to have confirmation. "Where is he keeping her?"

"I don't know."

Randy swallowed his frustration. "What has he done to her?"

"She is a vessel."

"A vessel? What kind of vessel?"

"A vessel for the *baka*," she replied.

Randy was more confused than ever. This woman was speaking gibberish. But he had to persist—she was his only hope. "What is a *baka*?"

"A very powerful, evil spirit. It usually manifests in the form of an animal, but can also appear as a human."

So Panama X and this Amir person are trying to curse me? What do they expect to accomplish by doing that?

"What is this *baka* supposed to do to me?"

The woman had been responding with her eyes half open, but they suddenly widened. "The *baka* will destroy you and your family."

We'll see about that. "How do I stop it?"

"You can't."

"Who can?"

"Only Panama X is strong enough to control the *baka*."

A new question occurred to Randy. "How does Lincoln Baker fit into all this?"

The woman started to speak, and then purposely bit down on her tongue. All that escaped was a pained wail.

Randy repeated himself. "Tell me what Lincoln Baker has to do with this kidnapping."

"He…He is Juanita's son. Panama X promised to find him."

She had to be talking about Juanita Simmons. Randy hadn't heard that name in years. And this Baker thug was her son? Impossible.

The next question rolled off his tongue, propelled by the flood of resurrected memories. "Is Lincoln…my son?"

Her pained expression vanished. She tried to look away.

Randy held her face in his hands and screamed, "Answer me!"

"Possibly."

Randy quelled his temptation to choke the life out of her. He collected himself and asked, "If I kill him, will the spirits be satisfied?"

"I don't know if anything will satisfy them this time," she said slowly.

"What the hell does that mean?"

"Looks…are deceiving."

Randy paced around the suite. So far all she'd given him was a name and some bullshit about *bakas* and spirits. He needed something more tangible to corroborate her claims. "How are you involved in all this?"

"Snake Roberts."

Randy flinched. *Snake has betrayed me? Motherfucking double-crossing bastard!*

Yet, it made sense. Snake was the inside man. How else could the kidnappers have known the details of Karen's schedule and routine? Snake had positioned himself to profit off both sides of this little plot.

Randy took a deep breath. He had to stay calm. Anger wouldn't help him stop whatever Panama X and Snake had planned. "What is Snake's plan?" he asked.

"Snake will go to the prison to get Lincoln. Then he will bring Lincoln to you so Lincoln can kill you, if the *baka* doesn't get to you first."

Now that Randy had the answers he needed, he knew what he had to do. First, he called his men back into the room and told them to dispose of Jhonnette Deveaux. Then he called Bill Edwards in Lake City.

"Bill," he said when his friend picked up. "Tell me more about these discrete FBI guys."

CHAPTER EIGHTEEN

Monday
Lake City, LA

M oses Mouton stared down at the tombstone. The granite inscription was blurry at first, then cleared to reveal the words:

Lincoln Baker
1974-2002

The strength went out of Moses' legs. He collapsed before Lincoln's grave.

How did this happen?

"What a shame, Moses," a female voice spoke from behind him. "We couldn't save him."

Moses turned to see Juanita as she'd been in the old days with Walter, at the height of her beauty and strength. Her butter pecan skin glowed with health, and her curly, auburn-tinged hair was pulled back into a bun, accenting her high cheekbones and strong jaw line.

"Juanita?"

"It's okay, Moses. It's not your fault. You did more for him than anybody."

"But it wasn't enough," Moses pleaded.

"This was all my doing," Juanita replied. "I couldn't find him in time. And now Malcolm has filled his head up with hatred and sent him off to his death." Juanita's face contorted as guilt and sorrow took over her facial muscles. "Lincoln was supposed to avenge me…for the life that was supposed to be mine. We all have ghosts, Moses."

"What is that supposed to mean, Juanita? Juanita!"

Moses' voice pierced his silent bedroom. The nightmare clung to him like a wet parachute and his shirt was soaked with perspiration. He peered into the darkness, trying to hold on to the essence of the dream. There was an immediate sense of relief realizing Lincoln was still alive, but it was quickly replaced by a growing feeling of dread.

This was the second night in a row he'd awoken from this terrifying dream. Moses had to stop fighting Fate. He knew what he had to do. After leaving a note for his stepson, Brandon, he got dressed and headed out.

The early morning sun illuminated his path. When she put on her best, Louisiana truly was beautiful. The so-called "Sportsman's Paradise" was more than the sum of wetlands, swamps, and tracts of farmland. This morning it was reflective lakes, endless fields of rich green foliage, and sweet, pine-scented air. He contemplated his mission as he sped by all this, trying to outrun the ghosts from his past.

Something epic was happening and Moses could feel Malcolm Wright's fingerprints all over it. They'd grown up together, best friends, but over time Malcolm had changed, growing into a monster Moses barely recognized. Ironically, Moses had been the bad one when they were coming up.

Malcolm had been the leader in those days. He was charismatic, extremely intelligent, and born devoid of the "love for his fellow man" chip. He channeled his anger into a fierce and focused hatred of whites which was always getting him in trouble. Moses, who'd always looked up to Malcolm, had been his willing accomplice.

Walter Simmons had been a breath of fresh air when he moved into the neighborhood. Walter spent his days trying to figure out ways to build up his community while Moses and Malcolm spent most of their days trying to figure out what they could destroy. Whenever Malcolm or Moses wanted to skip school, Walter convinced them to attend. If the two troublemakers were planning to rob a store or go across town to jump some white boys, Walter put cash in their pockets and persuaded them to play pool until they forgot about their anger and frustration.

Due to Walter's influence and persistence, Malcolm cleaned up his act and started applying himself in school. Moses, who didn't share their interest in books, grew jealous of Malcolm and Walter's bond and continued going in the opposite direction. After Walter and Malcolm went off to college at Dillard University in New Orleans, Moses got caught in a botched burglary attempt. The judge sentenced him to fifteen years in the Louisiana State Penitentiary at Angola. Moses spent the next twelve years in what was, at that time, the bloodiest prison in America.

While Moses served out his sentence, Malcolm and Walter became swept up in the burgeoning Civil Rights Movement. Moses tried to imagine Walter, the devout Christian, and Malcolm, Elijah Mohammed's latest convert, traveling all over the South, helping out their fellow brothers and sisters in the struggle.

One night, just outside of Jackson, Mississippi, Walter's car broke down. After walking nearly a mile, they were offered a ride by two white girls coming from a dance in the black section of town. Malcolm was staunchly against the idea, but Walter convinced him they had no other choice. Besides, they were just getting a lift to the nearest gas station. Not five minutes later, they were on the side of the road again, getting frisked by two angry Mississippi state troopers.

The officers let the girls go, leaving Walter and Malcolm alone with the cops. Walter knew they had broken the worst of the unspoken rules between black men and whites—fraternizing with white women—but he tried to remain confident. A few blows to his head and shoulders shattered his poise.

As Walter collapsed in a lifeless heap, Malcolm snatched away the other officer's revolver. Malcolm shot the cop in the back. The cop that had hit Walter received a bullet right between the eyes.

A week later, Walter was at Angola confessing the whole thing to Moses. Walter was concerned. After killing those two officers, Malcolm became convinced he'd discovered the key to breaking Black people's chains, once and for all. He was obsessed with the idea of an army of Blacks trained in military tactics and ready to die for their freedom. In his mind, it was now kill or be killed. Somehow killing white men— and getting away with it—had made Malcolm fearless.

When Walter was finished, Moses scolded him for being so stupid. The last thing he wanted was to see his friends joining him in prison, or worse.

Amazingly, Malcolm and Walter were never caught. The authorities had bigger snakes to handle now that the Civil Rights

Movement was in full swing and Afro-Americans from coast to coast were screaming for freedom. Walter wanted nothing to do with Malcolm's plans to form a Black militia, and this caused a rift in their friendship that was never repaired.

Shortly thereafter, Malcolm received the dreaded draft card in the mail. Project 100,000 had found another soldier for Lyndon Johnson's Vietnam War. In his last letter to Moses before setting off to fight in America's first racially integrated conflict, Malcolm described his fears of dying in some strange place. He also detailed how, if he lived, he would use his military training to become a General, leading Blacks out of oppression into something greater.

While Malcolm was away at war, life went on. Walter continued to visit Moses in prison, and through the scratched panes of prison glass, a bond was formed. Eventually, Walter married Malcolm's childhood sweetheart, a beautiful woman named Juanita. Juanita was the love of Malcolm's life and Moses often worried about how Malcolm would react when he found out the news.

After twelve years of hard time, Moses was finally released from prison. Committed to forging a new path, he served as a deacon at Walter's church back in Lake City. Walter, still fighting the good fight, decided to give up his law practice to immerse himself in local politics. Meanwhile, Malcolm continued to fight for a country that had no respect for him or his rights.

At some point, Moses' letters to Vietnam started coming back undelivered. After a year of no news, word came down that Malcolm and several other black soldiers had deserted.

Malcolm eventually resurfaced, not long before Walter, now mayor, was brutally assassinated—burned to death in his office with his white secretary. The police found evidence linking the crime to Juanita, who had disappeared the night of the crime, along with Malcolm. When Moses learned the two of them were living together outside of Houston, he'd confronted them with some tough questions.

Questions Malcolm had not been inclined to answer.

Moses, convinced that Malcolm had fully succumbed to the dark side, made it his life's work to undermine Malcolm at any cost. He'd been lucky to find Lincoln before Malcolm could get to him. Moses had managed to keep the boy on the straight and narrow for two years before that day at Simmons Park. But now that they were both sharing an address at Angola, Lincoln was under Malcolm's thumb.

The dream was clear—Lincoln's association with Malcolm would be the death of him. Unless Moses could intervene.

"We all have ghosts."

Moses turned onto Tunica Trace—the narrow byway also known as Hell's Corridor that dead-ended at the front gates of the Louisiana State Penitentiary. He had to stop Malcolm's plan, today, or else Lincoln would pay the ultimate price.

CHAPTER NINETEEN

Monday
Lake City, LA

Coral lay next to her snoring husband, staring into the darkness. The weekend had passed in an unbearable crawl. Despite Randy's assurances to the contrary, Coral firmly believed that Karen was dead. There was nothing left inside her now.

She wasn't strong enough to bear even the remote possibility of losing another child. Not like this. And since she couldn't save Karen, maybe she could do something even better, something that would reunite her with her children once and for all.

She got up and walked across the suite to the bathroom, closing the door behind her.

What if you're wrong? What if Karen is still alive?

Coral tried to ignore the voice, but it continued to badger her.

What if you're her only hope? A girl needs her mother, doesn't she?

Coral grabbed the bottle of Xanax. She filled her glass with water. Sweat broke out on her brow. Her hands shook uncontrollably. The walls were closing in on her.

She saw her own terrified reflection in the mirror. She had around twenty pills left; she prayed it would be enough to do the trick. Coral closed her eyes and popped the first little white pill into her quivering mouth...and then the next...and the next.

But she hadn't even opened the bottle of pills yet.

Her hand was empty and the glass was still full.

Coral fumbled to open the bottle, but the top was stuck. She twisted the cap with all her might and it finally spun off. She turned the bottle over to shake pills into her palm but nothing came out.

Randy must have taken the last one.

Or maybe it's just not your time.

Coral threw the empty container on the floor in a fiery rage and sat down on the toilet seat.

Stop being so weak!

The voice in her head sounded just like her long dead grandmother, the famous disciplinarian and matriarch of her family.

The only way Karen survives is if you're strong for her—for the both of you! There's no more time to feel sorry for yourself. Maybe Kristopher would still be around if you'd spent less time whining.

"Stop it, just stop it!" Coral screamed. She looked at herself in the mirror, half expecting to see the ancient face of her grandmother, but the tired face staring back was hers alone.

"What's going on in there? Stop making so much noise!" Randy yelled from the bedroom.

Coral collected herself and tried to straighten out some of the mess she'd made. As she drank down the glass of water, she noticed the empty bottle of Xanax she'd thrown on the floor. The bottle was overturned and there were pills scattered everywhere.

Coral slid to her knees and put the pills back into the bottle—twenty-two in all. Placing the bottle in the medicine cabinet, she returned to bed.

It was a long time before sleep found her.

CHAPTER TWENTY

Monday
Location Unknown

"My boys are on their way," Snake said. "Is the girl ready for delivery?"

Amir paced inside the dilapidated school where his crew was holed up. "Everything is under control."

"It better be. Everything's been set in motion on my end. If yuh try and fuck me, it's gonna get ugly."

"Don't threaten me," Amir replied in a calm, even tone. "We are both going to get exactly what we want."

"I want to know where yuh have the girl," Snake demanded. "We pahtners, right? What if something bad happens to yuh boys? Yuh know Lafitte can't be trusted."

"We've been over this a million times...the girl is my responsibility; you just worry about keeping Lafitte in check. Where are you now?"

"Rayne."

"Good. Now let's go over things one last time..."

Moments later Amir hung up and exhaled deeply. Things were slowly falling into place.

The hardest part had been convincing Lincoln to join their cause. He wasn't exactly the trusting type. But eventually his curiosity got the best of him, and after Panama X explained how Randy Lafitte had not only killed Lincoln's father, but ruined his mother's life as well, Lincoln was in.

The first plan had been to incite a riot and use the commotion as a distraction so Amir could sneak Lincoln out of the prison. Panama X quickly vetoed that idea—far too risky. After much strategizing, the three of them had come up with the perfect plan. Actually, it was more than perfect, it was damn near elegant.

Juanita Barber would finally be avenged. Amir visited his mother's grave in Lake City often. Even though he knew he could speak to her spirit from anywhere, he felt closer, more connected, at the spot where her physical remains lay at rest. One day after one of his regular visits, he returned to his car to find a note pinned between the windshield and wiper. It read:

Meet me at The Island of Capri. 7:00 p.m. Lucky Wins. I have information you need.

Lucky Wins was a cheap Asian restaurant populated by septuagenarians who let slot machines digest their retirement while they consumed smelly chinese food. Amir gazed around the crowded space, searching for anyone staring at him with recognition. A fair-skinned beauty with dark hair nodded and waved at him from the far side of the room.

With a face that could stop a war, her beauty pulsated towards him like a star about to go supernova. He tried to play it cool, but his stomach was hoola-hooping around in his mid-section. As lust stirred in his loins, Amir realized how blinded he had been by his mission. Seeing this woman was like seeing food after starving for so long he'd forgotten he was even hungry.

Amir made his way over to where she was seated. Not knowing what to say, he sat down and tried unsuccessfully not to stare.

"You don't get out much, do you?" she asked with a slight smile. Amir looked her over. She was a bewitching woman, probably in her early thirties. Her eyes were downright hypnotic—dark, piercing, and seemingly all-knowing.

"I get out enough," he replied. "This is my first time in a casino, though."

"Not a gambling man?"

"I prefer to play people, not cards, slots, or dice."

"Interesting," she replied. "How is that working out for you?"

"Some people are easier to play than others, and some people are best not to play with at all."

She nodded and smiled. "And which type of person are you?"

"I think you know." He returned her smile. "So, what's this all about?"

"Let's have a drink before we get to business," she replied. She summoned the waiter and ordered a bourbon on the rocks. Amir ordered a cranberry-orange juice.

"Don't drink?" she asked.

"Nothing with alcohol."

"You must get that from your father."

Amir was caught off guard by the mention of his father. "You need to start talking, lady."

"Yes drill sergeant! Wow, you military types are a mess." She chuckled, revealing a mouth of healthy white teeth. "Hmm...

where do we start? Clearly, I know some things about you, yet you know nothing about me. Let me get you up to speed. My name is Jhonnette Deveaux and I want to help you."

The waiter returned with their drinks. "Help me with what?" Amir asked, taking a sip of juice.

She grabbed a napkin, wrote something down, and passed it across the table. Amir read the name she had scrawled: Lincoln Baker.

"What about him?" he asked, trying to control his annoyance.

"Come on, Amir. Stop being so stoic. How am I supposed to help with you acting all nonchalant? Look, I know all about you, your father, and our friend there." She pointed to the napkin. "I also know how you can set him free and why that is so important to you."

"Go on," Amir replied.

"What do you know about Kristopher Lafitte?" she asked between sips of her drink.

"Besides who his father is and how he died? Not much."

"Did you know our beloved Governor's father died three days after he turned eighteen?"

"And?"

"You think it's a coincidence Kristopher Lafitte died on the exact same schedule?"

Amir was intrigued. "What are you saying?"

Jhonnette grabbed another napkin and scribbled something. Then she finished off her drink, stood and replied, "Karen Lafitte turns eighteen in two years. Think about it."

Amir did more than just think about it. In the weeks that followed his encounter with Jhonnette Deveaux, he became obsessed with the history of the Lafitte clan. She'd left her number on the napkin and when he called, she didn't sound the least bit surprised to hear from him.

"How did you figure all this out?" he asked.

"That's none of your business," she replied. "What you need to focus on is how you can use this information to free Lincoln and officially take the reins of the Black Mob from your father. That is your ultimate goal, right?"

She had him there. Everything Amir had done since he turned eighteen had the same objective: to prove his readiness to lead.

"I will help you," she continued. "All I ask in return is a small percentage of the ransom."

"Whoa, lady," Amir replied. "Who said anything about kidnapping anybody?"

"How else do you expect to force Randy Lafitte to issue a full pardon for Lincoln's release…"

So as brilliant as the plan was, Amir could not claim credit. At every turn, Jhonnette Deveaux had been there providing valuable insight and guidance. Unfortunately, his attempts to turn her into more than an advisor had fallen flat. She was not interested in mixing business with pleasure. And whenever Amir inquired about her reasons for helping him, she'd simply say, "Randy Lafitte has ruined many lives; your mother wasn't his only victim." Due to Jhonnette's cajoling, Amir finally conjured up the courage to perform the ceremony on Karen Lafitte known in Vodun as the *sending of the dead*.

The *sending of the dead* ritual would result in a brutally slow death for Karen. First, she would undergo rapid weight loss, then she would cough and vomit blood. Finally, she would lose all strength, succumbing to the demon. Once this process was complete, Amir would return Karen's inhabited shell to Randy so the *baka* could destroy Lafitte and return to the spirit realm.

Punishment at its finest.

Amir's father had taught him the guiding principles that molded his philosophies and framed his purpose. Vodun was the recognition that all things, events, and living beings were inextricably bound together. The only religion borne out of revolution, this universal spiritual system rested on the common principles of magic. When dealing with a *baka* there was always a blood contract involved.

With the *sending of the dead*, Amir, as the invoker of the *baka*, would be obligated to serve the *baka* in the afterlife. But in the case of a lost soul from the transitional realm like Kristopher Lafitte, the traditional contract could be waved by allowing the spirit to exact revenge against a common enemy with no negative consequences for Amir.

Today the *baka* would complete its mission. Amir played out how the day's events would unfold. At eight o'clock, Lincoln would be released from Angola. Once Amir received confirmation that Lincoln was safely out of prison and on his way back to Lake City, Amir would give the order for his men to make the final drop.

The rest was up to Snake. Apparently, Jhonnette had Randy Lafitte's enforcer under her thumb. When Amir had questioned the need for Snake's involvement, Jhonnette was characteristically vague. "It never hurts to have a man on the inside," she said. "Insurance."

Amir made his way down a narrow corridor to the control room where Moose, Zire, and Reef were posted up.

"What the fuck are you guys doing?" Amir asked.

The men looked at each other.

Moose spoke up. "We was just discussin' who was goin' to deliver the last drop."

Amir rubbed the back of his bald head. "Then it looks like I'm just in time. Where the hell are the Stooges?"

"Trump and Salsa are 'sleep," Zire replied in his chronic smoker's whisper. "Fat Pat just left to pick up our gal from the park."

"Thanks for the update, Zire. Just for that, you get to stay here with me while Moose and Reef deliver the drop."

Moose and Reef's expressions did not betray any concern. These were good men. Ex-military, just like him. Dependable and disciplined.

"Now here's how it's gonna go down...I want to speak to the Stooges once Fat Pat gets back. They're Team One and ya'll are Team Two. While they take care of the girl, ya'll deliver the drop. Then ya'll high tail it to the meeting point."

Moose and Reef nodded, then cleared out to carry out their mission. Amir turned to Zire. "You get those things I asked for?"

"Of course. You ready for them now?"

"Yeah. Thank you, Zire."

Once Zire's footfalls faded, Amir grabbed a flashlight and made his way into the prayer chamber. Amir's life had changed so much since his mother revealed the truth to him about his brother.

"Set Lincoln free, Amir."

His ears rang with the last words his mother ever spoke.

Running his flashlight over the room, Amir took inventory of the materials Zire had provided. The salt was clearly marked.

There were three tall black candles. A box of fresh chalk sat on top of two packages of Karen's blood. He touched the top package. Room temperature. Perfect.

But where is the knife?

He turned in a circle looking for his instrument and found it sitting in its leather sheath on a hook by the door. With all of the materials accounted for, Amir could proceed. Amir felt all the *loa* smiling down on him.

It was time to begin. Using the chalk, Amir drew a large intricate design on the floor.

The design (called *vèvè*) was required to summon a *loa*, in this case Guédé Barons or Baron LaCroix—the *loa* of the dead. Amir carefully sprinkled the salt in a complete circle around the *vèvè* (for his own protection). Then he stepped into the center with the blood, candles, and knife. He squeezed Karen's blood onto the large rectangle at the base of the *vèvè*.

As he did so, he felt the ground beneath his feet tremor ever so slightly. He lit the candles, placing one atop each of the three asterisk-like symbols. He chanted in French as he did this, and each time he repeated the mantra, he sprinkled more of Karen's blood on the candles.

Once the candles had been doused with blood, Amir sliced his palm with the knife and pressed his hand to the heart-shaped face. Then he stood, straddling the symbol, and waited for Baron LaCroix to manifest. He would need the *loa's* strength to control the *baka*. If not, the results would be disastrous for everyone.

Thirty minutes later, Amir lay on his cot, exhausted. He'd tried everything he knew to bring the spirit to him, but Baron LaCroix never showed. Maybe he didn't yet have the strength. Perhaps it was an omen. Either way, he would try again once his men returned with the girl.

Amir was nervous—Fat Pat should have reported back by now. Amir was in the middle of typing a message to Fat Pat on his two-way when he heard someone approaching. In moments, Fat Pat stood before him, sweating profusely, his face twisted with a wild look of fear.

"What is it?" Amir asked, anticipating the worst. Fat Pat's reply, however, was so far out of the realm of possibilities that it took Amir a few seconds to comprehend what he'd said.

"Come again?" Amir asked.

"It's th-the girl…" Fat Pat repeated. "She's gone."

CHAPTER TWENTY-ONE

A tickling sensation in her ear brought Karen into consciousness. With her eyes closed, she felt pressure on her chest like someone was giving her CPR. But the hands were concentrated on her breasts, not her breastbone.

A male voice attached to those hands grunted, "Damn, girl."

His tongue probed her ear cavity as he humped her hard and fast. Karen's pelvis convulsed in a sharp cramp.

He twitched frantically on top of her and after a few shudders rolled away.

Karen opened her eyes. She felt separated from what was happening to her body, as if it was another girl getting raped.

How did I get here? Where is here?

The charley horse galloping inside her abdomen brought her back to reality. Her lower back felt as if a migraine migrated there for the winter. She clutched and then rubbed her sore pelvis.

"You aight, yo? Whassamatta?"

"Cramps." Karen exhaled as they subsided.

"Cramps from what?"

She pointed down.

"You fo' real?" He moved a few spaces away. "Damn. What we gone do now?"

"Where...am I?" The past few hours were a blur. She vaguely remembered someone talking to her, telling her to get up in harsh whispers. She remembered the smell and feel of wet grass, too. Pain and wet grass.

Where is my fucking shot? I wouldn't be feeling this way if I had my shot...

"I rescued you," the voice said.

Karen rolled over, gazing upon her hero—a short, bald-headed, black kid who looked to be around her age. The word "Shorty" was written in Old English lettering on his inner forearm. "Who are you?" she asked.

"Don't worry bout all that. I'ma take good care of you."

"How did I end up here?"

The boy ignored her question and got to his feet. "You want somethin' to drink?"

"Is that your name on your arm?" Karen persisted.

The boy walked out of the room without answering.

Karen tried to focus. Bit by bit, snatches of memory began to return to her. Her new captor had liberated her from the small, windowless cell where the fat, sweaty black man, a.k.a. Flashlight Man, had been holding her prisoner. She'd been refused everything but the stuff in the syringe as they prepared her for the "ceremony." Every time she tried to remember details about the ceremony, she saw she and Kristopher on the swings in their backyard beneath the curved branches of Melinda Weeps.

Karen looked around the boy's room. It was unremarkable except for a huge gun sitting atop the dresser.

That gun is my ticket out of here.

Karen was about to reach for the gun when Shorty reappeared. "Here, drink this." He stood over her with a dixie cup full of thick, pink liquid.

"What is it?"

"It's called Lean. It'll make you feel real good. Slow everything down a bit."

Karen's heart flip-flopped with excitement, the gun completely forgotten. She greedily gulped down the contents of the cup, praying it would numb her senses again. It tasted like watered down cough syrup with a kick.

Thankfully, the drug worked fast. As she lay back and closed her eyes, a plan began to form. She just had to find a way to make the boy leave.

But she couldn't think straight; she kept nodding off. A vision of her father's screaming face being ripped apart by a black panther forced her eyes open again.

"I need tampons."

"Huh?"

"I'm on my period, gonna bleed all over myself if I don't get one."

"My moms got toilet tissue…that cool?"

"No…is there a store…you know, around?"

"Yeah…yeah, I'll handle it." He pulled on his sweats.

Karen scanned the floor for the condom she prayed he'd used. There was none in sight.

"When I get back, we'll figure out what to do next."

Once the boy was completely dressed, he dug around in his closet and emerged with a roll of duct tape.

"Sorry, bruh. I can't trust you to stick around while I'm away," he said as he bound Karen's hands to the posts of his bed in a spread eagle position.

Karen didn't resist.

"Gots to make sure I get that reward, ya feel me?"

Karen fixated on the word "reward." In a brief moment of clarity, as she looked at her increasingly thinning arms, the idea that her life meant something to her kidnappers hit home.

Her captor grabbed the gun off the dresser and left. Hopeless, Karen tried to maintain her high. The tears streaming down her face made it difficult, but she managed to drift off, even as her arms began tingling from the loss of circulation.

CHAPTER TWENTY-TWO

Monday
Angola, LA

"Baker? Baker! I know you hear me, boy! Time to wake up. The warden wants to see you."

Lincoln jumped at the sound of the man's voice. He opened eyes caked with sleep and saw a redneck guard yelling at him through the cell bars.

"What did you say?"

"Are you deaf *and* dumb, Nigger? The warden wants to see you. *Now*. Let's go."

Lincoln stretched. "What time is it?"

"Time to get yo' black ass over to these here bars and 'sume the position."

After securing the handcuffs—every prisoner's least favorite accessory—the guard yelled down the corridor. A moment later, Lincoln and the guard were only separated by air and opportunity. Lincoln held a happy vision of slitting the man's throat with a used razor blade. He smiled at the balding, pudgy, white man before him.

"What does the warden want to see me for? I've got to pack up my stuff. You know I'm fin to get out today."

The guard told him to shut up and yanked him out of the cell.

Walking down the corridor of Camp J, Lincoln looked into the cells of the other lifers waking up to another day on the block. They all had variations of the same story. To outsiders, twenty-three hour lockdown might seem unbearable, but to the prisoners of Camp J, there was a worse alternative. They could be at the injection center waiting for the poisonous kiss of the needle.

Moments later, Lincoln walked out into the humid Louisiana morning. As his eyes adjusted to the morning light, he smiled broadly. He usually only got to spend three hours outside per week.

When I get outta here I'm gonna sleep outside for a whole month! That'll be the life!

Lincoln got into the backseat of the patrol car and rested his head against the window, watching the other inmates trudging out for another day of work in the fields. He managed to get one hand inside his jeans pocket and fished out the crinkled photograph he carried with him at all times. Staring at the old picture of Juanita, given to him some years ago by Amir, he felt a mixture of anger and hope. Anger because she died before they could meet, and hope that he could do her memory justice upon his release. They had the same eyebrows, nose, chin, and mouth. And now they had the same dream. Revenge.

Amidst his collection of wallpaper was an article Amir sent him a few days after their initial introduction. Lincoln requested proof of Amir's authenticity and Amir had produced a worn article from 1973. The article accused a woman, Juanita Simmons, of killing her husband—the first black mayor of Lake City—and his secretary.

The assassinated mayor's name was Walter Simmons. Amir had circled his name and written **YOUR DAD** in the margin. Lincoln couldn't believe that the park he had played, grown-up, and killed on—Simmons Park— was named after his biological father.

At the end of the article Amir had written the phrase, **MOM WAS FRAMED.**

Panama X filled in the rest of the blanks, telling him about the man responsible for Lincoln's loneliness, pain, and suffering over the years. The man who'd robbed him of the chance at a better life. The man who had built an empire on the decayed bones of his father.

Listening to X, it all clicked for Lincoln. He immediately began to read anything and everything he could get his hands on about Randy Lafitte. The more he learned about his enemy, the more he fantasized about the day when he would confront him and make him feel pain like he'd never known. He didn't know if it was "his destiny," like Panama X always said, but he was committed to vengeance, consequences be damned. First step: get out of Angola. Second step: get to Lafitte. Third step: kill him.

Then improvise the rest.

The car pulled up to the prison administrative office, but instead of stopping, the guard drove around to the back of the building.

"What the fuck is goin' on?" Lincoln asked.

The guard ignored him.

"I'm axin' you a ques—" Lincoln swallowed the rest of his sentence as the guard turned around brandishing his bully club.

"The warden told me to give you this."

Lincoln started to protest, but a bully club to the temple shut him up. All he saw was a flash of light before his world turned black.

CHAPTER TWENTY-THREE

Monday
Lake City, LA

"I'm comin'," Brandon Mouton shouted at the front door. "Quit ringin' the friggin' doorbell, would'ja?" Brandon shuffled from his bedroom to answer the buzzer. After fumbling for a minute with the three locks on the door, he opened it with a jingle from the cowbell tied around the handle. The early morning sunlight burst into the dark cave of the modest house, blinding Brandon and illuminating a narrow hallway with brown tile floors.

Brandon rubbed his eyes until they adjusted to the morning sun. Then he recognized the short, bald-headed kid on the other side of the locked screen door.

"Whassup, Shorty?" Brandon opened the screen door and greeted his homeboy with a pound handshake and a half hug.

"What it do?" Shorty replied. "When you get back to the L.C.?"

"Late last night. The trip was off tha slab! We won the tournament and guess who got that MVP?"

"Yeah?" Shorty grinned. "That's cool. Real cool. Proud of you man."

"Thanks. So what's up? I know you didn't wake my ass up to talk basketball."

Shorty lifted his wife-beater slightly, revealing the unmistakable black grip of a Glock .357. He was no longer grinning as he said, "I need your help, bruh. You gonna let me in?"

Brandon suddenly wished he hadn't gotten out of bed. He looked up and down the street trying to think fast. An old, burgundy Oldsmobile Eight-Eight turned the corner in front of his house.

"Come on," Brandon interrupted, feeling exposed. He gestured for Shorty to enter.

Once they got to his bedroom, Brandon sat down on the bed. "Aight Shorty, what we got to talk about?"

"Man, you shoulda seen yo' face when you saw my piece. Looked like a scared little beeyatch."

"Why you walkin' around in the street with that goddamn gun anyway, Shorty?"

"Why else? It's for protection." Shorty reached into the small refrigerator on the floor of Brandon's closet and took out a Coke.

"Protection from who?"

Shorty got quiet and then said, "I found somethin'. Somethin' important."

"You gonna tell me what it is?"

"I'll tell you what it's about." Shorty rummaged through his backpack and Brandon could have sworn he saw what looked like a box of Playtex tampons. Seconds later, Shorty handed Brandon the newspaper.

"You seen this yet?"

Brandon read the headline glaring back at him from that morning's Lake City Advocate: "Governor Lafitte to Grant Lincoln Baker a Full Pardon." He had tried so hard to shut out the memories of that awful day at Simmons Park. He could barely stand to look at the picture of Lincoln. Long gone were the days of looking up to his older brother, the basketball superstar-turned-murderer.

Why did you do it, Link?

"When is he gettin' out?" Brandon felt a headache coming on.

"Eight this mohnin'."

Brandon's world was spinning. "Word?"

"Yeah, Bruh. I can't wait for Link to get back on the block." Shorty beamed with admiration.

Brandon thought he was going to be sick. "How…how is this possible?"

To his surprise, Shorty answered, "Come wit' me and I'll show you."

CHAPTER TWENTY-FOUR

Monday
Lake City, LA

"Okay," Brandon said. "Where is this thing you gotta show me?"

"My house. Let's cut through the woods."

They walked in silence through the forest, following a path that had probably been carved out by boys much like themselves years earlier. Eventually the woods cleared out and the path disappeared, revealing Shorty's backyard.

"Aight. This is what's up," Shorty said. "Somebody snatched the Governor's daughter two days ago."

"Karen Lafitte? Bullshit! That woulda been all over the news."

"Not if they had a ransom. I caught them bringing her to Simmons Park, and then I followed them back to their hideout..."

Shorty had been headed to school Friday morning when he got a text from one of his "customers." He took a slight detour to Simmons Park to unload a couple of dime bags before class. After he made the drop, Shorty smoked a little of the product and then continued on his way to school. He was about to jump the fence (put up after the killings to keep trespassers out) when he detected movement out of the corner of his eye. A fat guy and a musclehead were unloading a sleeping bag from the trunk of an Oldsmobile Eighty-Eight. The sleeping bag had a lock of blond hair sticking out of the top.

"Really?" Brandon asked. "Then how did Karen get *here*?"

"Well, I had a feeling that they might be watchin' the place, know what I'm sayin', so I pretty much just watched them come and go until I got their schedule down pat. Then last night I decided to check out the gym. You know I ain't been up in that piece since before the shooting, bruh?"

"Me either."

"Yeah, man. It was dark as shit up in there. That place used to be a lot bigger when we was kids, bruh..."

It had been easy to open up the gym door, but not nearly as easy to find his way around in the dark once he was inside. The sliver of light coming through the door from the single functioning streetlight was swallowed by the darkness. Shorty wished he had something to prop open the door, but he couldn't risk someone seeing the door ajar and coming in to investigate. He pulled out his flashlight and took a few cautious steps forward. The outside door closed behind him.

The flashlight illuminated a paper-strewn hallway. He looked around for clues as to where they'd stashed the body. Shorty paused after finding a blond hair on the stairwell.

He stopped and listened.

Upstairs, someone or something was whimpering.

He took a few more steps.

A female voice cried, "Where are you, Kristopher? I wanna see you."

⟨❧⟩

"Come on, Shorty, that ain't true," Brandon interrupted. Shorty had told some tall tales in his life, but this had to be like Manute Bol tall.

"You don't believe me?"

"Does 'hell no' mean anything to you?"

"That hurts, B, really. But I knew you wouldn't believe me, that's why I brought you here in the first place. So come on if you comin'."

Brandon followed Shorty into the house. The place was a mess, as usual. Shorty's rarely present mother was a packrat who had never found a piece of junk she didn't love.

Brandon checked his watch. He was going to be late for school for sure. Coach Torelli would ream him out if he missed the morning meeting. "We got to hurry this—" Brandon started to say as he stepped into Shorty's bedroom. He couldn't believe what he was seeing.

A blond-haired white girl lay spread-eagled on Shorty's bed. This couldn't be Karen Lafitte. He had just seen her at Jessica Breaux's homecoming after party. Karen had been named Homecoming Queen.

There was no trace of that girl here. Her wrists and ankles were taped to the metal posts. Brandon saw track marks up and down emaciated arms. She looked like the concentration camp victims in his world history textbook. He stared at Shorty dumbfounded.

"See. Told ya," Shorty said smugly.

Brandon took a step backward. He wanted to bolt, but was held transfixed by the scene before him.

"What did you do, Shorty? What did you do?"

"What the hell you talking bout? I saved her life!"

Brandon looked away—Karen wasn't wearing any panties. "This is sick, Shorty. What the hell is wrong with you?"

"Wrong with me? You got this twisted, bruh."

Brandon barged past Shorty and started undoing Karen's bonds.

"What the fuck you think you're doing? Stop!"

"Make me." Brandon had almost gotten Karen's left ankle loose when he felt the gun pressed into his back.

"I said, stop."

"You gonna shoot me, Shorty?"

"I don't want to, so don't make me. Now turn around. Real slow."

Brandon's heartbeat doubled as he got his second look at Shorty's glock. "Come on, Shorty, you know me. We can work this out."

"I thought so," Shorty said, taping Brandon's hands behind his back. "But I guess I was wrong. Now sit down and cross your ankles."

Shorty took his eyes off Brandon's face for a moment to tape up his legs.

Brandon jerked his knee into Shorty's jaw. It was a solid hit. Shorty tumbled off him, temporarily unconscious. Working his wrists, Brandon freed himself, tied Shorty up, then went back to work on Karen. Once he had her loose, he gently pulled her to her feet.

Karen rolled her head back and looked up at him. "Isaac?"

"Shhh. I'm fin to get you out of here."

"Brandon! Fuck, bruh!" Shorty groaned. "What you do that for. Let me go, bruh."

"No way, Shorty. I'm gonna get Karen out of here and then I'm calling the police."

"I'm telling you, I didn't do this! All you have to do is go over to Simmons Park and see for yourself. That's where they had her. Just check it out before you do something crazy, please!"

"You're no good, Shorty. We're getting out of here. I'm taking the gun, too, so don't get any ideas."

As Brandon dragged Karen outside he realized he was in way over his head.

CHAPTER TWENTY-FIVE

Monday
Baton Rouge, LA

"Give me some good news, Bill," Randy said, answering his phone. He gave up on his tie momentarily and sat on the edge of the tub inside his suite at the Marriott. He'd been waiting for Bill's call for over an hour.

"My FBI contacts have located Amir Barber," Bill replied. "And he is Juanita Simmons' son."

Randy slapped his knee with pleasure. Jhonnette Deveaux had turned out to be extremely helpful after all.

"Bulls-eye. He's the guy. Where is he?"

"We're triangulating his exact location right now."

"Excellent work," Randy replied.

"What are you going do to about Snake Roberts?" Bill asked.

It was a good question. One Randy had given serious thought to over the past eight hours.

"I've got Snake covered," Randy replied. Snake would soon learn the penalty for disloyalty. "Bill, Karen's fate is in your hands now. Bring my girl home to me."

"You can count on me, Ran. I'll keep you posted."

Randy hung up, splashed his face with water, and finished his tie. He was going to need the power of positive thinking to get through all of this. Since Karen's kidnapping, he'd just barely managed to keep from unraveling as the kidnappers continued to torture him. They'd sent two more DVDs, each one further documenting Karen's regression from a healthy teenager to a pale, emaciated zombie.

In the videos, Karen scratched at her arms, lined with the tell-tale marks of heroin use, while talking to herself like a schizophrenic. The look in her eyes was the worst though, like she was losing hope and humanity with each passing day. Randy just wanted her back alive, no matter what the condition. He was terrified of what today might bring if Bill couldn't find her first.

His cell phone rang again.

Randy stared at the words, UNKNOWN CALLER, staring at him from the display. It was the kidnappers. He could only imagine what they would have to say.

As he flipped open the phone, he was completely unprepared for the word that floated through the telephone receiver.

"Daddy?"

CHAPTER TWENTY-SIX

Monday
Angola, LA

"Wake up, Lincoln. Rise and shine."

Lincoln crawled out of the darkness as if he'd been buried alive under six feet of nightmares and confusion. His head throbbed and his hands and feet were strapped into a chair of some sort. Strange voices spoke in hushed tones near him.

There was a mask over his head, the kind of mask placed over an inmate's head just moments before he imitated the "this is your brain on drugs" commercial from the eighties. Judging from the echo in the room, he knew he wasn't in a holding cell.

Where the hell am I?

Rational thought gave way to adrenaline as fear bolted to the surface of his psyche.

I'm strapped into the electric chair!

His breath grew raspier as the mask stuck to his sweat-soaked skin.

Suddenly, it was ripped off his face.

Lincoln blinked as he tried to adjust to the bright lights. He heard snickering and laughter all around him. A tall figure in a dark suit stood before him. Lincoln immediately recognized his captor.

"You? You're responsible for this?"

"I don't know why you're so surprised, Lincoln," Kristopher Lafitte whispered. His sharp blue eyes shimmered crazily. "Did you really think they were just going to let you walk out of Angola?"

"This ain't happenin'." Lincoln squirmed against the rough wood of the electric chair. "This ain't real. You're dead!"

Kris stared back at Lincoln. "Death is relative, Lincoln. You should know that better than anyone. Remember? You killed me."

"Why...how...is this happening?" The smell of formaldehyde flooded Lincoln's nostrils. The last time he'd seen Kris, his best friend had been laying at the base of the lone tree in Simmons Park, clutching his stomach, blood blooming between his long pale fingers.

"Maybe I'm just a figment of your imagination, Lincoln. Maybe I'm your guilty conscience. Or maybe *this...is...real.*"

"I don't understand," Lincoln mumbled. Suddenly they were back in Simmons Park. Lincoln leaned over Kris as his friend bled to death from a bullet wound in his stomach. Lincoln inched forward so he could hear what Kris was trying to tell him between his wheezes and gasps.

Kris grabbed the back of Lincoln's head in one bloody palm, pulled him within kissing distance and gasped, "It's seven o'clock, Baker. You know where yo' pardon is?"

Lincoln opened his eyes. His head ached and nostrils burned. A voice spoke up in front of him. Swimming in confusion, he raised his head with some effort, the blur before him slowly materializing into solid form.

Warden George Winey sipped his coffee and stared at Lincoln like he couldn't decide whether he was pissed off or constipated.

A guard stood beside Lincoln's chair waving smelling salts under his nose.

Lincoln pushed the man's hand away from his face. "Assault is a criminal offense, you know."

"Save it for someone who cares, boy," the warden replied.

Lincoln gazed at the man who had presided over the prison with an iron fist for the past thirteen years. Lincoln refused to give Winey the satisfaction of seeing him sweat. Mind over matter, as Panama X liked to say. He leaned back and smirked like he was privy to an inside joke.

"What's so funny, boy?"

"Nuthin', bruh. I was just thinking about how wild you looked in that press conference the other day, but you lookin' good now, boss— lost a little weight. I guess your wife's Parkinsons is rubbin' off."

The warden looked primed to jump over the desk and strangle Lincoln to death. "You ain't outta here yet, you black idiot!"

"You can't do nothing to me and you know it, bruh." Lincoln maintained his smirk. "I got a pardon signed by the Governor and I'm walking out of here, whether you like it or not. I bet you want to know how I managed to get myself pardoned. Sucks to be you then, cuz that's one magic trick you'll never figure out."

"Magic, huh, boy? You must be crazier'n a shithouse rat if you think you're just walking out of here." Winey sauntered around to the front of his desk holding a copy of Lincoln's pardon. "The Governor gave us very specific instructions not to let you out until we heard from him. How you like the sounda that, boy?"

"Sounds fine to me, bruh. It's gonna be the last time you see me anyway, so you might as well get your fill."

"Oh, I've had my fill," Winey replied. "You actually have a visitor."

"A visitor?" Lincoln asked.

"Yes. Mr. Roberts. He's a friend of the Governor." The warden's smirk now mirrored his own.

Lincoln remained stoic but his stomach ached. *Something is wrong.*

The guard grabbed Lincoln by the arm and ushered him down a short hall to a small, windowless room. Lincoln met the steely gaze of a rugged-looking white man with long, silver hair and an equally unkempt silver beard.

"Mr. Roberts," the guard said. "Do you need me to stay?"

"No, you can go." Roberts fixed his faded gray eyes on Lincoln's face. "Have a seat, Link."

"Name's Lincoln. You don't know me, bruh, so don't try me."

"Come on, Link, I thought you were expecting me."

Lincoln stared back at the stranger. Something clicked. "You the Panther?" Lincoln asked, referencing Amir's codename for their partner.

"In the flesh."

Amir, you brilliant motherfucker. "Well, why the fuck didn't you just say so?"

Initially, Lincoln had been against partnering with someone from the outside, but once Amir explained that they had recruited one of Lafitte's own men as an accomplice, it became Lincoln's favorite aspect of the plan.

"So what happens now?" Lincoln asked.

"Well, that's the easy part. The Governor should be calling the warden right now, ordering your release. When you get the word, go check out yuh things. I brought yuh some cash and left yuh a car parked just outside the gates. A silver sedan."

"Anything else?"

"There's tons of reporters outside. I suggest yuh don't say shit to nobody. Just get to that car, and haul ass to the location in the envelope with the money."

"What then?"

"Then we'll meet up and head back to Lake City, together."

Lincoln considered this. Roberts didn't get his portion of the ransom until Lincoln touched down in Lake City, so all seemed good.

"Okay, I'm witcha. We done here?"

"For now."

Moments later, a guard led Lincoln to collect his things. Lincoln took stock of all the material possessions he had in the world—barely enough to fill a shoebox. He took a deep breath—he was now just three doors from freedom.

Lincoln noticed two strange envelopes mixed in with his personal effects. One was thick, stuffed with cash. The other was thin. He opened the thinner envelope as he made his way toward the front gates.

Inside the envelope was a note containing a single sentence. Lincoln stopped in his tracks just fifty feet from the front gate as his palms went cold. He read the note again, just to make sure his eyes weren't playing tricks on him. They weren't.

It read, "Congratulations! You're a dead man."

CHAPTER TWENTY-SEVEN

B randon stood in his bedroom, cordless phone in hand. Karen lay in his bed, sleeping peacefully. He wanted to call the police but Shorty's words gave him pause. What if Shorty was telling the truth and he'd really been the one who *rescued* Karen? Though they had different ambitions in life, Brandon had a soft spot for Shorty. After all, they'd both lost brothers in the Simmons Park Massacre. Brandon owed it to his troubled friend to try and confirm his story.

Leaving Karen to rest, he headed over to Simmons Park. The park, surrounded by a rusted chain-link fence, had been officially condemned after the killings took place, but everyone in the hood still used it to play ball, smoke out, and drink. But not Brandon. He hadn't set foot on this cursed ground since that day.

Everything looked just as he remembered, although weathered and worn from years of neglect. The faded, rainbow-colored jungle gym still stood beside the abandoned gymnasium—once a place of summer pool parties and community activities, now a hulking, beige husk with busted windows and cracked peeling walls.

If a building could catch leprosy, this was it.

Brandon hopped the fence and saw a burgundy Oldsmobile Eighty-Eight turning the corner. He instinctively ducked, knowing that any neighbor would have more than a few choice words to say to Moses if they saw Brandon going into Simmons Park.

Brandon pushed through the first pair of doors of the run-down gym and was immediately assaulted by stale air and the stench of rot. He headed up the stairs where Shorty had supposedly heard Karen's cries. Soon Brandon stood in front of the only closed door in the corridor. He pushed it open and entered the tiny room.

There was a mini refrigerator nailed to the floor, a toilet with no seat, and a giant Jamaican flag covering the entry. Brandon noticed a camcorder sitting atop a tripod in the far left corner. There was a crashing sound from below.

Someone had thrown open the doors downstairs. They sounded like a herd of elephants as they approached the stairwell. Panicked, Brandon only had one thought—*these must be the real kidnappers!*

They were now on the landing and rapidly approaching the guest room from hell. Brandon flattened himself against the wall next to the door opening, trying to calm his breathing and heart-rate with little success. In his head, he sounded like a broken vacuum cleaner each time he inhaled.

Then Brandon remembered Shorty's gun.

The door blew open. An obese, dark-skinned man barged in, a sweaty black blob with gigantic bulging eyes. His huge eyes nearly tripled in size after Brandon hit him in his baby-making factory with the butt of the gun.

All the intruder could say was a very surprised, "Ooof!"

Brandon got tangled up in the Jamaican flag as he tried to flee the room. A large hand clamped on his ankle and he fell to the floor, halfway between salvation and imprisonment.

Brandon squirmed and tried to get out of the man's reach. After bashing the man over the head with the butt of the gun, Brandon jumped up and ran toward the stairs. Unfortunately, he was so focused on what was behind him that he missed the first step. Badly. Brandon flew down the stairs headfirst.

As his forehead came into contact with concrete, he heard gunshots.

CHAPTER TWENTY-EIGHT

Baton Rouge, LA

"Yes, that's right, Bill, I spoke to Karen…just a couple of minutes ago." Randy sat in his Town Car on the way to the Louisiana Capitol Building.

"So she escaped?"

"Somehow, yes." Randy's mind returned to the all too short conversation he'd had with Karen as the motorcade glided through traffic. Her voice had been weak, wobbly, and shrill. She'd tried to tell him something, but with little success. He asked her over and over where she was, but her responses were incoherent and nonsensical. Then the line went as dead as Randy's heart.

Was this some sort of trap?

"My men are ready to move in as soon as you give the word," Bill said.

Randy could barely contain his anxiety. "That's good. Very good. But…please be careful, Bill. My daughter might still be caught up with them. Bring her back to me safely."

❧

Baton Rouge, LA

From far away, Coral heard someone banging on the door to her suite. It was probably the maid. "Go away!"

"Mrs. Lafitte?" a familiar voice called from the other side of the door.

Coral looked through the peephole. It was Larry, the chief of her husband's extra security detail. His bald, cone-shaped head looked extra pale in the incandescent light from the hallway. Randy was the first Governor in Louisiana's history to hire his own security, in addition to the secret service. Larry was the fifth chief of security to serve the Lafitte family since Kristopher died. He rapped on the door again.

"I'm not dressed, Larry."

"Come on, Mrs. Lafitte. Give me a break here. I've been out here banging for like five minutes."

"Okay, just give me a second please." Coral put on her silk robe in a fluster. She opened the door and said, "Thanks for your patience."

The large man loomed over her like a canopy. The bulges of his concealed weapons peeked out from under his oversized sports coat.

Something is wrong.

"I need you to get dressed, Mrs. Lafitte. Something has happened and I need to get you out of here."

Coral knew the routine and went into the bathroom to grab her things. The morning newspaper sat on top of the toilet. She read the headline on the front page in disbelief.

"Lincoln Baker Granted Full Pardon."

What the hell is going on?

Five minutes later, she was dressed and heading out the front door with Larry behind her.

Angola, LA

The clamor outside Angola grew. Panama X listened intently. The volume of the screams indicated they were getting a first glimpse of their villain. But Panama X knew who the real villain was, and soon the public would, too. He waited patiently for the phone to ring down the hall, the signal that Lincoln was clear.

The phone finally rang. Panama X stood and walked to the bars. A guard picked up the phone and nodded in Panama X's direction. Panama X smiled from ear to ear.

Angola, LA

Moses got out of the SUV and began the walk toward the penitentiary gates. Even though it had been years since his incarceration, the sight of the gates still brought on an intense loathing. The one benefit of his twelve-year stay, however, was that he still had allies on the inside who owed him favors. He was counting on them to get him access to Malcolm. The thought of acting the part of a prisoner, even for a cause as righteous as this, made him queasy. Nonetheless, he had no other choice. Lincoln's life depended on it.

Moses took a deep breath and pushed through the crowd gathered around the prison opening.

What's this protest all about?

Then he saw his adopted son emerge from the security gate.

What is going on here?

Angola, LA

Lincoln took his first steps toward freedom. He felt very exposed standing alone outside the security entrance. Armed guards had cleared a path for him to walk through the crowd of people behind the gate, but once he was outside, he would have no such protection from the angry mob. He'd received more hate mail and death threats than any other prisoner in Angola.

Sweat bloomed on his skin. Lincoln noticed the line of reporters waiting for their chance to speak to him. Cameras would once again project his face all over newspapers and television sets across the fifty states. He felt like he had hungry piranhas swimming around in the pit of his stomach.

"Did you think you were just gonna walk out of here?"

Lincoln couldn't find one friendly face amidst the hoards of people spitting and cursing at him. They had to be the families of the police officers and children killed during the Simmons Park Massacre. Lincoln's sweat flowed freely. Head held high, he stared into the sea of hate-filled faces. Hopefully Amir was having better luck.

Lake City, LA

Amir noticed movement on one of the security monitors before him. Was that a man crouching in the bushes before the gate?

"Yo, Moose," he ordered. "Go check out the perimeter."

Amir squinted at the monitor. He did not need any more surprises—it was bad enough that they'd lost the girl. He glanced at his watch—8:05 a.m. Good. Lincoln should be free by now.

Amir's cell phone vibrated on his hip. His calm evaporated when he read the truncated text: "Somebody followed us…"

Amir spun around to look at the monitors. Moose was at the front gate, on his back, with his hands covering his throat in a choking gesture. Spouts of what looked like oil spurted between his locked fingers. Four men stepped over Moose's body and scaled the gate.

Amir's eyes opened wide as he yelled, "Ambush!"

CHAPTER TWENTY-NINE

Lake City, LA

"There you are, maufucka."

Brandon was slowly regaining consciousness. The world had exploded all around him as the building was hit from all sides with a barrage of careening bullets.

"Get the fuck up!"

Brandon was jerked to his knees and he felt his shoulder pop out of the socket. He was pushed against the wall.

His oppressor ducked down saying, "Gotta get the fuck up outta here." He poked at Brandon's dislocated shoulder with his gun. "Trump! Salsa!"

Gunfire was the only response.

"There a back way outta here?"

Brandon shook his head.

"Fuck! Okay...when I say, we gonna bust up outta here."

Brandon knew this was a horrible idea, but he was in too much pain to fight back. He was yanked to his feet as he contemplated the final minutes of his life.

Using Brandon as a shield, the man shoved him toward the double doors. Death awaited them on the other side.

Brandon mouthed the Lord's Prayer.

"Our Father,"

Bullets obliterated the front windows to the left of the main entrance. Shards of flying glass cut into Brandon's cheek.

"Which Art In Heaven,"

The man checked his clip and safety.

"Hallowed Be Thy Name,"

Car doors slammed shut. Men yelled at each other to surround the building.

"Thy Kingdom Come, Thy Will Be Done, In Earth As It Is In Heaven,"

The man commanded Brandon to kick the doors open.

"Give Us This Day Our Daily Bread,"

Sunlight blinded Brandon as the doors burst open into the day. He stared up into the mournful blue sky.

"And Forgive Us Our Trespasses, As We Forgive Them That Trespass Against Us,"

His captor once again yelled, "Trump! Salsa!" Brandon saw two men lying nearly on top of each other, their weapons in death clutches as blood pooled around them.

"Lead Us Not Into Temptation, But Deliver Us From Evil,"

Shorty appeared from underneath the bullet-laden Oldsmobile. Their eyes met for a long moment. Then Shorty ran across the field as the man pushed Brandon toward the car, shooting in every direction.

"For Thine Is The Kingdom,"

Shorty was decapitated by a shotgun blast at close range.

"And The Power,"

A burning sensation like ten hot irons tore open the flesh of Brandon's shoulder.

"And The Glory,"

They were at the car, opening the doors.

"For Ever And Ever,"

The man pushed Brandon into the passenger seat and started the car. Brandon closed his eyes as they plowed through the fence surrounding Simmons Park.

"Amen."

Lake City, LA

Karen slept for an indeterminable length of time after she called her father. The boy, Brandon, who she barely remembered, had left her a note that he went out for food so she nodded off again. When she opened her eyes the second time, she was looking at the face of her dead brother.

Kristopher smiled a strange, sad smile, his blue eyes full of pity and shame. Kneeling next to her, he blew the hair from her eyes. Karen tried to speak but Kristopher put one finger over her lips and shook his head.

He motioned for Karen to follow him out of the house and they walked, side by side, brother and sister reunited.

Until the sky exploded in a thunderous cacophony of gunfire.

Karen fell into a ditch on the side of the road and put her face in the dewy grass, hands covering her ears. The gunfire boomed for what seemed like forever, but the silence that followed was far more ominous.

Kristopher beckoned for Karen to get up, but she was terrified. Crawling on her hands and knees, she sought refuge in her brother's arms. With his help, she found the strength to rise.

Some part of her knew this couldn't possibly be real, but she could smell her brother and feel his essence.

A car rattled their way. Kristopher looked at Karen.

"Trust him," she heard him say in her head. Then he faded away.

Through tears Karen watched a burgundy Oldsmobile approach. It looked like it had been used for target practice. Then she saw Flashlight Man's eyes and mouth widen in surprise and anger. The car skidded to a stop just a few feet away.

Kristopher's words rang in her ears as she locked eyes with Brandon clutching his arm in the passenger seat.

Trust him.

Lake City, LA

With arrest or death imminent, Amir took one confused moment to wonder how the hell they'd been found out. Then he sprung into action. He picked up his military issue UZI and hunkered down.

The front gate exploded in a whine of metal. Amir heard the unmistakable bark of bullets leaping from the muzzles of Zire and Reem's street sweeper shotguns. He knew they would rather die than go to prison.

He wished it was that easy for him.

Got to stay patient. Let them get past the first line of defense, waste some ammo, and then get what I've got for them.

Crouching low, Amir switched off the safety on his weapon. A terrific boom shook him to the floor.

What the fuck was that?

Amir thought of his mother's beautiful face and his resolve hardened. No matter what happened, he could not die before fulfilling his mission.

The intruders fired incessantly at the school, but Amir was at peace. *Come and get it, boys.*

Angola, LA

Panama X's smile dissolved into a grimace as the crowd noise grew into an uproar outside the prison gates. On the television monitor outside of his cell, the local news interrupted *The Price is Right* to broadcast the Governor's much-anticipated press conference. The reporter was speculating about what the Governor was going to address.

Panama X wondered the same thing.

He watched Randy Lafitte step out of the Louisiana State Capitol Building and approach the podium at the top of the famous stairwell. Panama X was struck by how ragged the man looked after eight turbulent years in office. Then he saw something only he could see. Randy Lafitte was infected. He'd had an encounter with a *baka*. But how?

Amir.

His son apparently had changed the plan.

It still might not be too late.

Lafitte opened with, "People of Louisiana…"

The prison alarms sounded. Gunshots rang out. There was screaming.

Panama X stared at Randy Lafitte on the television monitor and chanted under his breath.

Baton Rouge, LA

"People of Louisiana," Randy began, glancing down at his prepared remarks. "I called this press conference so I could address several topics of interest and put some rumors to rest." His cell phone vibrated in his jacket pocket. "Regarding rumors that my daughter has been kidnapped," he said, lips drawn in a tight smile, "those rumors are…unfortunately true." He clenched and unclenched his fist in his pocket. "My daughter, Karen, was kidnapped two days ago. The good news is that she was returned to us safe and sound this morning. She's currently in the care of some of the best doctors in this great state of Louisiana.

"She's fine, but the people responsible will pay dearly for this transgression of the law and invasion of my family." A black eagle of fear spread wings inside his chest. "The mastermind behind this deplorable act is already in custody. Death row inmate Malcolm Wright, also known as Panama X, a man convicted of killing thirty-two innocent people in a botched assassination attempt, planned the kidnapping of my daughter to try and pressure me into granting a stay of execution. Well, I do not take kindly to being blackmailed. Malcolm Wright lost his latest appeal to the Supreme Court and an execution date will be set as soon as the paperwork clears. My policy of swift justice for deplorable criminals like this is in full effect."

Randy's desire to watch Malcolm Wright in his death throes was nearly as great as his desire to see Karen alive and well again.

"I have to thank Chief Bill Edwards and the entire Lake City Police Department for their hard work during this investigation. Moving on, it appears that Hurricane Isaac will make landfall to the west of Baton Rouge sometime between eight and ten o'clock this evening, though, as we all know, this storm could change direction at any time. The President has declared states of emergency for Texas, Louisiana, and Mississippi.

"Evacuation plans are in effect for Baton Rouge and surrounding areas. Evacuation teams are going door to door passing out hurricane preparedness pamphlets and encouraging the people in the low lying areas to leave. I urge everyone to take the necessary precautions. Remember, you can replace material things, but you can't replace life."

He felt the crowd stirring with nervous energy.

An image of Kristopher flashed in his mind. "Last, but certainly not least, is the question of why I have chosen to show Lincoln Baker clemency. The answer is not as difficult as you may expect. I've recently reviewed new evidence proving Mr. Baker's innocence. This information was also reviewed by the Louisiana Pardon Board, which recently convened to go over the case. They have agreed that Mr. Baker should be released immediately and I cannot, in good conscience, let my personal feelings get in the way of doing the right thing. The moral thing."

Randy was immediately pelted by a barrage of questions from the cadre of reporters.

Enjoy your brief freedom, Lincoln. Because it's all going to be over for you soon.

Angola, LA

The reporters were lined up like a firing squad just outside the exit. They reminded Lincoln of a kennel of rabid dogs barking for attention. Lincoln stared past them at a woman holding up a sign. Her expression was so frantic, Lincoln's pulse jumped.

He squinted trying to read the black lettering across white poster board. It said: **DEAD MAN WALKING**

What the fuck?

Lincoln felt a whoosh of air by his right ear. A bullet had just narrowly missed his head. A second bullet hit home and imaginary hands pushed Lincoln face forward.

Blood seeped from the exit wound in his left shoulder. Chaos filled the air as people scattered, desperately trying to get away from the shooting. Some even ran toward the prison as if it were a safe haven.

Lincoln got to his feet and made a dash for the front gate, more determined than ever to get the hell out of Angola once and for all. He got within reach of the gate when he was shot again—this time through the left bicep. Lincoln lost his balance and fell to the concrete, his skull bouncing off the pavement.

White lights of pain burst in his field of vision and he closed his eyes against them. With his last lunge, he'd made it just outside the prison gates, but things had changed. The gate in front of him looked nothing like a prison gate; in fact, it resembled another gate he knew all too well. Lincoln tilted his head skyward. He read the bullet-riddled, square yellow sign posted a few feet above his head:

Welcome to Simmons Park.

No Cursing.

No Fighting.

No Horseplay.

No Fence Climbing.

Have Fun!

The concrete had morphed into gravel. Weeds sprouted through in several places. The alarms had stopped. There was no more screaming.

The only sound was from someone nearby bouncing a basketball on concrete.

Lincoln got to his feet. His injuries had vanished, and so had the pain. He gaped at his surroundings in bewilderment.

The park before him was immaculate.

Everything was exactly how he remembered it. The lawn was manicured. The gate was rust-free. The recreation center looked like it had been built yesterday.

A familiar sound interrupted his thoughts. He hopped the gate with ease, just as he'd done as an adolescent. As he made his way toward the basketball courts, he was struck by how the place smelled, like wet copper.

He rounded the side of the building and saw a bouncing basketball. The ball bounced at half-court, straight up and down, all by itself.

What the fuck?

Goosebumps covered his forearms. He had to exert real effort to move from the spot where his feet had taken root.

His feet eventually propelled him toward the bouncing ball. He felt eyes crawling over his skin as he moved closer and closer to touching the ball. He looked around one last time and on its next up-bounce, Lincoln snatched the ball out of the air.

Everything changed.

The sky turned from cloudless to overcast. The spotless park was gone, replaced by a trash- and junk-strewn place, with red graffiti sprayed everywhere. Upon closer inspection, Lincoln realized the graffiti was actually chalk outlines all over the basketball court. There were words written by each outline. The names of the chalk people.

He held the basketball to his chest and looked around wildly. The wind howled. Sudden acid rain pummeled him. Lincoln watched in horrid fascination as the chalk outlines disintegrated and pooled toward him in the center of the court.

It didn't look like spray paint anymore. He was ankle deep in a puddle of blood which had begun to run up his legs as the rain rolled down them.

How is this happening?

The pain from the bullet wounds was back. Lincoln had been holding the basketball in a death grip and let it go. The ball fell to the ground and continued bouncing on its own. The park immediately changed back to the clean, serene environment.

But not everything was the same. There was a message written in the bloody spray paint on the spot where the basketball bounced. Though tempted to grab the ball again so he could get a better visual of the message, Lincoln thought better of it. Instead he read between bounces:

LOOKS ARE DECEIVING

I'm going crazy.

Lincoln looked back down at the message. It now read:

HE WILL DIE

Who will?

Lincoln's hands were on fire, like they'd been dipped in acid. He turned them palm side up and saw two shapes burning into the flesh. He screamed in agony even as he saw what the final design would reveal.

On one hand was the bloody outline of a body, and on the other was a name:

Moses.

Lincoln closed his eyes. A single tear escaped and rushed down his cheek. Then a sound like metal grating against metal crashed in his ears. His eyes shot open.

He became painfully aware of two things: he was back at the prison lying on the ground, and someone was kneeling over him.

He stared into the unmistakable gray eyes of Snake Roberts for the second time in an hour. Roberts grimaced and said, "Time to go, Link. We gotta get you outta here."

Lincoln grasped Snake's hand and then hesitated.

Is this a trap?

Snake looked back at Lincoln and smiled coldly. "Either you come with me right now, or you die here. The choice is yours."

PART II: REVELATION

"You know as well as I do that people that die bad don't stay in the ground."

~Toni Morrison
Beloved

CHAPTER THIRTY

12 Years Earlier
1990
Lake City, LA

Karen sat beside her brother on the old bench under the shade of Melinda Weeps. This had been their Sunday ritual for as long as she could remember. After attending first mass at Our Lady Queen of Heaven with Momma, she and Kristopher would spend the afternoon relaxing under the curved branches of the old live oak tree with Abby, their nanny.

Today was Abby's birthday. She wore a pretty flower-print dress that she had made herself. Her many bracelets and bangles clanged together as she filled their cups with homemade iced tea.

"How old are you?" Karen asked. Abby was a Cay-jun, which Abby had once explained meant she was part Indian and part Acadian. Karen thought it was silly that it wasn't spelled the way it sounded, and had no idea what an Acadian was. It sounded like a race of aliens. Kristopher said Acadians were just Canadians who had migrated south, like birds did in the winter.

"Make her guess your age," Kristopher interrupted before Abby could respond.

"If I knew, I wouldn't be asking, duh," Karen said.

"Calm down, chillun," Abby replied with a smile. "Today I turn sixty-eight."

"Quick, Karen," Kristopher said. "How much older than you is Abby?"

Karen looked at Abby's wrinkled skin and black hair (she confessed to Karen that she still dyed it) and thought she must be a thousand years older. Karen knew it was a simple math problem and after doing some quick figuring said, "That's easy. I'm six, so that means Abby is sixty-two years older than me."

"Very good, kiddo," Kristopher replied.

"And you're fifteen, so she's...umm, fifty-three years older than you." Karen stuck out her tongue at her brother and he tried to snatch it out of her mouth. Karen evaded him and took another sip of the delicious iced tea.

A sharp rustle shook the limbs above them and a few leaves fell into Karen's cup. "Aww no," she whined.

Kristopher jumped up to investigate.

"What is it?" Karen asked.

"Probably just a squirrel or the wind," Kristopher reported, unable to find the culprit.

"Or it could be Isaac," Abby said.

"Isaac?" Karen and Kristopher asked, almost in unison.

"Who is Isaac?" Kristopher asked.

"Isaac is a ghost who haunts Melinda Weeps and this land."

"A ghost!" Karen exclaimed.

"Yes," Abby said, standing up to clear her dress of leaves. "It's about time ya'll learned of yo' family's hist'ry here. What ya'll know about ya'll ancestor, Luc Lafitte?"

"Besides the fact that he founded Lake City?" Kristopher replied, rolling his eyes.

"Yes. Besides dat."

"Well, he was also a pirate who got shipwrecked in Lake City while fleeing from the Spanish," Kristopher said.

"Dat all you know?" Abby asked.

Kristopher shrugged. "Pretty much."

Abby gestured for the children to follow her to the swing set nearby. "Chillun, let me tell you what really happened after Luc Lafitte landed on dese here shores."

Abby cleared her throat as she pushed Karen on the swing. "When Luc Lafitte landed, dere was already people living here. Lake City was a meetin' place and safe house fo' runaway slaves in dose days. Da Injuns dat lived here had been helpin' da slaves dat came through by providin' 'em wit' food and shelter while dey waited for da ferryboat to take dem out to da Gulf of Mexico. Back den, Mexico was free territory dat extended all da way into wat ya'll know as Texas. Did you know dat Karen?"

Karen shook her head.

"Luc Lafitte and his men wrecked dere ship and came to shore to steal some supplies from da Injuns. Dey found da camps of da runaway slaves instead. Luc Lafitte was a very cleva man and somehow convinced da runaway slaves dat had been livin' peacefully with da Injuns for some time, dat dey was being set-up by da Injuns and da Spanish."

"How do you know that?" Kristopher asked.

Karen could tell from his challenge that he was very interested.

"You gonna let me tell my story?"

"Sorry," Kristopher replied. "Please go ahead."

"Okay. Well, Luc told da slaves dat he and his men had come because dey wanted to help dem defeat da Injuns and help dem to freedom. Dis couldn't be furda from da troof. Luc's crew was outnumbered and he was just tryin' to stir up trouble cuz he knew he would need protection from da Injuns and da Spanish. It took him a little while to convince da slaves to stop runnin' and start fightin', but soon Luc Lafitte and his army of runaway slaves had killt almost every Injun and Spaniard."

Karen's mind was alive with visions of pirates shooting arrows at Indians as they tried to throw their tomahawks at them.

"Durin' all of dis," Abby continued, "Luc took a fancy fo' one of da Negro females in da camp and wouldn't you know it, she turnt up pregnant befoe long. Luc decided to put down roots and create a safe port for French commerce through West Lake and Prien Lake. He and da slaves built da first house in Lake City right chere, and dat's how da Lafitte Plantation was born."

Karen was reminded of another Sunday when Abby had explained that their home had once been the site of the Luc Lafitte Civil War Museum. Their grandfather, Joseph Lafitte, had torn down the museum and built a mansion. After he passed away, Daddy tore that house down to build the home in which Karen and Kristopher grew up.

A thought occurred to Karen and she asked, "Did they kill all those Indians right here? Is that where the Ghost comes from?"

Abby looked over at her and replied, "I'm sure some a' dose Injuns met their maker here, but dat's not da story of da ghost."

"Come on, Karen," Kristopher said. "Let Abby finish."

"Okay," Abby said. "So where was I?"

"Luc Lafitte built his plantation and fell in love with a slave," Kristopher replied.

"Ahh, yes. Thank you, chile. So as I said, Luc and da slaves had a deal. But as more and more Frenchmen and Cajuns migrated into da area, da runaway slaves lost dere equality. Lafitte married da daughta of a rich French settla' and quickly forgot about his chile by da slave. Dat chile grew up workin' in da first version of what would later become da Port of Lake City, unloadin' and reloadin' French ships all day."

"Good story so far, Abby," Kristopher interrupted. "But what does all this have to do with the ghost?"

"Yeah, Abby," Karen agreed. "We wanna hear about the ghost."

"Alright, alright. My grammie told me dis story when I was jes a lil' girl, even younga dan you, Karen. Grammie used to say dat histr'y always repeats itself, and dat knowing yo' histr'y helps you to avoid making da same mistakes in da here and now."

"Mom says that too sometimes," Kristopher interjected.

"And yo' momma know what she's talkin' bout. But I bet da reason she never told ya'll dis story is because she's forgot a bit about yo' family's hist'ry."

"What do you mean?" Karen asked.

"I mean dat obviously Luc Lafitte's descendants didn't keep as good of records as dose slaves dey tricked and betrayed. Luc Lafitte's illegit'mate child, a boy, grew up in da shadows of dis here plantation, pretty much forgotten by his real fatha. His name was Isaac...Isaac Lafitte, as was da custom for slaves to take on da last name of dey massa. Isaac and his motha worked in da big house until he was big enough to start workin' at da port. You know sweepin' and moppin', stuff like dat."

Karen's eyes widened and she looked over at Kristopher. She knew it wasn't a coincidence that Luc's son was named Isaac, just like the ghost. She just couldn't figure out how he went from working at the port to becoming a ghost.

"Da Lafitte Plantation and da Port of Lake City was bustlin'," Abby continued. "Befoe long, da township of Lake City was born, but in dose days it was called Port City. Port life was toughenin' Issac up and he was growin' into quite da young buck. His momma died on his seventh birthday, leavin' him to raise his baby brotha and sista by himself."

"That's so sad that his mommy died," Karen said. "Isn't that sad, Kristopher?"

"Yeah, a real tear-jerker," Kristopher replied. "Go on, Abby."

Abby continued. "Da story behind da ghost of Melinda Weeps begins when Isaac was around twenty years old. He only had one more year to work off his family's debt, and was one of da best employees down at da port, still providin' for his younga brotha and sista who was workin' as servants in da big house.

"One day Luc's youngest daughta, Melinda, showed up at da port. She wanted to see her daddy's business, but as soon as she saw Isaac throwing dose fifteen pound rice bags with dat muscular frame of his, da sightseeing tour ended. It seems like she had inherited her fatha's taste fo' dark meat." Abby cackled.

Karen didn't get the joke but let it go.

"That's nasty, Abby," Kristopher said, scrunching up his face. "Isn't that incest? That's disgusting."

"Yes, I guess it was incest," Abby replied.

"Incest is nasty," Karen agreed, wrinkling up her face. She thought incest was a kind of bug.

"Anyway, Melinda and Isaac was gettin' together fo' maybe two or three months befoe anyone found out," Abby continued. "Actually, I tink someone tattled, probably one a' Melinda's jealous suitors. You can imagine what happened when ole Luc found out his daughter was creepin' around with one of his slaves."

"He killed him," Kristopher said in a serious tone that gave Karen chills.

Abby nodded and continued. "Luc had to handle da situation delicately because he didn't want anyone findin' out about his daughta's indiscretions. Poor Isaac didn't know what hit him. Da angry mob dragged him from da port one day while he was workin'. Dey dragged him all da way to da Lafitte Plantation, beatin' and cursin' him—calling him a rapist."

"Issac just let them take him?" Kristopher asked. "Why didn't he fight back or tell the truth about what was going on?"

"Because he was outnumbered and had his brotha and sista to worry 'bout," Abby replied. "Luc Lafitte didn't even know dem kids was also his chillun or dat dey was related to Isaac, and Issac wanted it to stay dat way. Da lynch mob wanted to hang him right away, but Luc had otha plans. He told da men to tie Isaac to da tree fo' da time bein' 'cause he wanted him to suffa befoe he died."

Abby looked at Karen and said, "Karen, I don't tink you should be hearin' dis part. Why don't you go play over in da sand pit?"

"No ma'am, I'm okay. Right, Kristopher? Tell her I'm okay."

"She's alright, Abby."

Abby looked skeptical but said, "Alright now, chillun, I'll go on but ya'll got to promise not to say anything to Missus Lafitte, okay. We got a deal?"

"Deal," Karen and Kristopher said in unison.

Abby stopped pushing the swing and divided up the last of the tea. "Follow me, chillun."

She led them around to the other side of the large live oak. "Dey tied Isaac to dis tree right around da trunk here and proceeded to do some awful, horrible tings to da poor chile."

"Like what?" Kristopher asked.

Karen saw a strange look in his eyes.

"For starters, dey whipped him senseless. Den dey dug up red anthills all around da yard, coated Isaac with honey, and dumped fire ants on him. Dis was after dey had castrated…uhh cut off his…nevermind."

"It's okay, Abby," Kristopher said. "Karen doesn't know what that means. Do you, Karen?"

Karen didn't know what castration meant, but that didn't stop her from getting a horrible case of the squirmies. "I hate fire ants. Icky, icky, icky bugs…I hate them."

"I know, chile," Abby comforted. "I know."

"So what happened next?" Kristopher asked.

"Well, dey let da ants have dere fun with Isaac fo' a while, den dey doused dem off him wit' a bucket of scaldin' hot water and left him fo' da night. He shoulda died from da shock of it all, but all da years of labor had made him very tough. Lata dat night, Melinda came to him, feelin' guilty I guess, and told him dat she would not let him die, dat she had a plan. She said dat she loved him and was pregnant wit' his chile and would save him.

"Da next day came—Melinda's eighteenth birthday, by da way—and Isaac learned dat he would be hung from da very same tree after breakfast. I imagine dat at dis point he couldn't wait for it to be ova', but it was far from ova'.

"Isaac found out about Melinda's grand plan a few minutes befoe his life ended. Dere was a big crowd gathered here and Isaac was strung up prob'ly right around here." Abby pointed to the second layer of branches. "He was placed on a horse and made to face da crowd. Luc Lafitte, dressed in his French captain's wear, stood to da side of da horse and addressed da crowd.

"'Ladies and Gentlemen,' Luc began. 'This slave has been accused of raping my beautiful daughter, Melinda. As the owner of this land and founder of this township, I am exercising the authority vested in me by God, and am hereby punishing him to death by hanging for his crimes.'"

Karen giggled a little at Abby's angry Frenchman impersonation.

Abby wasn't smiling, however. "So da story goes dat Luc Lafitte turnt roun' and looked at Isaac, his illegit'mate son, and asked, 'do you have any last words?'

"Isaac looked down on da fatha dat was never dere for him and said, 'You may kill me today, but da stain of yo' guilt will burn in yo' soul foreva. He who kills his own shall be cursed 'til his death.'"

"Luc had messed wit' da wrong one. Isaac's motha was what dey call a *mambo* in voodoo. She had taught him da way of da left hand."

"What's a *mambo?*" Kristopher asked the exact question on Karen's mind. She hoped Abby would explain what voodoo was, too.

"Sorry, chillun, I forgot who I was talkin' to for a second. Voodoo is a religion, just like bein' Catholic, but it's practiced by people from Haiti. Haiti is an island south of Louisiana, Karen."

"Oh, okay," Karen replied, trying to imagine where it could be. She resolved to look it up on Daddy's maps as soon as the story was over.

"What's the 'way of the left hand'?" Kristopher asked.

"Well, it's what you would prob'ly call black magic. But magic don't have no color, and if it did, it wouldn't be black. Isaac's motha was in touch wit' da earth and da spirits, and taught Isaac in dese ways as well."

Kristopher nodded with understanding. Karen was lost, but wanted to hear the rest of the story.

Abby continued, "When Isaac said dese words, Luc Lafitte looked at da bleeding, condemned man atop da horse, saw his own eyes starin' back at'm, and hesitated. Den a blood-curdlin' scream from da roof of da big house broke up dat father and son moment. Everyone turnt to see what da commotion was, and what a sight it must'a been.

"Melinda Lafitte was screamin' at da top of her lungs from da roof. Screamin' and standin' naked as da day she was born. Obviously, Luc Lafitte had no idea what was goin' on, and rushed closer to da house.

"Melinda screamed, 'Father please, I love him, don't kill him, I love him!'" over and over. She was threatenin' dat if Isaac was killt, she would kill herself.

"Luc quickly yelled for servants to get her down as he stared up at his daughter, scared to deaf. Da man who had been holdin' da horse steady all dis time let go of da reins to see what all da commotion was about. While Luc was tryin' to calm Melinda down, da horse, startled by all da action, bolted. Isaac let out a short scream dat was cut off by his neck snappin'.

"Melinda watched in horror as Isaac swung and twitched in da wind. Den she threw herself from da roof—killin' herself and her unborn chile."

"Wow!" Kristopher said with noticeable admiration. "I can't believe all that really happened right here!"

"Yes chillun," Abby said solemnly. "Da descendants of Luc Lafitte are doomed to be haunted by Isaac and Melinda. Dere first victim was actually Luc Lafitte. You see, he killt himself exactly three days after Melinda's suicide. Da servants found him lyin' naked at da foot of dis tree one mohnin'. He was holdin' a revolver in his right hand and a tear-stained slip of paper in his left."

Abby touched the old tree gently and said, "Come on chillun, dat's enough for today."

"What!" Kristopher exclaimed. "Come on Abby, you gotta tell us what that letter said. Pleeease?"

"Okay, okay," Abby said after more pleading from Kristopher and Karen. "It was some kinda weird suicide note. On da back were two words: Melinda Weeps."

Karen backed away from the tree as if she might get infected if she got too close. She didn't think she would ever think of that tree the same way again.

Abby must have noticed the concern on her face because she quickly said, "It's a good ting da curse died off well befoe ya'll was born, cuz you see dere's something strange about dat house, a pattern of sorts. Many Lafitte chillun dat lived in dis house never lived past dey eighteenth birthday."

CHAPTER THIRTY-ONE

Monday
Lake City, LA

Trapped, Amir ducked and ran back into the supply room to get more weapons to make his last stand, but there was no ammo anywhere inside the closet. The masked attackers were inside the school. Amir heard the unmistakable hiss of teargas grenades going off, as glass shattered all around him.

Gas filtered through the door.

Shit!

Amir slid his cell phone inside a hidden compartment in his cargo pants and fingered the seven-inch stainless steel switchblade he kept for emergencies. His reaction to the gas was violent and immediate. He ripped the sleeves off his t-shirt and covered his mouth, already tasting metal in the back of his throat. His nostrils burned, as if he had snorted ethyl alcohol.

Moving from the direct path of the gas, Amir closed his eyes, started spitting, and blowing his nose like he'd learned in boot camp. He panted, taking in short shallow swallows of acid air. Soon doubled over, he vomited up his breakfast.

Four masked men charged into the room and in moments he was disarmed, handcuffed, and being marched through the ruins of his failed operation. The men moved with military precision. Once they made it outside, Amir surveyed the destruction through sandpaper eyes.

The air was thick with smoke, the old school completely obliterated. The yard was littered with scattered bodies. His captors stepped over the corpses of their fallen comrades and Amir's men without batting an eye. At least Zire and Reem had taken some of the motherfuckers with them.

Two men standing before a camouflaged Hummer H-2 led Amir out of the compound and shoved him into the backseat of an unmarked black Crown Victoria.

Who the fuck are these guys? Who sent them?

The handcuffs were the only thing preventing Amir from choking one of the men in the front. If he could just get one arm free.

One of the masked men spoke through an earpiece and microphone, presumably to the others. "Timber Pack…this is Red Wolf…Jackal acquired. Proceeding to drop-zone."

Drop-zone? Jackal? What the fuck is this, the Nature Channel?

Amir discretely struggled with the plastic, double lock cuffs, most likely made by Monadnock, national sponsor of police brutality everywhere.

The only reason I'm still alive is because they need information.

Red Wolf mumbled a few other words and signaled the troops to move out. Abrupt car movement tossed Amir backward, temporarily derailing his escape efforts.

"Sit up," Red Wolf demanded without taking his eyes off the road.

Amir righted himself. The caravan drove by the abandoned train district. Each car followed two vehicle lengths behind the other. He wondered again about the identity of these men. They were clearly not cops, and were too precise to be Feds.

Who does that leave? SWAT? Snake?

The answer became readily apparent.

They got to Jhonnette.

She was the only person who knew Amir was in Lake City, although she didn't know where they'd been keeping the girl or how to get to the money. That's where Red Wolf and Anvil Head came in.

Did she give up Snake, too?

If so, Lincoln was in for a world of trouble.

How could I have been so stupid?

Doubt crept into Amir's mind for the first time since embarking on his mission to save Lincoln. Why hadn't he been able to move on after his mother's death? Why hadn't he contacted the authorities instead of rounding up a gang of thugs to bust Lincoln out of prison by any means necessary?

The answer was obvious.

Dad.

His father had preached his entire life about how a black man in America had to live by his own laws and create his own rules because the "system" was built for the black man to fail. Amir had grown up with a romanticized vision of what his father and the Black Mob stood for. Now that the veil was lifting, he could see his father for what he really was—an angry black man who'd taken the eye for an eye mentality to insane lengths. This revelation surprised Amir as much as it hurt.

Now, here he was, ringleader of his own Black Mob, attempting to prosper on the pain and suffering of others. He had kidnapped an innocent teenage girl and turned her into a monster. If his mother were still alive, Amir would not be able to look her in the eyes. On top of that, he was probably going to end up dead or in jail for his trouble. What a way to honor her final wish.

Red Wolf's chatter brought Amir back to his predicament.

He listened intently. Something was going on at St. Mary's Hospital in the center of town.

Lake City, LA

Scenery blurred past the bullet-riddled, burgundy Oldsmobile Eighty-Eight speeding through Lake City. Brandon lay slumped in the passenger seat, his sprained left wrist cradled on his lap. He couldn't believe he'd nearly been shot. He was lucky to be alive — far luckier than Shorty.

He stared out of the broken front windshield as shattered glass danced on the dash. Trees, traffic lights, and random billboards flashed in and out of his field of vision. He wanted to turn around and check on Karen, but the man he now thought of as Gordo, was watching him. So instead, he focused his mind on his last conversation with Shorty, replaying it over and over like a skipping CD.

Karen lay curled up in fetal position on the backseat. She thought of Kristopher's message to trust Brandon. Yeah right — she'd never trust anyone ever again. Besides, Kristopher was only a hallucination brought on by the drugs. Her cramps flared up and she found herself praying for drugs. She coughed violently for the second time in less than a minute. Her blood-tinted mucus splattered the seat.

God, what is happening to me?

Fat Pat focused on the road as the steering wheel dug into his generous belly. All the streets appeared alike. He smacked the steering wheel repeatedly in frustration. Trump had been the driver, not him.

Fat Pat glanced over at the lanky kid in the passenger seat with dried tears on his face. Then he checked on the girl in the backseat.

How the fuck did this happen?

Fat Pat looked at what was left of his watch. It had stopped at 8:23 a.m. Unbelievable. The whole saga at the park had lasted less than ten minutes.

He examined his options. Salsa and Trump were dead, and he assumed the same was true for Amir and the boys back at headquarters. Yet he had gotten away pretty much unharmed. And, he still had the girl.

What kind of dumb luck is this?

The original plan was fucked. It was up to Fat Pat to make the best of a bad situation. The girl was his ticket out of this whole mess. Nothing could happen to him as long as he kept her close.

Fat Pat's mind turned to the ransom. Amir hadn't told anyone in the crew where the money was. If Fat Pat could just figure out the location of the dough, he'd be set for life. He needed information though, information he could only get from one place.

"Kid," he began. "Kid! Look at me. Wake up."

The kid rolled his head toward Fat Pat's voice.

"Where the hell are we?"

All he got was a blank stare.

I'll wake your ass up.

Fat Pat dug his pointer finger into the bullet hole in the kid's shoulder until he howled in pain.

"Good. You're awake. Now tell me where the fuck we are?"

"Ain't telling you squat." The kid rolled his head back toward the window.

"Wha—maufucka is you crazy? You think you in pain now? You don't know pain, kid."

The car drifted off the pavement toward a ditch. Fat Pat hit the brakes just in time. The car skidded to a halt.

"See what you made me do, lil' nigga? I should just blast yo' ass right now."

The kid met his gaze. "Go ahead."

Skinny lil' nigga got balls. Either that or he's crazy.

Fat Pat grabbed the gun and pressed it against the kid's sweating nose.

The kid's eyes showed no sign of fear as he whispered, "Do it."

Fat Pat applied pressure on the trigger. Then the girl popped up and grabbed for the gun.

Aw hell naw. These maufuckas done lost they minds.

He wrestled the gun back and grabbed the white girl by the throat, choking her until she went limp.

The kid let himself out of the car and rolled down into the ditch.

Fat Pat watched the kid pick himself up off the ground. His scream caught in his throat as he took in the deserted surroundings.

They were smack dab in the middle of the train district—the perpetually deserted train district. Amir had actually considered setting up shop around here before deciding on the old school, which gave Fat Pat some sort of reference point. He was close to HQ!

"Nice try, maufucka," he said, leveling the gun at the kid. "Now let's try this shit again. You gone tell me how to get where I wanna go or am I gone have to end yo' life right here?"

"Okay, okay," the kid replied. "Where you trying to get to?"

"The ole' schoolyard," Fat Pat replied without hesitation.

Baton Rouge, LA

"Why are we stopping here?" Coral asked, confused. Larry had pulled the sedan over in front of a small building. The tattered sign declared its name as **Here Today, Gone Tomorrow**.

"This is the safe house I told you about," he said.

"A pawn shop?"

Larry got out and opened Coral's door, ignoring her question.

Coral looked from the open door, to the pawn shop, then back to Larry. She pulled out her cell phone and started dialing.

Larry snatched the phone out of her hands and stashed it in his suit pocket. "No cell phones."

"What are you...you have no right! I want to speak with my husband!"

"Strict orders, ma'am. No contact from cell phones."

Coral was fuming. "So when can I speak with him?"

"We have a secure line inside, ma'am. You can call him from there."

Grumbling, Coral took Larry's extended hand and got out of the car.

A man in his late twenties with long, unkempt dark hair met them at the door. He glanced at Coral and then fixed his gaze on Larry. "About damn time. What took you so long?"

Larry shrugged and ushered Coral inside.

"And you are?" Coral asked, once across the threshold. She'd been wrong to call this a pawn shop. It was actually an Army/Navy store.

"Shaw Roberts."

"Snake's brother?"

"Bingo."

"Is this your store?"

"Correct again. Just got discharged from the service. Bought this place off this crazy Vietnam Vet. Poor guy's daughter had him committed."

Larry cleared his throat. "The phone is in the back, Mrs. Lafitte."

Shaw led her through the store, which was cluttered with enough camouflage and rupsacks to equip a small army. Larry brought up the rear. Soon Coral found herself in a storage area that seemed to have everything *except* for a phone.

"Where is it?" She asked.

Shaw pivoted and thrust a rag over Coral's mouth. "It's right here."

Coral plummeted toward unconsciousness with one thought assaulting her.

I've got to warn Randy!

Angola, LA

The Reception Center, also known as Death Row, was in chaos. The narrow corridors echoed with the screams of condemned men. Some were throwing flaming reams of toilet paper at the guards, while other banged on their cell bars with tin cups and sticks.

Panama X observed the pandemonium from his cell. Stoic on the outside, internally he was concerned about Lincoln. He hadn't expected his young protégé to escape from Angola without incident, but all this screaming and shooting had not been part of the plan.

Panama X shut his eyes, blocked out the commotion, and dove inward to the place inside himself where time did not exist. From this contemplative space he considered what he'd detected in Lafitte while watching his speech.

Lafitte's aura had been orange-brown, a clear indicator of spiritual infection. But from whom?

The answer revealed itself in the form of a picture.

He saw a dark room. Tied to a high-backed chair was a girl in a sheer white dress. Behind her was the shadowy figure of a drummer dressed in ceremonial garb. A deep, inhuman voice was chanting. Panama X pushed himself into the mind of the girl. She was trapped in a steel cage watching a figure emerge from the shadows of her subconscious. The figure was very familiar to the girl; she did not fear him. But this presence in her head was not alone.

She's the doorway.

Panama X got a brief glimpse of the spirits overtaking the girl's mind and body before being violently expelled from her psyche and coming face to face with his own son.

Amir?

The vision froze. Amir stood before the girl with a horsewhip in his hand. Flecks of blood were suspended in the space between the whip and the girl's upturned face. Amir's expression was triumphant. He clearly had no clue as to what he'd done.

Why did you do this, Amir? Why couldn't you be patient?

"He's doing it for you," Juanita spoke from a corner of his mind.

He turned to find her standing behind him in his cell. His breath caught in his throat as he gazed upon her. She wore a flowing white gown and looked like an Orisha goddess—so beautiful his chest ached.

"Juanita," he whispered. "My love. Why have you come to me now?"

She turned away. They were no longer in his cell. They were standing in their old kitchen in Frenchtown. This was only a memory.

"He looks up to you, Malcolm," Juanita said. *"Sometimes I think he wants to be you."*

He remembered. This was the fight they had after Amir announced he was going to enlist in the army.

"I've already spoken to him," he said. *"He won't listen."*

"I know there's a part of you that's pleased," she replied. *"You finally have what you've always wanted—your perfect soldier."*

He winced at her words. "You know I can't control him. He has his own path to walk, just as you and I have. But yes, maybe the military will finally instill some discipline in him."

Juanita faced him. "He's going to follow you to his death. I refuse to be a part of your insanity any longer."

"My insanity? The same insanity that has protected this family for over 20 years? You are the one who refuses to move on, Juanita. You are the one who has never fully embraced your own son because you can't get over the child and life you lost."

"Damn you, Malcolm," Juanita replied, as tears streaked down her face. "I wish I had died in that fire. Then I wouldn't have to live with a coward for a husband—a man who talks revolution but refuses to strike back at his enemy. A man who sends his own son to fight his wars for him..."

"This was not a part of my plan," Panama X whispered, alone again in his cell. It was pointless to torture himself in this way—what was done was done. He needed to find out everything he could about the spirits he'd sensed back in Karen Lafitte's mind. Only then could he set things back on course.

Amir was going to have to suffer the consequences for overstepping his abilities. Lincoln, he knew, would fend for himself.

Sometime later, the riot guards stormed into Death Row to collect him. Panama X was ready. As the guards clamped on the cuffs and walked him out of Death Row, he prepared himself for the final phase of the journey he'd begun 29 years earlier.

CHAPTER THIRTY-TWO

29 years earlier
1973
Lake City, LA

M oses read his sermon for the mid-week service at Old Emmanuel Baptist Church for the fifth time. It was good, but missing something. He picked up the phone and dialed Walter Simmons—the most gifted orator he knew. Walter always gave great advice on how best to communicate God's message.

He dialed three times and got a busy signal on each try. Moses decided to swing by Walter's office on the way to church.

The scent in the air reminded him of the lilacs he'd once planted on the grounds of the Angola prison cemetery. As he rounded Lake Shore Drive and the Civic Center, he saw thick smoke pouring out from the top floor of the City Father's building. Moses' heart-rate spiked in response.

There were three cars in the parking lot: Walter's yellow T-Bird, Juanita's Cadillac, and a beat up Pinto he knew belonged to Walter's secretary. The smoke was coming from a generous crack in Walter's favorite window. Moses sprung out of the car and raced up the stairs to the top floor.

The fifth floor landing was abandoned; a dark curtain of smoke rapidly coated the ceiling. Moses looked around frantically for something to break down the door to Walter's office. He'd decided on the secretary's chair when something hit the door with tremendous force from the inside. A moment later, another battering force banged against the door and it buckled.

A black man spilled out, head first, wielding a heavy metal chair. The man hit the ground and sprung back up, turning back to pull someone else through.

Juanita!

Even through burning eyes, Moses knew she was unconscious. He peered into the doorway as sweat poured into his eyes and smoke scorched his throat. Except for an all-encompassing flame rapidly devouring the office, he couldn't see anything.

Moses managed to pull the couple back to the stairwell. Then he closed the reinforced door to put one more obstacle between them and a fiery grave. The temporary reprieve gave him an opportunity to see who he'd saved.

Malcolm Wright opened his good eye and stared at Moses with a furious desperation that chilled Moses' blood. Malcolm tried to speak, but only a cough escaped.

"Where's Walter?" Moses screamed.

Malcolm looked away.

Moses pushed at the door. Intense heat seared the palms of his hands and he screamed with pain and frustration. Fire engines still some distance away matched his wailing.

Moses backed off the door and saw Malcolm half dragging, half carrying Juanita down the stairs like a heavy suitcase.

Did Malcolm have something to do with this?

Moses shook off the ridiculous thought. Instead of letting his mind wander down crooked paths, he lent Malcolm a hand. Soon the three of them burst out the front door into an orange-brown Louisiana dusk. Moses wanted to stay and wait for the firefighters, but Malcolm made it clear he was getting out of there.

After a few violent coughs, Malcolm said, "I'm taking Juanita with me."

"What happened up there, Malc? Where's Walter?"

"You don't want to know," Malcolm said grimly. "And I don't have time to tell you."

With that, Malcolm carried Juanita over to her car, put her in the backseat, and sped off without looking back.

CHAPTER THIRTY-THREE

Monday
Baton Rouge, LA

Randy stepped back from the podium atop the steps of the Louisiana State Capitol building, the tallest capitol building in the United States. He'd survived another round in the boxing ring of public opinion by bobbing and weaving through flurries of tough questions. Credibility intact, Randy's thoughts returned to Karen. He prayed that the Lake City arm of his sting operation had been successful.

Randy's cloak of calm threatened to slip away, but he held it together by sheer will. He was deathly afraid of the consequences if he lost his head. Gazing down at the grand staircase, one step for each of the fifty states (listed in the order of their admittance to the Union), he steadied himself. His eyes settled on the quotation chiseled in stone beside the main entrance:

"We have lived long, but this is the noblest work of our whole lives...The United States take rank today among the first powers of the world."

Flanked by his usual secret service escort, Randy re-entered the Capitol and strode down the striking Memorial Hall, adorned with the likenesses of several Louisiana luminaries. When he made it to the bank of elevators, he waved off the secret service man shadowing him and entered the elevator alone.

He straightened himself out in the reflective metal of the elevator doors as the numbers jumped in gleeful diagonals. The elevator settled to a halt on the twenty-seventh floor and Randy exited onto the promenade of the Observation Deck, which overlooked the city of Baton Rouge.

Here he would have complete privacy.

His thoughts turned to his old adversary. Panama X had assumed that Randy would be so distraught by Karen's kidnapping that he'd make a mistake. He probably hoped Randy would just lie down and die. Somehow, Randy always beat the odds.

Panama X's luck, however, had run out. At this very moment, he was being moved to the solitary confinement wing in Camp F, the Injection Center. Imagining Panama X in his final death throes brought a rare smile to Randy's face.

The bars were back on his cell phone. He dialed Bill Edwards to find out the outcome of the morning's activities. Voicemail picked up and Randy left a quick message for Bill to call him back with an update.

Storm clouds billowed around the needle of the Capitol tower. The hurricane would be the perfect cover for the Lake City and Angola operations. This time tomorrow, no one would ask too many questions about what had happened in Lake City, and no one would care that Lincoln Baker had been killed while trying to exit the prison. He'd be just another dead nigger in the right place at the wrong time.

His cell phone vibrated. It was Snake Roberts. But that was impossible because Snake Roberts was supposed to be dead.

"Snake?"

"Yuh fucked with the wrong one, Boss."

"Excuse me?" Randy asked, trying to figure out how Snake had survived.

"Your boys missed. Now we're comin' for ya, Boss. And we've got your wife."

He has Coral? How?

"Bullshit," Randy said, stalling for time.

"Yuh willin' to call my bluff?" Snake asked.

"Let's say I believe you," Randy replied, wondering how he'd lost the upper hand. "What do you want?"

"At first, all I wanted was yuh money," Snake said. "Now that yuh tried to have me killed, that won't do anymore. Not at all. Yuh gonna have to do much better."

Randy could tell that the backstabbing bastard was really enjoying this.

"Are you afraid to get your hands bloody?"

He heard the echo of Madame Deveaux's question in his mind. She'd been right all along, of course. If he'd taken care of things himself from the beginning, none of this would be happening. He remembered the tall, black man who'd shot his father.

A voice spoke up in his head, *get him close and then bleed him like the leech he is.*

"Yuh still there?" Snake asked.

"I'll match the seven million dollars I've already paid your friend, Amir Barber," Randy said. "Meet me at my place in Lake City at 6 p.m. tonight and I'll make you a rich man. You bring my wife, I'll bring the money, and we'll make a trade."

"Yuh must think I'm an idiot."

"Clearly, I'm the idiot for not seeing you for the snake you really were all these years," Randy replied, surprising himself by stating the plain truth. "This is my best offer, Snake. You can't run and hide forever. Plus, you've got the most recognizable woman in the state in tow. There's no place you can go. And if you kill her that will only give me the increased incentive, public support, and resources I need to hunt you down. Truthfully, I'm tired, Snake. I just want my wife and daughter returned safely. Think about it and call me back."

Randy hung up and leaned his forehead against the floor to ceiling window overlooking the Capitol Gardens. Had he just signed Coral's death certificate?

Movement amongst the roses below caught his attention. Some lanky punk teenager was trying to pull an act of vandalism on the State Capitol in broad daylight. The shaggy, brown-haired kid had come out of nowhere and was wearing a baggy white velour sweatsuit favored by rappers and suburban white kids dying to be niggers.

With growing anger, Randy watched as the wigger looked around, then pulled up roses like a slave bailing cotton.

How can he do that without cutting his palms to shreds? Where the hell is the gardener or security or somebody?

Randy banged on the window before realizing from this high up, even the birds wouldn't hear him. The murder of the roses continued. Randy was going to have to take care of the damn kid himself. He was going to have to take care of everything. All thought ceased when the adolescent looked up at the great white phallus, making eye contact with him all the way up on the Observation Deck.

Randy felt a sensation similar to a dull ice pick stabbing him in the eye. He lost his grip on the phone and it slapped against the floor and shattered.

Kristopher!

His testicles crawled into his small intestine; his saliva evaporated. Gasping for air, he leaned on the railing before him.

The brunt of the shock did not come from seeing his long dead child materialize before him. The shock came from seeing blood-filled, eyeless sockets streaming red tears down pale cheeks, forming a morbid mask.

Randy walked toward the elevator in a trance, strangely compelled to meet his son—a lunatic voice speaking in his mind.

"Come see what I've seen, dear old Dad. Come walk the promenade of the blood forests of Sheol with me. I'll show you your fate. Sure, it might drive you a little batty, but we'll have ourselves a time. I'll be waiting for you…"

CHAPTER THIRTY-FOUR

Monday
New Roads, LA

Jhonnette Deveaux sat in an uncomfortable blue bucket seat in the waiting area of the hospital Emergency Room. She read the news on her laptop and bit her left pinky compulsively. The taste of acetone assaulted her taste buds. She'd forgotten about the nail solution she coated her nails with to break the bad childhood habit.

Jhonnette glanced at the TV in the corner. The ten o'clock news was on. The anchorman had interrupted the interminable hurricane coverage for a breaking news story.

Although set to low volume, she could make out the anchorman stating, "Well, we've got another Fox 29 News superstory for you. Exclusive footage from the Louisiana State Penitentiary at Angola, where Lincoln Baker, the man convicted ten years ago for the Simmons Park Massacre, was released earlier this morning. You're not going to believe your eyes…"

As this was the second time she'd seen this report, Jhonnette only gave it half her attention. She'd already heard the ridiculous explanation from the warden about how someone had opened fire on Lincoln from the crowd and the guards had returned fire to *protect* him. The only part she agreed with was just how lucky Lincoln had been.

After getting shot multiple times, Lincoln somehow managed to make it out of the prison, only to later fall off the bow of the Angola ferry. They'd fished him out of the Mississippi River a few hours ago and rushed him to the hospital.

This was definitely *not* how Jhonnette had foreseen events transpiring. Both Snake and Lincoln should be dead as a result of her meeting with Randy Lafitte. Instead, Lincoln had miraculously survived. Because she believed everything happened for a reason, Lincoln must be alive because he was *supposed* to live, just as Randy Lafitte had survived his bout with brain cancer due to her involuntary assistance. There was something greater at work here, and the only thing she could do was work with it, not against it.

Besides, keeping Lincoln among the living presented several interesting opportunities for her to capitalize on.

Another intriguing story getting a lot of coverage was how one of the four civilians injured during the commotion was Lincoln's adopted father, Moses Mouton. He was in critical condition receiving care in the prison infirmary, the R.E. Barrow Treatment Center.

Jhonnette knew she could use this news to get Lincoln on her side.

"Miss Deveaux?"

Jhonnette jerked her attention from the television and looked over her shoulder toward the triage station. The charge nurse waved her inside the double doors that led to the ER. Jhonnette was anxious to confirm her theory that Lincoln was still breathing because he was somehow a part of the Lafitte curse, too. Lafitte hadn't exactly taken the bait when she teased him with the possibility, so she couldn't be sure, but it was the only explanation that made sense.

By now Lafitte was probably waking up to the fact that he'd been duped, but it was far too late for him to change the course of events she'd set in motion. Jhonnette had amplified Amir's spiritual capacity so much that the *baka* he'd unleashed would be far too powerful for anyone to control. And if the *baka* didn't finish Lafitte off, Lincoln would. It was his destiny. Jhonnette understood that now.

The charge nurse pointed to room number 243. "He just came out of surgery. You've got an hour, not a minute more." The nurse looked her up and down. "What news station did you say you were from again?"

"Channel Nine News in Lake City," Jhonnette replied, suppressing her disappointment. Lincoln was no good to her if he wasn't conscious, and she was running out of time. "Just try not to aggravate him too much, okay?"

Jhonnette thanked the nurse with a fifty dollar bill and paused in front of the door. She longed to bite her nails again but remembered the acetone polish.

"Not a minute more," the nurse reminded her as she walked back to the nurse's station.

Jhonnette took a deep breath and gave two short knocks on the door before entering.

CHAPTER THIRTY-FIVE

This school shit is for the birds.

Lincoln groaned. He had just finished his second official basketball practice and was sitting on the curb in front of the St. Louis Preparatory Academy boy's gymnasium. Lincoln had been back in high school for two weeks and didn't see himself surviving another two. He just didn't have the patience to deal with the upper-crust 90210 wannabes that attended classes with him. Going back to juvenile detention was not an option, however.

Moses was the only reason he hadn't completely shown his ass yet. *Where the fuck is Moses?*

Moses knew practice ended at 6 p.m., but for some reason was not on time. Lincoln decided to call Murda or Stacy from his gang to come scoop him up. He moved his six-foot-five-inch frame in the direction of the entrance.

It was locked.

Maybe Danny the janitor was still working. Lincoln walked around to the other side of the gym toward the sports faculty parking lot.

No cars. No lights. No dice.

Lincoln gave the door handles a few healthy shakes.

Gonna have to break in if I wanna use the payphone.

The school's lay out was in alphabetical clustered pods labeled A to G. Each pod had a different academic focus. Although only 6:30 p.m., the school's many entrances were already barricaded.

Somebody has to be around, right?

Lincoln circled the perimeter of the school, checking each entrance for vulnerability. He saw a black vintage 1963 Corvette parked in the honors lot. Could have belonged to a teacher, but Lincoln knew better. This was some spoiled rich kid's car.

An almost uncontrollable urge to jimmy the car door and take the ride off said rich kid's hands overtook him. Instead, he ran his palms over the Vette's metal curves in appreciation and awe.

Then he saw it.

A teacher had left their classroom window open. Lincoln was inside in an instant and quickly made his way toward the gymnasium.

The payphone was just outside the boy's gym, where the St. Louis Crusaders did their business on Tuesday and Thursday nights. Lincoln jogged down the hall and picked up the receiver. The payphone was dead.

Fuck!

He was about to make his way back through the silent school when he heard a strange noise coming from inside the gymnasium. Lincoln pushed through the double doors into the gym. Empty.

Something clattered to the floor inside the men's locker room. Lincoln followed the sound. Nothing could have prepared him for what he found behind the second set of double doors. A chair lay on its side in the middle of the room and a white boy dangled from a rope tied to the rafter, his face swollen, and bluish red.

Lincoln froze.

Oh shit. Is he alive?

The kid's body spun lazily.

Lincoln reached the teenage boy in three long strides. He righted the chair, removed his switchblade, and grabbed at the rope, hoping to cut through it. The kid kicked him in the solar plexus.

Still alive.

Lincoln rose with renewed purpose and sawed at the rope. The noose was notched tight—the kid must have been a boy scout. Lincoln looked into the boy's face. He recognized him.

Kris Lafitte?

They played on the team together.

Lincoln cut through the last strand of rope and Kris fell to the floor. Lincoln quickly maneuvered the noose from around the boy's neck. Kris let out a sputtering breath before pouncing on Lincoln—slobbering and sobbing like a wild man. It took Lincoln a moment to regain control of the situation.

He soon had Kris pinned with his face against the floor, arms behind his head. Lincoln struggled to hold Kris down. "Fuck is wrong with you, bruh?"

"Fuck! You!" Kris spat.

"Look! Calm the fuck down, man. I just saved your fuckin' life."

"Didn't...ask...for...no...fuckin'...help."

"You're welcome."

"I'm supposed to die," Kris gasped. He stopped struggling and went limp.

"We all gonna die, bruh. But ain't nobody dyin' today."

Lincoln released Kris's hands and pulled him to his feet. One thought was on his mind.

Why the hell is this silver spoon rich white boy trying to kill himself?

CHAPTER THIRTY-SIX

Monday
New Roads, LA

Jhonnette entered the dark room. Her eyes took a moment to adjust. Slowly, she advanced on her target.

Lincoln lay in the hospital bed like a corpse in an open casket. Except for the simple fact, his eyes were open. He was hooked up to multiple I.V.'s. The incessant beeping of the heart monitor informed the world that life still pulsed through the veins of America's Worst Nightmare.

"Who the fuck are you?" he croaked.

Jhonnette smiled and approached the bed.

"Hi," she said, pointing to the chair at his bedside. "May I sit?"

"No."

"Okay. Can I ask you some questions then?"

"Do I look like I feel like answerin' any fuckin' questions?"

Jhonnette took a deep breath. "My name is Jhonnette Deveaux. I'm a friend."

"You ain't no friend of mine. What the fuck are you doin' here?"

"I'm here to save you."

"From what?"

"I was there at the prison. You can't trust that long-haired man you were with."

"But I can trust you?" Lincoln turned his eyes on her for the first time.

The pain she saw in his eyes made Jhonnette flinch. His eyes reminded her of marbles she'd played with as a young girl. She saw something else as well. Lincoln's eyes were identical to Randy Lafitte.

"Lincoln, your life is in danger and I'm the only person who can help you."

"Next you're gonna tell me how you can never tell a lie, right?"

"Okay, you want the truth?" she replied, sitting down against his wishes. "We're wasting valuable time here. Every moment you bullshit me is one more that Moses Mouton loses—"

"What the fuck happened to Moses?"

Now she had his attention. "We can help each other, Lincoln."

"I asked you a question, lady."

Jhonnette looked at her subject. He sure talked tough for someone with tubes coming out of his nose. "How about we take turns answering each other's questions. I'll even let you go first. Deal?"

Lincoln appraised her like an experienced diamond jeweler— another Lafitte trait.

"Okay," Lincoln said finally. "Tell me everything you know about what happened to me this morning, starting with where the hell I am."

Jhonnette nodded. "You're in a hospital near the prison."

"How did I end up here?"

"Apparently you dove off the bow of the Angola ferry. You almost drowned. What were you thinking?"

Lincoln offered a confused expression and Jhonnette could tell he had no memory of diving off the ferry. She waited patiently for his next question.

"Tell me where Moses is," Lincoln said.

"Moses was there this morning, too. He's been shot. He's inside the Angola infirmary and he's going to die there if we don't do something quick."

"There's nuthin' I can do to save him," Lincoln replied.

"Lincoln, you can't know that."

"Who the hell are you anyway?" he snapped. "And why do you care so much about what happens to me and my father?"

"Amir never said anything about me?" Jhonnette asked.

Lincoln's gaze sharpened at the mention of Amir. "You know Amir? How?"

"Think of me as his silent partner," she replied. "I want the same thing as you and your brother, Lincoln. I want to see Randy Lafitte dead. But we have to get you out of here to do that."

Lincoln groaned with sudden pain.

"Are you okay?"

"Be aight," he mumbled. "Can you do me a favor?"

Jhonnette nodded.

"Get somebody to bring me some pain drugs. My goddamn side hurts like a bitch."

"Alright." Jhonnette stood up to fetch the nurse. She opened the door into the hallway and saw her time was almost up.

CHAPTER THIRTY-SEVEN

Monday
Lake City, LA

"I'm going to ask you some questions," Red Wolf said, staring at Amir in the rearview mirror. "If you choose not to answer, my colleague here is going to hurt you."

Anvil Head brandished a nasty-looking taser.

"We'll do this dance until we get the information we need or until you're incapacitated," Red Wolf said. "Understand?"

"Fuck you," Amir replied with resolve.

Red Wolf nodded slightly. Anvil Head jabbed the taser at Amir's right shoulder.

Amir lost control of his muscles and writhed in the backseat like an epileptic.

"That's enough," Red Wolf commanded. Anvil Head withdrew the taser.

Amir's heart galloped in his chest. He swallowed the glob of saliva in his mouth. He'd nearly pissed his pants and his thoughts were scrambled like eggs.

"I don't know why people always insist on doing this the hard way," Red Wolf said. "Hopefully we have your attention now. Let's get to my first question. Which bank did you put the money in?"

Only Amir and Lincoln knew the location of the ransom money, but Amir knew it was only a matter of time before they broke him. He needed the kind of help he could only get from one place. Closing his eyes, he breathed deeply. Then he started chanting the prayer his father taught him.

Red Wolf ordered Anvil Head to shock him again, but their words came from far away. Amir could barely hear them over the drums...

CHAPTER THIRTY-EIGHT

18 years earlier
1984
Houston, TX

Amir couldn't sleep. There was too much noise coming from his parent's party in the backyard. He crept out of his bedroom and down the hallway, following the loud frenetic drumming.

The backyard was right off the kitchen. Amir crossed the chilly linoleum floor and peeked out the screen door. Someone had built a bonfire and ten or eleven people were dancing around the fire pit. He located his mother. Juanita wore a loose-fitting, white summer dress with white flowers in her long, curly brown hair. Beautiful and free, she swayed to the drum's rhythms, dancing so close to the fire her flowing locks appeared to be ablaze.

Amir searched for his father. They needed to warn his mother about the flames. Amir stepped onto the porch, not taking his eyes off Juanita for an instant.

She turned to face him and her eyes opened knowingly. Then, a shadow crossed over her features as she gyrated with greater urgency.

Amir screamed and ran toward her. His fingers touched the soft cotton of her dress and then he was flung back to the porch. It took him a few seconds to realize he was being held in his father's arms.

"Let me go, Dad! Something's wrong with Mama!"

"Shh, Son. Everything is okay. Your mama is okay."

How can Dad say these things?

Juanita jumped up and down like a human pogo stick. She was dangerously close to the fire again.

"What's wrong with her, Dad?" Amir looked into his father's dark, lined face and saw not a trace of worry.

"Nothing is wrong, Son. Your mother is just being ridden."

"Like a horse?"

"Exactly. Except she's being ridden by a spirit. A *loa*."

Amir was confused.

"This is a special moment for your mother," his father explained. "She's finally accepting the teachings of Vodun and now she's joining with her special *loa*, Loko."

"Loco?" Amir asked, reminded of the Mexican kids at school. "Mom's going crazy?"

She looked crazy bouncing around the blaze like a human moth.

His father looked confused for a moment, but then his face lit up. He chuckled. Whenever he laughed, his eye patch shifted.

Amir reached up and gently corrected it. "What's so funny?"

"Your mom's not loco, Amir. Her *loa*'s name is Loko, with a K. He's the *loa* in charge of nature, sanctuaries, and most importantly, justice. Do you understand?"

Amir understood his father's words, but he didn't get how a ghost could ride a person. "Loko is a ghost?"

"Not a ghost. A spirit. Do you remember your invisible friend? What was his name again?"

"Arnold."

"Arnold, right. Well, was Arnold a ghost?"

"No way. It was just that I was the only person who could see him."

"Exactly, Son. The *loa* are just like that. You can't see them, but that doesn't mean they're not there."

"But why is she dancing like she's possessed or something?" Amir asked.

"Because she is. Your mom's been possessed by Loko. But it's okay. Look at her. Does she look like it hurts?"

Amir focused on his mother. She appeared happier than he'd ever seen her.

"Okay. I get it. Do I have a special spirit, too?"

His father smiled down at him. "You are a descendant of Simba, and Simba rules the sea. When you are older, I will show you how to contact him and many other *loa*."

"How many spirits are there?"

"Too many to count. There may be as many *loa* as there are humans. Whole families in fact."

"Are they all good like Loko?"

His father looked away and stared at Juanita for a long instant. "No, Son. They're not all good. But they all have a purpose. Like you and me and your mother."

"What's my purpose, Dad?"

Again, his father turned away as if in deep thought. "Son, I think you and Loko have a lot in common. You both exist to make sure there is always justice."

Amir thought about his father's words and asked, "Dad, when I'm older, will I have to dance around a fire like Mom to talk to the spir...I mean, the *loa*?"

"No, Son. *Loa* just like a good party. But if you ever truly need a *loa*, you only have to call them..."

CHAPTER THIRTY-NINE

Monday
Lake City, LA

"Where the hell is it?" Fat Pat asked. They'd been driving around for almost twenty minutes.

"I could have sworn it was on this street," the kid replied. "It's around here somewhere, I'm sure of it. Make a left at the next light."

Fat Pat knew when someone was giving him the runaround. He eased the car into the next lane. The structure on his left was definitely not headquarters.

"What the fuck is this shit?"

"St. Mary's Hospital…that's where you wanted to go, right?"

"You skinny fuck…I told you to take me to the old school!"

"Listen man, I've lost a lot of blood, I got a hurt arm, and you expect me to be able to pay attention?"

"You ain't slick, kid." Fat Pat looked at his captive with new eyes. The kid was definitely in bad shape and besides, Fat Pat could use some stitches of his own. He'd gotten a few deep cuts in his scalp when those bastards shot through the glass at Simmons Park.

How the hell am I supposed to walk into a public hospital with guards and everything and get out in one piece? It's a fucking hospital. They got doctors everywhere. Creep in, hijack one of them maufuckas, and then move the fuck on.

Fat Pat was never good at planning, but he felt good about this one. On impulse he grabbed his cell phone and called Amir. If anyone could have made it out alive, it would be Amir. No answer. Fat Pat closed the phone. He was on his own.

"Aight," he said. "We go in, but if you try any slick shit, a lot of innocent people gone die, including yo'self."

"Scout's honor," the kid replied.

Fat Pat just had to figure out what to do with the girl. She was still passed out in the backseat, but he knew she wouldn't stay that way for long.

"Don't try no shit," Fat Pat said to the kid as he got some rope out of the trunk to tie her up.

Brandon watched as Gordo walked around to his side of the car and yanked the door open.

"Get the fuck out."

Brandon did as he was told.

"Now take this rope, Boy Scout, and tie this bitch up."

Brandon took the rope, leaned into the backseat, and manipulated the rope into slipknots—easy to create and easy to get out of. He had a vested interest in protecting Karen. She was the missing link in this whole mystery, the only person who could answer his questions about whether Shorty had kidnapped her or if it had been someone else.

After he finished her knots, Gordo pulled Brandon to his feet and steered him toward the hospital entrance. Brandon's legs were warm jello as they walked; Gordo's large gun bore into his left side.

Two paramedics stood by the entrance smoking cigarettes. Brandon inhaled deeply, held the air there, and allowed faintness to take over his body.

Fat Pat ignored the stares and raised eyebrows assaulting him as he dragged the kid toward the Emergency Room with bloodstains all over them. When a toy cop security guard stared a bit too long, Fat Pat prepared to act. Unfortunately, he was not ready for what the kid did less than ten feet from the Emergency Room.

They'd been moving along at a good pace when the kid's body went limp and he crumbled.

Fat Pat froze. One of the paramedics saw Brandon collapse and jogged over to them. Fat Pat hid his gun inside the back of his sweats. He knelt over the kid and pretended to check the kid's breathing.

Fuckin' amazing day. This is like a fuckin' movie. I guess I'm the bad guy.

The hero arrived a second later.

"Let me check him out."

Brandon felt Gordo move out of the way, counted to five Mississippi, and opened his eyes. He stared into the paramedic's face.

The guy was clearly confused by the liveliness he saw in Brandon's eyes. Then the paramedic fell over on top of Brandon.

Brandon squeezed his eyes shut and tried to control his racing heartbeat. *Thank God Gordo didn't catch me with my eyes open. What now?*

Brandon waited for the sounds of more people approaching. Surely someone had seen what happened. The only sound was Gordo's hoarse breathing. The paramedic's body rolled off him. Brandon was pulled up by his t-shirt.

Brandon recalled a game he used to play with Lincoln when he was a kid. He'd act like a corpse and Lincoln would have to lift him up and carry him around the house, showing the "body" to everyone. What a fucked up game.

Brandon applied the principle now and completely relaxed every muscle in his lanky frame. He quietly rejoiced at the sounds of Gordo's mighty struggle to get him over his shoulders. Opening his eyes and looking down Gordo's expansive back, he saw the lump of the man's weapon and grabbed for it.

Fat Pat was fed up with all the discomfort he'd suffered at the expense of Amir's stupid plan. He resolved to start shooting the next time something went wrong. All this knocking people out, quiet revenge tactic shit was not his forte. Fuck a plan, he was going to walk into the ER, brandish his weapon, and make some shit happen.

He paused for a moment under the blessed shade of the hospital awning and then approached the second paramedic. It took a very long time for the paramedic's droopy eyes to make it from Fat Pat's shoes to the body slumped over his shoulders.

This kid must be stoned out of his mind. Either that or he's a retard.

"You…see what…happened?" Fat Pat said, out of breath.

"Nawww, man," Droopy replied, dragging out his words.

"Your boy fainted out there." Fat Pat pointed at the other guy. "You should go help'm out."

"Yeah? Oh shit, yeah." He glanced at Brandon. "Whasswrong wit' the kid?"

"Heat stroke," Fat Pat replied, surprised at his own cleverness.

"Damn. I feel'm. It's hotter'n two fat hos trapped in a Pinto in the desert."

"Fo' sho'," Fat Pat said, digging in the back of his sweats for the gun. He came up empty.

Where is it?

The stoner left to help the other paramedic. A moment later, Droopy yelled for help.

Fat Pat reached for his gun again. Strike two.

The fuck?

Fat Pat glanced back at the paramedic. Droopy was looking down at his fallen comrade. He held Fat Pat's gun in his hand like some alien artifact.

Fat Pat groaned and dumped the kid on the ground.

As soon as Gordo's back was turned, Brandon dashed into the hospital. The ER was half-full, but the people seeking help were too absorbed in their own problems to be concerned with him. Brandon did a full 360-degree turn before finally locating the inter-hospital phone on the wall. He ran over, picked up the receiver, and quickly punched zero for the operator.

An automated voice politely told him that all lines were busy.

Fuck!

Brandon's eyes scanned his surroundings. He needed to find

a place to hide. He spotted a door marked 'Hospital Employees Only' and slipped inside. Gordo staggered into the building, gun back in hand. He turned around in a slow circle until something on the linoleum floor caught his attention.

Brandon backed off the door as Gordo followed the trail of Brandon's blood to his hiding spot. In moments, he ran toward the door like a wild bull at the rodeo. A bullet whizzed by Brandon's ear and slammed into the wall as he turned toward the empty hallway and ran for his life.

CHAPTER FORTY

Monday
Baton Rouge, LA

Coral watched her father carving in the woodshed adjacent to their home. He was making the pony he promised for her fifth birthday.

"The wood tells a story," he said. Shavings fell to the floor by his work boots. "I walk through the woods out back. I see a tree stump. Tree stump starts talking. Says…I'm no tree stump. I'm a footstool. I'm a jewelry box. I'm a birdhouse. But I ain't no tree stump."

He looked down at Coral. He wanted to know if she understood.

She nodded, even though she couldn't figure out how a tree stump could talk without a mouth.

"So I listen to Mr. Tree Stump. I let'm tell me his story. While I'm carvin', I'm listenin'. And the story comes down like all them shavings you got there. Can you hear'm talking?" He held the clump of wood that had grown horse legs out to Coral.

She pretended to listen.

"What's he sayin', Curly?"

She shrugged.

"Well, one day when you're older I'll teach you the secret. My pop—your Granpop—taught me when I was just a bit older than you. He taught me how to be still and silent and how to listen…oh so carefully. Would you like me to teach you?"

Coral imagined all the ponies, frogs, butterflies, ladybugs, and unicorns awaiting her in the woods behind their house. "More than anything," she replied.

"Would you like to try now?" he offered.

Coral was frightened. He held the knife out to her, hilt first, but she shook her head no. He pulled the knife back out of sight.

"Maybe when you're older," he said, shrugging. "Lemme show you how. Gimme that piece of wood over in the corner, Curly."

She got up and lugged a sizeable piece of firewood over to her father's workbench.

He secured it in his hands and started carving. Carving so fast his hands became a blur. Smoke rose from the desk. Her father's face took on a dark shade of concentration.

Coral backed away, afraid.

"He's talkin' to me, Curly. Talkin' fast. Can't hardly keep up. It's that tree, Curly. Melinda Weeps. It's the doorway. Oh God. So much death." He was sweating and crying as he carved.

Coral had one foot out the door of the shed. She didn't want to hear what her father was telling her. She wanted out of here. She wanted Mommy.

"Spirits wouldn't leave him be. They drove him to it. Tried to kill himself, he did. Lincoln stopped'm. Spirits didn't like that. They wanted him so they used Randy to get him."

Wood fell to both sides of the workbench in a torrent as her father twisted and turned the log in his big, calloused hands. It was starting to take shape.

"They want Karen, too. It's her turn."

"How do I stop it?" Coral screamed, an adult voice emanating from her child's frame.

Her father carved on, then suddenly went rigid. "All done," he whispered. "Beautiful." He spun around in the chair.

Coral looked up into her father's face and found Kristopher gazing down on her. She screamed.

"I want you, Mommy," he said, grinning. "I want you and Daddy." Kristopher grabbed the carving off the table and showed it to his child mother. He dangled the severed head of a bald, black man in front of her. The eyes bulged, the nose snorted, and a long, pink tongue lolled from blue lips.

Coral couldn't stop screaming.

"Go ahead. Scream all you want. No one is coming."

Coral opened her eyes. Shaw Roberts sat on a stool across from her, watching some morning game show on an old 1970s era TV. It took her a moment to regroup, but then she remembered where she was. **Here Today, Gone Tomorrow**.

"Bad dream?"

Coral looked away. Her nose was running. She touched one nostril tenderly and gasped when she saw red blood superimposed on the pale skin of her finger.

The dream was fading. It had felt so real.

Coral could smell the remnants of the chloroform he'd used to subdue her. She was bound to a chair. A wave of despair washed over her.

"You can ignore me now," Shaw said. "But you'd better get used to talking to me. I'm the only friend you got."

"What are you talking about? You're just a no count thug-for-hire under your brother's thumb." Her words surprised her.

Shaw stood and glared menacingly. "What did you just say?"

"You heard me. What's your cut? Or are you just the fall guy?" She shook her head in disgust. "You're just too dumb to see what you've gotten yourself into."

The back of Shaw's hand connected with the side of her face. Coral's head rocked; she saw stars. Fresh blood bloomed on her busted lower lip.

"Told you to watch your mouth." Shaw stomped out of the room.

Gotcha.

Coral closed her eyes and let her head clear. Once her ears stopped ringing she caught the television announcer saying, "We interrupt our coverage of Hurricane Isaac to bring you a Fox 29 News Breaking Story."

Footage rolled of Lincoln Baker's release from Angola.

A connection fired deep in her synapses as she watched her son's killer walk to his freedom.

How did he get free?

Randy. Pardon. Karen. Kidnapping. Kristopher. Murder. My. Fault.

The words chased themselves through her subconscious, until she finally put it together. Randy lied to her about Karen because he hadn't thought she could handle the truth. He'd been right to lie.

What kind of partner am I? What kind of mother?

Coral had been passive for too long. Prayer and meditation, solutions she'd preached in her book, would not get her very far in this situation. For the first time since the day before her son's murder, Coral was wide awake.

CHAPTER FORTY-ONE

As Jhonnette exited the room, Lincoln tried to remember his last moment of clarity.

He'd been lying on the ground just outside of Angola—people screaming all around him. Roberts was kneeling over him.

"Either you come with me right now, or you die here." The words seemed to be coming from a voice right next to his ear.

Lincoln bolted upright in bed and glanced around wildly. For a second, he swore he smelled the sour tobacco scent of Roberts' breath.

What happened next?

The only thing he remembered was waking up in this hospital bed. He needed to stay focused. First things first, he had to contact Amir and confirm Jhonnette's story.

Jhonnette paced in the hallway searching for a nurse. She needed a few minutes to clear her head, as well as take a much-needed potty break. She'd been running pretty much non-stop since three o'clock in the morning. Her bladder's burden relieved, her mind returned to Lincoln. She was still a long way from gaining his trust and needed to accelerate the process before it was too late.

While Jhonnette stood patiently in the corner, a short, petite nurse named Monica checked Lincoln's monitors and administered morphine into his intravenous line. Lincoln paid no attention to the nurse, his eyes fixed intently on Jhonnette.

The nurse finished her duties and glided out of the room.

Jhonnette approached Lincoln's bedside and asked, "Feeling better?"

"I need to use your phone."

"To call who?"

"It's none of your business. Listen, I'll tell you whatever you want to know. Just let me borrow the phone first."

"Okay." Jhonnette dug through her purse for the cell phone.

She watched as Lincoln searched for the dialing pad. "How you work this thing?" he asked.

"Let me," she said, taking it back. "What's the number?"

After dialing, she returned the phone to him. Lincoln held his breath as the phone rang and rang.

"Amir not answering?" she asked.

Lincoln's eyes widened. "How did you—"

"Amir has been compromised. You're going to have to start trusting me, Lincoln, because I may be the only person left that can get you out of this."

"What the fuck you talkin' 'bout lady?"

"Like I said, I'm here to help. I have information you need."

"Yeah? Well you can start by telling me what the fuck happened to Amir."

"We'll get there, but first things first. You need to understand your past to make sense of what is required of you now. What was Kristopher Lafitte doing on the wrong side of town on the day of the Simmons Park Massacre?"

"I hate when people call it that. It wasn't no massacre. It was a set up."

Jhonnette seized her opening. "But set up by whom?"

Lincoln was silent.

"You and Kristopher Lafitte were friends, weren't you?"

Lincoln rolled away from her. "You think you know me just because you've read some articles? You don't know shit."

"I know we share a common enemy, Lincoln," she said. "And we are running out of time. But I need to know why you killed your friend. Or why you allowed yourself to be framed for the crime if you didn't."

"Why is that important?"

"Because you are the key to bringing Randy Lafitte to his knees and you don't even realize it. But first you have to stop blaming yourself."

Lincoln stared at her for a long time. Then he started talking. His words came painfully slow at first, but soon he lost himself in his own story and Jhonnette got lost with him.

Chapter Forty-Two

Ten years earlier
1992
Lake City, LA

Lincoln's life had come full circle since moving in with Moses. On New Year's Eve, two years after his house arrest sentence began; Moses finalized Lincoln's adoption and announced his engagement to a wonderful, loving woman named Lois Payne. For the first time in his life, Lincoln was part of a real family. Lois had a child from a previous marriage, six-year-old Brandon who idolized Lincoln from the moment he entered the house.

Lincoln was a senior at St. Louis Prep, popular and well liked—the Fresh Prince of Lake City. His exploits on the basketball court had become legendary and rabid, cheering fans packed the Crusader's gym every game night.

Now that he was somewhat of a local celebrity, he had a lot of new friends and associates, chief among them—Kris Lafitte. Lincoln had never met a crazier white boy in his whole life—and he'd never befriended or trusted a white person, ever. Despite their differences, they forged a bond almost as strong as his gang brotherhood because Kris had his demons as well. They never discussed Kris's suicide attempt, but every so often, Lincoln would glance at Kris and see a tortured shadow pass over his friend's face.

After Lincoln led the Crusaders through the Class 5A state playoffs to the championship game, reporters, agents, scouts, and college coaches started calling the house every day. Everyone started treating him as though he was the second coming of Michael Jordan. People speculated about whether Lincoln would go to some college powerhouse or do the unthinkable and leap straight from high school to the pros, something no high school player had done since Moses Malone in the late seventies.

Kris constantly talked about them attending North Carolina, Stanford, or Duke together and how big they would be living. "Imagine living on our own, Link. College girls, our own supped up dorm room, no curfews..."

Lincoln loved seeing Kris making plans for the future, but didn't share his friend's joy. Lincoln, having been largely ignored most of his life, was not used to being the center of attention. He couldn't verbalize how terrified he was of leaving Lake City and the sanctuary of Moses' home.

As the deadline for him to declare his eligibility for the NBA draft approached, Lincoln was unable to sleep, eat, or concentrate in class. One afternoon, he and Kris left school early and went out to Barton Coliseum near the airport to smoke a little weed and talk.

They drove Kris's car into one of the horse stables next to the domed building and parked. "So what are you gonna do?" Kris asked, firing up a joint.

"I really don't know, bruh."

Kris passed the joint to Lincoln, then reached into his backpack and produced an envelope.

"What's that?" Lincoln asked.

"Open it."

The letter was from the Louisiana State University registrar's office. Lincoln patted Kris on the back excitedly. "Congrats! You're a college man now. I thought for sure you'd end up at UNC though."

"LSU is gonna let me play ball."

Lincoln nodded. Another thing they had in common—their love for the game. Being able to play ball was their reason for breathing. Basketball was life. "Look, Link," Kris said, growing serious. "I know you're worried about leaving Lake City, but you gotta get the hell outta here before something bad happens."

Kris was referring to fallout from the brawl during the semifinal game against crosstown rival Lake City-Boston. Several Scorpions were standout athletes on that team and a bench-clearing brawl had broken out in the middle of the third quarter. Lincoln and Kris were both suspended for their role in the fight and ever since, Kris had been obsessing over whether or not the gang would retaliate.

"I think they're planning something, man, I really do."

Lincoln laughed. "Kris, what the hell do you know about gang activity? Are the gardeners going to war with the butlers in your hood?"

Kris wasn't laughing.

Lincoln took another puff off the joint. "You're serious?"

"As a heart attack, man. If you stay around here, they will get you back eventually."

"I ain't worried," Lincoln said with a shrug. "The Skulls still have my back."

"I hope so, for your sake. Anyway, man, you coming with me to LSU or not?"

"Kris, I been meaning to talk to you about that. You're my boy so please don't take this the wrong way, but we didn't come from the same place, and we ain't goin' to the same place."

"What's that supposed to mean?"

"It means you got it made, bruh. You've always had it made. Look, you're prob'ly gonna go to college, meet some spoiled rich girl, graduate, go to law school, get married, build a huge house, and live happily ever after. Ain't none a' that gonna happen to me."

Kris stood. "It's always the same thing with you, man. It always comes back to my family's money. Yeah, I come from money and yeah, you don't, but that doesn't give you an excuse to ruin your life, does it? You people are so dense sometimes."

"*You people?* Fuck you! You're just like the rest of these corny whitebread trust fund motherfuckers. Go home and count your money, rich boy. Even if I decide to go to college, ain't no way in hell I'm following your lame ass to LSU. Forget about me. Go get some new friends…"

The next day was Senior Skip Day and Lincoln was grateful. He couldn't deal with any more questions about his decision and desperately needed to get the fight with Kris off his mind. He met up with some other senior skippers and headed out to Prien Pines Beach for an afternoon of sun and fun.

Everything was going fine until Kris stumbled into the party, disheveled and drunk. Lincoln felt a pang of sorrow for his friend, but his pride wouldn't allow him to break the silence between them.

Kris, bolstered by his belligerence, was on a warpath. When he spied Lincoln, he went on the attack. "Hey, look at the big star everybody! Big Link Baker, number one draft pick. He's a fucking coward everybody! Look at'm!"

Lincoln tried to ignore the venomous accusations pouring from Kris's lips, but that only made Kris angrier.

He headed toward Lincoln. "Yeah! Fucking Lincoln Baker, the savior of Lake City! Everybody loves Link, right? He's a fuckin' fraud! You're a fuckin' fraud, Link, you hear me?"

Lincoln had heard enough. He attempted to remove Kris from the premises.

Kris swung at him. His punch landed just below Lincoln's eye. Then it was on.

It took four football players to pull Lincoln off Kris.

Kris, bleeding from a busted lip, continued to scream as they escorted him away. "Bet I got your attention now, Link, huh? Bet now you'll hear what I gotta say! You ain't got any friends, Link! None of these people give a damn about you! You're a joke, man. A bad fuckin' joke!"

Lincoln nursed the cut under his eye and stared at Kris from across the sand with murder on his mind. As embarrassment and hurt set in, Lincoln couldn't resist a final verbal jab as Kris left. "I shoulda let you kill yourself that day, Kris. You know that, you ungrateful motherfucker! I shoulda let you die!"

CHAPTER FORTY-THREE

Monday
New Roads, LA

Two knocks on the door interrupted Lincoln's train of thought.

A heavyset nurse entered. "Times up, Ms. Deveaux. Please follow me."

"We just need a few more minutes," Jhonnette replied. "Can we work that out?"

"Let's talk outside, Ms. Deveaux."

Jhonnette followed the nurse into the hall.

"Sorry," the nurse said. "The police just called. They're coming to move the patient."

"Where are they moving him?"

"I don't know, but he might be able to help you out." She nodded at someone over Jhonnette's shoulder.

Jhonnette turned just in time to see Snake Roberts enter Lincoln's room.

❧

The drug's effects overtook Lincoln, helping him understand the hunger in the eyes of all those painkiller addicts he'd sold to over the years. Morphine was the shit. Not feeling any pain was a strange sensation.

The door opened and he looked up in anticipation, ready to share this revelation with Jhonnette.

"Guess wha—"

"Don't you mean guess who?" Snake Roberts smirked.

Ok, this is it. You can do this.

There was only one way to ensure Lincoln trusted her enough to give her what she needed. Jhonnette pressed her ear to the door.

Poor Snake. He'd been an essential part of her plan, but had served his purpose. Still, a part of her ached at the thought of what she was about to do. Over the past few months, she'd developed a soft spot for the man. This was no time for sentimentality. She had to focus.

She removed a small handgun from her purse. After screwing a silencer onto the barrel, she opened the door as quietly as she could.

CHAPTER FORTY-FOUR

Monday
Baton Rouge, LA

"Governor! Governor!"

Someone shook him. Randy opened his eyes. One of his secret service guards, Jack, leaned over him with a look of extreme alarm.

Randy's vision doubled for a brief second. He shook his head from side to side to remove the grogginess draped over his body like a rain poncho. He attempted to tell Jack he was fine, but nothing came out.

Something was inside his mouth. The something slipped a few notches as if in reaction to his thinking about it. Randy gagged in response.

Jack groaned.

Randy made the universal choking gesture.

Jack came to his senses and moved behind Randy. He wrapped his arms around Randy's midsection and pressed on Randy's solar plexus with his thumbs inverted performing the Heimlich maneuver.

Randy's vision cleared dramatically upon the first pressure. He looked upon his surroundings in amazement. He sat before

Huey P. Long's tombstone in the southeast corner of the Capitol grounds—a good ten minute walk from the Observation Deck. He looked up at Louisiana's first and only assassinated governor, and for a moment swore the statue was staring down at him.

Rumor had it Huey Long was actually killed by his bodyguards, not the dentist blamed for the crime.

A dark tint clouded his vision as Jack pushed again. Randy felt the first tickle of panic. Sane people didn't lose track of ten minutes of time. They didn't sleepwalk down twenty-seven flights of stairs.

Jack pressed a third time. Randy felt like his chest was going to cave in.

What's happening to me?

Jack pressed again, with more force.

The object in Randy's throat dislodged and blasted off into the open air. He took a few deep breaths, ignoring the pain coming with each inhalation. Then he looked at what he'd just expelled.

A blood red rose, wet and shiny with saliva, lay on the manicured lawn.

CHAPTER FORTY-FIVE

Monday
Lake City, LA

"Wake his ass up," Red Wolf commanded Anvil Head. "We're almost there."

Their captive couldn't take the tasering. He'd been unconscious in the backseat for over five minutes. Now he was convulsing.

"He don't look so good."

Red Wolf looked at Amir in the rearview mirror and cursed under his breath. He pulled the car into the yard of a one-story red brick home.

"Go straighten him out," Red Wolf ordered.

Anvil Head got out and opened the back door. Not taking any chances, he trained the taser on Amir while ducking into the backseat.

Red Wolf got out on the other side. They were wasting valuable time here. "Hurry up," he barked.

As traffic flowed past him, he heard a strange guttural noise. Drawing his gun, he bent down to get a better look inside the car. His eyes widened as he witnessed the scene in the backseat.

Blood spurted from Anvil Head's ruptured jugular, painting the window red. Then the driver's side door burst open, catching Red Wolf in the forehead. He rocked on his haunches and fell backwards into the busy avenue, dropping the gun in the process. Immediately aware of the danger of being run over, Red Wolf rolled until he was safely out of the road. As soon as he made it onto the grass, someone grabbed his neck. Expert fingers pressed and squeezed his windpipe as if it were an accordion

Red Wolf tossed his head around until he was staring into the face of an adolescent white girl with jet black hair. She had a pretty face and creamy unblemished skin but wore a distressed expression.

Anvil Head's blood dripped into Red Wolf's eyes from the girl's clenched ruby red lips. He bucked in an attempt to knock the girl off him. She rolled with him but maintained her death grip.

As the life drained from Red Wolf's body, the girl smiled sweetly at him. He heard her voice in his head.

"It will all be over soon. It's better on the other side. Follow the sound of the drums."

Drums? What drums?

Then he heard them—soft pounding beckoning in a slow rhythm that matched his declining heartbeat.

Who are you?

Her name came.

Melinda.

His phone chirped. He barely heard his men advising him that they had arrived at the hospital. He was too busy staring into Melinda's angelic face. He felt no pain; she had taken his pain away. Until the girl's face morphed back into the face of Amir.

A crushing sensation collapsed his lungs.

Amir stood up, got into the Crown Victoria, and drove away.

With no breath left, Red Wolf's eyes lost focus and glazed over as he expired.

CHAPTER FORTY-SIX

Monday
Baton Rouge, LA

"Sorry about earlier. Here." Shaw untied Coral and handed her an ice pack.

Coral pressed it against her busted lip. Of course it wasn't cold enough. This guy couldn't get anything right.

"We got off to a bad start," Shaw said. "Of course you're angry. But nothing's gonna happen to you."

"A little late for that, don't you think?" Coral snapped. "You, your brother, and Larry have committed a capital offense. And that's not even the worst part! You kidnapped a teenage girl and forced my husband to pardon a convicted killer. The man who killed my son. Oh man. You guys are gonna fry."

Shaw paced before her. She could almost hear his mind working.

"It wasn't supposed to happen like this."

"What do you mean? You didn't mean to kidnap my daughter and me? Just like you didn't mean to slap the Governor's wife?"

"Look. What do you want from me? I got these medical bills. Something got into me over there in Iraq. Some bad shit."

"And Snake promised to take care of everything, right? All you have to do is hold the Governor's wife in your place of business for a few days. Well I've met your brother—he's worked for my husband for a long time. Never did strike me as a guy playing with a full deck."

Shaw put his face in his hands. "Aw man. Aw man. Shit. What am I supposed to do?"

Coral knew it was now or never. She stood and placed her hand on Shaw's shoulder. "Listen to me. You didn't think this through. Let me help you. If you let me go now, we can forget about this whole thing. We can act like this never happened."

Shaw looked at her with tears in his eyes. She almost felt sorry for him.

"I can't do that. Snake'll kill me. Oh God."

"Where is he now?"

"He went to take care of that Baker kid. At the hospital in New Roads."

"You got him pardoned just to kill him? That doesn't make much sense."

"No. Not kill him. He has to live."

Coral was confused. "Why?"

"She needs him for something."

"Who's she?"

Shaw ignored her question.

Coral should have known Snake Roberts couldn't have planned something like this on his own. "What if I told you I could take care of everything?" she offered. "Your medical bills, get Snake off your back. Everything."

"How you gonna do that?"

"Well, the medical stuff is easy. My husband is Governor, remember? And Snake? Snake may just have an accident. What do you think?"

Shaw nodded with understanding. "What do you need from me?"

"Well to start, a car and a gun."

And a prayer!

"What do you need the gun for?"

"We have to make it look like I escaped..." Coral detailed her plan as Shaw nodded in agreement. It was a long shot, but her plan just might work.

CHAPTER FORTY-SEVEN

Monday
Baton Rouge, LA

Randy sat in the back of a sedan en route to Baton Rouge Municipal airport where his chopper was waiting. The car abruptly slowed to a crawl and Randy observed a line of cars in the fast lane with their hazard lights blinking—a funeral procession.

The lead car was a hearse decorated with vibrant red roses. He groaned. Randy never wanted to see a rose again.

A large black bird landed on the back of the hearse. A phrase came to his mind:

Crows are the carriers of the dead.

The bird shook and flew off to Randy's delight. He popped two Advil. He'd given himself a headache trying to get back those precious minutes between seeing the ruffian (*Kristopher... it was Kristopher!*) in the rose garden and waking up in front of Huey P. Long's tomb.

Okay, say it was Kristopher. What now? Am I supposed to believe that my dead son came back from the grave to kill me?

Maybe it wasn't to kill him, though. Maybe it had been a warning.

He came to warn me about Karen.

The driver maneuvered around the caravan and put them back on a crash course for the airport.

Randy was desperate for an update on Karen's whereabouts, but his cell phone was in pieces on the floor of the Observation Deck and the car phone would not afford him with a secure line. Any imbecile could trace the call and that would be no good...no good at all.

And what to do about Snake?

If Snake was dumb enough to show up at the Lafitte mansion, he was a dead man. Randy pictured himself strangling Snake to death with a piece of chicken wire. Yes. Tonight his hands would get plenty bloody.

But first, Randy would take the relatively short helicopter flight back to Lake City so he could be there when they found Karen. He wanted to be the first face his daughter saw. He blocked any morbid thoughts of warnings from beyond the grave with a lucid vision of their reunion.

"We're here, sir."

He blinked and his daughter's face vanished, replaced by the dark leather interior of the vehicle. Randy looked around the car as if seeing it for the first time.

The driver stared at him in the rearview mirror.

Randy wanted to crawl into a hole and die. He shuddered as he recalled the way Kristopher had looked at him with those bloody eye sockets. Though the helicopter was waiting, he had no desire whatsoever to get out of the car.

What if he's out there?

Instead of moving or giving the driver further direction, Randy sat and watched the helicopter blades rotate. He had flown by chopper hundreds, maybe thousands of times without a problem, but today each helicopter blade was a razor sharp guillotine waiting to chop his head off.

"Sir?"

"Yes, of course, Joel. I'm ready."

Joel opened his door. Randy's eyes watered as a whippet of wind slapped him in the face. He rocked on his feet.

Joel grabbed his arm to steady him and asked if he was okay. Each word seemed to come in slow motion, barely audible though Joel was yelling in his ear.

Randy blinked his heavy eyelids and continued watching the blades. The rotating motion was so...hypnotic. Just when he thought he was going to pass out, the scene before him shifted.

"This is one election you can't steal."

The words echoed in his mind as he stared down at Juanita Simmons lying unconscious before him.

He was inside an official-looking space he knew very well—the Lake City Father's Office. Randy shook his head to clear the fog and felt the weight of the telephone in his hand. He'd just knocked Juanita out with it. Her husband, Walter, struggled mightily in the closet, trying to free himself.

Randy didn't have much time. He shut the closet, cutting off Walter Simmons' protests, and dragged Juanita over to his desk. After handcuffing her arm to the desk, he inspected the rest of his handiwork.

Carla Bean, Walter's secretary, stared up at him with unseeing eyes as blood darkened her green, silk blouse. Even dead, Carla was a very attractive woman—it was no wonder Walter had fallen for her. He positioned her in the chair and then picked up the twenty-two caliber pistol he'd used to kill her.

Wiping the weapon down with a rag, he placed it in Juanita's outstretched palm. There was something exciting about being this close to a woman other than Coral. And a black woman at that. Had he ever been this close to one? He couldn't recall.

Randy examined her face and body, so foreign, yet so familiar. He traced her handcuffed arm but she did not stir. He could understand how these full, sensual lips and round and supple bodies had seduced so many slave owners. Walter Simmons was a fool, he decided, unbuttoning his pants.

I should make him watch.

Randy opened the closet door and mounted Juanita as Walter's rage-filled grunts filled the room. When he entered her, thorns tore into his naked shaft.

Randy screamed and jumped up to find he was in the Capitol Rose Garden with his pants down. Streaks of crimson were smeared all over his tie and dress shirt.

That's going to stain.

Randy had to fight the urge to giggle.

I'm going crazy.

"Don't be ridiculous, Dad," a voice said from behind him. "You going crazy would be as likely as the Beatles rapping."

Randy turned to see Kristopher, the way he'd looked the last time he'd seen him.

"Here, let me give you a hand." Kristopher extended his right arm.

Randy reached out to touch his son's face but Kristopher stepped back out of range.

"You started this," Kristopher said. "You brought this upon your own family. Why?"

Randy realized Kristopher's lips weren't moving. Still, he heard his words loud and clear.

"I...I don't know what you're talking about."

"Can't bullshit me, Dad. I'm dead. Just like you are going to be if you don't open up. Now open up!" Kristopher demanded.

Randy, having lost control of his mind and faculties, felt his jaws spreading open. The unmistakable aroma of thousands of roses singing their fragrant song filled his nose. Kristopher placed a rosebud in his mouth.

Randy gagged. The flower smelled just like a rose, but tasted like blood. Randy closed his eyes against a wave of tears.

"You alright, sir?"

Randy forced his eyelids open and saw concern slinking its way across his driver's face. Randy's eyes were still watering from the wind swirling off the helicopter. He gladly accepted the handkerchief Joel offered.

"Of course I'm fine, Joel, why wouldn't I be?"

"Well, sir, you kind of spaced out on me there for a sec..."

"It happens from time to time," Randy replied, looking at the rotary blades again. *What is happening to me?*

Jhonnette Deveaux's words came like a whisper. *"Only Panama X is strong enough to control the* baka.*"*

Once inside the helicopter, Randy put on his headset and said to the pilot, "There's been a change of plans."

"Where to, Sir?"

Randy had made a career of following his instincts and they'd never led him astray. He prayed the trend continued. "We need to make a stop at the Louisiana State Penitentiary."

CHAPTER FORTY-EIGHT

Monday
Lake City, LA

Fat Pat watched the kid sprint down the corridor. The lanky bastard ran in a zig-zag pattern like it was going to stop him from catching a bullet.

Fat Pat tried to take another shot but the gun jammed. Cursing, Fat Pat took off down the hall. He had to get his hands on that kid. In his haste, Fat Pat tripped over some wires and belly-flopped on the linoleum floor. The weapon flew out of his hand and discharged when it hit the ground.

The sound was louder than a grenade going off in an aluminum trash can.

The kid stopped dead in his tracks when the gun went off. He patted his body to see if he'd been hit anywhere, then ran back to retrieve the gun, which had come to a rest midway between the two of them.

Fat Pat watched helplessly as the kid picked up the gun with a quivering arm and aimed it at his head.

"Hey kid, put the gun down, man. You ain't gonna shoot nobody. Come on, man, I'll take you wherever you wanna go. We can get a doctor and I'll get you back home..."

"What about Shorty?"

"What the hell you talkin' 'bout?"

The tremor in the kid's hand was gone. "Ya'll think you can just kill whoever you want," the kid said, tears streaming down his face. "Now I see how it works. You take a gun like this, point it at some defenseless person and you've got the power, right? Killing helpless little kids…that make you feel like a man?"

"I ain't kill nobody, man!"

"Who's the man now, huh?" The kid was less than ten paces away from Fat Pat.

"Please," Fat Pat pleaded. He wondered if he could outmaneuver a speeding bullet.

The kid's arm relaxed slightly as he lowered his eyes from his target. For a second, Fat Pat thought he might avoid Trump and Salsa's fate, but then those eyes came up blazing with resolve.

"It's funny, you know," the kid said without a trace of humor in his voice. "All my life I've thought I was different than Lincoln. Now here I am with this gun and I think I know exactly what he was feeling that day."

A nurse appeared in the hallway behind the kid. "Hey!" she yelled.

As the kid turned to look at the nurse, Fat Pat made his move. He grabbed the barrel of the gun and tried to wrestle it out of the kid's hand. Fat Pat's fingers flirted with the trigger as he inverted the gun toward the kid's chest.

The nurse hit Fat Pat over the head with something hard and he lost his grip on the gun. As he fell backwards, he watched the barrel swing back toward his chest.

The kid stumbled backward as well, and when his back hit the wall, his finger squeezed the trigger.

The bullet sliced through Fat Pat's sizeable gut, exiting out the other side. The pain was intense, like being stabbed with a molten hot fireplace poker. His heartbeat drummed in his head as he slid down the wall. Fat Pat coughed violently and pus-filled blood dribbled down his chin.

The nurse stared at him in horror; the kid's expression was a blank mask of shock.

Fat Pat wondered if this was how Salsa and Trump had lived their last moments—thinking about how nothing they'd ever done in their entire lives had meant anything. He struggled to get up.

Several men burst through the Employees Only entrance.

Fat Pat watched them approach in slow motion, guns drawn. He waited for another bullet barrage that never came. These were the strangest looking cops he'd ever seen, with their slicked-back hair and dark suits.

Must be undercover.

The cops trained their weapons on the kid and commanded him to drop the gun. The kid stared back at them like they spoke a foreign language.

Fat Pat shut his eyes as a cold wave washed over him. When he opened them, the men were slapping handcuffs on the kid. The nurse lay on the floor beside him, in her own pool of blood.

Fat Pat stared at the unconscious girl in the hospital hallway as he slowly bled to death. He knew this was it, but still felt glad he wasn't going wherever they were taking the kid. He'd spent enough time in the streets to know that whoever those guys were, they were very bad news.

CHAPTER FORTY-NINE

Ten years earlier
1992
Lake City, LA

"Wake up, kiddo, wake up." Karen rolled away and pulled the covers over her head. "Leave me alone, Kristopher."

He shook her gently. "Come on, Smurfette. I need to tell you something."

Karen groaned and turned back over. "I told you to stop calling me that! I'm gonna tell Mom."

"Okay, okay. I'm sorry. How are you doing?"

"I'm sleepy. Whaddaya want?" She sat up in bed and rubbed her eyes. Kristopher's face was all bruised up. He'd fallen off his bike a couple of days ago. Karen had just gotten the training wheels off hers.

"I need you to listen to me very carefully, Karen. Can you do that?"

His tone was so serious Karen became afraid. She looked him over again. Though it was dark outside, he was fully dressed.

"Where are you going, Kristopher?"

He looked away. "I need to do something, Karen. Something to keep you safe."

"Safe from what?"

Kristopher sighed. "You remember that story Abby told us?"

Karen remembered. She'd had nightmares for a week after. "What about it?"

"I need to do something about the curse."

Now Karen was really scared. "But Abby said the curse was dead."

"What if it isn't? What if I don't do anything and Dad drops dead, or Mom, or…you?"

"What…what are you gonna do?"

"I'm gonna go see Abby tonight and I need you to cover for me. Can you do that?"

Normally Karen would challenge him, but this was serious. She nodded.

"Good girl. Don't worry, kiddo. Everything's gonna be alright. I'm sorry if I scared you." Kristopher stood and walked toward the door. "Oh, one more thing. I got you something."

"What?"

"Look on top of your TV."

Karen squinted in the dark and saw Kristopher's prized Sony discman resting atop her SuperNintendo. She was immediately suspicious—he never let her touch it. "What's going on, Kristopher?"

"Nothing. Mom got me a newer one yesterday for my birthday, remember? Besides, I'm going off to college in a couple of months and I know how much you've always wanted this. So think of it as a present."

Karen jumped out of bed and hugged Kristopher hard. "You're the best big brother ever!"

"And you're my favorite sister."

"I'm your only sister!"

"I know, kiddo. And I love you. There's a CD already in the player, but you gotta promise me that you won't play it until I say, okay?"

"Who is it?"

"You'll see soon, kiddo. You promise not to listen?"

Karen pouted. "Promise."

Kristopher hugged her tight again. "Have sweet dreams, kiddo."

CHAPTER FIFTY

Karen's eyes shot open. After a moment of disorientation, she rolled onto her back, not at all surprised to find she'd been tied up again. She manipulated the knots around her wrists. Her neck throbbed from the Penguin's rough choking.

If I make it through this I'll have one hell of a career as an escape artist.

She coughed up more blood and peered out the window. Two men, wearing blue and yellow paramedic uniforms, lay prostrate in the middle of the parking lot.

Karen pounded her head against the window, to no avail. She was getting a headache from the head butts, so she refocused on her hands. There was one upside to having lost so much weight — it made it easy to escape most wrist bonds. Moments later, she opened the car door, emerging into the humid Louisiana afternoon soaked from head to toe.

Okay, Karen, now what?

Two unmarked black sedans galloped into the parking lot from a side entrance, coming to an abrupt halt in front of the ER. Four men in dark suits got out and conferred with one another. Karen flashed back to that day ten years ago when cars just like these pulled up outside of her house.

Karen was playing tea time on the porch with Abby. Two cars pulled up and a man with long silver hair and a thick gray beard got out of the lead car. He reached into the backseat and emerged with the limp body of her brother Kristopher. Kristopher's head lay upside down in the cradle of the man's arms. His shocking blue eyes were wide open, but even at the tender age of seven, Karen knew Kristopher wasn't seeing anything anymore.

The memory dissolved as Karen observed the situation unfolding before her. After a quick huddle, two of the men ran inside the hospital. The remaining two stood sentry outside. They reminded her of her father's security guards.

Karen didn't know whether to hide from them or run. The roar of an engine caused her to whip around. A third black sedan was speeding into the parking lot.

Karen froze as the car sped toward her.

CHAPTER FIFTY-ONE

Lake City, LA

Amir regained his freedom as abruptly as he lost it.
This was the first time he'd been inhabited by a spirit. It
was like being locked inside a cage within his psyche—as if he was
standing in a cold cell with a movie screen before the bars watching
himself viciously attack Anvil Head. Though disconnected from
his body, he tasted the man's salty skin, coppery blood in his
mouth, and felt the tension in his neck and jaws as he held on
until the man was lifeless. He spread his fingers around the rough
unshaven skin of Red Wolf's neck, helpless to stop himself from
choking Red Wolf to death.

What have I unleashed?

Jhonnette had convinced him that bringing Kristopher Lafitte
back to destroy his father was the only fitting punishment. She
told him she could boost his spiritual powers so that he'd have the
strength to control the *baka*. But Kristopher Lafitte wasn't the only
spirit who'd escaped.

The doorway is open.

While entrapped he'd sensed Melinda's presence as well. He
was unfamiliar with this *loa*, but being ridden was a two-way

street. Some of her essence remained—a swirling static buzz in his mind. She was very old and had died tragically.

Amir found his bearings. He was speeding down Third Avenue, on a collision course with St. Mary's Hospital. From the sound of Red Wolf's phone conversations, something important was happening at the hospital.

That fight was no longer Amir's. Without the girl, the plan was fucked. It was time to cut his losses; he needed to get the money, contact Lincoln, and get the hell out of dodge.

It was amazing how fast the situation had degenerated. Things had gone from bad to worse and from worse to shit and it was no use blaming anyone but himself. He'd have plenty of time for self-flagellation later; right now he needed to figure out the fastest route to the cash.

The hospital parking lot came into view.

Amir attempted to turn left at Guinn and get back on Highway 14, but the steering wheel did not obey his command. His body was rebelling against him. Amir was powerless as the car continued straight. His right foot jammed the accelerator to the floor.

The car entered the St. Mary's parking lot at fifty miles per hour. The buzzing in his head was now a locust swarm. Blood dripped from his nose as he fought to regain control of his faculties.

After a short struggle, he reached into his cargo-shorts pocket and retrieved the switchblade. Everything slowed as the blade clicked open. The car veered drastically to the left and then hit a pothole listing back to the right. Amir's eyes widened. He was headed directly for Karen Lafitte.

What the fuck is she doing here?

Their eyes locked. Karen smiled a knowing smile.

I won't do this.

Amir screamed and buried the knife down to the hilt in his thigh, then slammed his foot down on the brake pedal with all the force in his body. The car fishtailed as the shriek and smell of burning rubber consumed him.

He missed Karen by inches, but didn't miss the downed paramedics a few feet away from her. The car bunny-hopped the bodies and Amir was thrown forward, his head smacking the steering wheel. His foot found the accelerator again. An instant later the car slammed into a pair of black sedans parked in front of the Emergency Room.

Amir flew.

The next thing he knew, a roaring, wave-like noise battered against the sloshing insides of his gray matter. It sounded like he was inside a cavern behind Niagara Falls. Disconnected from his body, his whole world was consumed by the noise.

Someone close-by screamed. Then the earth-shattering sound subsided, replaced by something like a scrambled FM frequency. He wasn't quite on the station, but could hear the announcers trying to reach him anyway. He strained to decipher the words.

"Shut…move…here…slow…careful…burst…back," was all he got at first.

Slowly but surely, the blanks began to fill in like a game of Hangman.

"Clear…off his eyes…hemorrhaging…CCs…more oxygen… please shut…"

Whoever they were talking about sounded pretty fucked up.

"What's your name?" A female voice cut through the static clearly. "Can you speak?"

Someone screamed, "It's gonna blow!"

The air quality changed. Amir felt a strong influx of hot wind whistle through his ear cavity. He was rammed back into himself like a square peg banged into a round hole with a sledgehammer. Invisible arms lifted him and he was casually tossed aside, like he'd encountered a patch of bad turbulence. Except, instead of dropping down, he was keenly aware of moving on up to a De-Luxe Apartment in the sky.

Then radio silence.

"Just try to make him comfortable." Words emanated from his left side some time later. "Don't try to move," the voice said.

Amir attempted to open his eyes but the burning sensation in his left eye forced him to close them immediately.

"You're going to be okay."

"Where…" he attempted to ask, but only hoarse groaning emitted from his throat. An overwhelming claustrophobia made it difficult to breathe. Amir couldn't feel anything from the neck down.

"Shhh…don't try to speak. You've been badly hurt. You need to rest now."

Amir knew she was right, but he couldn't rest. Sleep was the cousin of death. Despite the pain, he forced one eye open and flinched from the light. His mother's beautiful face came into focus.

It was like seeing heaven frowning down at him. She applied a compress to his face and gently wiped away shining fragments of glass.

"That's it," Juanita whispered softly. Her expression was soothing as she stroked the cool cloth against his feverish skin.

"I'm so sorry, Mama," he moaned. "I messed…everything up."

"It's gonna be okay."

"No…it's not," Amir gasped. "Lincoln…"

"You saved him," Juanita said. "You saved them both."

"Both?"

"I want you to rest now, Amir. Soon you will be able to tell me all about it."

CHAPTER FIFTY-TWO

Monday
New Roads, LA

Roberts' face brought everything back.

At the prison, Roberts had offered Lincoln his hand, but instead Lincoln took his gun and bashed him over the head with it. Then he took Roberts' car and drove to the Angola Ferry. Lincoln was practically home free, but for some inexplicable reason he decided to dive off the top deck of the ferry and almost drowned. Roberts was obviously here to finish the job.

"Help!" Lincoln yelled.

Roberts was on him in a flash. "Shut the fuck up, goddamnit!" He pistol-whipped Lincoln in the face.

The pain the morphine had subdued came roaring back. Church bells gonged for Sunday service in Lincoln's head.

"That's better," Roberts said. "Why did yuh run from me? I'm tryin' ta…"

"Stop and turn around!" Jhonnette commanded.

She'd gotten the drop on Roberts. Standing in the doorway, she had a handgun pointed at his head.

"Give the gun to Lincoln and kneel on the floor," she ordered.

Snake placed the gun on the bed with a surprised chuckle. "So it was you all along," he said, dropping to his knees.

Lincoln brought the butt of the gun down on Roberts' head with as much force as he could muster. Roberts toppled over like a blow up doll.

"We gotta get the hell out of here," Lincoln said.

The movies made escape look so easy.

They never showed the blood spraying on the heroine's favorite summer suit while she jerked I.V.'s out of the hero's arm. They never showed the heroine struggling to support a man nearly twice her size as they limped, crawled, and rolled their way to freedom. No, movie escapes were infinitely more graceful.

Jhonnette was now navigating the rented Jeep Liberty toward Baton Rouge. The clock on the dashboard read 11:30 a.m. They needed to figure out their next move. She jerked the car across two lanes of highway and brought the vehicle to a halt on the shoulder. Lincoln lay in the backseat glaring at her in the rearview.

"Lincoln, I know you're in pain but you've got to talk to me. The police have probably found your buddy back there and are most likely hot on our trail right now. We've got to come up with a plan."

Before everything went to pieces at Angola, Lincoln had a very specific agenda. Now that everything had gone to shit, Lincoln was rethinking his priorities. According to Jhonnette, Moses was in the Angola infirmary, one of the most dangerous places for any inmate to wind up, much less a civilian.

How the hell am I supposed to get Moses out of there? And where the hell is Amir right now?

Despite the odds, Lincoln refused to believe that it was too late.

"Lincoln, I know you hear me talking to you."

Lincoln regarded her silently. Jhonnette had shown up mysteriously that morning with information about Moses, claiming to be an ally. But what was in it for her? Sure, she'd saved him from Snake, but could she really be trusted?

"Who are you?" Lincoln asked.

"I know you're having a hard time trusting me, Lincoln. Believe me, I do. And I'm ready to come clean."

"I'm waiting."

Jhonnette continued. "Lincoln, I hate to be the bearer of bad news, but you've been lied to and manipulated by those closest to you."

"Like you're lying to me right now?"

"I know you think I'm full of crap, but I'm telling you—you've put your trust in the wrong people. Walter Simmons is not your father."

"And I'm supposed to just take your word for it?" Lincoln pulled himself into a seated position. "I'm getting out."

"Getting out and going where? You won't last two hours out there."

"I'll take my chances." He grabbed the door handle.

"Lincoln. Stop. I know why you tried to kill yourself this morning."

"What are you talking about?" Though he couldn't remember exactly *why* he'd jumped off the ferry, there was no damn way he was tryin' to commit suicide. Not when he finally had his freedom back.

"My mother was…special. She could read minds…and tell the future. A long time ago, your real father came to her and started something. Something that has affected your entire life."

"You better start making sense, lady."

"Your father resurrected a family curse to kill his father, Joseph."

Lincoln laughed and got out of the car. He made it four paces before her hand caressed his shoulder.

"There are no coincidences, Lincoln. If you hear nothing else I say, hear that. Your father knew this the moment he learned Karen had been kidnapped…"

She's lying. She's lying.

"He tried to ignore the curse even after his father, and then his son, succumbed…"

No!

"I had to come save you before Randy found out about you, Lincoln…"

No!

Lincoln grabbed Jhonnette by the throat and slammed her against the Jeep. He resisted the urge to crush her larnyx, to stop her from uttering these lies. Her words were impossible.

"Stop it, Lincoln!" Jhonnette screamed. "You're hurting me!"

Lincoln let go. They stared at each other, each out of breath.

Jhonnette broke the silence. "Lincoln, three days after a member of the Lafitte family turns eighteen, someone dies. You have Lafitte blood in your veins. If you want to live, you're going to have to make a choice."

Lincoln felt like he was going to faint. "And how do you know all this?"

"Your mother wasn't the only woman ruined by Randy Lafitte's ruthless ambition. He ruined my mother as well, and I've committed my life to making him pay. I uncovered the truth about you during my research."

Lincoln stared ahead in stunned silence. *Could this be true?*

"If you don't believe me, that's on you," Jhonnette continued. "But the fact remains Karen Lafitte turned eighteen two days ago."

"So?"

"So, Karen's birthday started the clock. And Lincoln, things have changed. The curse has gained strength. Normally, one person's death is enough, but not this time. It's being fed by someone."

"Who?"

Jhonnette looked away. "That's what I don't know. What I do know is that Moses didn't come to Angola for you."

"You're not making any sense!"

"You can run away from your destiny, Lincoln, but if you do nothing, a lot of people are going to die today."

"I don't give a damn about that family. Let them all die."

"That family is your family too, Lincoln. Don't you understand? You are at risk as well."

Lincoln examined Jhonnette carefully. She sounded crazy, but if she was telling the truth, it changed everything.

Kris was my...brother?

It was too much for Lincoln to handle. His mind was closing. "Even if I did believe you, it's too late to do anything now, right?"

"Focus, Lincoln. Seventy-two hours after a family member reaches eighteen, someone has to die. That leaves us with you, Karen, and your father. Unfortunately, it's not your choice who lives or dies, but if Karen survives, then either you or Randy will meet death."

Lincoln looked at her with resolve. "I ain't goin' nowhere."

"You sure about that? You've been shot and nearly drowned already. Karen must be doing pretty well for herself. I can't speak for the Governor."

A part of Lincoln always knew it would come down to this.

It's either him or me.

"Tell me what I need to do."

"Well, you can't face your father in this shape. You need proper medical attention."

"I don't have time for that!"

"Well, we're going to have to make time. You have to trust me now, Lincoln. We're on the same side here. Now get in."

Lincoln gazed at her for a long while, trying to gauge whether she could possibly be telling the truth. He thought of Kris Lafitte trying to kill himself and remembered Kris's warnings. He needed to get to the bottom of this, and Jhonnette Deveaux offered a path to the answers. Deciding to play this out, he got back in the Jeep.

"Okay," he said. "Where to now?"

CHAPTER FIFTY-THREE

Monday
Lake City, LA

B ill Edwards slammed the phone back in its cradle. He should have exerted the same force when talking to Randy, but passive aggressive was about as aggressive as he got where the Governor was concerned.

"Keep things quiet for me, Bill," Randy had said in that subtle Machiavellian way of his. *"Keep things quiet and reap the rewards for your loyalty."*

That was Randy's standard line whenever he needed one of his "favors," and Bill had definitely been compensated well for his discretion over the years. This time, however, the risk was not worth the reward.

"Today is going to be a day of tests for all of us, Bill... Can I count on you?"

Bill paced the length of his modest office contemplating the answer to this question as the phone rang and rang. Every now and then it would stop ringing abruptly, only to start again a few seconds later. He had to tread carefully so as not to pull a serious C.L.M.—Career Limiting Move. Bill had not gotten as far as he had by pulling C.L.M.'s. He was smarter than that.

The phone rang again.

Since speaking with Randy earlier, he'd called off all city patrols. He also had Dispatch routing all emergency calls directly to him so he could screen everything that came through. Dispatch packed his voicemail and he listened to call after call, writing the pertinent details down in his logbook. So far, this morning had brought in six cases of drunk and disorderly; two burglaries (one that turned out to be a dispute between two lesbian roommates up at Lake City College); ten car-related emergencies; and three fires. By themselves, these calls would have made the morning a doozy, but these were in addition to a series of other calls—the calls he'd been screening for in the first place.

One call was from Morris Fontenot, who was screaming over loud bursts of heavy artillery to report a drive-by shooting at Simmons Park. "It's a war zone out here!"

Another call was from Evan Leday, a truck driver, reporting the spontaneous combustion of the old schoolyard. "There was a friggin' mushroom cloud over that place, man!"

But the morning's winner went to Ms. Beulah Boudreaux. She'd reported seeing the ghost of a white girl walking down her street wearing nothing but a Houston Rockets jersey. "One second she was floatin' down the street and then there was this loud blast. When I looked up, the girl had disappeared into thin air."

"Bill, the last thing we need is one of your guys trying to play supercop on this one."

Easy for Randy to say. He didn't have to explain to his superiors and constituents why he was letting a group of rogue FBI agents, kidnappers, and gangbangers run wild all over the city. Which is why Bill needed to keep a lid on the chaos until things were back under control.

Regardless of what his conscience said, Bill did not have the luxury of saying no to Randy Lafitte. Ever. After all, if it wasn't for Randy, Bill would be rotting in jail for the murder of his wife, Paula. A fact Randy *never* let him forget. When Randy made a mess, Bill reached for his broom—no questions asked.

Still, this was a mess of epic proportions. Bodies were piling up all over town. It was only a matter of time before the press got wind of it.

Right on cue, Bill's cell phone rang. It was Captain Rick Morgan, head of Lake City's SWAT division.

"Chief," Rick Morgan began in his usual grave baritone. "Big explosion over at St. Mary's Hospital. My wife called me hysterical. She swears it was a terrorist attack."

"Shit!" This was going to be all over the news within the hour. "Any casualties?"

"Four dead and two injured, but that's not all."

Bill swallowed. "Go on."

"Sheila says there's a white girl that looks an awful lot like Karen Lafitte sitting in the hospital parking lot…"

Lake City, LA

"So after the fat guy grabbed that nurse you shot him once at point blank range," Officer Jeff Abshire said. He stared at the slack mouthed, skinny, black kid slouched over before him.

Jeff heard footsteps running down the hall and wondered what the hell else had gone wrong. It was like martial law had broken out in the city. There were barricades everywhere; cruisers and fire trucks were racing from crisis to crisis. Half the city was on fire.

This must be what it's like to be one of those big city cops in New York City or something.

He turned his attention back to the skinny black kid they'd apprehended at the hospital. He was up to his neck in this, but hadn't said a word. Even though there was no way the kid could possibly have been in all those places at the same time, the Chief was trying to pin all the murders on him. Sixteen and counting. Abshire had been charged with the impossible task of securing a confession, but the kid wasn't talking.

Karen Lafitte was in the Chief's office. They'd found the blond-haired, living skeleton in the hospital parking lot behind the apparent getaway car, crying and scratching at her biceps like a heroin addict. She wasn't talking either.

"Is he dead?" the kid asked, finally breaking his vow of silence.

"You shot him from less than a foot away. What do you think? You were definitely trying to kill him. Make it easy for yourself and tell me what the hell happened out there."

The kid grumbled again.

Jeff slammed his fist on the table. "Take the goddamn marbles out your mouth and speak the fuck up, Goddamnit!"

The kid recoiled and drew his lips tight.

Jeff sighed. "Listen, kid, I'm sorry for yelling. But you've got to give me something or you're gonna leave me to draw my own conclusions."

Their eyes met. The kid gave him a look that said, *who are you kidding, you're gonna do that anyway.*

Jeff rubbed his forehead in frustration. *Why do I always get the shit assignments?* He was far from being the most experienced interrogator in the department. Stokes, Landry, and Boudreaux were all better choices, but they were on special assignment. The same kind of special assignment that led to so many cop deaths back at Simmons Park ten years earlier.

"So what's it gonna be, kid? We're almost out of time here."

No reaction.

"Okay, fine. I'm gonna leave you here and check out those hospital surveillance tapes. I'm also gonna take the statements of the dozens of eyewitnesses who can place you at the scene of sixteen murders and one kidnapping. Then we're gonna lock you up and throw away the key, and you can explain your side of the story to the other killers on the inside. I'm sure they'll be sympathetic."

The Chief burst in with Captain Morgan in tow. Jeff was ushered roughly into the hall as Captain Morgan approached the kid and unclipped his service revolver.

Monday
New Roads, LA

Monica Babineaux was getting worried. She wanted to take a smoke break, but couldn't find Big Bertha. Nurses who reported to Big Bertha had to ask permission to pee, and this was doubly true when they were short-staffed. Because of the impending hurricane, half the nurses had called out. *I should have called out, too.*

To keep her mind off her nicotine craving, she walked to the nurse's station to check the telemetry monitors. John Doe in room 243's monitor was off. Monica stalked toward the room with purpose. If something happened in her section she could kiss her job goodbye.

Monica reached for the door handle. Crashing and thrashing noises emanated from behind the closed door.

Don't go in there.

A man groaned.

Turn around and call security.

Monica's curiosity overcame her fear and she pulled the door open a crack.

"Goddamn that hurts," the man said. "How many times I gotta say it? I can't fuckin' help yuh!"

"For some reason, Snake," a woman replied. "I just don't believe you."

Monica pulled the door open and the light from the hallway illuminated the characters within. Her John Doe was nowhere in sight. Instead, a bearded, silver-haired white man in a rumpled suit lay on the floor in a tangle of wires. It took her a moment to realize he was tied up.

Monica stood transfixed in the doorway. Seated directly across from him was a familiar-looking white woman. She held a silver handgun in her left hand. "I don't think you realize the position that you're in," she said. "You think I'm here to talk? I'm through talking."

"I can't tell yuh nothing, Coral, because I don't know nothing."

"Well in that case." Coral extended her arm and pulled the trigger. The gun barely made any noise on account of the silencer attached to the barrel.

Monica gasped as the man called Snake slumped over, a crimson stain spreading through the sleeve of his jacket. Coral whipped her head around, staring Monica in the face.

"Who the hell are you?" she demanded.

"I'm s-sorry," Monica stammered. "I'm just a nurse. Please don't kill me!"

"Get in here and shut that door."

Monica froze.

"Shut the goddamned door!" the crazy woman yelled.

Monica stepped inside the room, allowing the door to close behind her. Snake groaned again. He wasn't dead.

Coral returned her attention to Snake. His teeth were bared, giving him the appearance of a werewolf.

"What are you going to do now, tough guy?" Coral said to him.

"Gonna kill yuh. Cunt bitch." He grunted with a ferocious grin. "Just like I killed yuh son. Then I'm gonna kill yuh daughter. And Randy's gonna get blamed for the whole thing."

"You shut up! Just shut the fuck up!"

"Truth hurts, don't it?"

Coral stood. Tears streamed down her pale cheeks. "Why? Why did you do it?"

Snake looked at Monica for the first time. "You should get out of here and call security, don't yuh think?"

"Don't even think about it," Coral admonished, swinging the gun in her direction.

Monica's knees went weak. It took everything in her not to topple over. "Do you have kids?" Coral asked.

"Yes," Monica replied shakily. "I got twins. A boy and a girl."

"What are their names?"

"Lashonda an' Taykwon." Monica wondered if she'd ever see them again.

"Nice names. I've got a boy and girl, too. Kristopher and Karen."

Snake looked at them like they'd lost their minds.

Coral trained the gun on Snake once again. "He killed my son. He killed Kristopher. What would you do if someone hurt your kids?"

Kill them, Monica thought.

The woman must have read her mind because she said, "I knew you'd understand."

Monica stopped shaking.

"Well, Snake, it seems as if we are in agreement here. I'll give you one last chance to tell me why you did it. Otherwise, I'm going to play target practice with your face."

Snake struggled mightily to escape his bonds, but to no avail. He looked up at both of them in exasperation. "I was just following orders, yuh know?"

Coral took two steps toward him. "Well I've got an order for you to follow. Go to hell." The bullet tore into Snake's chest.

Monica and Coral stared at each other for a long time. Finally, Coral said, "I've got to save my daughter. All I'm asking for is a thirty-minute head start. I don't care what you tell the authorities after that."

Monica looked down at Snake. "I'll give you an hour."

Lake City, LA

"I want everybody out of this room!" Dr. Patricia Lyles screamed. Her patient was dying and now was not the time for casual bystanders.

Dr. Lyles had just finished calling the spousal abuse hotline on behalf of a battered woman when the first explosion shook the floor around the nurse's station. She and several nurses ran through the double doors separating the ER from its waiting room.

The smell hit her first—a pungent bouquet of charred flesh, gasoline, and roasting metal. She covered her mouth and nose; the nurses did the same. After her nose adjusted she surveyed the extent of the damage.

Her critical eyes missed nothing.

A burning three vehicle pile-up filled the ER waiting room with smoke. A skinny black kid lay against the wall with blood all over what was left of a yellow Nike t-shirt, just a few feet away from a man wearing one of the waiting room chairs around his fractured neck like an oversized necklace. Another man was on fire from the waist up, lying half in and half out the wrecked automatic doors separating the ER waiting room from the rest of the world. She didn't see the fourth man, the patient who was now, some two hours later, dying in her Emergency Room, until she had put the burning man out with a fire extinguisher. From the look of things, her patient had been ejected from one of the black sedans. He'd landed in a spray of shattered glass just outside the waiting room.

She and her team had just pulled him clear of the wreckage when a second explosion rocked the hospital. The red ER awning came crashing down, a large chunk of metal just narrowly missing her.

She dusted herself off and surveyed the scene outside. There was even more carnage in the parking lot. Two paramedics lay motionless on the ground, their skulls popped like grapes, probably by one of the smoldering cars to her right. Her gorge trembled and she vomited her breakfast all over the pavement like a first-year med student during cadaver lab.

Once the nausea passed, she felt better, until she saw the emaciated teenage girl rocking back and forth on the pavement just a few feet away from the paramedics. Patricia was about to see if the girl was all right when a police cruiser came tearing into the parking lot. Before Patricia could intervene, the cops grabbed the girl and put her in the back of the cruiser. As Patricia dizzily made her way over to the vehicle, the driver turned the car around, hit the siren, and bolted out of there like he was riding on a lightning bolt.

Another officer appeared out of nowhere. "You in charge here?" he asked.

She nodded.

"I need you to clear this area of non-police personnel immediately."

"What's happening, Officer?"

"Just clear the area, please."

"But—"

"I'm not going to repeat myself again," the officer interrupted while pulling out his service pistol.

He escorted her back to the ER. The teenager in the tattered, yellow Nike t-shirt had regained consciousness and was sitting against the far wall. The officer gestured to one of his colleagues and the kid was handcuffed and loaded into another police cruiser.

"Excuse me, Sir," Patricia interjected. "That boy needs medical attention."

The officer ignored her plea. "Where is the hospital security room?"

She sent him on his way, wondering what the hell was going on in Lake City today.

Patricia went back to check on the man who'd been ejected from his car. But not before placing a call her brother-in-law over at NBC Channel 9 News.

Her trauma team had stabilized the patient, but they needed to get him into surgery. As she checked his vitals, he looked up at her with glazed eyes. "Did Lincoln call?"

"Don't worry about that now."

"Tell him…" the patient continued urgently, "tell him that it…wasn't worth…it."

The patient's pressure dropped; he was going into cardiac arrest. Patricia motioned for the defibrillator. She shocked him twice and his heartbeat came back on line.

Close call.

The nurse backed away from the patient, eyes wide. "Um, Dr. Lyles…" She pointed. The patient's face contorted as thick ropes of blood descended from his nose and ears.

Patricia bent down to check his breathing. A clicking noise emanated from his throat. She leaned in further.

The patient grabbed her face with both hands and whispered, "Can you seeeeeeee?"

She stared paralyzed into his contorted face. Patricia's eyes dilated as images played before her.

She saw an enormous live oak tree in front of a plantation home. A fair-skinned black man hung from one of its many curved limbs. An older white man sat at the base of the tree with a gun to his temple. A young teenage girl lay crumpled a few feet away in the shade of an enormous house. Her water had just broken.

A car pulled up and a silver-haired man carried the body of a lanky, blond-haired teenager into the home. The mother burst into tears. The father averted his eyes and looked toward the tree. A young blond-haired girl peeked out from behind her father's legs with a look of confusion on her face. Patricia was riding shotgun in a fast moving vehicle. The patient was driving. She looked through the windshield and saw they were entering the hospital parking lot. A teenage girl appeared in front of the car. He was going to run her down...

"Doctor Lyles!"

Patricia's eyelids fluttered. She looked around in a daze. Her patient had flatlined. She tried to resuscitate him, but it was too late. Time of death, 12:11 p.m.

The door burst open and a colleague poked his head in.

"Hey, there you are. We've got a situation out here."

"What's going on?" Patricia asked, composing herself.

"It's the hurricane," he started. "It's shifted this way. We're gonna to need all hands on deck and the Lord's good grace, because ready or not, Isaac is coming."

PART III: REVOLUTION

"I didn't know I was really alive in this world until I felt things hard enough to kill for 'em... I feel alright when I look at it that way..."

-Richard Wright
Native Son

CHAPTER FIFTY-FOUR

39 years earlier
1963
New Orleans, LA

"You really think this is a good idea?" Malcolm whispered to his brother Ronnie as they made their way through the bustling house in the Magnolia Projects.

"These people are lost," Ronnie replied. "They're damned near Catholic with all these gods they pray to. They need to hear the teachings of The Honorable Elijah Mohammed as much as anyone. Besides, I'm hungry, and these ceremonies are serious chow throw downs."

"You're always hungry," Malcolm quipped, checking out his surroundings. The walls were adorned with African warrior masks, the bookshelves lined with foreign titles. The air heavily perfumed with musky incense. Everyone wore white from head to toe, and Malcolm felt woefully out of place in his black suit, starched white shirt, and bowtie, even though no one seemed to notice or care about his attire.

Malcolm had to admire Ronnie's commitment to the cause. Who else but his brother would dare recruit prospective converts to the Nation of Islam at a Voodoo ceremony?

Malcolm had always been intrigued with Voodoo. When he was a child, his older brother Duke told him the story of the Haitian Revolution—how slaves had organized and revolted, ultimately defeating both the French and British in a war that took over 12 years and cost hundred's of thousands of lives. The Revolution began with the Bois Caïman ceremony, where the various factions of slaves solemnized their pact in a voodoo ritual Duke said began with animal sacrifice and concluded with a huge storm—as if the Voodoo deities were roaring their support for war. Though Malcolm's rational mind knew it was impossible for a human being to control or communicate with the dead, a part of him wanted it to be true. He had often longed to be so powerful no white devil would ever threaten his family or loved ones again.

After they'd each devoured two plates of fried chicken, potato salad, and green beans, they headed outside toward the sound of the drums. The first thing Malcolm noticed was the tree, an enormous live oak that seemed to suck up all the space around it. The trunk, covered with intricate designs and patterns, created mostly in chalk. The drummers sat in a semicircle around the tree, their palms a blur in the moonlight. The sound seemed to emanate from the tree itself.

Positioned in front of the drummers were four women and two men. Each of them swayed and vibrated at their own pace, some in rhythm, and others just off the beat. They moved as if they were completely unaware of the other dancers, or the group of people watching. Malcolm turned to ask Ronnie if he knew what was going on, but Ronnie had headed back into the kitchen to talk to the young man who'd invited them here.

Bearing witness to a voodoo ceremony for the first time, Malcolm realized that the public really had it all wrong. This just seemed like a nice gathering of folks. There were no animals being slaughtered in sacrifice to some pagan deity, no witchdoctors turning random people into zombies; only food, drums, dancing, and that enormous tree.

And her.

The woman emerged through the midst of the dancers like a wraith, almost as if the tree had spit her out. She, too, wore a white dress and matching white head wrap that covered much of her rich, curly black hair. Her fair skin was quite a contrast as well, with everyone else's skin tone somewhere between brown and "blue-black" as his mother called extremely dark-skinned folks. This woman could have passed for white were it not for that African nose and full lips. She was the first woman he'd ever seen more beautiful than Juanita.

Malcolm's breath caught in his throat at the sight of her.

"Welcome friends," the woman said in a commanding voice that reverberated throughout the crowd. "Tonight we come together to celebrate new life." She gestured toward a woman who was clearly three or four months pregnant. "Tonight let us dance with the *loa* in celebration. Tonight let us call out to Papa Legba to protect this woman, to protect her new family, to protect all of us in these trying times of change and persecution." Her eyes linked with Malcolm's as she said this.

Malcolm stood transfixed. He probably would have remained that way had Ronnie not dragged him into the house to meet with three young men, who wanted to know more about the Nation of

Islam. After a truncated version of his standard speech about the
need for black people to unify and learn the truth about their white
oppressors (he had to get back outside), Malcolm handed each man
fliers containing information about the two area mosques. The men
headed out back. Malcolm followed them until Ronnie stopped
him.

"So what do you think?" Ronnie asked.

All Malcolm could think about was the woman, but he said
nothing.

"What's got you so quiet?"

Malcolm was about to answer when the reason for his silence
walked into the kitchen.

Ronnie glanced between them and gave a slight chuckle before
saying, "Forget about her, Malcolm. She's way too far gone to
convert."

Malcolm couldn't have agreed more but he replied, "Couldn't
hurt to try." He walked over to where she stood pouring herself a
glass of water.

"Hello, Sister," he said. This was the customary Muslim greeting
toward a woman.

She glanced up at him, and smiled provocatively. "If I were
your sister, that would be most unfortunate, don't you think?"

Malcolm took a step away, too aware of Ronnie's eyes boring
into his back. Islamic women didn't dress or talk like this one.
Islamic women were modest to a fault. Malcolm doubted she could
even spell modest.

"It's okay, Brother," she mocked. "Thank you for coming to
our little gathering tonight. What questions do you have?"

Is she trying to convert me?

Malcolm decided to play along. "Those people, the dancers, I noticed they seemed a little distant. Is that normal?"

"They were each being ridden by a *loa*."

"What is a *loa*?"

"You would call it a spirit, I guess."

"Reminds me a bit of people speaking in tongues in church, except for all the dancing," he replied, smirking against his better judgment.

"So you do have a sense of humor, Brother X." She smiled in return.

"Can you tell me the significance of the etchings on the tree?"

"The *vèvé* on the *Poteau Mitan*, you mean?"

His face must have reshaped in confusion because she laughed again. "It's French, Haitian French to be exact. Certain ceremonies in Vodun require a *Poteau Mitan*, or tree, as you called it. It is the doorway through which the *loa* exit and return. The *vèvé* are used to call them forward."

Malcolm nodded as if he understood a word of what this crazy woman was saying. He'd decided approaching her was a bad idea until her next question stopped his thoughts cold.

"Do you believe in coincidence, Malcolm?"

"How...how do you know my name?"

"I know a lot more than that," she replied. "My name is Desiree Deveaux and I am going to show you your destiny."

CHAPTER FIFTY-FIVE

Before sunrise, Hurricane Isaac had been on a trajectory to make landfall in Southeastern Alabama and along the Florida panhandle. A little over six hours later, the storm had been upgraded to a Category Five and changed course. Isaac was expected to make landfall at approximately 8:00 p.m. near Baton Rouge. The National Storm Center contacted the Governor's office advising full-scale evacuations from New Iberia to Lake City.

Monday
I-10 West

"Can't yuh make this bucket go any faster?" Snake screamed at Shaw from the backseat of the Crown Victoria.

Shaw nodded, but his jaw tightened as he gripped the steering wheel.

Larry sat next to Snake and tried to diffuse the situation. "Boss, the tracking device shows her about twenty-four miles ahead of us."

"So, step on it!"

"We're doing almost ninety-five," Shaw interjected.

"We're gaining on her, Boss," Larry added. " She's been sitting still for the past twenty minutes."

"Sitting still? I feel the same way! First you dickwads take an hour to locate me. A fuckin' hour!" Snake glared at his hapless employees. "Fuckin' incompetence. One a yuh's should've been tracking Coral, while the other got me. And I don't wanna hear no excuses outta you, Shaw. You were the one that let her get away from yuh with the gun she shot me with. Twice!"

Snake clutched his chest, still sore and raw from Coral's bullets. How the fuck had Lafitte's zombie of a wife gotten the drop on them all? Thank God for Kevlar and Coral's shitty aim. His head hurt more from Lincoln's bashing.

He was gonna make that bitch pay. They'd had an airtight plan, and it had all gone to shit. What was most shocking was the way he'd been played by Jhonnette. He should have known better than to trust a damn woman. Women had been the downfall of great men since Adam and that cunt Eve.

"We still gaining?" Snake asked.

"Fifteen miles and closing, Boss."

Snake nodded. Getting Coral back was the key to making Randy pay. Then he'd turn his attention back to Jhonnette.

I'm not out the game yet.

I-10 West

Coral was trapped in bumper to bumper traffic. The missing pieces to her son's murder and daughter's kidnapping were falling into place and the picture unfolding horrified her. Snake's confession that he'd been ordered to kill her son rattled around in her mind incessantly.

Ordered by whom?

The answer was obvious. The answer was hell.

After everything that had happened and everything she'd learned, Coral found it hard, but not impossible, to believe Randy could do such a thing. Randy had a special talent for shielding his thoughts and feelings from the outside world. Shoot, he'd been keeping her in the dark for years.

Randy had never handled tragedy in a positive manner. After Kristopher died, she'd seen a side of Randy that scared her so much she'd blacked it out. But seeing him on TV and how he'd been behaving lately brought back memories of Randy locking himself in the bathroom and coming out with a rash of razor slashes all over his bare arms and chest, a terrifying blankness in his eyes.

Years later, she finally understood the feeling.

My marriage is over.

No comfort came with this realization. She grabbed one of Shaw's guns and put it in her Gucci bag. There was comfort in that, at least. Her eyes glazed over as she saw herself shooting Snake over and over again. There had been such a rush of exhilaration when she'd pulled the trigger and watched him slump over.

Traffic moved forward a quarter-inch. Coral groaned in frustration. There was no escape. She remembered the first time she heard her son using those exact same words. It had new meaning to her now. What had Kristopher feared most in those last days?

The answer was the key to solving the mystery surrounding his death. Still, solving Kristopher's murder wouldn't save Karen. Would it? Watching the stalled traffic, Coral realized only a miracle could help her now. On cue, the gas light flashed on the dashboard. She was in luck because there was a service station up ahead.

Lake City, LA

Brandon feared for his life. There had been no ruse or subtle introduction before the torture started. The two cops (one wearing a Chief's badge) burst into the holding cell and kicked the younger officer out. The Chief pistol-whipped Brandon twice before he could blink.

The pain was like running face-first into a brick wall. The man not wearing the Chief's badge stood behind Brandon and picked him up. He locked both hands underneath Brandon's chin and pulled his neck while arching his back. The cop inserted his fat, mustard-tasting fingers into Brandon's mouth and spread the corners open into a grotesque clown's smile.

The Chief wiped off the bloody butt of the gun and twisted a silencer muzzle on the tip of the barrel.

Brandon attempted to yell, but the officer behind him applied more pressure to his windpipe, choking all sound into a senseless gurgle. Brandon's vision blurred and sharpened like there was a TV antenna embedded in his skull.

The Chief shoved the muzzle of the gun inside Brandon's mouth. Drool dribbled down both sides of his lips and met with salty tears pouring from his eyes and snot dripping from his nose. The veil of security had been jerked from Brandon's eyes. No one was coming to save him.

Brandon looked into the frigid eyes of the Chief and saw no humanity—only murderous purpose. A corpse couldn't argue or plead innocence.

"How long does this take?" the cop behind him asked.

"He'll be unconscious any minute now."

"And what then?"

"Then, we get Ran's girl to identify—" A knock on the door interrupted his speech.

"Shit," the Chief groaned, pulling the gun out of Brandon's mouth. Glorious amounts of air poured in, nearly choking Brandon as bad as the man's hands. He took a huge breath that left him dizzy, then started yelling. As the sound escaped Brandon's lips, the man behind him squeezed his larynx without mercy, transforming his yell to a guttural moan until Brandon lost consciousness.

LA-1 South

It was starting to rain. Jhonnette remembered the hurricane and turned on the radio to get an update. Rather than a progress report on the storm, however, the reporter was detailing the sad state of affairs in Lake City. Apparently, a young black man had gone on a killing rampage.

He'd begun the morning at Simmons Park where he'd shot seven people dead. Then he'd strolled into the Emergency Room at St. Mary's Hospital with a bomb, detonated the device, and killed six more. He was currently in custody at the Main Branch of the Lake City Police Department.

The reporter ended his commentary saying, "And most interesting of all, the shooter has been identified as Brandon Mouton, the adopted brother of Lincoln Baker, pardoned just this morning by Governor Lafitte. It appears Mouton was working in conjunction with a man named Amir Barber, who died earlier in St. Mary's ER. There are also accounts that Governor Lafitte may have been lying this morning when he stated that his kidnapped daughter, Karen, had been found. We have eyewitness accounts from several physicians who saw Karen Lafitte in the St. Mary's parking lot at the time of the explosion. More to come..."

Jhonnette switched off the stereo. None of that had been part of her plan.

Lincoln spoke up from the backseat. "I don't give a damn what they said, he didn't do it. Brandon's a good kid."

"This is really bad, Lincoln," Jhonnette said. They've already released his name and they're tying these crimes to him. The plan is collapsing. Amir is dead and Karen Lafitte is in their custody. It's time to cut our losses, don't you think?"

Lincoln looked at Jhonnette, eyes hardened by resolve. "I've gotta get back to Lake City and save Brandon. That's what I gotta do."

"Lincoln, Lake City is like…one hundred and fifty miles away," Jhonnette replied, dismissing his idea. "There's a hurricane on the way. And besides, that would be playing right into their hands. He's in custody! You think you can just walk into the LCPD and break him out of there?"

"I know it sounds impossible," Lincoln replied. "But I have to do this."

"What about Moses?" Jhonnette asked. "You can't save them both, you know."

Lincoln considered her words for a moment and then said, "That's why we gotta split up. You go to Angola. Get to Moses. I'll head back west."

"How am I supposed to reach Moses? Won't the prison be on lockdown after this morning?"

"You got to me, didn't you?"

Fair point.

"Turn the car around and I'll tell you everything you need to know to get into Angola."

Jhonnette locked eyes with him in the rearview. "You sure you want to go through with this? If you change course now, then Lafitte gets away and all this was for nothing."

"How do you know so much about everything?" Lincoln challenged. "What are you after here? Why are you helping me? What's in this for you?"

"It's not enough that we share a common enemy?" Jhonnette replied, deflecting the inevitable question.

"I need to know *why*?"

Jhonnette made a decision. If she didn't give Lincoln something, she would never get what she wanted out of him. "Okay…fine… you and I are more connected than you know, Lincoln. We are connected by our fathers' war against each other."

"Our fathers?"

"Yes. I learned some things about Randy Lafitte years ago that led me to investigate my mother's life." Jhonnette vividly recalled reading the letters between her mother and father while he was in Vietnam: letters that had guided her mission.

"What kind of things?" Lincoln asked.

"For starters, I learned that Randy Lafitte came to my mother to resurrect a curse on his own father. The same curse that is plaguing all of us today."

"Why would someone want to kill their own father?"

"Don't you want to kill yours?"

"Good point..."

"Anyway, meeting Randy Lafitte ruined my mother's life. My mother and Randy had a lot in common, you see. Both opportunists. She saw using Lafitte as a way to strike a blow against the system. But he must have found out that none of it was real."

"Wait, I thought you said the curse *is* real."

"Curses are powered by belief, Lincoln. Randy stopped believing in the curse years ago, but there are enough others who still believe to keep it alive."

"Like you?"

"And my father."

"I still don't get where your father comes into this. Who the fuck is he?"

Jhonnette was silent for a moment. Then she said, "When they met, my father was calling himself Malcolm X."

"Wait, Malcolm X?" Lincoln laughed. "I hate to drop this on you, but he's dead."

"His given last name was Wright."

Lincoln did a double-take. "What did you say?"

"Malcolm Wright...is my father."

Lincoln felt a tightening in his chest at the mention of Panama X. His head pounded from the pain of his bullet wounds and the mental stress. This was too much.

"I know this is a lot to handle..."

"No shit," Lincoln replied. Jhonnette was Panama X's daughter? Amir's half-sister? Finally, everything clicked. She wasn't here for him at all. She was here to get to Panama X. But to do what?

"You don't look too good. You have to let me help you." Jhonnette pulled the car over. She got out and opened Lincoln's door.

"What are you doing?"

"Helping," she replied, pressing her hands to his shoulder wound.

Lincoln's headache lifted as soon as she touched him. A wave of heat moved through her fingertips into his shoulder. He felt giddy and faint at once. Then the tingling started—a maddening sensation, like hundreds of insects dancing beneath his skin.

"What are you feeling?"

"My...skin is crawling," he replied, finally understanding the expression.

"That's good. You're a fast healer."

"You...you're doing this?"

She nodded.

"Why?" Lincoln groaned.

"I know this hurts, Lincoln, but it will be over soon. Just keep your eyes on mine. I'll guide you through."

Lincoln stared deeply into her eyes and gave in.

"We're here," Jhonnette announced, pulling up to the prison gate. It was 1:00 p.m. The only sign of the morning's chaos was the gleaming shards of glass clustered around the dented penitentiary portal.

"Turn right toward the visitor processing center."

Jhonnette complied and minutes later she parked in front of a wide brick building with a faded maroon roof. She cut off the engine and offered Lincoln her sunniest smile. "So, what's this big plan of yours?"

Lincoln had been thinking about just that. There was only one way to get inside to Moses. He detailed his plan slowly, making sure she got every nuance.

"Do you know why Moses was here this morning?" she asked as he finished.

Lincoln had been chewing on this question all morning. "You were right. I don't think he came for me. I don't think he knew I was getting out. That means he came to talk to Panama X."

"About what?" she asked.

"They have history..." Lincoln trailed off.

"There's something you need to know about Amir," Jhonnette said.

"What?" Lincoln asked, preparing himself for another bombshell.

"Amir didn't die in vain," Jhonnette said. "The girl is the key. If she gets back to her father, the rest will take care of itself."

"How?" Lincoln asked, aware that he was now referring to his sister—no longer the deserving victim of punishment. His headache was returning.

"She has a special present for your father," Jhonnette replied cryptically. "A final present from Amir and me." She exited the Jeep and then turned to say, "I healed your physical wounds, Lincoln, but only you can heal your real scars."

Lincoln watched her walk away, pulled himself into the front seat, and turned the car around. The prison dwindled in his rearview, but not in his mind. Jhonnette's final comment echoed in his skull.

What did you do to Karen, Amir?

He might never know. Amir was dead and whatever he'd done had died with him. Lincoln pressed down hard on the accelerator. Regardless of what trials lay ahead, Lincoln was finally headed home.

CHAPTER FIFTY-SIX

Angola, LA

A helicopter proudly bearing the seal of Louisiana on its side touched down on the helipad at the Louisiana State Penitentiary. Two of the warden's staff greeted Randy. He made small talk with the men as they escorted him to the warden's office for a meeting.

Panama X sat on his cot inside of Camp F reading over the last page of his memoir. His new cell was only a short walk from the lethal injection chamber and the end of the line. But not for him. That poison dart would never mark his flesh.

The memoir was a story of tragedy detailing the lynching of his father, his brother Duke's murder, his killing of two policemen in Mississippi, and the assassination of Walter Simmons. It was a tale of transformation that described his conversion to Islam during college, his time in the Army during Vietnam, his discovery of Vodun after defecting, and his return to America as the general of the Black Mob. It detailed his failures and successes as a husband to Juanita, and father to Amir. In it, he confessed his inadequacies and frustrations—chief among them his inability to kill Randy Lafitte during the River Boat bombing. Finally, it was a saga of spiritual awakening during Panama X's self-imposed exile in prison.

Thinking on his memoir, two words flashed in his mind's eye—**duty** and **destiny**. Behind each word lay a path, and before each stood a woman. His dear Juanita represented the path of duty, while Desiree Deveaux embodied his destiny. The message was clear. He was going to have to choose.

Panama X remembered all Desiree had done for him. She had predicted Duke's death, Malcolm's entry into the military, and the journey he would have to take to become the leader of his people. Malcolm strayed from the path she laid out when he chose Juanita, which resulted in the thirty year detour from his destiny. With Lincoln's release and Randy Lafitte's inevitable demise, it was time to refocus.

His ears caught a snatch of the radio broadcast from KLSP; the Angola radio station was always playing at low volume from the radio in the corner of his cell. Upon hearing Amir's name, he turned it up to learn his son had been killed in Lake City. A wave of disorientation crashed over him. *Amir, dead?* He closed his eye and felt Amir's spirit painfully ascending onto the spiritual plane. Amir would be damned to wander eternally without a proper burial.

What have I done?

When they formulated their plan to free Lincoln, Panama X knew the risks were high. Still, a father could never prepare for the death of his child.

Is this what you felt, Lafitte?

The Governor was very close. The *baka's* presence was like a locating device. But what was he doing here?

Panama X managed a grim smile. It was destiny.

Warden George Winey settled into a plush, leather chair opposite his brother-in-law, Randy Lafitte. "So, Randy, what brings you to my little corner of the world on such a bad day?" he asked.

"Did you catch my press conference this morning?"

"Of course."

"Good. Then you know about Malcolm Wright's new situation."

"Yes, and I've already made the appropriate provisions."

"Good. That's real good. What's not so good is how your men managed to miss Lincoln Baker this morning."

George winced. "They didn't miss, Randy. Baker had help." He reached into his desk and handed over a photo.

The picture showed Snake Roberts carrying Lincoln past the prison gates.

"I should have told you earlier, but it's been crazy around here."

"It's okay, George." Randy stared at the photo. He was looking at two dead men.

"I'm sure this is just me being a worrier," George began. "But is Coral okay?"

Was Coral okay? That depended on whether or not Snake would uphold his end of their deal. The good news was that after speaking to Bill Edwards on his flight over, he got the great news that Karen had been recovered. That was enough for him for now. He'd deal with Snake and Coral later. Randy looked back at his brother-in-law soberly. "Your sister's…fine." *I hope.*

George visibly relaxed. "Is Malcolm Wright really behind all of this?"

"I'm afraid so. He's been targeting our family for some time."

"Well, we've got him now."

"Yes," Randy replied carefully. "When can I see him?"

"Anytime you want. We moved Wright to solitary just this morning. I can take you over now."

Panama X opened his eye at the sound of footsteps. He met the guard at the cell door. A moment later, he was being ushered down a long corridor into the visitation chamber.

The visitation chamber consisted of a lone table with one chair on each side. The peeling walls were a dingy white. Gloom intruded through three barred windows cut into the wall. Two armed guards stood on either side of the door; a third escorted Malcolm to the empty chair opposite Randy Lafitte.

Panama X was slightly surprised to see his longtime adversary, but made sure his expression betrayed none of this to the enemy he'd actually never met face-to-face. In Randy, he saw the mob that had killed his father and brother. He saw the racist cops he'd killed. He saw the white officers he'd fragged with grenades before defecting. He saw the CIA agents who'd tried to infiltrate the Black Mob in Houston.

His enemy was weak. Randy's eyes were sunken from his battle with the *baka*. He was in a terribly vulnerable state. It was time to capitalize.

"Welcome to Angola, Governor," he said. "To what do I owe this privilege?"

"Well, if it isn't my favorite flunky," Randy said. He coughed, covering his mouth with the back of his hand.

They both saw the bloody phlegm he'd spewed. Randy tried unsuccessfully to cover it up by putting his hand under the table.

"You don't look too well, Governor," Panama X replied. "Actually, you look like death warmed over. Is it your cancer?"

"You bastard," Randy said. "You're doing this to me."

"Governor, I'm disappointed in you. How could I infect you from a prison cell?"

Randy leaned forward. "I know what you're up to. Jhonnette Deveaux told me your plans."

Jhonnette Deveaux? Desiree had a daughter? "I don't know who or what you're talking about."

"Don't play dumb with me, Wright. You put a curse on me."

"A curse?" Panama X asked. "I thought you were a rational man, Governor. What would your loyal constituents say if they heard you spouting off about a curse?"

"I don't give a fuck about what people think," Randy yelled. "You have to stop this!"

"Now why would I do a thing like that? And even if I could help you, what can you possibly offer me in return? You are planning to execute me, remember?"

"Don't patronize me, Wright. You and Desiree Deveaux were in on this together from the very beginning. You were there the night my father died, weren't you?"

He's putting it together. Good.

"Governor, all these unfounded accusations. I'm appalled. Besides, didn't your father blow his own head off with that old revolver?"

"How did you know the kind of gun he used?"

Panama X laughed. "Okay, you've got me there."

"You…tricked me."

"If only I had that ability," Panama X replied. "How was I supposed to know that an eighteen-year-old punk would stumble into my woman's place of business talking craziness about a family curse he wanted to resurrect to kill his racist father?"

He watched Randy's eyes widen.

"No, Governor. It was all you. You refuse to take responsibility for your actions, even now at the end? Amazing."

"I…saw you there. You did this. All of it," Randy stammered.

"I was there that night, I won't deny it," Panama X replied. "Just like I was present when you came to see Desiree Deveaux. I also followed you when you went to see your father at Commander's Palace to collect a sample of his hair and clothing for Desiree. I comforted Desiree later that evening after she slept with your father in the place of his usual mistress. Then years later, I used a vial of your blood you'd provided to Desiree to cause the cancer which you miraculously recovered from. And we both know about the River Boat bombing and how your daughter saved you by trying to kill herself. But you must believe me when I tell you that your father ended his own life because of the curse that *you* brought back. And you are destined to share the same fate."

Randy looked shell-shocked by Panama X's admissions. He opened and shut his mouth as he tried to process what he'd just heard. Finally, he managed, "You made me."

"No, Governor. Your anger and rage toward your father made you. Your cowardice and refusal to get your hands dirty made you. Trust me, I do understand why you want to direct your animosity toward me—we have been tied together for a long time. Believe me when I say I wish our paths had never crossed."

Unfortunately, what had begun as a plan to blackmail Randy had resulted in the deaths of Joseph Lafitte, Walter Simmons, Juanita Barber, Kristopher Lafitte, and now Amir. Destiny was an unforgiving road with a singular destination. It was time to send Randy Lafitte on his way.

"It will be over soon, Governor," Panama X said. He sucked in an immense amount of air and released a dark, cloud-like substance into Randy's face. Randy choked and clutched at his throat. Panama X watched Randy struggle to maintain control of his faculties. Of course, the skirmish was over before it even began. Panama X stood and walked around the table.

"By the end of this day, you will know my pain, Governor," he said. "Your punishment is just beginning."

Panama X snatched a strand of the Governor's hair, some dead skin, and a piece of thread from his blazer. Then he bent over and whispered in the man's ear. When he finished, he sat back down across from Lafitte.

"You came here begging for help, but all you did was sign your own death warrant. From the moment you leave this place, you will be completely vulnerable to attacks both spiritual and physical. Your strength is now my strength, and your weakness has been increased one-hundred-fold. I can see the shift in your aura."

Panama X smiled with satisfaction as the color drained from Randy's face. "When you awake, you will remember nothing. You will return to your Lake City home. And when the sun sets, you will take your own pitiful life. Nod if you hear me."

Randy's head went up and down.

"Good."

Now came the hard part. Panama X calmed his heart-rate. When it reached the desired rhythm, he uttered a guttural command.

Randy's face went from slack to livid. He jumped across the table and attacked. As they fell to the floor, Lafitte pummeled Panama X with his fists. He scratched Panama X's face and arms, biting his hands and neck.

Panama X did not resist or cover up.

Finally, Randy sat on his chest and clamped his hands around Panama X's throat.

Panama X looked at Randy. The man's face was a mask of rage, but his eyes were passionless.

Good.

The light in the room began to darken as the life was slowly squeezed out of his lungs.

Panama X visualized Juanita's face.

My duty to you is done, Juanita. It is time for me to embrace my destiny.

Before succumbing to the beckoning darkness, Panama X whispered another command. Then his body went limp.

"You've got to get out of here, Randy. I can't keep this quiet for long." George put his hand on his brother-in-law's shoulder.

Randy couldn't believe what he was seeing.

How did this happen?

Malcolm Wright lay motionless on the floor of the visitation chamber. His face had been bludgeoned.

Randy stared at his bloody knuckles.

Did I do this?

One second he was talking to Wright—the next he was sitting on the man's chest with his hands around his throat. After the initial disorientation, he called George from his cell phone.

"Randy, did you hear me? Get the hell out of here! I will cover for you."

"Thank you, George. I'm really sorry about this. He…he said some bad things about your sister. About my daughter. Then he attacked me. I had no choice. You believe me, right?"

George gave him a long, doubtful look and replied, "Of course, Randy. Now go home to your family."

The medical team arrived as Randy made his way out of the chamber. At first he thought the man had hope, but then Randy saw the haphazard way they threw the body onto the gurney. He glanced back at George and raised his eyebrows.

George gave a slight tilt of his head.

It was as bad as he'd feared. Panama X was dead.

CHAPTER FIFTY-SEVEN

US-61

Lincoln arrived at the intersection where Tunica Trace met US-61. He was at a crossroads. A right turn would take him into the eye of the storm. A left turn would lead somewhere else, to some other future.

I'm a free man. I could just head north and never look back.

Lincoln thought about Brandon locked up in the Lake City Police Department. He pictured Moses laid up in the Angola infirmary. He'd rather slit his wrists than abandon the only people who'd ever given a fuck about him. Lincoln gave one more glance toward the left and the sweet unknown. Then he turned right.

After a difficult hour and a half, his choice put him in the middle of a completely gridlocked highway. Cars packed to the hilt with suitcases, kids, and pets smothered I-10 West.

Where the fuck is everyone goin'?

A sign announced a rest stop ahead. It couldn't have come at a better time.

Lincoln struggled to remain conscious. Whatever Jhonnette had done to him had his body in a state of shock. She'd warned him that he might suffer a reaction to her healing. He had been stupid to trust her. She'd probably put some voodoo hex on him because, after all, she was Panama X's daughter.

He could see the rest area up ahead on the right, but the stalled traffic was not allowing him to get any closer to it.

Fuck this.

Lincoln pulled over onto the shoulder. A few seconds later, he parked crookedly next to a station wagon that had also pulled off the road. Most of his remaining strength had drained out of his body. Shivers overcame him, his heart beating weakly in his chest. He could barely keep his eyes open.

Jhonnette's parting words came back to him, *"I healed your physical wounds, Lincoln, but only you can heal your real scars."*

Lincoln closed his eyes and saw stars. Moments later, he was snoring loudly inside the Jeep.

CHAPTER FIFTY-EIGHT

Ten years earlier
1992
Lake City, LA

"Test, one two…can everybody out there hear me okay?" Principal Jefferson asked. "Great. Well, I'd like to thank you all for your prompt attendance this afternoon. Today is a momentous occasion for St. Louis Prep Academy, for Lake City, and for this young man seated to my right. Since joining us two years ago, Lincoln Baker has been a model student and athlete, helping to put the St. Louis Crusaders on the map. It's going to be tough next season without him, but we're happy to report that he's moving on to bigger and better things…"

Lincoln tried not to gawk at his principal, who hadn't spoken more than two words to him since he transferred to St. Louis Prep.

Moses' warning rang in Lincoln's head. *"Watch out for leeches, Son. You can't walk through the woods without catching a few."*

Where was Moses? Panic descended over Lincoln the closer it got to his turn to speak. All of the saliva in his mouth had dried up. He rubbed his sweaty palms on the new Dockers slacks Lois had bought him for the occasion. His clip-on tie choked him. Sweat pooled in his armpits.

"Lincoln? Son?"

He glanced over at Principal Jefferson's clown-like face. Lincoln was supposed to say something, but needed water. Then he remembered the speech he and Moses had written together the night before. Pulling the neatly folded piece of notebook paper out of his pants pocket, he stepped up to the microphone and cleared his throat.

"Good afternoon, everybody." The microphone squawked loud feedback as the crowd stared back at him expectantly. Lincoln finally found Moses' face in the throng. Moses gave him a nod and a smile.

You can do this.

"I'm kinda nervous," Lincoln continued. "But here goes. This season was one of the best fuh me. Winnin' the state championship and everything. Plus, the education and support I've received from St. Louis has been great. I 'preciate everything everybody has done fuh me. Now it's time fuh me to give back. I've decided to skip college and declare myself fuh the NBA draft next month. I wanna play against the best and learn from the best and give back to my fam'ly and my city. That's all…"

Thirty minutes later, after dropping Moses off at church, Lincoln navigated Moses' Cadillac over to Simmons Park to pick up Brandon. Long gone were the cold sweats, dry mouth, and other symptoms of anxiety. He felt great.

In a few months he'd be in the NBA, and everything would change. Moses would quit his job and move with Lincoln to wherever he was drafted. He'd have more money than he could spend. His days of drug dealing, robbing, banging, and struggling would be a distant memory.

Lincoln would have to get used to being an overnight celebrity, but he could handle it, especially after all the shit he'd been through. He even envisioned reconciling with Kris; they were both rich now. Anything was possible on a day like this.

There were five entrances into the Village from Highway 14. Lincoln took the shortest route, turning right after the newly opened Shoney's. It was a straight shot to Simmons Park from there. He hoped Brandon would be on the lookout for him so he wouldn't have to get out of the car.

The kids always swarmed Lincoln whenever he came by. Not to mention old Mr. Diaz, the park manager, who acted as if Lincoln owed him something because he learned his game on the Simmons Park courts. Lincoln didn't like Brandon being around Diaz; there was something odd about the man.

Lincoln pulled up to the stop sign on the corner of Simmons Way and General Bradley. A police cruiser was stopped there also, making no effort to move. Lincoln had the right of way, but he stopped for an extra beat—he didn't need trouble with the po-po today. While he waited for the cruiser to move, Lincoln turned his attention to the small forest that bordered Simmons Park. He thought he saw movement in the woods. Staring hard into the dense foliage, he made out several figures creeping toward the outer edge.

The men moving through the forest appeared to be brandishing semi-automatic weapons.

What the hell?

Lincoln got out of the car, only to be slammed against the hood, cheek pressed to warm metal, arms pinned behind his back.

"What the fuck I do?"

The cop cast an anxious glance toward the park. "Shut the fuck up, Superstar."

Lincoln couldn't believe this shit; yet another white boy running around with a badge and a Napoleon complex. He was probably jealous a black man was going to make a come up and wanted to teach Lincoln a lesson.

Another police cruiser pulled up behind Moses' Cadillac, boxing Lincoln in.

"What we got here, Smitty?" the other cop asked, his hand resting lightly on his weapon.

As the second cop approached, someone clearly screamed from the park, "You…put the gun away!"

Bad shit was happening right behind them, but the cops were more concerned with fucking with Lincoln than stopping whatever was going down at the park.

Brandon's in danger.

Lincoln tried diplomacy one last time. "I tried to tell yo' pahtna here that somethin's goin' on ova' at the Park!"

"You know what, Boy? You're exactly right!" Smitty pulled out his Beretta and pointed it in Lincoln's face. "The question is… what are you gonna do about it?"

"Smitty," the other cop said, "let's throw him in the back of the cruiser. This shit is about to go down."

Smitty glanced at his partner.

Lincoln took advantage of the man's momentary distraction and grabbed the barrel of Smitty's gun. As his hand touched steel, a peace descended over him like everything that had happened in his life—the hunger, loneliness, abandonment, orphanages, foster families, group homes, juvenile detention centers, gang initiation, and years with Moses—had led to this.

He twisted Smitty's arm downward, along with the weapon. Smitty's wrist snapped like a dry twig. He howled with pain and released the gun.

Lincoln pointed the gun at the other cop.

A lone gunshot rang out from the park like the start of a one-hundred-meter dash.

Someone screamed, "Stop fighting! Can't you see? You're being set up! This is exactly what they want!"

Lincoln recognized Kris Lafitte's voice.

The second cop reached for his gun. Before Lincoln realized what he was going to do, he pulled the trigger. The cop's hand exploded in a mess of blood, skin, and bone.

Smitty was trying to crawl back to his car. Lincoln put a bullet in the back of each of his legs.

In the distance, several guns boomed in response.

Lincoln ran across the street into a warzone. A rush of wetness on his cheeks made him wonder if it had started raining, until he realized the moisture came from the tears streaming from his eyes.

CHAPTER FIFTY-NINE

Flying over Baton Rouge en route to Lake City

Randy looked down on the Capitol building from the air, numb all over. He couldn't get Malcolm Wright's death mask out of his head, no matter how hard he tried. To top it off, Larry was also M.I.A, which had to mean he was in cahoots with Snake. Everything was coming undone and the blank spots in his memory were driving him mad. Even through his bout with brain cancer, he'd managed to fully maintain his mental faculties. What had happened at the prison was eerily reminiscent of another time he'd blacked out.

"Governor? Governor. Are you listening to me?"

Randy blinked hard. He stared down at the starfish-shaped speakerphone in the middle of the console. Several key members of his staff were on the line for one massive conference call—his Assistant Chief of Staff, the Chief of Homeland Security, and the Public Safety, Social Services, Transportation, and Development Chairs, as well as the mayors of Lake City, Lafayette, and Baton Rouge.

"This is unacceptable, Governor," the voice of Lake City's mayor yelped at him through the speaker. Randy calmly reached toward the speakerphone and pressed a button to unmute the phone.

"I'll tell you what's unacceptable, Mayor Robiceaux," Randy began. "I've been hearing about the mess you're making over there. If I've told you once, I've told you a million times—you're a goddamned Mayor! In times of crisis, you have the power and authority to make decisions under the Pelican Ordinance. You don't need to hear from this office. All of you have been sitting around twiddling your thumbs for two days now. Two goddamn days! That's forty-eight hours we've lost where a significant number of citizens could have been evacuated."

"Governor, that's not completely accurate—"

"Listen to me, goddamnit! This situation has reached a crisis point and I, for one, am tired of your excuses. As of this moment, all of your authority and power returns to this office. You've lost your chance to do something. I'm giving the orders now. But rest assured, the blame for this calamity—and trust me, we're talking about a calamity of biblical proportions here, will rest squarely on each of your shoulders!"

Several voices chimed in at once. "What do we do now?"

"Either get on the road to higher ground with your constituents, or learn how to swim. That's all." Randy pushed the disconnect button and sat back in his seat. A thin line of spittle rolled down his chin. He wiped it away with the back of his hand. He may have lost control of his personal situation, but he was still the boss around here.

The speakerphone rang twice before he picked it up.

"Sir," a voice he recognized as his Chair of Transportation ventured. "Sir, what just happened?"

"In France, I believe it's known as a cluster-fuck. Now please excuse me." Randy hung up again. Tightness in his chest and shortness of breath assaulted him. Randy had friends who'd suffered heart attacks. They'd described the onset as a little guy in your back playing the accordion with your lungs and heart. That sounded about right.

The helicopter cabin was collapsing. His hands were clammy. His tie was a python around his throat and he couldn't catch his breath.

He banged on the divider between him and the pilot in a panic. The pilot needed to land so he could get out of this chopper before it was too late. His heart thudded in his ears. He was seeing everything through a reddish glaze.

Why isn't the pilot responding?

Randy fell over, staring helplessly at the pilot's cabin. The pilot wasn't alone. Another man sat beside him.

Randy looked up into a long-forgotten face. The old man wore a straw hat slightly cocked back on his forehead. Randy blinked.

The dead man was still staring at him.

James Diaz smiled at Randy. "Won't be long before you join me, Governor. Payback's a comin' for the raw deal you gave me..."

CHAPTER SIXTY

Ten years earlier
1992
Lake City, LA

Randy sat at his desk in the Lake City Senatorial office across from James Diaz, the park manager from Simmons Park. He studied the piece of paper the older black man had just handed to him.

"So you finally got it done," Randy said, after reading the one-page agreement in its entirety. The document was a peace treaty signed by the leaders of Lake City's two most notorious gangs, the Dirty Skulls and the Seville Scorpions. Among other things, it stipulated that Simmons Park was officially a cease-fire zone.

"Yessiree. Them boys want ta do tha right thing."

"Well, you're doing the right thing, too. When it's all said and done you're going to be a wealthy man, Mr. Diaz."

The old man shifted in his seat. His eyesore of a tie was going in two different directions across his short-sleeved, button-down shirt. Randy could smell the desperation oozing from his pores.

"Is there something else you want to get off your chest?"

Diaz looked up, unsure of himself, but finally said, "Why do it have to happen during the week? We could 'complish tha same thing on Satuhday, right?"

Randy stared back blankly.

"I mean, there's gonna be kids out there that day. I don't want nuthin' to happen ta my...ta them babies. You unnerstand?"

Randy offered a thin smile as he said, "You and I have a deal, Mr. Diaz. As you know, until the park is officially shut down and condemned, I can't repossess the land. No land equals no casino. No casino equals no money for me and my friends. And it certainly means big problems for you. Do you want problems?"

"Well I—"

"Well what, Mr. Diaz? You're in too deep to start second-guessing now. If you back out, your career and your life will be over." Randy unfastened the top of a manila folder sitting on his desk. He slid the contents across the table.

He watched as Diaz examined the photos with an expression of bewildered fury. The photos depicted Diaz in compromising situations with several young boys. Randy's father had taught him a lot about negotiating. The chief lesson was, dirt was the best bargaining chip when negotiating.

Mr. Diaz looked up with tears brimming. "So now you blackmailin' me?"

"Call it what you like, Mr. Diaz. I like to think of it as insurance. We wouldn't want Mrs. Diaz to find out why you love your job so much, now would we? All you've got to do is make sure both gangs arrive at the designated time. We'll take care of the rest. You're doing such a valuable service here...ridding your community of ruthless killers and opening the door for a casino that's going to bring jobs and prosperity to the city. You should feel good about that..."

Later that evening, Randy stood before Lake Francis shooting skeet—his favorite pastime between hunting seasons. He was focused on pulling, tracking, and shooting.

Two up, two down. Let's go for three. Pull. Track—

"Dad?"

Randy wheeled around, shotgun pointed at the intruder's head.

Kristopher's eyes were wide with fear, his hands raised in a defensive gesture, like a common thief caught red-handed at the coffers. That damn Sony recorder Coral had bought him for earning A's in his AP classes was cupped in the palm of his bruised right hand. Kristopher's face was still swollen and discolored from the scuffle he'd gotten into playing basketball yesterday.

"Goddamnit, Kris! How many times have I warned you not to sneak up on me while I'm shooting. Huh? How many goddamn times?"

"You gonna shoot me, Dad?"

Randy was still pointing the gun at his son's head. He lowered it to his side.

Kristopher looked down at his shoes, took a deep breath, and then looked up again. He had his grandfather's piercing blue eyes—a hereditary trait that almost got him smothered in his crib.

"You want to talk so bad you had to come out here and interrupt. So talk!"

"This was a bad idea..."

He had his mother's sensitivity to boot. "No. I apologize, Kristopher. It's been a long day. Let's start over. What's on your mind, Son?" Randy's eyes flicked back to the tape recorder. He didn't really want to hear what his son had to say, and was annoyed when Kristopher started talking.

"Dad, what's going on at Simmons Park?"

"I don't know what you're talking about."

"I'm just trying to understand. I've been recording your conversations for a week now, and today, I heard you blackmailing that old black man, the caretaker of the park..."

Speechless, Randy examined the man-child before him. Just yesterday they'd celebrated Kristopher's eighteenth birthday. He'd taken his son out for a round of golf and at the end of the day they'd gone down to the Elks Lodge and talked over a couple of beers. Kristopher was supposed to go to LSU. Become a lawyer. Follow in his old man's footsteps. Shit, go farther.

Kristopher could have been president, but he had to stick his nose where it didn't belong. It grieved him to admit it, but by the time his son finished speaking, Randy's mind had already conjured up a strategy to keep Kristopher quiet for good.

CHAPTER SIXTY-ONE

Monday
Lake City, LA

Karen couldn't move. Her muscles weren't responding to her commands to sit up, get up, and get out of Uncle Bill's office inside the Lake City Police Department's main branch. Even stranger, she'd been hearing soft drums keeping time in her head. The drums reminded her of something. Something she desperately needed to remember.

Say hey!

Flashes of the Penguin came back to her. The delicious feeling that came after the needles, as her cares floated away. The odd sexual encounter with Shorty. The blood that came after. Nearly being run over.

Seven stabs of the knife, seven stabs of the sword.

Big salty tears dropped from her eyes. Karen hadn't felt this helpless since Kristopher's death. She had a sense that her brother was very close to her. She closed her eyes, letting her mind wander back to those dark days.

Karen was tormented by horrific nightmares after Kristopher's burial. She'd see his bloody corpse in her closet and hear his feet thudding about in his bedroom. She started avoiding sleep altogether; then the visions started torturing her days as well.

It was her father's idea to send her to Dr. Gerard Faustus, the child psychiatrist of choice for Lake City's affluent. Faustus offered psychiatric immersion to cure everything from early signs of homosexual behavior to eating disorders. Even at her young age, Karen had heard horror stories of normal kids going to Dr. Faustus and morphing into blabbering lunatics locked inside padded chambers where no one could hear their screams.

Her father drove her there that first and only time. It was one of the few moments of her childhood where she could remember being alone with him. She idealized her father and it was easy to understand why. He was tall and strong, with a laugh that could make anyone smile. When he looked at her, it was like staring in the mirror.

He could also be playful, but that day he was sullen and brooding. Karen begged him not to leave her there alone, but he just kissed her forehead and turned her over to a smiling female attendant.

After checking in with a pretty, dark-haired receptionist, another attendant led Karen down a dark, narrow hallway lined with doors. Each psychiatrist's domain had a nameplate identifying him or her. A much wider door with no nameplate stood at the end of the hallway. The other doors were painted white, but this last entrance was a deep brown mahogany.

It looked like the kind of portal that people got lost behind.

The attendant rapped on the door. After a brief moment, it opened. The room that revealed itself turned out to be far less imposing. Several bookcases lined the wall closest to her. Child psychology books with titles like "Speaking to Children So They

Hear You" and "Adolescent Depression" lined the bookshelves. Against the opposite wall was a steel square that Karen recognized as a vault. Artificial light emanated from an ornate crystal chandelier hanging in the center of the room. There were no windows.

A slim man with a gaunt face and dark hair stared at her through black, passionless eyes. He sat at a modern desk underneath an inkblot mural that seemed to shift as Karen looked at it.

Karen turned to run back the way she came but the attendant blocked her way. The attendant carried her into the room against her will, and seated her in a high, straight back chair, built to put her eye level with Dr. Faustus.

He smiled. "So," he spoke in a firm yet boyish voice. "What do you think of the place?" Karen shrugged.

"It's the mural, isn't it? You saw something that scared you?"

She looked at the painting above his head. The inkblot now resembled a giant sea turtle.

"Tell me...what do you see, Karen?"

She was too confused to speak.

"This is a magic painting, Karen. You do like magic, don't you?"

She nodded and thought of Kristopher's obsession with magic. He had loved pulling tricks on people. Cold sweat accumulated in the cups of her underarms despite the robust air conditioning.

"Your brother wasn't scared when he was here visiting me."

She looked back at him in surprise.

"What? Daddy didn't tell you that Kristopher and I were friends? For shame. He was a bit older than you are now when he came to see me. How old are you, Karen?"

"Sev...seven." Her words came out in a low whisper.

"Ahhh…yes, seven. You're too young to die, Karen. Just like your brother. He thought he was saving you. Yet here you are getting weaker by the moment. It's the sending of the dead, you see. Oh, how I will enjoy seeing Kristopher again."

The vault burst open.

Karen looked into the vault's black maul and saw hell.

Faustus was right next to her. He grabbed her by the shoulders and pushed her chair toward the vault.

Karen struggled mightily while he chanted an oddly familiar song:
Say hey!
Seven stabs of the knife, seven stabs of the sword.
Hand me that basin, I'm going to vomit blood.
Seven stabs of the knife, seven stabs of the sword.
Hand me that basin, I'm going to vomit blood.
Hand me that basin, I'm going to vomit blood.
But the blood is marked for him.

Karen was in the vault, surrounded by the overpowering stench of death. The walls inside the vault were lined with shelves flush with the decapitated heads of children. Their purple-black tongues lolled from petrified faces. She tried to get up from her chair, but she was petrified, too.

All the while Faustus continued chanting:
I say hey! I'm going to vomit blood, it's true.
Seven stabs of the knife, seven stabs of the sword.
Hand me that basin, I'm going to vomit blood.
Hand me that basin, I'm going to vomit blood.
My blood is flowing, Dantò, I'm going to vomit blood.
My blood is flowing, Ezili, I'm going to vomit blood.
My blood is flowing, Karen, you're going to vomit blood.

Faustus's face shifted into that of a bald-headed black man with a compassionate face. The man looked genuinely sorry for what was taking place. Then the door slammed shut.

Karen opened her eyes. She was back in Uncle Bill's office. Her stomach twisted and tightened as her abdomen expanded almost to the splitting point. She opened her mouth to scream and instead emitted a solid stream of putrescent blood and bile that coated the ceiling. Her eyes bulged from their sockets like round, white solitaires.

She vomited until she couldn't see the white ceiling paint anymore. Until she couldn't breathe or feel anything except for the acid-filled corridor where her esophagus and throat used to be. Until she became one with the darkness inside her.

Jeff Abshire had to find out what was going on in his precinct. And the answer was a door away. All he had to do was open it and look inside.

If Chief Edwards catches me, I'm fucked.

That left Jeff with one option. *Don't get caught.*

Using a lock pick kit, he worked on the knob to the chief's door. After jimmying it a few times, it came open.

A wet, coppery smell wafted out into the hallway. His eyes watered as he wrinkled his nose.

What died in here?

The answer became clear once his eyes settled on the Chief's tattered couch. Karen Lafitte lay on her back, eyes wide open, choking on her own bloody vomit.

Christ!

Jeff rushed into the room and quickly turned the girl on her side. He slapped her back, gently at first and then harder until she coughed away the remaining regurgitation.

It was like the exorcist in here.

What could have caused this type of eruption?

Karen's eyes opened and focused on him. One of her irises was hazel and the other was a sharp, shocking blue.

Is that natural?

"Karen, it's gonna be alright," Jeff reassured her. "I'm gonna get you some help. We're gonna get you outta here. Hold tight."

Jeff left her on her side, realizing that the only person who might be able to explain what was going on was the black kid. It was time for some answers.

CHAPTER SIXTY-TWO

Ten years earlier
1992
Lake City, LA

B randon opened his eyes. Shorty was staring at him. "Hey ya, Brandon. 'Bout time you woke up."

Brandon sat up on his floor mat and looked around the gym. Most of the other kids were asleep. Mr. Diaz was standing near the gym doors speaking in heated whispers with Miss Beatrice, the after-school program supervisor. He looked in their direction and Brandon quickly ducked back into a sleeping position.

Why the hell were they having nap time anyhow? Hadn't they stopped that last year? Usually at this time, he and the other kids were outside playing dodge ball, baseball, or basketball. But when the bus dropped them off in front of the park today, Miss Beatrice was there waiting for them. She quickly ushered the children into the gym, as she did on days when it looked like rain. But there wasn't a cloud in sight.

How long have I been asleep? Lincoln was supposed to pick him up early for tee ball practice.

"Brandon...Bran?" Shorty tapped him on the shoulder.

"Yeah, Shorty?"

"I'm tired of layin' here. Let's go outside and play."

Brandon should have seen this coming. His friend was incapable of obeying the rules. "We'll catch a whuppin' for sure if we do that."

"Not if everybody goes."

"How?"

"Through the back," Shorty answered, gesturing toward the double doors in the back of the gym.

"What about the alarm?"

"Broken," Shorty replied. He snaked over to the back wall and pushed one door open. Brandon held his breath waiting for the alarms to shriek, but they didn't. Still, something was telling him not to go outside. He attempted one last excuse. "Miss Beatrice is makin' cookies."

"Don't nobody want them hard-ass cookies."

"Okay," Brandon replied, giving in. He looked around one last time for Mr. Diaz, but he was no longer in the gym. After giving Shorty the all clear, they crept from mat to mat waking up all of the kids, pressing their index fingers to their lips so everyone would keep quiet.

Once everyone was awake, Brandon took over the operation. He bubbled with the excitement of doing something wrong and possibly getting away with it. Lincoln, Mr. Diaz, and even Miss Beatrice, were the furthest things from his mind.

He got all the kids lined up and told them to wait for the signal. Then he and Shorty led everyone outside as quietly as they could. Brandon made it to the jungle gym in record time. A second later, Shorty tapped him on the shoulder.

Shorty pointed at the basketball court. Mr. Diaz was talking to an older boy Brandon had seen somewhere before.

"That's Murda," Shorty whispered in admiration.

Brandon knew Murda was the leader of the Dirty Skulls, which meant the other boys with him must've been the rest of the gang— except for Lincoln. Lincoln never spoke of his gang days, but Shorty had told him all he needed to know. Brandon recognized Shorty's older brother, Stacie, standing next to Murda. The wind carried faint snatches from the conversation, but not enough to piece together what was being said.

"Ole Pooh Butt looks nervous," Shorty whispered in Brandon's ear.

Normally, Shorty's nickname for Mr. Diaz would crack Brandon up, but not today. Something just didn't seem right.

Mr. Diaz abruptly turned his back and walked away from Murda and the gang, with Murda yelling at him. The other Dirty Skulls were laughing. Then someone called out to Murda from the fence.

It was a white kid. Kris something. Brandon knew him better as number forty from Lincoln's basketball team. What was he doing here?

"Oh shit, they got guns!" Shorty shouted.

The Skulls pulled out weapons from the front of their pants as the white boy approached. A lump of fear grew in Brandon's throat. Something very bad was about to happen.

His friend Jennifer gripped his hand and pulled him away from the crowd of eager kids, back toward the gymnasium. When the shooting started, it came as suddenly as a summer rainstorm.

CHAPTER SIXTY-THREE

Monday
Lake City, LA

"Wake up, Brandon. Wake up!" Brandon snapped out of unconsciousness. He looked up into the face of the young officer who'd been interrogating him, Jeff Abshire. The cop's face was flushed and he was out of breath. He stared at Brandon with a crazy gleam in his eyes.

"Okay, kid. No more games. I'm gonna ask you one question and if you lie to me, I'm gonna kick your ass, lock you up, and throw away the key." He paused to take a deep breath. "What the hell is wrong with the Governor's daughter? What did you do to her?"

Brandon studied Officer Jeff's strained face. There was a fifty-fifty chance the man would actually believe him. "I didn't do anything. We're both victims here. I'm the one who saved her..." Brandon recounted the morning's events as faithfully as he could remember them.

Once Brandon finished telling the story, Officer Jeff blinked for what seemed like the first time since bursting into the cell. "Okay, kid. I believe you. Somebody in here doesn't want you talking, but you're the only witness I've got. I've got a deal for you. I'm gonna help you get out of here, and you're gonna help me put away the bastards that are tearing our city apart. Deal?" Brandon nodded. "Get up and follow me."

"Is she okay?" Brandon whispered to Officer Jeff, as they made their way down a corridor lined with holding cells.

"She's alive. Now shut the hell up. You're supposed to be a dangerous killer."

I'm out of the net and into the barrel.

Officer Jeff escorted him through a throng of officers and inmates. Brandon wondered if this was a trick designed to further implicate him by making it seem like he'd tried to escape. Unfortunately, Brandon didn't have many other options. It was either trust this man, or go back to his cell and wait for the Chief to finish the job.

As if sensing Brandon's unease, Officer Jeff whispered, "We've just got a little farther to go."

They emerged into the central containment area where they'd fingerprinted and photographed Brandon hours earlier. There were cops everywhere. Brandon couldn't distinguish friend from foe.

"Keep your head down no matter what. Just keep your feet moving."

Brandon did as he was told. Even if he got out of here, he would be living on borrowed time. No matter how he spun it, without the girl to prove his innocence, he'd be replacing Lincoln in Angola.

CHAPTER SIXTY-FOUR

Ten years earlier
1992
Lake City, LA

Lincoln's mind was gone and he was glad. He gripped the cop's gun tighter. There was no time to think. Killing was the only thing that made sense.

Running to the park, his mind's eye saw everything with the cold calculation of an assassin. The Dirty Skulls stood in a semicircle around half court, shooting across the park at the men Lincoln had seen coming out of the woods. Lincoln veered toward the second group of adolescents he recognized as Scorpions by their black t-shirts.

Then, he saw the children clustered around the jungle gym. Everything started moving faster.

Lincoln hopped the fence and charged across the field as bullets whizzed by his head. He caught a Scorpion by surprise and shot him in the back.

Grabbing the kid's piece, Lincoln raised both guns and started blasting, cutting down one Scorpion, then two, then three. His left gun jammed so he dove onto the grass to take cover. Then he saw Kris duck down behind a park bench.

One of the Scorpions pointed his gun at Kris. Lincoln took aim and shot the Scorpion in the chest. With kids out here, he couldn't afford to miss. So he didn't.

Unfortunately, he wasn't the only one shooting.

More cops arrived and opened fire on everyone. Helicopters flew overhead.

A bullet grazed Lincoln's forehead and knocked him off his feet. He landed on top of another gun. Good. He shot at the black t-shirts from the ground. When he ran out of black t-shirts, he shot at cops. He pushed forward, crawling over bodies. He had to make it to Kris and Brandon.

He reached the basketball court, just a few feet away from his friend. Murda and the other Skulls had fallen back to the gymnasium and most of the Scorpions had congregated around the jungle gym. Kris stared at Lincoln and tried to get up, completely unaware of the Scorpion rounding the tree behind him.

As Lincoln aimed at the Scorpion and pulled the trigger, a bullet fired from somewhere behind Lincoln pierced his shoulder, throwing off his aim. Lincoln's bullet passed through Kris's midsection, pinning Kris against the tree. The bullet that hit Lincoln spun him around. He locked eyes with a rugged-looking white man with long gray hair.

Out of the corner of his eye, he saw a grinning Scorpion moving in to finish Kris off. Lincoln charged across the court, oblivious to the crossfire. He painted the tree trunk grayish-red with the Scorpion's brain and skull fragments. Kris was gasping for air as Lincoln reached him. Lincoln stared at Kris's stomach in disbelief. There was so much blood. Kris reached up and pulled Lincoln toward him.

"Shh...don't talk."

Sirens filled the air around them.

Kris smiled and blood dribbled down his chin. His eyes shot up over Lincoln's shoulder.

Lincoln turned and put a bullet through a Scorpion no older than thirteen. He grabbed the gun from the kid's hand and looked around. The helicopters were still there, but most of the cops were down, or calling for more backup. Black boys dressed in red and black littered the park. All dead?

Desperate hands tugged his shirt.

"Isaac?"

Lincoln turned back to his friend and said, "Kris! Stay wit' me, bruh! Stay wit' me!"

"Can't. Hurts. Breathe."

"I know, Kris. Helps on the way, man. Just hold on. Please."

"I'm...ready."

"No you're not, Kris! You're not going anywhere."

"Will...Karen be safe now?"

"Stop talkin', Kris. You wastin' too much energy."

"Melinda...Weeps!"

"Just relax, Kris...you ain't makin no sense, just relax."

"Cursed," Kris gasped. He slumped over.

"Kris?" Lincoln shook him. "Kris!"

Kris stared past Lincoln, past pain, past life.

Something wet caressed Lincoln's ear. He looked up to see Murda standing over him with blood dripping down his right arm. Another gun blasted and Lincoln was bathed in his gang brother's blood. Murda fell on top of Lincoln and Kris, the three of them locked in an embrace of death.

Lincoln remembered Brandon. His strength waning, he threw Murda off him and got back to his feet. More cops had arrived. Lincoln grabbed a gun off another dead body and started blasting. How many dead? He'd lost count. Only the living counted.

He couldn't locate Brandon, and now there were too many police and not enough Skulls. Lincoln stood at half court, his clip-on tie swung over his shoulder, his powder blue, button down Oxford and khaki Dockers covered with blood. The police surrounded him and ordered him to drop his weapon. Why didn't they just shoot?

Kris was right, I am cursed.

Lincoln put the gun in his mouth and squeezed the trigger. Click. Click-click. Click-click-click. Empty—

Then they were on him, beating him with clubs, guns, fists, and feet. He didn't resist. From the ground, he stared at Kris's startling blue eyes glaring back at him. As he passed out, he envied Kris. Sometimes death was a gift...

CHAPTER SIXTY-FIVE

Tap.
Tap-tap.

Lincoln opened his eyes.

Someone was tapping on the windshield. Lincoln rolled his sore neck and stared into the eyes of a dead man. Kris grinned down at him like a lunatic.

Kris had a billy club in his hand and started hammering against the windshield.

Lincoln flinched and closed his eyes. When he opened them again, Kris was gone. Something was still tapping on the windshield, however. There were also loud metallic plongs. The Jeep vibrated as large chunks of ice battered the car from all directions. The rational part of him wondered how in the hell it could be hailing in Louisiana.

Lincoln sat up in the seat, groaning from the effort. His butt was asleep and he was sore in muscles he never even knew he had.

Plong-plong!

Ice bashed the Jeep. Then, crack! A spiderweb formed in the upper right-hand corner of the windshield after a baseball-sized chunk of ice exploded there. It sounded like a firing squad was shooting at the car.

Outside, people ran for cover.

Lincoln expected the hail to slack off, but after another few minutes, it grew in intensity. His instinct was to dive into the backseat and ride it out, but as his body awakened, so did his bladder. If he didn't make a move soon, he would urinate on himself.

Finally, the storm calmed down a bit. Lincoln tucked Jhonnette's gun into the waistband of his hospital pants, grabbed the car keys, and opened the door. He limped from the Jeep to the Quick Stop rest area in bare feet. His bladder kept him from returning to the vehicle.

At least it wasn't as packed now as when he'd first parked. Highway traffic was moving quite nicely.

How long was I out?

He entered the convenience store and swiped three boxes of Band-Aids, aspirin, and a bottle of peroxide from the shelves. Slipping into the restroom, he relieved his bladder's burden, and then focused on his wounds.

The hospital had done a nice job dressing him, but there was some leakage from the bandages on his shoulder, right bicep, and left thigh. He poured the peroxide on his wounds and placed fresh Band-Aids over the bullet holes. Then, he re-dressed them with the hospital bandages. Lincoln swallowed a handful of aspirin. The ribs on his left side were still tender from his fall off the ferry that morning.

For the first time since all the craziness back at Angola, he was sure his injuries weren't fatal. Jhonnette really had healed him. Lincoln didn't dwell on this miracle too long, however, because he realized he was starving. Another good sign.

He looked around and saw a pizza place, Baskin-Robbins, Burger King, Popeye's, and Starbucks. What the hell was a Starbucks?

His mouth salivated, as he smelled the wonderful aromas of fried chicken and fresh biscuits. But like an idiot he'd left the money Jhonnette gave him back in the Jeep.

Damnit!

Lincoln burst out into the rain. He was halfway to the Jeep when he saw Snake Roberts step out of a dark blue Crown Victoria parked two cars down. Vertigo gripped him as Snake's present-day image merged with the younger version of him Lincoln remembered encountering that day at Simmons Park. It had been Snake's bullet that caused Lincoln to shoot Kris!

Lincoln ducked behind a small compact car.

Did they spot me?

Snake walked right past his hiding spot, clearly in some pain.

We must have hurt him worse than I thought.

Lincoln's head swam as he tried to maintain focus on the present.

At least I've got this gun.

He glanced through the driver's side window and saw two other men getting out of the Crown Vic. One man was huge, bald-headed, and ugly. The other man was younger, with long, shoulder-length dark hair. Neither man looked like they were here for a potty break.

How did they track me here?

He and Jhonnette had left Roberts hog-tied in the recovery room, sure the police would have picked him up by now. It was either dumb luck that they had ended up in the same place at the same time, or they had some sort of tracking device in Jhonnette's car. On the other hand, maybe Jhonnette had double-crossed him.

Was that why she'd agreed so willingly to his plan?

Lincoln's ears perked up as the men moved closer to his position. They didn't even look at the Jeep as they passed it, confusing Lincoln even more. He had the gun in his palm now. His index finger flirted with the trigger.

He could rise up and put bullets through each of their heads before they took their next step, but something told him to wait and see. Snake growled something that sounded like, "Where is she?" But he couldn't have heard that right. He'd probably said, "Where is he?"

Lincoln peeked out from behind the car and saw they were carrying their pieces as openly as he was.

Then he heard, "There she is!" The younger man took off running toward the facility where Lincoln saw Kris Lafitte's mother, Coral, filling up a white Ford Taurus.

They're after her? Why?

Lincoln watched in amazement as the younger man called out to Coral. She turned, eyes growing wide as she saw who was calling her. She pulled out a huge gun.

What the fuck is this, the Wild Wild West?

Coral squeezed the trigger but nothing happened.

The young man took one shot. Coral swatted at her neck and then collapsed.

Lincoln looked around. Amazingly, he was the only person watching this go down. Roberts and Big Bald Ugly humped it double time back to the Crown Vic. The young man put Coral in the passenger seat of her own car, replaced the gas nozzle, and got into the driver's seat. Then both cars took off.

Lincoln's instincts told him to follow them. He ran back to the Jeep.

You're not getting away from me this time, Snake.

CHAPTER SIXTY-SIX

Lake City, LA

"Governor Lafitte? Can you hear me Governor?"

Randy opened his eyes and blinked hard to clear his vision. "Where am I?" he asked through a mouthful of sludge.

"You're home."

Randy sat up and saw his Lake City mansion looming over the chopper.

"I apologize for the turbulence," the pilot said. "This hurricane is a tricky one. It's turned again and is picking up speed and heading toward Lake City. I know you told me to drop you at the LCPD, but there's a riot going on down there. Chief Edwards said he'd bring Karen over as soon as he can. I hope that's okay."

Randy tried to process the pilot's words. The hurricane was headed to Lake City? Karen was still at the LCPD? People were rioting?

He watched Melinda Weeps come alive in the foreground as the wind whipped through the leaves. There appeared to be an ominous red aura surrounding the tree.

"Will you need me for anything else, Governor? I've got to get this chopper back to Baton Rouge before it's too late."

Randy got out of the helicopter transfixed, by the glowing tree in his yard. As the chopper lifted off, he reflected on the pilot's words. Things were finally starting to make sense. Isaac was tracking him, though he couldn't tell if it was Isaac the hurricane or the slave Luc Lafitte had hung from the branches of Melinda Weeps. Not that it mattered.

What mattered was that his father had actually killed himself that night. And Randy had sacrificed his own son's life to this godforsaken curse as well. Karen would not suffer the same fate. It was time to end this. Randy strode toward his home, knowing what had to be done.

CHAPTER SIXTY-SEVEN

Angola, LA

The Louisiana State Penitentiary complex was a study in organized confusion. But that was prison. Jhonnette was just happy she wasn't outside in the stifling heat like the inmates she'd seen working the expansive fields.

Who needs a time machine? All I ever needed to know about slavery is right here.

She walked into the Reception Center, a small building set up like an airport security checkpoint. It was empty except for two guards. "Where is everybody?" she asked. "What's going on?"

"Big storm's comin'."

They x-rayed and searched her belongings. The guard took extra pleasure in patting her down.

"You should get a job at the airport," she said to the guard as he disassembled her laptop bag and purse. "Terrorists wouldn't stand a chance against you."

The guard smirked, giving sign of an actual human heart beating beneath that navy blue uniform.

Jhonnette desperately tried to distract him from finding the note Lincoln had told her to get to a trustee named Bishop.

"He'll be the old, toothless, bald guy sweeping up around there," Lincoln had said. *"All you have to do is make sure the guard doesn't find this note. For your sake, I hope it's Combs' day off. He is one meticulous motherfucker."*

Unless Combs made her pull down her panties, he'd never find the note. Lincoln was right though, this guy wasn't messing around.

"So what's the deal with this storm?" she asked the more relaxed guard at the confiscation desk. He was staring at her as if she were a T-bone at a backyard barbecue.

"It's Category Four right now, or whatever that means. Prob'ly gonna hit close to Baton Rouge sometime tonight."

"What if it comes this way?" she asked.

"Warden has to make that call. Evacuating five thousand killers ain't no easy task, you feel me?"

"I can imagine."

"No, you cain't," a thin voice said from behind her.

Jhonnette turned and faced an older black man about her height. His head was bald, his eyes yellow and jaundiced. After looking her over for a second, he revealed a toothless grin.

"Had us a big stohm a coupla yers back, maybe twinty yers ago. Warden dint evacuate. Quite a few of da boys in her drount."

"Shut up and go on ahead with that crap, Bishop," the guard replied.

Bishop gave the man a cursory glance and focused on Jhonnette. "You shouldn't even be her," he warned. "Dis stohm gonna make dat un look like a summa drizzle."

"Really? Wow." If he was right, Jhonnette would be trapped inside a prison during a hurricane with thousands of crazed lunatics. Still, she wasn't fazed.

Panama X will protect me.

Other than the letters between her mother and Malcolm Wright, Jhonnette had no physical evidence to prove he was her father. But she'd known the moment she'd seen him during the River Boat bombings trial that they were blood, and when Panama X saw her, he would know, too.

It was clear from her mother's letters that she thought him a great man. There had been no angry or bitter messages — just undying faith that he would one day return to her.

Jhonnette would bring him home. Right after she neutralized Moses Mouton.

"Hey," she said, turning back to the guard. "How much longer?"

"Any minute now, Boo. Warden's just finishing up a meeting."

"Can I, you know…is there a bathroom in here?"

"It's right ova heah, Miss," Bishop replied. He pointed toward a bland brick wall.

Jhonnette quickly stashed a pen in her pocket before the guard took her things. The door had no lock on the inside; she figured she had about five minutes before the guards came knocking. She unzipped her skirt, revealing pink panties that covered the note, warm from her body heat. She transposed the message onto the toilet paper.

She was ushered into the warden's office twenty minutes later. He sat behind a modest desk, poring over a series of maps.

The warden greeted her with a look of unguarded lust. "Well, hello there," he said, clearing his throat. "What can I do for you?"

She took a seat. "What have you got there?" she asked, pointing at the maps.

"Oh these? These are just some things I'm working on. Not important. Now what can I do for you again, Miss—"

"Mouton. Jhonnette Mouton. I drove up from Lake City to see about my father, Moses."

"Well, it looks like you picked a decent day to get out of the city."

"What's that supposed to mean?"

The warden smirked. "Take a look-see at this here satellite photo." He slid a map-sized photo across his desk.

It was a diagram depicting the size and projected path of Hurricane Isaac. A deep feeling of unease settled into the pit of her belly. The storm was on a collision course for Lake City. Was this Amir's doing as well?

"Oh," was all she managed.

"Oh shit, you mean?"

"Yeah."

"Now, Miss Mouton, my time is very short. You said you were Moses Mouton's daughter?"

"That's right. How is he?"

The warden crossed his arms over his chest. "He's being treated in the hospital as we speak."

"When can I visit him?"

"I'm terribly sorry, Miss Mouton, but I can't allow that. My assistant will contact you after your father has been moved. It is not safe for you to be in the prison. Some of these animals would love nothing more than to rape a pretty girl like you. So, once again, I'm saying this as nice as I possibly can, you need to leave."

Jhonnette and Lincoln had discussed the high likelihood she would get kicked out of the prison without seeing Moses. But

Jhonnette was not easily deterred. The warden was no match for her powers of persuasion.

Jhonnette locked into the warden's eyes and pushed a thought at him: *This will become a public relations nightmare.*

Next, she amplified his anxiety, showing him the National Guard swarming into the prison, taking over as thousands of angry citizens, screamed for his resignation.

The warden flinched as the thoughts flew at him. His pupils dilated as the images played in his mind's eye.

"Warden, I'm not going to take no for an answer," Jhonnette said emphatically. "I know people. Important people. People who can make life difficult for you. Neither of us wants that, right?" She smiled sweetly. "I want to see my father. Now."

Minutes later, Jhonnette stepped out of his office, escorted by a young prison guard. As they walked toward the infirmary, a sudden image flashed of Panama X being zipped up in a body bag. Jhonnette's breath caught in her throat.

No!

She was reminded of the time she'd healed Randy Lafitte and learned of his relationship with her mother. The feeling of knowing was unshakable. Jhonnette desperately tried to deny what she'd seen, but knew it was the image of her father as the Warden had seen him.

How had this happened? Was Moses Mouton involved?

Picking up the pace, she realized just how right Bishop had been. There was a huge storm coming Angola's way. This time, however, there would be no survivors. If something had happened to Panama X, Jhonnette would make sure of it.

Chapter Sixty-Eight

Six years earlier
1998
New Orleans, LA

Moses descended into a room that contained a bullpen that once held slaves prior to auction. The air was thick with the stench of mildew and rot. The only light emanated from a small crack in the door behind him. If the boogeyman had a hideout, this would be it.

He spotted the real boogeyman sitting against the far wall. "Malcolm," Moses called into the black.

Nothing returned. Moses took a few cautious steps in Malcolm's direction.

"Stop right there," a gravelly voice commanded.

"Malcolm, it's Moses."

A sigh from the wall. "So you've finally come to save me, that it?"

"Only God can save you, Malcolm, you know that."

A curious pause and then, "Truer words were never spoken."

He's mocking me? Under these circumstances. The man is amazing.

"So how long do we have, Moses?"

"It's not a question of time, but more a question of how we utilize what's been allotted to us. You remember who said that?"

"Of course I remember. And I remember how little Walter did with what he had. What a waste!" Malcolm spat on the packed earth that constituted the floor of his cell.

Moses reminded himself to stay calm. Malcolm always knew how to push his buttons.

"So you're here to do what exactly?" Malcolm asked. "Gloat? Offer sage advice? Or perhaps some misguided spiritual counseling?"

"Living on the lam has made you bitter, Malcolm. Or maybe it's just the reality of finally getting caught. What do you think?"

"You should know better than that, Tabs."

As a joke, Malcolm had nicknamed Moses "Tabs"—short for stone tablet. He'd invented the name after Moses became a minister.

Malcolm continued, "I'm here of my own free will, of sound body and mind. My conscience is clear. Yours, I'm afraid, is not. I can smell your guilt and regret from here."

"Guilt? What do you know about guilt? You've been a sociopath for as long as I've known you!"

Dammit, he pulled me in again. Moses took a deep breath to calm down.

"Don't confuse my lack of sorrow for lack of conscience, Tabs. The difference between us is that I've found a way to make peace with my past, while you continue to drown in the world's blood. You're wondering what I'm up to, yes?"

Moses nodded at the darkness.

"We all atone in different ways, Brother. I've got to atone for my sins of arrogance, pride, and wrath. It's just my time."

"But why now? And why did you try to kill Lafitte?"

"Because it's time for me to go where I'm most needed."

Moses laughed out loud. "You always were great at justifying your actions, you know that?"

"Where you see justification, I see purpose. Something that you've clearly lost over the years. But not from a lack of trying. No sir! Take Lincoln Baker for instance...what a great deed! You must've felt like a true angel for taking on that challenge. You think you're serving the greater good but all you're doing is creating tomorrow's heartache, tomorrow's cautionary tale, tomorrow's regret. I'm no saint, but at least I've lived a regret-free existence. First Walter, and now you. Do-gooders doomed to fail due to a lack of purpose—"

"That's enough!" Moses commanded. "I'm not here so you can unload your anger and frustration on me. I'm here to warn you... stay away from my son. Stay the hell away from him!"

Now it was Malcolm's turn to laugh. "You came all the way down here for that? Man, you really are lost, aren't you? Tabs, there are things in motion here that you could never understand. I won't have to bother Lincoln. When the time comes, he'll seek me out. I'll teach him the meaning of purpose. And when the Big Picture becomes clear to you, Tabs, which I hope it will in time, you will understand the power of my purpose as well. And as usual, you'll be too late to stop it..."

CHAPTER SIXTY-NINE

Angola, LA

A nearby commotion awoke Moses. His vision was blurry, but he didn't need eyes to know Angola had him in its bloody clutches once more. He was lying on a hard bed inside the R.E. Barrow Treatment Center, the place where only the very unfortunate few survived. The lucky majority were unceremoniously buried in Point Lookout Cemetery, their crimes forgiven if not forgotten.

In addition to distorted vision, Moses' temples throbbed. He was blessed to have survived being shot. God was truly with him. He touched the bandage over his upper leg that covered his gunshot wound. A sharp, sudden pain shot up from his thigh.

How am I supposed to get to Malcolm like this?

Moses shut down his pessimistic thoughts. He was here for a reason, and that reason would reveal itself in time. Across from him, a group of EMTs lifted an occupied body bag onto a steel slab with a resounding thud. There was no official prison morgue at Angola, and many bodies were held inside the infirmary awaiting autopsy and eventual internment.

Rattling wheels nearby broke his train of thought. Moses turned to see a mountainous black inmate trudging toward him with the food cart. He caught the man's eyes and what he saw sent shivers of gooseflesh over his body. He saw death in the man's eyes.

Moses attempted to maneuver his injured body into a seated position as the inmate moved in for the kill. No stranger to prison-style murders, Moses spotted what looked like a shank cupped in the palm of one of the big man's large mitts. Back in the 1950's, during Moses' incarceration, this type of killing was the preferred method. He was surprised at how little things had changed.

The would-be killer was three beds away. Moses looked around frantically for a guard, nurse or, doctor. No luck, the EMTs were long gone. Moses had no chance of defending himself against an enemy of this caliber, so he cleared his throat and called out to the inmate. "Excuse me. Yes you. Can you help me out with something?"

The inmate stopped in his tracks. Moses noticed something strange about the man's movements. He tilted his head to the left, as a dog did when called.

"Did you hear me? Please, I need your help."

The inmate drew closer.

Moses heard him mutter something under his breath. It wasn't until he was a bed away that Moses realized the man was humming the song "Roughside of the Mountain," one of Moses' favorite hymns.

Moses could tell something was wrong with him. His eyes shone dully and he kept ducking his head as he pushed the cart. This boy was as retarded as he was big. Unfortunately, the revelation did nothing to ease Moses' fears.

The inmate adjusted his grip on the shank. "Whadaya want, suh?"

Moses knew it wouldn't be long before the simpleton buried a shank in his neck or chest. His body tensed as he braced for impact.

"Sorry to bother you," Moses said, his voice shaking. "Where is the doctor? I'm in terrible pain."

"Doc's busy." The man stood at the foot of the bed scratching his head. His face went blank as a sheet of paper. Then, all the life rushed back in. "I gotcha lunch here."

"I see that. What else do you have for me?"

The inmate drew a blank again, and then offered a beautiful smile that lit up his whole face. He pulled out a green tray from the back of the cart that held a plate of pineapples, grapes, and cantaloupe along with a small plain yogurt.

Well, if it's my time to go, I go with my eyes open.

Moses considered his life and recalled the pain of losing his parents to a serial burglar at age eleven. He felt each of the twelve years he lost rotting in Angola for his own stupidity. His remorse over not being able to save Walter overwhelmed him. He re-experienced his choking regret when Lincoln was sent away to prison as a teenager for the rest of his life. He'd almost given up all hope when Lois, his beloved wife, died of breast cancer just three years into their marriage. And now, instead of redeeming himself, Moses was going to die inside the Angola infirmary. It wasn't fair.

"You look jus like my ole granpappy," the man said, intruding on Moses' thoughts of fatality. "He from ova in Nawlins, like me. You from Nawlins?"

Moses didn't know where this was going, but decided to play along. "What's your name?"

The man scratched his head again. "Names Rodrick, but they all call me Man."

Moses could see why. "Well, Man, I'm not from Nawlins like your granpappy, but I've been there."

"I ain't been dere in a long time," Man said, downcast. He looked down at his hand. Then his face lit up again as he brandished the weapon in Moses' face.

Moses was immediately confused. Most shanks consisted of a sharply filed toothbrush, piece of glass, or other penetrating object protruding from a napkin or rag-wrapped handle to mask fingerprints. But this shank was missing the sharp object. Man placed the folded napkin on the tray and went back to his cart. He looked at Moses and raised his pointer finger over his lips.

Moses mimicked the gesture as Man looked sneakily from left to right like a child with a secret. Then he straightened up and said, "Betta eat up."

Moses stared at the wad of paper and saw that it wasn't a napkin but a carefully folded note, written on toilet paper.

"Storm's comin'. I hate the rain. Be makin' crazy shadows in my cell." Man took another furtive glance around the room, "You gone need yo' strength, suh. Bishop tole me so. I'll go and see 'bout that doc fo' ya'. He get you nice and strong again."

Moses waved his thanks as Man pushed the cart down the corridor toward the exit. Moses stared at the folded paper for a full minute before opening it. Words were scripted on the inside in a careful hand. He gave the infirmary a quick scan and read it:

Pop, if you're reading this it means it's not too late to make things right. Brandon's in trouble back home. I'm going to try and save him. I'm going to make up for last time. For my whole life really. I'm going to set things right, Pop. You can trust the woman. She's gonna try to get you outta there. I can never repay you for what you did for me, all I can do is try to make things even. After that, who knows?

> *Your son forever,*
> *LB*

Lincoln's words brought tears to Moses' eyes. He read the note again through blurred vision to confirm just how grave the situation had become.

Brandon's in trouble, the note said.

When Lincoln used the word "trouble," it was not the same as when the average person used that word. Moses had to assume the worst.

There was a commotion in the infirmary. A civilian woman entered and rushed over to Moses.

The woman.

Lincoln had written that she could be trusted, but Moses had a natural ability for reading people. This woman, whoever she was, could not be trusted. Trustworthy or not, a moment later she jumped into his arms.

"Daddy! Thank goodness you're okay!"

Chapter Seventy

Lake City, LA

Brandon's suspicion of a trap strengthened when Officer Jeff left him unguarded in his small cubicle.

"Stay here and stay quiet. I'll be right back for you."

Brandon gripped the cop's uniform in his sooty palm. "Where are you going?"

"I'll be right back. I've got to create a little distraction. Now, for christ-sakes, keep quiet, alright?"

Here we go.

Brandon searched for possible escape routes. Who was he kidding, he couldn't outrun a sloth. He examined Officer Jeff's cubicle and the first thing he noticed was a small vanity mirror. Brandon lifted it and stared at a stranger.

He was a wreck. His neck was swollen, eyes blackened, nose bloodied, and scalp bruised.

Officer Jeff's computer beeped, taking Brandon's attention off himself for a moment. Brandon touched the mouse and the screen lit up, revealing the MSNBC homepage.

"Monster Barrels toward LA Coast," the headline screamed.

Brandon clicked on the local news link on the left toolbar to read the headline; *"As Issac Approaches, Chaos Erupts in Lake City."*

Brandon read the short article, realizing two things. One—the media sensationalized everything. Two—he was truly fucked. He winced at a photo depicting body bags laid out on the Simmons Park basketball court. For a moment, he lost track of where, or more importantly, *when* he was.

"It's all happening again," a resident of the Village was quoted as saying.

After finishing the article, Brandon pieced together the rest for himself. A series of improbable coincidences had conspired to leave sixteen dead bodies across town and one suspect. The article didn't mention him by name, but described a black male, approximately six-foot-four inches, as the prime suspect.

All happening again.

That day, Mr. Diaz had known something would happen. He had gathered the Skulls in one spot, in the center of the basketball court. Then the Lafitte kid showed up and tipped Murda off that the Scorpions were hiding close by, all hell broke loose. By the time Lincoln arrived, it was almost over.

He wouldn't have even been there if it weren't for me.

Guilt pierced Brandon's soul. He'd treated Lincoln terribly these past ten years, upset that first his role model and then his mother had abandoned him. As he cycled through various "what ifs," he could hear Moses in his head saying, *"Everything happens for a reason, Brandon."*

And really, what could Brandon do about any of this? Under the current circumstances, nothing. But if he could find out why

Kristopher Lafitte had shown up that day, at least he might be able to find closure, and possibly prove Lincoln's innocence.

Brandon had lost all faith in the cop—he'd been gone too damn long. He nervously tapped his feet. Was there any worse torture than hope?

Brandon was half-tempted to break for the door. Remembering what had happened to the kids who ran at Simmons Park, Brandon remained still, waiting for the inevitable.

Fire engine sirens punctured the walls of the police department.

Officer Jeff reappeared. "It's time to get you out of here, Brandon."

Brandon stood. Officer Jeff peeked out into the corridor and gave Brandon a hold signal. The noise outside had reached an all-time high, the roar of sirens mixed with the elevated voices of an angry mob. Intermittently, he could hear someone on a bullhorn trying to maintain order, but not having much success.

"Okay, this is what we're gonna do..." Officer Jeff quickly explained his plan. He handed Brandon a bundle of clothing.

Brandon ripped off his tattered Nike t-shirt and put on the purple tuxedo pants and matching top with the letters LHS imprinted diagonally across the front. Generous vomit stains ran across the front as well. Brandon reluctantly pulled on the Dr. Seuss-esque top hat that was the final touch of any good marching band uniform.

Officer Jeff looked him over and lowered the brim of Brandon's top hat so he could barely see, or be seen.

"Okay," Officer Jeff said. "You look great. Time to roll. Just don't forget what I told you."

Officer Jeff's plan worked out so well they walked right past the Chief who was returning to his office in a huff after dealing with the press and convincing the fire department that everything was under control. Moments later, they stood in the adjacent parking lot. Brandon wanted to kiss the pavement he was so happy. Officer Jeff directed him to an unmarked police cruiser.

Brandon wondered again why this cop was taking such a huge risk. Then he remembered how Lincoln had been that day at Simmons Park. For some people, there was no halfway of doing things. Officer Jeff was like that.

As Brandon stepped into the cruiser, he saw Karen Lafitte sitting in the backseat with her head turned toward the window. She wore a black wig, dark sunglasses, pink miniskirt, and white halter top.

Brandon tapped her shoulder gently. "Hey, you okay?"

"Leave her be. She'll be alright as soon as we get outta here." Officer Jeff pulled out of the lot, leaving the LCPD behind in a cloud of dust. Once the station was out of view, Officer asked, "So, where to?"

Karen lifted her head from the window and said, "Home."

Brandon's arms broke out in gooseflesh upon hearing the voice emanating from Karen's mouth. That voice, definitely not feminine, barely sounded human.

Officer Jeff stared at him in the rearview, clearly as unnerved as Brandon.

Brandon swallowed the fear lodged in his throat. "You heard her, Officer. Take her home."

CHAPTER SEVENTY-ONE

I-10 West

Lincoln sped down the highway, maintaining a comfortable distance between his Jeep and the Crown Victoria containing Snake Roberts and Big Bald Ugly. The younger man and Coral were about five miles ahead of the Crown Vic in the white Ford Taurus. Rain pounded the cars without mercy.

They were the only cars headed toward Lake City; the eastbound lanes were gridlocked. The shifting traffic patterns confirmed what Lincoln was hearing on the 640 AM weather advisory. A detour thirty miles ahead would re-route them either north or east. All traffic entering Calcasieu Parish had been cut off.

This news was completely unacceptable. Lincoln had to take out the Crown Vic and its occupants, and then stop the Taurus, without hurting himself, his car, or Coral Lafitte. He checked the gas gauge—half a tank left. The dashboard clock read 3:10 p.m. The darkened sky overhead made it seem much later.

Twenty-five miles to the detour.

If Lincoln didn't move now, it would be too late. He flew past a sign lit up in a flash of lightning: Atchafalaya Bridge 2 miles. The Atchafalaya Bridge was a fifteen- mile stretch of concrete hovering above the Atchafalaya Swamp. The eastbound and westbound lanes were very narrow, with very little shoulder. On this dark, rain-soaked evening, it would be easy to run the Crown Vic over the side. It was his only chance.

He sped past another sign—the bridge was one mile ahead. Lincoln jammed the gas pedal to the floor. The quality of the asphalt changed as he moved onto the bridge. The sound of the wind over the Jeep and the road underneath melded into a symphony of action. The taillights of the Crown Vic grew bigger, much like Lincoln's eyes as he anticipated contact. If he was right, Big Bald Ugly would see him in his rearview and get over into the slow lane.

Snake relaxed. He finally felt like things were back under control. Unhooking one velcro shoulder of his bulletproof vest, he peeked at the damage. His shoulder wound had turned into an ugly black circle of charred flesh and was beginning to smell. The only consolation was that soon, he'd be a rich man with the best doctors money could buy. As they passed the sign announcing the Atchafalaya Bridge, he drifted off to sleep with a smile.

Larry's face was all concentration. He hated driving in the rain and wasn't a huge fan of driving at night, either. But now, because of this damn storm, he got both. He glanced in his rearview mirror and saw Snake with his head against the window, legs stretched out on the backseat, snoring. Then he saw the headlights of an unidentified vehicle gaining on them. His first instinct was to accelerate, but instead he slowed down.

Let the asshole pass. At that speed, he'll be sleeping with the swamp gators for sure.

Larry smiled, imagining the unidentified car barreling off the highway in smoke and flames. A moment later, the Crown Vic entered the Atchafalaya Bridge.

Snake twitched in the backseat as a nightmare enveloped him.

He watched the cops beat down a tall, black kid in prep school clothes who'd been standing at half-court in Simmons Park. Snake scanned the carnage and admired Lafitte's ruthlessness. It took a seriously imbalanced motherfucker to plan out something this crazy. Snake tripped over a corpse in a black t-shirt and almost fell. He kicked the corpse in repayment.

He would have to watch his step. There were bodies everywhere. For his contribution to the body count, Snake was going to make a quick fifty grand. Not bad for a few hours work. Still, he had to admit, he hadn't expected to jump out into Vietnam...

Lincoln closed the remaining distance. Sure enough, the right turn signal flashed as the Crown Vic eased into the other lane. Lincoln floored the accelerator to connect with the left rear bumper of the Crown Vic, hoping to send the vehicle into a hydroplaning tailspin over the edge.

He held his breath anticipating contact. But he'd miscalculated the distance. Instead of ramming the car, he missed completely and sped past with an expression of naked dismay. Soon he was well out in front of the Crown Vic.

The speeding car behind them was dangerously close. Larry was pissed. If it wasn't for the rain, he'd race the bastard all the way to Lake City. But he didn't want to wake Snake—it was too damn peaceful without his snarling and growling.

Larry hit his right turn signal and eased over, just as the asshole flew by.

Fucker nearly hit me!

Larry watched the Jeep Liberty barrel ahead and thought to check in on Shaw.

Maybe Randy Lafitte was a sucker after all. Twenty-five thousand to make sure his son was dead and another twenty-five grand to bring him home. Sounded like a deal to Snake. And he'd just guaranteed his payout by shooting the black kid through the arm as he was trying to shoot a gangbanger preparing to kill Kristopher Lafitte.

Now that the commotion was over, he just had to collect the boy and bring him home. He hadn't bargained on all the bodies or the rotten stench of shit and early decomposition, however. Snake was wading through a sea of death as he made his way toward the one non-black corpse in the vicinity. There were so many bodies he couldn't see the grass. The dead were lying on their backs with their eyes and mouths open. Their open eyes watched him as he stepped over their legs, chests, and heads to get to that singular speck of pale flesh...

"Fuck! Fuck!" Lincoln took his frustration out on the steering wheel and roof. "What now?"

"Revolution," someone on his right said.

Lincoln looked over at Kris Lafitte's smiling corpse sitting in his passenger seat. He nearly drove off the side of the bridge himself he was so freaked. After avoiding disaster, Lincoln turned to see Kris was still there.

He's just in my head.

"You're damn right I'm in your head," Kris said. "And there's a shitload of empty space in here."

"What is happening to me?" Lincoln asked, not really expecting much explanation.

"Well," Kris replied. "For starters, you need to learn how to drive. How could you have missed that car so badly?"

"I know, and it's too late now."

"It's never too late, Link. Revolution, remember? You can turn this whole thing around."

"I ain't no stunt car driver, Kris."

"Quit whining and turn the fuck around!"

Lincoln decided to take Kris's suggestion, even if he was a figment of his imagination. With less than five miles of bridge left, he threw the car into reverse and slammed on the brakes. He braced himself and turned the steering wheel dead right.

The Jeep lost contact with the road.

The next instant, Lincoln was hydroplaning on a sheet of water. The centrifugal force pinned him to his seat. He tapped the brakes furiously. Mercifully, the Jeep slowed.

Lincoln slammed the car into neutral and put his full body weight on the brakes. The Jeep shuddered, rocked right, and finally settled in place. Lincoln let out a shaky breath and looked left, directly into the blinding headlights of the Crown Vic.

"Blue dog two, come in, over," Larry said into his Nextel.

"Blue dog two here," Shaw replied.

"Watch your six for a speeding Jeep, over."

"Gotcha. There's a barricade up ahead."

Larry had anticipated something like this. "Okay, we're gonna jump off in…Oh shit!"

"Blue dog one, come in. Blue dog one!"

Lincoln stared down death, as he had so many times in his life, truly unafraid. He shielded his eyes from the high beams coming at him and prepared for the impact of a mass of steel moving at least sixty miles per hour.

Lincoln could smell the burning rubber as Big Bald Ugly slammed on the brakes and jerked the steering wheel to the right to avoid a collision. The Crown Vic fishtailed and smashed through the barricade, barely missing the Jeep.

With that mission accomplished, Lincoln put the vehicle back in drive and peeled out in the rain and oil slick pavement. He had to catch the Ford Taurus before they reached the detour.

Snake heard thunder overhead. He tugged at the white arm buried underneath the black bodies. At first, he only saw an endless arm, but then the top of Kristopher's shaggy, dirty blond hair appeared.

Snake grabbed a handful of hair and pulled the boy out of the pile. He felt a tugging sensation on his pants leg. Snake looked down to see five or six black hands pulling him into the pile. He was sinking into the corpses, like they were a pit of quicksand. He struggled, but the hands were too strong.

Kristopher's head twisted in his grip. It spun around until Snake was face to face with a dead, smiling Kristopher Lafitte.

"Hi Snake," the head said amiably. "Hey, I always wanted to axe you something. Why do they call you that?"

"This ain't happenin'."

"Right, right. What's the longest river in Africa? De Nile! Is this my sweet dream or your nightmare?"

Snake groaned. He was buried up to his waist. The hungry hands ripped off his clothes, pulled his hair, and scratched his naked flesh. Then, one hand found his right eyeball and plucked it out of his head. Another hand ripped off his left ear.

He heard Kristopher speaking.

"Congrats, Snake! You're now a rich man. You're gonna have more money than you know what to do with. You know how we use money in hell? We eat it. We eat and eat until we're stuffed. And then we eat some more. We eat until we can't speak. Until we can't breathe. Until we can't smell, see, or hear anything but the maddening rustle of paper. So, eat your heart out!"

Chapter Seventy-Two

Coral awoke one heartbeat at a time. Rain smacked against metal like a steel drum. Eyes closed, she experimented with movement, but her entire body was frozen. She was paralyzed.

It all came back. Someone had kidnapped her, just like Karen. A stifling, gaseous smell washed over her. Gasoline seemed to be in her pores. It took enormous will to open her eyes, and even then, they wouldn't open all the way. She blinked the dashboard clock into focus and read the time: 4:05 p.m.

The seatbelt alarm dinged. The driver must have exited and left the car running. Shouting from outside the car confirmed her theory. The gas smell was getting worse. Sweat trickled down Coral's cheeks and neck, pooling inside her blouse.

Maybe I'm at a gas station.

Her captor probably needed a bathroom break. Kidnapping was thirsty work and taking a mother and daughter had to be twice the trouble. Coral dreamed of a reunion with Karen. She felt some hope in the thought. But the hope evaporated when a burning smell joined the gas.

We've had an accident!

Coral envisioned a multi-car pileup on the rain slick highway. Out of the corner of her eye she caught a flame igniting. Any minute there would be an explosion, and after that, none of this would matter anymore. She almost welcomed the thought.

More yelling. Probably paramedics, firemen, and police trying to save some lives but scared to get too close because of the gas leak. Something was definitely burning now. It would all be over soon.

She heard a loud popping noise that came in bursts, like gunfire. *Who's shooting?*

Coral attempted to move again. Her fingers quivered slightly but nothing more.

The popping abruptly ceased but there was still plenty of gas, fire, and smoke. Coral coughed violently, her throat and sinuses burning.

Someone ripped the passenger door open. Because she was facing her left side, she couldn't see him or her. She felt a wave of relief. She was going to live! Coral hadn't realized how much she wanted to live until the strong arms wrapped around her waist pulled her from the car.

A man's gasping breath was hot against her neck. His face was hidden to her peripheral vision, but his strength told her everything she needed to know. He was good. He was a hero. And he was too late.

The explosion crept up on them like a bully behind the new kid on a swing set. A mighty push of air sent them skyward. The hero's grip tightened but he wasn't strong enough.

Coral floated in the dark, landing on her back in rough gravel and glass that tore at her skin and clothes. The rain tried to drown her from above. Coral couldn't move her head to avoid the murderous droplets attacking her.

Something shifted in the gravel next to her. A hand grabbed her arm. The face attached to the hand swum out of the darkness and Coral gazed upon her savior. The shock of seeing Lincoln Baker's distinct features inches from her own was too much. A mournful sound emanated from the darkness. As she stared at her son's killer, Coral realized the sound was coming from her.

CHAPTER SEVENTY-THREE

After the staged embrace, Moses held Jhonnette with his piercing, mahogany gaze. Moses was a wise man; she knew he wouldn't believe a word she had to say. And why should he really? For all he knew, she might be the culprit behind his current pain and suffering. She hoped their mutual need for survival could thaw his frosted glare.

Jhonnette became aware of the growing chaos around her. Doctors and nurses filled the treatment center, running around like hyperactive preschoolers as they grabbed medical supplies. The warden had said there would be no evacuation, so why all the commotion?

Jhonnette stepped into the corridor to catch an orderly, nurse, or anybody who could tell her what the hell was going on. They flowed around her as if she were a boulder in a river.

"You better move before you get trampled," a smooth, even voice spoke from the bed.

Moses was smiling at her. Jhonnette returned to his bedside. "Thanks for the heads up."

"I should really be thanking you," Moses said, his eyes never leaving her face. "I can't have my savior getting taken out of the picture, now can I?"

So he read Lincoln's little note. Good.

With firmer footing to stand on, Jhonnette asked, "Do you know what all the fuss is about?"

"Looks like they're moving supplies to the camps to prepare for the hurricane."

"The warden said they were going to try and ride this one out."

"Very unfortunate for us, isn't it?"

Jhonnette nodded. "How are you feeling?"

He mulled the question over like a professional wine taster and then said, "When I was a kid, a friend's cousin dared me to climb a tree and try to knock down an old wasp's nest we all thought had been abandoned. I got up there, showboating and what not, and hit that wasp's nest with a stick. Before I could blink, six angry wasps were on me. I fell out of a tree and landed on the roof of a neighbor's old car with wasps stinging me the whole way down."

"Ouch!"

"Right. Now multiply that pain times ten and you'd be close." He smiled again, in spite of the pain.

Jhonnette was charmed, but reminded herself she was there for information, nothing more. In this condition, Moses was no threat to her father. He could rot here for all she cared.

"Don't worry about that," Moses said, misreading her expression of concern. "We're not going anywhere either."

As if to confirm this, an orderly walked over with a clipboard in his hands. "Takin' dinna orduhs," he said. "Sloppy Joe or Spam?"

Neither. Jhonnette caught Moses in the corner of her eye wearing the same expression.

"What's it gonna be?" he asked again.

"I'm not planning on staying for dinner," Jhonnette replied.

The orderly gave a knowing smirk. "Whetha' or not you decide ta' eat, you gone be here, Miss. Warden's got da whole prison on lockdown."

"I think what my daughter was trying to say was, is there anything on this evening's menu that doesn't come out of a can?" Moses asked. "I know that beggars can't be choosers, but…"

The inmate gave Moses a strange look. Then he said, "Lemme go check."

"Wow," Jhonnette said after he'd walked away. "You've really got a way with people."

"Some people," Moses corrected, a shadow crossing his features.

"If you're talking about Linc—"

"Shh! Not in here. You don't know who's listening."

Jhonnette looked around the near-empty infirmary and gave Moses her "who the hell are you worried about" look. Her eyes settled on what appeared to be a corpse directly across from Moses' bed.

Father?

"I apologize for being harsh," Moses said, "but we need to take certain, uh, precautions in here. You've already taken a huge risk in coming. I don't want that risk to be in vain."

"Uh huh," Jhonnette replied, barely hearing. Needing confirmation, she slowly unzipped the body bag. It was her mental image in the flesh. Panama X lay enshrouded in plastic, dead to the world.

Jhonnette searched his petrified features for proof of her parentage. Her shaking hands were drawn magnetically to his eye-patch. Without thinking, she removed it and shoved it down her blouse.

"What are you doing?" Moses hissed.

Silence was her only reply. Then the sirens started, and a surreal wailing sound emanated from the walls. Jhonnette jumped as a bedpan clattered to the linoleum floors

"Get back over here!" Moses beckoned.

Jhonnette let the image of her father's corpse sear into her brain. She felt the old anger swelling and stretching beneath her skin and relished the feeling. Then she calmly re-zipped the body bag and walked back to Moses.

"Here comes the dinner committee," he said. "That's strange…"

She followed Moses' gaze. Two armed guards in riot gear trotted toward them.

"What's happening?" Jhonnette asked the guard in front.

"We've got an, uh, situation. You both need to come with us."

"Like hell we do," she replied, gripping the railing of Moses' bed like she planned on swinging it at the man. "This ma—my father is injured and shouldn't be moved."

The guard gave Moses a cursory glance. "Sorry Miss, we've got our orders." With sneaky dexterity, the guard grabbed Jhonnette in a bear hug, despite her loud protestations. The other guard looked at Moses as if to say, "What's it gonna be?"

Moses didn't know if he'd be able to walk, so he made one request. A moment later, Moses lowered himself into a wheelchair. The guard told Jhonnette he'd let her push Moses if she shut up.

"Where the hell are you taking us?" Jhonnette asked for the fifth time. They had exited the Treatment Center into the waiting storm outside. Flanked by guards, Jhonnette pushed Moses in the rickety wheelchair.

The guard with the name Jones stitched on his uniform gave her a dirty look. "Miss, please shut the hell up and just follow us."

Jhonnette stopped. "Not until you explain what's going on."

"Listen Miss, we don't have time for this shit."

Moses' strong hand found her wrist and squeezed. Jhonnette managed to stop herself from screaming obscenities at the guard and let out an angry exhale instead. The wailing siren muted as they entered the prison camp. Jhonnette pushed Moses down a wide corridor until they reached a large basketball gym. Cots were laid out military style in twenty or so rows, each with a footlocker at the base.

"Minimum security," Moses whispered.

The inmates seemed docile as if they'd been drugged. She whispered this thought to Moses.

"They probably are," he whispered back.

Jhonnette could tell he wasn't kidding. Warden Winey had said they were going to try and ride out the storm. He probably ordered the cooks to mix some sedatives into the lunch sludge to calm the inmates.

"Stop here," the other guard named Burton ordered.

Jones unlocked a small cell with a triple-enforced steel door. SOLITARY was printed in block letters on the front.

"I'm not going in there," Jhonnette protested. "You might as well take us back to the Treatment Center right now."

"I was hoping you'd say that," Jones replied, bearing a determined smile. He swiftly removed something from his utility belt.

Moses saw this happen with the sluggishness of a bad dream. He screamed, "Wait! Don't! We'll go!" But he was too late.

Jones jabbed a taser into Jhonnette's midsection. She spasmed like she'd caught a seizure. She would have collapsed backwards busting her head on the door had Burton not caught her mid-faint. He dragged Jhonnette into the cell and placed her on the cot.

"What about you, Pops?" Jones asked. "Wanna do the 'lectric slide, too?"

"Why are you doing this?" Moses asked, hoping his voice didn't sound as full of fear and despair as he felt.

"Don't worry 'bout that, Pops," Jones replied. "The warden wanted to send a little message is all. Said he knew what you were planning and to tell you that it won't work. Not unless one a you's is related to Houdini." He rolled Moses into the cell.

As Burton shut the door, locking them in, Moses was consumed by a rage that left purple spots in his vision. He felt reconnected with the spirit of the nineteen-year-old boy who had once stabbed a guard to death inside this place.

CHAPTER SEVENTY-FOUR

Lake City, LA

R andy sat alone in his father's study. The room was as silent as a grave. The muted flat panel television screen on the far wall silently broadcast Isaac's rapid progress. The storm, which had inexplicably hung suspended in the Gulf of Mexico earlier that morning, had finally chosen its course. Swirling radar imagery depicted the hurricane's outer wall over Lake City and most of Southwest Louisiana. The bleak visual resembled a death scythe.

The meteorologists had it all wrong, though. The storm wasn't causing irreparable damage to the oil refineries along the Gulf Coast and decimating the wetlands. It was right here in this office. Randy felt its energy pulsating throughout his frame.

He stared at the expansive desk before him and stroked the solid, reassuring surface, remembering what he'd done to possess it. This desk had long ago belonged to Walter Simmons, the only item salvaged after that fateful fire. Randy took the desk places Walter could never have reached. He and Coral once joked, that Randy would one day replace the famous centerpiece of the Oval Office with this simple cypress desk from Louisiana. That dream had fizzled, however, after his failed presidential bid in 2000, his first unsuccessful political campaign since losing the mayoral election to Simmons back in '72.

Randy's thoughts turned to his father. "Well, Joseph, I didn't get to the White House," he said aloud. "But I got further than you ever thought I would."

And if he could go back in time, he'd do it all again. He had no regrets about the life he'd lived. He'd chosen this life path and set everything in motion, starting with the bullet that stopped his father's heart.

A small piece of him wished he could have handled Kristopher better. He wondered if his own father ever felt the same way after his mother's death.

Randy pushed back from the desk and turned toward the credenza behind him. There was a safe imbedded in the second drawer. Here Lafitte's had safeguarded important things, secret things, for over eighty years. Randy pulled out a slim, leather portfolio with the letters RL engraved in gold leaf on the cover.

He avoided his father's dingy old Klu Klux Klan hood, which stared at him from the back of the safe like a headless ghost. He gently opened the portfolio and stared down at several pieces of paper, ripped years ago from Kristopher's journal. Randy read slowly, digesting every syllable of every word, even though he knew them by heart.

There is no curse. Abby hit me with that one tonight. Just an urban myth invented by the slaves and recycled over the centuries to scare massa. But how can that be? Isaac and Melinda are in my head; they offer me no peace. They are real. I should run a knife through Randy tonight, just in case. But I can't risk getting caught. I've got to get to Link tomorrow. Once I save him, I'll take care of Randy once and for all. Curse or no curse.

A single tear fell onto the journal pages. Randy acknowledged these foreign tears as the first he'd cried for his dead son. Staring bleary-eyed at Kristopher's last recorded thoughts, Randy sat up rod straight. His tear had plopped down on top of a name he hadn't thought of in years.

Abby.

It had been Coral's idea to hire the old Cajun woman. Randy hadn't been particularly fond of having a black woman around his children, but he'd been too busy running for Senate re-election to offer much protest. And by all accounts she'd done a good job with Kristopher and Karen, hadn't she? Still, something tickled the back of Randy's mind, waiting to be scratched and sniffed.

He'd planted Carla Bean all those years back to seduce Walter Simmons. What if Abby had been a plant, too? Everything made sense now. Panama X had planted Abby inside his home. She had filled his children's heads with tales of the Lafitte curse. Kristopher had believed her and sacrificed himself to save Randy and Karen!

By orchestrating the events leading up to the gang war, Randy had succeeded in ensuring his own son's demise that day at Simmons Park. And why?

"Because I could," Randy said stonily.

Well here it was. The cold, hard truth, out in the open. And damn it hurt. But Randy knew how he could make things right again. He should have done this long ago.

He removed a smooth walnut box from the safe. Inside was Robert E. Lee's most famous gun, which he lifted out of its crevice with the care it deserved. He felt the weight of legacy and responsibility as he opened the chamber. Clean as a whistle.

The case also held six thirty-six caliber lead round ball bullets. Randy removed the bullets one at a time and lovingly placed each one into a sterling silver-lined chamber. The weapon had been the first piece of his enormous inheritance.

Randy placed the barrel into his mouth. It tasted like a billion bitter, black roses. Another tear snaked down his cheek.

Please forgive me.

Randy stilled his shaking hand and depressed the trigger.

CHAPTER SEVENTY-FIVE

Angola, LA

George Winey hung up the phone. He'd just learned the levees surrounding the prison were threatening to collapse. *What else can go wrong?*

There were nearly five thousand inmates and another three hundred staff members who wouldn't make it through the night if the levees broke. Plus, a dead inmate who, by all rights shouldn't have been dead until Winey executed him.

George should have been relieved at not having to worry about the man formerly known as Panama X, but his indigestion told him things were far from settled. The rain pounded the pavement as he exited his office and headed toward the Treatment Center.

God, let me make it out of this one okay, and I promise to get out of this business next year.

Thirty years in corrections was enough.

Dr. Abe Johnson, the head of his medical staff, met him halfway to his destination.

"Have you examined him?" George asked.

"Preliminarily. We had to clean him up first."

"Fuck. No chance we can pass this one off as an accident?"

Abe looked at him in surprise. "Not if I'm the person filling out the report."

That can easily be arranged, George thought.

Abe glanced down at his notes. "The inmate's face was bashed in pretty badly. His larynx was crushed. How did this happen?"

George ignored his question. "What's your recommendation?"

The doctor hesitated.

"Abe?"

"Sorry, George. This isn't your typical prison murder."

"No shit."

"No, I don't think you understand. I don't know how to tell you this, but here goes. It appears as if the inmate's body is..."

"Is what?" George barked impatiently. He didn't have time to play twenty questions.

Abe took a deep breath. "His body is disintegrating."

George surprised himself by laughing. "What the hell are you talking about, Abe?"

"I know. I know. It sounds improbable—"

"Improbable! That's an understatement. Just level with me. And use small words, Goddamnit!"

They were just outside the entrance to the Treatment Center, standing in rain up to their ankles. Winey wondered if maybe he'd made a mistake by not evacuating the prison. God, this was bad.

"You want simple, George? Go on in and see for yourself."

George stormed into the infirmary and headed to the far wall where a cluster of nurses were still working. "What's going on over here?" he demanded.

The frantic nurses looked up in unison, each with their hands extended, as if in offering. George looked at their hands. They were covered in dark, sooty substance that reminded him of ash.

"What the hell is this?"

"Exactly," Abe replied, coming up behind him. "As we were wiping the blood off his face, his skin began crumbling. He's as brittle as paper mâché."

George looked up at Abe. "What did you just say?"

"I said we were wiping—"

"No, after," George croaked. His saliva had evaporated.

"What? The brittle part? I said he's as brittle as paper..."

"Mâché. Right." George pushed a nurse out of the way and in one swift movement, plunged both of his hands into Panama X's chest cavity. Looking around wildly he said, "This body is hollow!"

Abe's eyes widened. "So if this isn't him...then where...Oh my God."

Exactly. If Panama X had escaped, God help them all.

As if in response to George's thoughts, speakers throughout the prison complex blared distorted music. George stumbled over to the gun cabinet in a daze. A moment later he and several guards emerged into the rain, shotguns in hand, eyes wild. They made their way through the prison complex as Winey wondered—how the hell are we supposed to kill a ghost?

It was easy to deceive people who only believed in what they could see. Most people, barely leveraging ten percent of their mental capacity for any given task, could never fathom what the world would look like if they could double their output. These people only knew what a pulse could tell them through numb fingers. They didn't know you smelled death coming long before you ever saw him. They didn't know death was untouchable.

Panama X pondered these things as he watched the nurses' fuss over what they believed to be his corpse. He was a little surprised at the commotion over this condemned man, until he realized the commotion was not for his life, but for their own. Still, their efforts would be for naught.

The teachings spoke of astral projection—of thrusting the spirit out of the body in a violent exhalation. Once accomplished, the body became a brittle shell that would decompose if the spirit did not return. Panama X had no intention of reclaiming that body. He was strong enough to subsist in his spiritual form for some time. And whenever he tired, he could always manifest more flesh, if needed.

Panama X realized he could feel the rain. Not like before with his hands out as trickles washed over him. He felt the rain from the inside of his spirit, understanding its purpose on that night. It buoyed him.

This storm was generations removed from the ancestors that drowned the world in forty days and forty nights, but it held the same intent. To the west, he could feel the power and presence of Hurricane Isaac, like him, a product of God's wrath. Anyone who had ever survived a hurricane understood the fury of God more than most.

Everything was happening as Desiree Deveaux prophesized.

After defecting from Vietnam, Panama X and his small band of outlaws—the original Black Mob, found asylum in Salvador, Brazil. There, Panama X was indoctrinated into the Candomblé religion, his eventual gateway into Vodun. One day he learned the story of Zumbi, a Brazilian slave who escaped to create the so-called Republic of Palmares—a colony of over twenty thousand free blacks who fended off the Portuguese and the Dutch for nearly one hundred years.

Desiree impressed upon him that he would accomplish the same mission in his lifetime. And now on this night, nearly forty years later, Panama X was going to free every inmate in Louisiana.

Randy Lafitte's death, combined with Isaac's destruction, would throw the state into complete disarray. Panama X's liberation army of freed prisoners would march from parish to parish until the entire state was his. They would take over the prisons, and then the Capitol. They would take out all telecommunications, cutting Louisiana off from the rest of the country. They would burn the banks and overwhelm the weakened military.

Panama X floated out of the Treatment Center, out into God. Just like the rain and Isaac, tonight he would also realize his purpose. Tonight his name would be spoken among the ranks of Zumbi, Boukman and Turner. Tonight, he would make the slaves of Angola believe in miracles.

CHAPTER SEVENTY-SIX

Lake City, LA

Somewhere, Randy could hear his father laughing.
I'm in hell.

He opened his eyes slowly and saw the underside of his desk. After a moment's confusion, a searing pain in the left side of his neck reminded him what he'd done.

I'm still alive!

He pressed his fingers against the back of his neck and felt the exit wound. It radiated with a sickly heat, but the blood flow seemed to have stopped. Randy looked to his right—the gun was still in his hand. It was some kind of miracle.

He heard the laughter again. The sound wasn't in his head—it was coming from the safe. He got to his knees and with shaky hands he entered the combination. The safe opened and Randy saw his father's Klan hood standing upright.

It stared at him and then spoke in his father's roaring voice. "Givin' up that easily, Boy? What the hell's wrong with ya?"

"It's over, Dad. I can't fix it."

"Whaddaya mean? You lied, killed, and stole to get here and now you just quittin'? I always knew you were too weak. Just like your goddamned mother!"

The disgust in his father's voice made Randy look down in shame. "But I'm too late. What can I do now?"

"The curse is real, Boy, and Karen will die unless you kill that nigger bastard."

Lincoln Baker!

Randy's thoughts were on fire. "Where can I find him?"

"Join with me, Son. I will take you to him so you can reclaim your legacy."

Yes. Randy could make up for his mistakes. He reached into the safe and retrieved the hood. Oblivious to the pain, he slipped it over his head. The shift of the hood connected with his neck, making an audible click.

It was a perfect fit.

CHAPTER SEVENTY-SEVEN

Lake City, LA

The rain commenced as soon as they pulled into Karen's driveway. All throughout the neighborhood, Mexican laborers lugged gigantic plywood boards to cover the large, expensive bay windows of the Lake City affluent. The affluent were nowhere to be found; they had gotten out at the first sign of trouble.

Brandon wondered who was boarding up the Mexicans' homes.

The Lafitte Mansion stood tall and pale under the rain's burden. Brandon had never seen its equal. A sense of foreboding filled him, even as he marveled at the home of Louisiana's Governor. He glanced at Karen, who'd fallen silent after her strange vocals outside the police station. She sat so still, he might have mistaken her for a corpse if not for the artery that pulsed in her temple.

"So...we're here, Karen." Officer Jeff looked at the teenagers in his backseat.

Brandon looked back at him with fear and uncertainty. Karen made no movement at all.

"Is she still—"

Brandon nodded.

"Ya'll sit tight," Officer Jeff reassured them, "I'll check things out."

Brandon wanted to scream *no*, but Officer Jeff had already shut the car door and walked toward the house.

Officer Jeff jogged up the swooping staircase to try the front door. It was locked. He then walked around the side of the mansion and descended a small slope that ran to the canal's edge and disappeared into the yacht's docking area.

Brandon studied Karen. She looked weird underneath that black wig with those dark sunglasses. The shades were too big, the angles of her cheekbones too sharp. She used to be a beautiful girl with a bright future, but now she had become something dreadful.

"Ya'll keep a spare key or something?" Brandon asked.

"No…key," Karen spoke again in that inhuman voice.

"Why didn't you tell him that?"

Karen turned her head slowly toward Brandon and removed the sunglasses. Brandon swallowed hard. Foreign blue eyes had invaded Karen's pale face. Although terrified, he couldn't break his gaze. They stared at each other as the rain poured.

Minutes passed like hours.

Brandon stared into the stranger's eyes and knew something bad had happened to Officer Jeff. "We have to get out of here!" he screamed, frantically pulling on the door handle. When that failed, he leaned against the creature and kicked at the side window. He gave up after six or so kicks and lay back in the seat exhausted.

The being that possessed Karen's body turned and opened her door. Karen's body then exited the car. When Brandon didn't immediately follow, the door on his side of the car flew open. Taking the hint, Brandon stepped out into the rain. Karen's body beckoned him toward the house.

The mansion bore down on them. It warned them to turn around and run away. Brandon looked up at the structure through wet eyes as they ascended the sweeping stairway to the front porch. The front door creaked open the moment they stepped onto the landing. A deceptively inviting orange glow emanated from the interior.

Karen wrapped a bone-cold hand around Brandon's wrist and led him inside.

CHAPTER SEVENTY-EIGHT

Angola, LA

Jhonnette broke out of unconsciousness and covered her ears. Music was everywhere. Completely disoriented, she opened her eyes. Moses leaned over her with concern.

"What's going on?" she whispered.

"I don't know. This music just started."

She tried to sit up. A blinding cramp tore through her abdomen.

Moses pushed down on her shoulder. "Stop trying to move."

Jhonnette remembered the taser and groaned. Moses shifted his wheelchair slightly and she heard an odd swishing sound, like water in a washing machine. She rolled onto her side and looked down at the floor.

Moses was sitting in water up to his calves.

How long have I been out?

The music blared. The water rose.

Fresh panic jumped into her eyes.

How can Moses be so calm about this?

Moses touched her face as she cried uncontrollably. She wasn't meant to die like this. This wasn't part of the plan. She was supposed to be on her way back to New Orleans with her father in tow, a much richer and happier person.

Where are you, Father? I need you!

The music stopped. A heartbeat later, the cell door sprung open. A bevy of dirty brown water rushed into the cell. Soon, Moses was covered up to his waist.

"Can you get up?" he asked, still calm.

Jhonnette didn't think so, but the rising water gave her renewed motivation. She stood on top of the cot and looked to Moses for further instruction.

"You're going to have to float me." He extended his arms out to his sides and put his head back like he was being baptized.

"What?" Jhonnette's face contorted in confusion.

"I can't walk. I tried when the water first started trickling into the cell. You're going to have to float me out."

"I…I can't," Jhonnette moaned. There were a million shards of glass glimmering in the water, waiting for her to step in so they could slice her to shreds.

Calm down. You're amplifying.

The tasering, coupled with her fear of drowning, had disrupted her ability. She commanded herself to breathe.

Throughout the massive complex, inmates screamed, cried, and moaned in their flooding cells as the nightmarish liquid poured in, bringing their deepest regrets and biggest fears to the surface. The killers, rapists, and molesters saw their victims floating in the water; the thieves saw serpents. And the innocent saw nothing, for no one was innocent in Angola.

Panama X saw it all and it crushed and confounded him. The prisoners were supposed to pour out into the open, but no one moved. It wasn't supposed to happen this way. This was *his* legion.

If he didn't do something, his liberation army was going to drown in their cells.

Summoning every ounce of concentration, Panama X focused on re-manifesting his flesh. His efforts required a target. He hurled his essence into the prison camp and pinpointed a drowning inmate. The impact of their collision jettisoned water from the dying man's lungs.

Many *loa* had ridden Panama X over the years. He was accustomed to the lightning bolt of amnesia that struck upon the *loa's* arrival. Now he knew how the other side felt.

At first, he had the immediate sensation of weight. It seemed like a billion small anchors tethered every molecule of his being to the earth. Raw electricity burst from the body's nerves in unison, as if to reject the foreign presence. To make room for the invader, the inmate's soul was rapidly squeezed out. Panama X could feel the man holding on for dear life. At last, the inmate let go; Panama X felt like he was rushing through a pitch black cave toward a tiny pinprick of light.

Panama X was aware of a paralyzing fear as he awoke. He opened his eyes underwater and saw a giant anaconda within striking distance. Gasping, he allowed more deadly floodwater into his fragile new system. While choking, he saw the snake dim and then dissipate altogether—a mirage.

With renewed focus, he burst through the water, finding a small pocket of air near the ceiling. He sucked in precious oxygen until his chest burned. There was an immense psychic force at work here. It was familiar to him. He hadn't experienced anything like this since...

"Jhonnette Deveaux told me your plans."

That was it. Desiree Deveaux's daughter was here somewhere. He had a feeling Jhonnette was deeply involved in everything that was happening. She'd manipulated Randy, and Panama X suspected she'd gotten to Amir as well. And why? To get to him— her father.

Why didn't you tell me, Desiree?

Panama X had to shut her down. But first, he would save as many men as he could.

"Jhonnette, listen to me. Whatever you're seeing isn't real. Do you hear me? This isn't real." Moses tried to maintain his calm but the water was now up to his chest. He was seeing things, too. The top of a human head had just emerged before him in the water. As the head rolled back, Moses found himself staring at Walter Simmons' corpse face.

"You really let me down, Moses," the head gurgled.

"Jhonnette, get down off the bunk!" Moses yelled. "One foot at a time. Close your eyes if you need to." Moses decided to take his own advice, but could still hear Walter talking.

"You just let Malcolm walk out with my wife," Walter said. "You let them go. Why did you do that?"

Jhonnette was now in the water, pulling him out of the wheelchair.

"Running away again?" Walter's head asked.

Jhonnette was trembling, sobbing, and muttering "Oh, God" over and over again. Moses couldn't imagine what horrors she was witnessing. If it was anything like Walter's charred death mask, then God help them both.

Moses had a flash of insight. He grasped Jhonnette's hand and yelled, "Jhonnette! Pray!"

Walter's head was relentless. "Look what happened to my face!"

Moses prayed out loud as Jhonnette wailed into his ear. The combined noise finally drowned out Walter's voice. Jhonnette pushed Moses out of the cell into the corridor. "Keep moving, Jhonnette!" Moses shouted. "No matter what you see or hear!"

That was easier said than done. All around them, men shrieked like pigs in a slaughterhouse because of the visions the water carried. They were standing on their bunks as Jhonnette had been, screaming as their ghosts laughed. All the cell doors were open but only he and Jhonnette were moving. As they approached the exit, he wondered how high the water was outside.

Jhonnette lost her footing and went under. Moses reached for her in the murky water and pulled her back to the surface. Her face was a mask of terror. Moses shook her but got no response. Her mind was gone.

Water rolled into his nostrils. He snorted it out. Moses knew he couldn't support the two of them, but refused to let go.

There's got to be some sort of roof access in here. Check the walls.

Most of the buildings in the prison were one story. Moses had read that after the last time the levees broke, they'd installed roof hatches for moments like this. But he didn't see anything.

Wait. There was a roof hatch a few feet away. How was he supposed to pull them both out of here?

Jhonnette was pulled from his grasp as he considered this. A voice said, "So you're the one causing all this trouble?"

Moses turned his head and laid eyes on a middle-aged, dark-skinned black man. "Who are you?"

The man stared back at Moses. "The universe works in mysterious ways, indeed. Looks like this time I get to save you, Tabs."

CHAPTER SEVENTY-NINE

Lake City, LA

Brandon and Karen emerged from the rain into a grand entry hall. Brandon stared in awe at the spiral staircase leading up to the second story and the large ornate carpets in the two front rooms that looked like they came out of a history book.

The ceiling hovered some thirty feet above them. White columns separated the entry foyer from the front hallway. A beautiful crystal chandelier dangled overhead. Everything smelled faintly of pine and cedar.

"Where…where are we?" Brandon stammered.

Karen led him into the great room. They were not alone. A slim, but muscular, fair-skinned black man sat on an archaic couch beside a beautiful, dark-haired, white woman. Their clothes were straight out of the colonial period. The black man reminded Brandon of Lincoln. They had the same eyes.

"Welcome home, Karen," the woman spoke. "We've been expecting you."

Karen moved toward the couch. Brandon had a strong feeling that something bad was going to happen when she got to them. Propelled by the urge to protect her, Brandon darted forward and blocked Karen's path.

Karen tossed him aside like an empty pillowcase. He hit the wall and crumpled to the floor, helpless.

"It's time, Karen," the woman coaxed. "Time for you to join us."

Karen stopped before them.

The man stood and opened his arms as if to embrace her, but then he recoiled. "You!" he yelled.

Karen's head tilted slightly, and she replied in that guttural voice, "You...can't...have...her."

The woman jumped up and stood toe-to-toe with Karen. "She is rightfully ours!"

Karen grabbed the woman by the throat and flung her across the room. Then she raised her hand as the man prepared to engage her. "Isaac. Others...are...coming."

"It's too late, Kristopher. We have chosen. Release her to us. Release this body, *baka*."

Isaac? Kristopher?

As strange as it seemed, it finally made sense. Brandon didn't have a clue who Isaac was, but Karen was clearly possessed by her dead brother. He was speaking through her like a bad ventriloquist.

What the hell am I thinking? That's impossible.

As Brandon got to his feet, Karen pointed at him. "Lincoln...will...come...for him. Make...them...choose."

Choose what?

For the first time Isaac marked Brandon's presence. Brandon did not enjoy having those bloodshot eyes looking at him.

Thankfully, Isaac turned his attention back to Karen and said, "And if they choose incorrectly?"

"Either way...you win."

The woman was back on her feet. Isaac looked at her for confirmation. She nodded her assent.

"Alright, then, we will conduct the reckoning in the old style, Kristopher. This time." As Isaac spoke, the house began to change. He and the woman began to fade as well.

In a matter of seconds, Brandon watched the interior of the house turn from an antebellum plantation to a modern mansion. The orange glow dissipated, leaving him in the dark. Shadowy darkness replaced the waning afternoon light as rain and wind swirled about the house.

"Brandon?" a weak female voice called out.

"Karen!" he cried. Relief coursed his body. "Are you okay?"

"I…can't move."

Brandon helped her onto the sofa. He tried to switch on the lamp but the power was out. "Karen, you have to tell me what's happening here."

Tears sprang from their deep, dark wells and streaked down Karen's face. "He said the curse wasn't real. He lied to me."

"Who lied? Kristopher? What's this curse?"

"Kristopher went to see Abby the night before he died, but he lied to me about what she said."

"Who the hell is Abby?"

"They talked about the spirit world. Curses, voodoo, ghosts… God. Our belief makes them possible."

Brandon was confused. "Then why do they say that voodoo can affect you even if you don't believe in it?"

Karen wiped her tears away. "My family has fed into this curse from the very beginning. We have made so many sacrifices to

Isaac and Melinda, each time hoping it would be the last time. But now I know, as long as we stay here, the curse will come back to haunt our children, and our children's children. Somebody has to pay for Isaac, Melinda, and their unborn child. Kristopher paid that price..."

"Then why don't you just leave?" Brandon asked.

"One of our ancestors tried that, and it actually worked for a while," Karen continued. "But they are so patient. They waited. Then our grandfather was born. They whispered to him as a child and he came back home. There's no escape. The only way is to give them an offering they can't refuse."

This was the craziest story Brandon had ever heard. Still, he believed her. He'd seen the ghosts with his own eyes. How could he doubt that?

Karen grabbed his shirt and pulled him down on top of her. "Quiet. Someone's here."

"Who's coming, Karen?" he whispered. "How can we stop them? How can we end this?"

"You can't," a gravelly baritone spoke from behind them.

Karen and Brandon looked up to see a tall man with a pointy white hood over his face glaring down at them. He removed the hood slowly with one hand; a strange gun was clutched in the other.

Karen gasped. The man's face was a grotesque mask of blood and charred flesh, but Brandon still knew him.

Randy Lafitte offered a grime-filled smile and regarded them with bloodshot eyes. "Daddy's home."

Chapter Eighty

Coral opened her eyes in time to catch a green sign announcing the arrival of Iowa, LA in a quarter mile. Lying horizontal in the backseat, she stared at the bald head of her driver. There was a whistling sound outside of the car she recognized as wind, though she'd never heard any wind sound like this before.

Adjusting her body into a more comfortable position, she noticed Lincoln Baker's eyes watching her through the rearview mirror. She'd seen him staring at her the same way in more nightmares than she could count, although this was the closest she'd physically been to her son's killer. Now, with only inches separating them, Coral didn't feel how she thought she would. For one, there was no hate. Strangely, she felt...gratitude. Besides, hadn't Snake Roberts confessed to the crime? The car was pushed violently across lanes and Coral realized they had much bigger things to worry about than hate and forgiveness.

Almost home.

Lincoln exhaled as they passed the Iowa exit. He couldn't stop thinking about Brandon. *If he was stuck in the police station during the hurricane...* Lincoln shut down this train of thought. He tried the radio again, but no news. All of Southwest Louisiana was deserted.

Coral's up.

Lincoln caught her movements in the rearview. Their eyes met. Then without warning, the wind whipped under the Jeep and lifted it off the highway for an eternal second.

Shit!

This storm was no joke. If they didn't find shelter soon, the Jeep was going to take flight.

"Where are you taking me?" Coral croaked suddenly.

"Home."

Coral nodded.

He wondered if she felt it too, the magnetic force that seemed to be pulling them back to Lake City. He was definitely on a mission—after he dropped Coral off he needed to locate Brandon and get him to higher ground. Thankfully, Moses' house was in one of the only sections of town high enough above sea level to withstand the inevitable flooding.

As Moses was fond of saying, "If we're flooded over here, the rest of Lake City is underwater."

Thinking of Moses, Lincoln had an attack of conscience. For the first time in his life, he felt the urge to confess and make amends. Lincoln knew this woman would never understand why he'd done what he'd done, but he felt compelled to try. He didn't know if he'd have another chance.

"Look," he started. "Did you know those men back there?"

Coral raised an eyebrow. "They work for my husband. Or at least they did. They kidnapped me."

"I know. I saw the whole thing."

"You were there?" Coral asked.

"Yes." Lincoln cleared his throat. "Mrs. Lafitte, how well do you know your husband?"

Coral fidgeted, clearly offended by the question.

"I mean...do you have any idea what he's capable of?"

Coral stared out the window, ignoring the question.

"Does the name Walter Simmons mean anything to you?" Lincoln pressed.

"Well, of course. He ran against Randy and won the election for Mayor."

"And then he was killed."

"Yes," she said. "It was a horrible accident."

"Was it?"

"What are you saying?" Coral asked, her skepticism and mistrust slowly subsiding

"I ain't sayin' nothin'. Just layin' out some facts. Tryin' to make sense of what she told me."

"She, who?"

"This woman, Jhonnette Deveaux. Claimed to be some kind of psychic."

"And you believed her?"

Lincoln looked away. "I've been seeing some crazy stuff today. Stuff that makes me want to believe her."

"What kind of stuff?"

"Well for one, I've been seeing your son, Kris. Everywhere. He's been talkin' to me. Showin' me things."

Coral looked away as a tear ran down her face.

"You too? I guess that makes some kinda sense." Lincoln lost his train of thought as something caught his attention from the corner of his eye. A huge billboard was skimming down I-10, directly toward them. He maneuvered out of the way, just in time to watch the sign roll down the highway like a giant tumbleweed.

They both exhaled in relief. Silence wedged between them once more.

"I was going to kill you," Coral spoke up abruptly.

"What?"

"This morning. I went to that hospital where they took you after you got out. But you weren't there. Instead, I found Snake Roberts."

So that's what happened.

Lincoln had wondered what went down after he and Jhonnette split.

"He got the bullets I'd reserved for you," she sighed. "Right after he basically told me my husband had ordered him...ordered him to kill...our son." Coral's lips quivered as she got the words out. Tears gushed from her eyes. "And then you come and save my life. I don't know what to think about anything anymore."

Lincoln considered this near miss as he put his eyes back on the road.

So Randy ordered Snake to kill Kris.

Lincoln rubbed his shoulder on the site of the wound he'd received right before he accidentally shot Kris.

"Gotta put it all together," Lincoln whispered.

"So what else did this psychic tell you?" Coral asked.

This was so crazy Lincoln had to smile. "This is gonna sound nuts, but what the hell, here goes. Supposedly, your husband…is my father."

"That's ridiculous!"

"Is it?" Lincoln probed. "I mean here we are talkin' about a man who may or may not have killed his political rival and may or may not have ordered the killing of his own son. Think about it. Cheatin' on his wife wouldn't be that far a stretch for a guy like that."

"I don't want to hear any more of this." Coral said, looking away.

Through the rain-blurred window, Lincoln observed the demise of Lake City as he navigated them slowly over downed power lines and around assorted tree parts lying scattered all over the highway.

"Turn off here," Coral directed as they arrived at the Lake Street exit.

They drove to the Lafitte homestead in silence. At last, they pulled into an empty driveway in front of an enormous home.

"Looks like nobody's home," Lincoln said. "You sure you want to go in there?"

This close to the lake, Coral could really feel the hurricane's fury. The Jeep rocked from side-to-side. The rain and wind battered all scenery. Coral tried to calm the panic uprising underneath her skin. No, she did not want to go in there. She had a bad feeling she was going to find corpses of her family in the foyer.

Lincoln must have sensed her hesitation because he said, "Look, if you want, I can go in with you and check everything out."

Coral looked back at Lincoln and thought about everything he'd said. If he was right, she'd been living with a stranger. A monster. She didn't want to be alone right now, but she also didn't want Lincoln in her house. Conflicted, she replied, "Thank you, but you don't have to do that."

"It don't feel right just leavin' you here. Come on, let's get you inside." With that said, Lincoln attempted to push open his car door, but the wind was too strong. "Okay, let's try the other side."

"Lincoln, wait." Coral put her hand on his shoulder to stop him. One last matter needed to be addressed. "I have to know something first. What was your involvement in my daughter's kidnapping?"

She watched Lincoln compose himself. He let out a shaky breath and said, "No matter what Snake said, I was there. Fate brought me and Kris together that day. And I shot him. It was an accident, I swear. But I paid for it. I spent the last ten years in prison beatin' myself bloody over it. And then I learned about Walter Simmons and how he was killed. Your husband became the target of all my anger. Taking your daughter was just a means to an end. I had to get out so I could kill him, and the only way to do that was to force his hand. So yeah, I was involved in your daughter's kidnapping. I guess it don't mean a lot to say that if I knew then what I know now, then none a' this woulda' happened."

Coral didn't know why this latest revelation shocked her. But his words rocked her core. The tears that had subsided came roaring back as Lincoln continued.

"I want you to know I'm real sorry for what happened to your daughter and son. I'm sorry for the part I played in all that. But I would've been to blame for both of those crimes, even if I didn't do them. I know now I was set up. Been set up from the very beginning of my life. But there's no point in laying blame at no one else's feet cuz I went along with it. Just like we're going along with this right now. And I don't expect your forgiveness or nothin' like that. That's not why I'm tellin' you all this."

"Then why?" Coral wailed.

"Because, this is all startin' to make sense to me now. Kris told me somethin' earlier. He said, 'Looks are deceiving'. Your house looks empty, but I don't think it is. I think we're supposed to go in there together, and the only way you were gonna let me get you in there was if I told you the truth, am I right?"

Coral looked up at her home and then back at Lincoln.

"I'll take that as a yes." Lincoln said, abruptly opening the passenger's side door and stepping outside into the elements. His hospital get-up billowed in the wind like a parachute as the rain soaked him. It took him a few moments to situate himself to open Coral's door.

Coral's body was still betraying her. Lincoln had to lift her out of the car like a groom carrying his bride. With her arms wrapped around Lincoln's neck, Coral once again felt Lincoln's strength. She thought about his confession and what it meant. Coral knew she'd never forgive him, she couldn't even forgive herself. But she was very glad of his company.

Making their way up the driveway, her eyes fixated on the old live oak tree behind them. She noticed something odd about that tree, but she couldn't place it. Then a gust of wind nearly knocked them down.

That's it!

The wind swirled all around them, but not a frond on that tree budged. Everything became clear. And the picture that manifested chilled Coral down to her marrow. This was about history. This was payback.

Lincoln got the door open on the first try and carried Coral out of the storm into the darkened foyer. The door slammed behind them on its own, like in a haunted mansion, and they both flinched.

"Where can I set you down?" Lincoln asked moving cautiously in the dark. When Coral didn't immediately reply, he asked her again. But Coral's focus was behind them.

Lincoln felt the barrel of a gun poke his skull and knew he wasn't going to save Brandon after all.

CHAPTER EIGHTY-ONE

Angola, LA

With an unconscious Jhonnette flung over his shoulder, the stranger led Moses to a covered guard tower adjacent to the building, one of the few dry places left in the prison complex. The last of the drowning prisoners' screams had stopped a few minutes before and the rain once again trumped all other sound.

Chest heaving with exhaustion, Moses looked at the strange man across from him. As they were making their way through the prison, the stranger had tried frantically and unsuccessfully to revive several of his fellow prisoners. Now he looked shell-shocked and whipped.

"It's okay, Son," Moses said in an attempt to console. "There was nothing more you could have done."

The stranger maintained his defeated posture.

"You know if you hadn't shown up when you did…" Moses shuddered. He'd danced with death too many times for his own comfort. Maybe silence was best.

The stranger got to his feet and dragged Jhonnette to the railing. As he hoisted her up, Moses realized he meant to throw her over the side of the tower to her death. He propelled himself into the crazed man's path. "Stop!"

They locked eyes. Moses saw more than lunacy in the other man's face; he recognized a deep reservoir of regret. "What are you doing? You just saved this woman's life and now you want to kill her?" Moses asked.

Jhonnette's torso hung precariously over the wooden banister. The man tried once again to finish what he'd started, but then let her body crumple back to the floorboards. He didn't even watch her fall back, his focus intent on the human soup below.

"Don't even think about doing anything foolish, now," Moses said. "Come on. Sit down. Let's talk things out."

"There's nothing left to talk about, Moses."

"How do you know my name?" Moses blurted, remembering how the man had called him Tabs.

The man leaned against the railing and sighed. "You know me, Moses. You knew the first moment you saw me. But I imagine that your faith won't permit you to believe what your mind already knows."

"What are you talking about?"

"Isn't your religion built around an unseen mystical figure no one can prove exists? Well look at me, Moses. I exist. Believe in me."

Moses stared at the man incredulously. The man even spoke in Malcolm's cadence.

"I know you haven't seen me without the eye-patch in a while..."

"This is impossible!" Moses proclaimed, eyes wide with fear. "How?"

"I told you there were things at play here you wouldn't understand. You remember that?"

Moses stared open-mouthed, finally seeing his old friend behind this new mask. "Malc? This…this is a…a miracle."

"If that's how you need to think of it."

Moses' mixture of confusion and elation was palpable. Questions swirled in his mind.

"You're probably wondering why I saved you," Malcolm said. "The funny thing is, I'm wondering the same thing. It wasn't supposed to happen this way."

"You had something to do with this disaster, didn't you?"

Malcolm met Moses' accusatory gaze. "And if I did? It doesn't matter anymore. Duty has denied me from reaching my destiny, yet again."

"What destiny? I thought you came to Angola because this was where you were most needed."

"I believed so, too," Malcolm exhaled. "And I see now that my beliefs have led me astray."

"Belief is a choice, Malc," Moses replied. "No one forced you down this path. Belief is an excuse people use to justify their actions. But we have to rise above our past."

"Rise above?" Malcolm asked. "I'm supposed to rise above the Middle Passage? How many of our brothers and sisters are covering the bottom of the Atlantic? What about the brutality? They killed off an entire generation, Tabs. An entire generation, gone, so they could cut us off from our ancestry, our languages, our religions, our home. We were beaten into submission. Dehumanized. Humiliated repeatedly. How many of our women were assaulted, mentally and physically? How many of our men became the strange fruit coloring the sadistic orchards of the South? I was a soldier. I bled for this nation! I killed for this nation! And what awaited me upon my return? Injustice? Inequality? Assassination of my leaders? Am I supposed to just let go of the hopelessness? The fear? The self-loathing? At least I stood up. At least I stood for something! And you…you expect me to forget!"

Stinging tears bubbled in Moses' eyes as he relived the collective history of Africans in America. He felt every physical, spiritual and psychological wound deeply, remembering every indignation and humiliation. Through his tears he finally said, "I never expected you to forget, Malc. I haven't forgotten—"

"Haven't you?"

"No, I haven't. But at some point you must forgive, right?"

"Forgiveness is so passive. Our people don't need to forgive anyone. Our people need action. A movement. And I gave them that."

"All you did was sink to their level," Moses admonished. "All you did was kill, terrorize our terrorists, and end up a slave again. Nothing you've done has changed anything. Not one foolish act."

Veins bulged in Malcolm's temples. "What do you know about sacrifice? You've been a follower all your life. You have no point of view worth exploring. It's almost like Walter's weak spirit took over your body when he perished in that fire."

"Well, looks like you've sunk to a new low this time, Malc, even for you. It took me awhile to come to grips with the truth, but I'm done denying it. I know you had a part in Walter's death. I just don't know why."

"Why, why, why," Malcolm mocked. "See, that's your whole problem, Tabs. You always get lost in the why. Why doesn't matter. Nothing matters anymore."

"Tell me the truth, Malc. It's time."

Malcolm stared at him. "You know what? I'd do it all over. Because after Walter was gone, those were the best years of my life. Raising a family. Walter didn't deserve Juanita. He was weak. Not the man to lead our people. Not the man to have a beautiful woman like that at his side."

Moses thought of the dreams he'd been having and Juanita's warning. "Juanita never forgave herself for leaving Walter."

A single tear escaped Malcolm's eye. He caught it in his palm and examined it like an exotic insect. "Walter betrayed her."

"So you killed him."

"No. But I wanted to. Randy Lafitte took care of that for me."

Comprehension dawned on Moses. "So Lafitte assassinated Walter? Why am I just learning this now? And what does she have to do with all this?" Moses pointed to Jhonnette. Then it hit him. "She's your daughter, isn't she?"

"Yes," Malcolm replied, turning away. "A long time ago, her mother and I came upon a way to solve our financial problems by using a young boy's hatred for his father to convince him we had the power to resurrect a family curse."

"But your plan backfired," Moses replied. "Lafitte never paid up, did he?"

Malcolm shook his head.

"So what does that have to do with Walter's assassination?"

"Up until this moment, I always believed them to be unrelated. But now I see that Desiree and I created a domino effect that has led us here."

"A domino effect?"

"Yes. Lafitte was the catalyst. Everything starts with him and his desire to kill his father. From there, his ambition only grew. He learned how to deal with people standing in his way."

"By killing them."

"Exactly."

"But what about you, Malc? You were there the day of Walter's assassination. You were inside the office. But you didn't save him. How was that Lafitte's doing?"

"Juanita was in so much pain after she found out about Walter's cheating," Malcolm continued, ignoring Moses' question. "I needed to comfort her. She was a devoted wife, so I had to deceive her. And once I'd had her, I knew I would do anything to keep her."

"What do you mean, 'once you'd had her'?" Moses demanded.

Malcolm was silent.

Moses looked at Malcolm's new form and gooseflesh broke out all over his body. "Did you," Moses began, not believing the words coming out of his mouth. "Did you take over Walter's body and lay with Juanita?"

Malcolm turned around to face Moses. "Yes. And it is quite possible that Lincoln was conceived the night of our union."

Moses believed everything happened for a reason, but the cruelty and depth of this betrayal rocked him to his core. Nothing made sense to him anymore. Nothing except the hatred rising underneath his skin.

Because of Malcolm's obsession with Juanita, Walter lost his life. Cause and effect? Malcolm was going to learn about cause and effect. Rage poured out of Moses in waves. He charged at Malcolm with both hands outstretched. As his hands connected with Malcolm's sternum, he shoved with all his might. Malcolm pin-wheeled backward over the railing, somehow managing to grab on to the banister with his left hand.

Moses stared down at Malcolm in his new incarnation. His fog of rage cleared long enough for him to realize he couldn't take the man's life, even though he deserved to perish. Moses leaned over the railing and offered his hand.

Malcolm smiled up at Moses and said, "We can't outrun the past, Tabs." Then he let go.

"Malcolm!" Moses screamed as Malcolm somersaulted down into the murky floodwaters below. He stretched over the railing, but it was too late. Malcolm's body disappeared beneath the surface.

CHAPTER EIGHTY-TWO

Lake City, LA

Randy was pleased with himself. Since he put on the hood, he'd been quite productive for someone with a bullet hole in his neck. He was tying up the loose ends very nicely—the first of which had been the cop. After shooting him in the back and watching him fall into the lake, Randy came back inside to find the black bastard with his daughter.

If he'd had more time he would have killed the boy. As it was, he left him bound and gagged in the living room and retired Karen to her bedroom, making a mental note to personally inspect her feminine parts later to make sure there'd been no tampering. Then he moved the cop's car.

Another vehicle pulled into the driveway. Randy cut the lights and found a place where he could see, but not be seen. What he saw made him drunk with bloodlust.

Lincoln Baker was carrying his wife's corpse toward the house.

Not only had his son's killer kidnapped Karen, he had murdered Coral as well? The man's gall was dizzying. To think, Randy had nearly ended his own life—believing the situation unsalvageable. No wonder Joseph had called him weak. Randy visualized the headlines he'd narrowly avoided: *"Louisiana Governor Commits Suicide After Murdering Wife and Child."*

Tears welled in his eyes at the very idea, but Randy contained his emotions. This was not the time. His second chance at redemption was here and he did not intend to let this opportunity go to waste. Randy couldn't believe his luck—that jungle monkey Baker had walked right into his own funeral. Randy felt a smug sense of satisfaction as he pressed the gun to the back of Baker's head. It took all his strength to resist pulling the trigger.

No, not yet. Everything has to be right.

Randy experienced a moment of confused disappointment when he realized Coral was still alive. She was just going to get in the way, as usual. But he'd have to deal with her later; it was time to get on with the show.

Randy turned the power back on. The first thing he saw after his eyes adjusted to the brilliant light was his father's portrait above the fireplace. He stared into his father's stern blue eyes and for the first time in his life, he felt his father's approval.

Kristopher should have been here for this.

But because of the bastard sitting on the floor before him, he wasn't. Striding across the great room, Randy projected all his rage, loss, and anger toward Lincoln Baker.

Lincoln had escaped from life in prison, near death collisions and shoot-outs, but he could not avoid Lafitte's trap. As soon as he felt that gun nuzzling the back of his skull, he knew his run of good fortune had dried up. Soon after, he was tied up and gagged, sitting on the floor in an enormous dark room.

The wind screamed and howled. Lincoln tried to free his hands from the plastic cuffs Lafitte shackled him with, praying for an inch of daylight, any smidgen of hope in which he could wedge his fingers to manifest a positive outcome.

Moses had always said, *"We may not control what happens to us in this life, but we do control how we respond to what happens."* Well, this was Lincoln's moment of truth. It was up to him to make the best of a bad situation.

The room lit up like an epiphany. Bright light poured down from the most beautiful chandelier Lincoln had ever seen. He sensed he was not alone in the room and turned to see Brandon, unconscious but alive, tied up in the corner. An overwhelming surge of joy overtook him.

His captor's rapid approach quickly squelched Lincoln's gratitude. The hurricane pressed and coiled itself around the mansion, as Lafitte moved toward him. Lincoln's teeth ached with the storm's vibrations. He heard the distinct sound of stretching glass. Soon the myriad of windows surrounding them would explode inward like a legion of poison-tipped arrows, if the groaning roof didn't peel off first leaving them exposed to the elements. That might be the sliver of opportunity he was looking for—the only chance he might get to save Brandon.

Randy's nightmarish face swam toward him. The man looked terrible. His eyes were so bloodshot Lincoln could barely find the iris beneath the veins. The left side of his once handsome face sagged as if the muscles had simply quit. His lips were blackened and chapped and he licked them with what appeared to be the green tongue of a snake.

So we finally meet. Face to face.

Despite what Jhonnette had told him, he still couldn't believe the man was his father.

"It's time," the ghoul said, pointing above them.

Fear transformed to adrenaline as he followed Randy's gesture and saw the noose hanging high above his head.

Coral didn't want to help Randy, but she didn't see any other option. The moment she laid eyes on her newly disfigured husband, she knew no one was leaving this house alive. The best she could do was try not to anger him, in hopes that he might grant her a swift exit.

"Coral, get over here," Randy barked.

Coral couldn't move. Her acute awareness of her impending demise, coupled with her visceral fear of the man she used to love had rendered her frozen and mute.

"Guess I'm gonna have to do this all by myself," Randy said. "Luc was a lucky bastard. He had a whole mob to help him. And I've got…you. Here." Randy placed a strange gun with a long, thin muzzle inside her shaking palm. "Make yourself useful and hold this."

She looked at the gun like it was a poisonous spider that would sink its stinger into her if she dared move. Hours earlier, she'd wielded a weapon much bigger than this and shot a man twice. But now, she was utterly paralyzed by fear. It was all she could do to control her bladder.

"You're fucking useless, Coral," Randy said, glaring at her. "You know that?" He spat on their living room floor to punctuate his point.

Coral lowered her eyes and saw a molar glistening up from the midst of his bloody saliva. "What...what do you need me to do?"

"One, I need you to stop being so damn skittish. We're in this together. Two, I need you to go and get Karen."

Coral almost cried with glee. "Karen? She's here?"

"Of course she's here. Now go run and collect her. I'll have everything setup by the time you get back."

Karen needed more energy. And more time. She'd already ransacked her room once looking for it. She didn't dare contemplate what might happen if she couldn't find it before he came for her.

From her bucking bedroom window, Karen saw a nightmare approaching. A giant funnel of wind and chaos moved across the lake with breathtaking speed. She knew it wouldn't be long before the tornado borne from the hurricane found its course. Isaac and Melinda were going to destroy everything this time if she didn't find that damned Sony discman!

Kristopher's words came swirling out of the past. *"There's a CD already in the player, but you gotta promise me that you won't play it until I say, okay?"*

Karen glanced nervously at the tornado. Was it closer? What if the maid had stolen the discman, or worse, Randy had it?

The Kristopher who lived in her subconscious spoke up. *"Stop playing around, kiddo. You know exactly where it is."*

"I've looked everywhere!" Karen whined, ready to give up. Then she noticed something out of the corner of her eye. Something blue and circular peeking out from behind her entertainment center.

The discman!

Of course, Karen had listened to the CD as soon as Kristopher gave it to her, but the cryptic message hadn't made any sense to her. Until now. Now it was the key to everything. Putting the headphones over her ears, she pressed play but got nothing. The batteries were long dead.

Was the damn CD even still in the discman?

Karen opened the CD player. Sure enough, it was empty. Where could she have possibly put Kristopher's CD? She sat down on her bed pressing her hands to her eyes, desperately trying to remember.

Wait. Hadn't she listened to it again after her appointment with Dr. Faustus? And hadn't her father caught her listening to it and she'd...yes, that was it! Karen ran to her dresser and removed the diary she'd begun after Kristopher's death. Quickly finding the lump in-between the pages, she removed the CD, put it in her combo CD-alarm clock and listened.

Kristopher's voice came through loud and clear.

Karen had just finished listening to his instructions a second time when her mother barged in.

"Good," Karen said after they embraced. "Everyone's here. Quick, we don't have much time."

Coral nodded fearfully as Karen explained what they had to do.

Before ascending the spiral staircase with Baker, Randy donned his father's hood again. Joseph had once told him that the origins of the Klan's hood and robe could be traced back to ancient European rituals signifying fraternal brotherhood and anonymity in doing good works. Tonight, Randy would perform *great* work.

He grinned behind the hood, silently lamenting his lack of a robe. The hood also represented a more practical aspect of his task this evening—that of executioner. Randy made sure to separate his personal feelings from the mission at hand. Joseph had been very clear about that point.

Joy would come in the morning; tonight was about solemn duty.

With the gun jammed in Baker's side, Randy pushed him up the stairs to the second floor landing where his death noose waited. Baker was struggled with his bonds to no avail. Finally, he gave up and stared at the ceiling.

Randy imagined he was praying, which was all right. Even a condemned man deserved a last glimmer of hope. Hadn't Randy offered the same oration in the seconds before he'd turned the gun on himself? Still, not even God could save Baker from this fate.

The closer he got to the landing, the more Lincoln knew the roof was about to peel away. The wind, which had sounded like muffled whistling from the first floor, was now roaring like the turbines of a 747 engine.

Even castles crumble.

He just prayed he could hold on until this one did.

Karen entered the great room and saw her father fixing a noose around Lincoln Baker's neck. Through the bay windows, she could see the beastly funnel was closer than ever. Karen fought to stay upright, her frayed nerves nearly overloaded. She honestly didn't know how much energy she had left, but it would have to be enough.

One way or another, it would all be over soon. She just needed to summon the strength and courage to follow Kristopher's instructions. But first, she had to set Brandon free. She was going to need his help.

"Hey kiddo," Kristopher opened the recording. *"You just couldn't wait, could you? It's okay though. I probably couldn't have waited either at your age. I really hope that after you hear what I have to say, you can call me in my dorm or apartment and we can have a good laugh at my expense. But something tells me that by the time you hear this, I'll be long gone. Either way, I need you to know what I know. The curse Abby told us about is very real, very alive, and very dangerous. If you don't do exactly as I say, when you turn eighteen, Isaac and Melinda will come for you, too. I'm not saying this to scare you; I'm saying this to prepare you. Now this next part is going to sound crazy, kiddo, but it is absolutely essential. You have to destroy that tree—Melinda Weeps. It's the anchor that holds the curse in place. If you're hearing this, chances are I didn't make it back from Simmons Park, which means the tree is still standing. You have to burn it to the ground, kiddo. Your children and grandchildren are all counting on you..."*

Kristopher went silent for a few moments and then abruptly said, *"One last thing. And I wish there was an easier way to say this, God I do. If you have already turned eighteen by the time you hear this, destroying the tree alone won't save you. You have to kill Dad. That's the only way to break this cycle for good. I really hope it doesn't come to that, but I need to prepare you for all the possibilities. I'm so sorry to burden you with this. I love you... Oh, and before I forget, I left you supplies. Check behind the secret panel in my closet. Everything you need is there."*

Randy wasn't the only Lafitte great at keeping secrets. Staring at the homemade bombs stockpiled inside Kristopher's closet, Coral wondered what kind of lunacy had possessed her son's mind in his last days. Karen insisted there was no time for her to listen to the recording; she was going to have to trust her.

Coral picked up two makeshift bombs and looked at them skeptically. Then she noticed four large kerosene canisters.

I don't even know how this stuff works.

"Duck your head, boy," Randy said. "Don't make this harder than it needs to be."

They stood at the summit of the stairs. Randy held the noose with one hand and urged the shuffling nigger forward with the other. Baker resisted the noose with all his might. Damn he was strong.

"Either you put your head in this here rope, or I shoot your friend down there," Randy said. That did the trick. Baker stopped fighting. His head was almost in the noose when Randy abruptly let go of the noose and slapped his thighs. "I knew I was forgettin' somethin'!" He went to a chair in the hallway behind him and picked up a serrated butcher knife he'd left there for this occasion. Brandishing it before Lincoln's wide eyes, he said, "Sometimes I can be too impetuous."

He gazed down on his father's portrait and steadied his grip on the knife's hilt.

Setting foot outside, Coral realized Kristopher had given them an impossible task. Staring at the two canisters of kerosene by her feet, she held onto the staircase railing for dear life. She was afraid that if she let go, she'd go flying off into the turbulent night.

For her children's sake, she had to make it to that tree. No matter how much the raging wind sounded like some giant, tentacled langolier with a jagged-toothed black hole for a mouth.

"I'm with you, Mom," Kristopher's voice spoke up in her mind. *"You can do this. You have to."*

Coral took one shaky step away from the railing's security and then managed another and another, until she stood beneath Melinda Weeps. At least the old tree provided some respite from the rain and wind.

God it was dark under here. Coral unscrewed the top of one canister of kerosene as leaves rained down on her. In moments she was buried up to her calves, the canister lost in a bog of soggy foliage. She heard something other than the wind and swishing leaves. It sounded like an angry mob.

Who would be crazy enough to be out in this kind of weather?

The noise was undeniable. Coral whipped her head left and right but saw nothing.

"Hurry up, Mom," Kristopher screamed urgently in her head.

Coral doused the base of the tree with the pungent liquid. She'd successfully soaked the roots and base of the tree when abruptly night became day.

She was now standing, not underneath, but in front of a large crowd gathered before Melinda Weeps. Her confused eyes landed on Randy standing a few feet away, dressed in an odd military uniform. He held a parchment in his hands. Behind him, a badly disfigured Lincoln Baker sat atop a large horse with a noose around his neck.

"Too late, Mom," Kristopher said from right next to her.

Coral stared at her son with tears in her eyes. "What's happening here, Kristopher?"

"This is how it all started," he replied sadly.

"We have to do something," she cried.

"They're too strong," Kristopher replied. "I thought I'd found a way to beat them, but I was wrong."

Coral refused to believe his words.

This isn't real. This isn't happening. It's night. I'm outside under the tree with leaves around my ankles!

Just like that, Coral could feel the rain and wind again. She felt split between two worlds but kept up her mantra.

The kerosene is in my hands. It's heavy.

She could feel the weight of the canister.

Randy looked at her, alarmed. "What do you think you're doing?"

"What I have to do!"

Randy, Lincoln, and the mob disappeared.

"Quick, Mom. Quick. The matches."

Coral dug in her pockets and found them. They were soaked. She collapsed to her knees sobbing as a voice said, "Ladies and Gentlemen…"

Coral looked up and saw Randy addressing the mob. "Don't do this, Randy!" she screamed.

He ignored her pleas and continued, "This slave has been accused of raping my beautiful daughter, Melinda. As the owner of this land and founder of this township, I am exercising the authority vested in me by God, and am hereby punishing him to death by hanging for his crimes."

Lincoln stared into Randy's eyes, noticing for the first time the similarity with his own. The ache at this realization somehow hurt more deeply than the gaping gash in his gut where Randy had stabbed him. Lincoln could barely focus. The pain was excruciating. He might bleed out if he didn't get pressure on the wound soon.

The rough twine of the noose scratched his neck as Lafitte encircled his head with the rope. Then the mansion fell away in a disorienting blur. One reality melted away, only to reveal another right behind the curtain. In this reality, Lincoln sat astride a horse, his hands tied behind his back. The heat was stifling. He and the horse were underneath the shade of a large tree in the front lawn of an antebellum plantation house, the mid-morning sun blinding him.

He looked at his naked body. The damage he saw took his breath away. He was mired in a screaming chorus of swollen insect bites. There was a circular wound of cauterized flesh where his manhood had once been. Lincoln nearly fell off the horse, the pain emanating from his groin was so profound.

What did I do to deserve this?

Lincoln couldn't remember.

He raised his head and looked upon an angry mob. Their eyes screamed for the sort of retribution only bloodshed could bring.

Before them, Randy Lafitte stood with his back to Lincoln, reading from some strange rolled up paper.

Please God, let them hang me and be done with it!

A wave of lightheadedness overtook him as his eyes fell on Coral Lafitte kneeling for some reason in a pile of wet leaves. She held a match. Irrational hope consumed him.

Light it, Coral! Blast this tree to fucking hell!

But Coral cowered as her husband turned to Lincoln and said, "Do you have any last words?"

Lincoln was struck by déjà vu. He'd been here before. He knew what he was supposed to say, but seeing Coral gave him pause.

Karen struggled to get to her feet. To her surprise it was daytime. Light streamed into the house from all angles.

Is it over?

She gazed around, hope turning into despair as she recognized where and when she was. They were too late. Something shifted within her abdomen. There was a kick. Karen looked down, mouth wide.

A baby!

She cradled her protruding belly in wonder. This wonder became dismay as she heard shouting from outside. She went to the open door and saw a crowd of people standing around the tree. A black man sat on a horse wearing a noose around his neck. Her father was addressing the crowd.

I'm not too late! I can stop this!

Karen ran up the stairs with purpose. She made her way into the attic and climbed out the one window, nearly breathless. She stepped out onto the ledge and prepared to jump. Then a voice spoke up from behind her.

"I've got you, Karen. Don't worry." Arms enfolded her waist pulling her away from destiny.

"No!" she screamed. "I love him. He can't kill him!"

"I don't have any idea what you're talking about, girl, but we gotta get out of here."

Karen turned to see Brandon holding her upright. But that didn't make any sense. How did he get here?

She looked around and realized they were standing in the living room. She looked up to see her father push Lincoln off the landing.

The first explosion rocked the house as gravity took hold of Lincoln's body.

Lincoln was cast out into space. He felt the freedom of weightlessness before invisible anchors tethered to his ankles began jerking him to his death. He wondered if the noose around his throat would snap his neck (bringing instant mortality), or slowly strangle the life out of him.

He'd rather go quick.

Everything morphed again as he fell. The great room gave way to the outdoors and the screaming mob. Then the full weight of his body was snapped rigid by the rope around his neck. The noose cinched tight against his jaw, creating an excruciating burning sensation. His already raspy breath was sucked from his lungs, as his neck muscles stretched to the breaking point.

But his neck did not snap.

Inertia swung his body in a semicircle, around to where he knew Melinda and their love child lay dead.

At least we will go together.

But Melinda hadn't jumped and something was burning. The darkness called to him and Lincoln followed. It felt like falling.

Coral had given up hope when, miraculously, her second-to-last match lit. If she'd been outside the protective canopy of the trees leaves there's no way the match would have caught fire. Clearly, someone or something was helping her. Unfortunately, it had a very short fuse. Before she could properly light the kerosene-soaked leaves, the fire was nipping at her fingertips. She dropped the match with a cry and was nearly blinded by a greedy burst of flame.

She shielded her eyes and fled from beneath Melinda Weeps, back out into the elements. Behind her, the ancient tree roared in agony. Coral was almost to the front door when an explosion from inside the house tossed her back into the night. Her home was torn open by brilliant bursts of fire.

The flames moved slowly until they located traces of spilled kerosene on her person. As her hair caught fire, instinct commanded her body to stop, drop, and roll. She writhed around on the ground until the flames were extinguished. Then she crawled back toward her burning home with one thought on her mind.

I have to save Karen.

Randy's elation became consternation as he watched Lincoln fall to his death.

Something was wrong. Things were different.

He looked around wildly.

Melinda isn't dead, he thought.

Through the window, Randy saw Melinda Weeps burst into reddish-orange flames. But that wasn't all that had gone wrong. Lincoln's rope had burned through.

I will finish him myself.

The explosion shook Randy to his knees. *What the fuck had exploded?* From this vantage, he watched the roof of his beautiful home start to cave in, chased to the ground by the relentless rain. He crawled to the banister and watched Lincoln's long fall to the first floor as his noose snapped. Randy got to his feet and hurried down the quivering spiral staircase to where Lincoln lay defenseless.

Brandon got Karen just outside the front door before the first explosion. But he'd lost his balance and dropped her as the force from the blast sent them flying.

Karen felt Melinda's presence dissipate as soon as she hit the ground. She felt lighter and freer until Kristopher invaded her mental space.

"*I'm back,*" Kristopher spoke inside her mind.

"What's happening, Kristopher?" Karen yelled as the roof in the great room crumbled.

"*You did it. Isaac and Melinda are gone. It's almost over.*"

It didn't feel anywhere close to being over. As the shockwave of the first explosion dispersed, three more ripped through the house. At least the bombs Brandon had placed were working.

"*It's time to finish this,*" Kristopher said, taking control of her mind.

CHAPTER EIGHTY-THREE

Lincoln awoke to large chunks of plaster falling from the ceiling in a torrent. He was lying in several inches of water that was rising steadily. His handcuffs had broken in the fall and he was able to rub his sore wrists. Remembering the noose, he reached for his throat. Then he thought of Isaac.

We broke the cycle. Somehow, we did it.

A blast of heat brought him back to reality. The mansion was on fire. He had to get out before it was too late.

What about Brandon? Coral? Karen?

Lincoln struggled to sit up and was greeted by a searing ache in his lower back. He didn't know if he could walk, but he had to get up or die trying.

Sharp metal sliced into his shoulder. Lincoln screamed.

"Thought you were rid of me, Boy?" Randy Lafitte said from behind him.

Randy swung the blade again, just narrowly missing Lincoln's torso. Another chunk of ceiling crashed down next to Randy, knocking him off balance.

As adrenaline coursed through his veins, Lincoln lunged at Randy, slamming him into the staircase. Randy lost his grip on the knife and Lincoln could tell his adversary was weakening.

A giant funnel of wind was headed directly toward the house. Another explosion divided the men and threw Lincoln onto his back. The floor rumbled beneath them as the tornado rushed onshore and tore through the house. The bay windows buckled and then imploded, sending thousands of glass shards leaping at him. The roof flexed downward as if something heavy had landed on it, and then rippled upward. Lincoln stared into the center of hell as rain and glass whipped him.

As the roof went, the chandelier broke free and nearly crushed him. Randy was not so lucky. He'd recovered the knife, only to be stopped in his tracks by the falling fixture. Randy grunted and went silent.

Thankfully, the knife was just out of Randy's reach. The collapse had also knocked off his mask. Amazingly, not only was Randy still alive, his hand was floundering for his weapon.

Lincoln made his way back to Randy, and the knife. He was about to pick it up and finish him off when a thought gave him pause.

"Who would want to kill their own father?"

"Aren't you trying to do the same thing?"

Was he? Lincoln had never hesitated to kill in the past. In the hood and in prison, that type of hesitation got you killed. He wasn't in prison anymore though.

The patio door blew open and the lake poured in, interrupting these thoughts. Before he could reconsider, Lincoln cleared the chandelier off Randy, pulled him to his feet and carried him to the front door before the water dragged them both to their deaths. He got Randy outside and closed the door on the chaos, only to see the tree where Isaac had died completely engulfed in flames.

He dropped Randy in a heap on the front steps. He couldn't believe what was happening right before his eyes.

The tree was burning and surrounded by an ominous red glow. There was a square opening in the trunk. It appeared to be a doorway. As he watched, Karen Lafitte ran across the yard and into the mysterious portal while Brandon held her hysterical mother back.

"Karen!" Coral screamed. "What are you doing? You'll die in there!"

A moment later, Karen was swallowed whole by the void. It might have only been his imagination, but as she entered, Lincoln swore he heard the tree howl in agony. Then the rain, raging wind, and fire shut off like someone threw a switch. Seconds later, Kris Lafitte stepped out of the hole and walked toward Lincoln.

Holy shit!

Lincoln's mouth gaped as his best friend and brother approached. He didn't know how to react. Coral had the right idea. She fainted away in Brandon's arms.

"Kris?" he stammered. "Is that really you?"

"Sure is," Kris said, smiling. "As real as I get these days anyway."

Lincoln moved to hug him and hesitated.

"Go ahead, Link. I'm real enough for that."

They embraced. Lincoln kept repeating, "I'm so sorry."

"It's okay, Link. I'm sorry, too. Sorry you got dragged into the craziness of this family."

"I was a little more involved than that," Lincoln admitted.

"Not really," Kris replied. "Kidnapping Karen wasn't your idea. You weren't even looking to get out of prison until you met Amir and Panama X."

"You know about them?"

"Of course. How do you think I got here? It was their belief that brought me back."

Lincoln hadn't been clued in on that part of the plan. Had he known, he never would have agreed.

"So, you're here to kill me, right?" he asked.

Kris looked disappointed. "Not even close. I'm here to finish what I started ten years ago. But this time I don't have to worry about getting sidetracked having to save your black ass." He smirked.

"So what happened that day at Simmons Park had nothing to do with the curse?"

Kris frowned. "After all you've seen, do you still believe in coincidences, Link?"

Lincoln looked back at his friend and replied, "No. I guess not. So Randy set you up then?"

"I set myself up," Kris said. "I believed in the curse from the moment I learned of it. I couldn't bear the idea of someone in my family suffering just because I had another birthday, so I figured I'd end it early. But you put a monkey wrench in that plan, didn't you?"

"If you would have died that day you tried to hang yourself…"

"It wouldn't have changed a thing for Karen when she turned eighteen. But because of you I got the chance to come back and finally set things right. Speaking of which, where's that devilish Dad of ours?"

Lincoln looked around to see that Randy wasn't where he'd left him. He heard a grunt and saw Brandon topple over in the yard. Randy stood with his arm around Coral's throat, pressing that strange revolver to her head.

"If you move," he growled, "I'm gonna blow your mother's head off."

"No," Kris whispered.

The gun flipped out of Randy's hand. One second, Kris was standing next to Lincoln; the next, he stood behind Randy.

"Let her go," Kris commanded.

Randy's arms flew up and Coral dropped to the ground. His body did a 180-degree turn until he faced his son. Lincoln saw how much he was straining to regain control over his body.

"Wow, Dad," Kris greeted his father. "Hate sure has made you ugly."

"You don't scare me," Randy said.

"You don't have enough sense to be scared, Dad. But don't worry, where you're going, they will put that fear back in you."

"Not. Going. Anywhere."

Kris looked at Lincoln and shrugged as if to say, *"See what I have to deal with?"*

"When you started this all those years ago, you had to know it would end this way, right, Dad? I mean, you have been a one-man wrecking ball for over forty years. Doesn't it get old? The lies? The money? The power?"

Randy glared back at Kris. "Never," he spat.

"Oh well, you clearly can't be helped," Kris said. "So I'm going to take you back to a time before all this. Back when you should have taken your own miserable life."

Confusion wrapped Randy's face and was abruptly replaced by horror. Lincoln saw stripes of blood begin to soak through Randy's shirt. They resembled knife slashes and Randy screamed with each new slash. His features began to change.

Lincoln watched the man regress backward through the years. His hair returned, his face lost its lines, and his frame diminished until he looked like the boy Kris had once been. The younger he became, the more bloody slashes appeared on his clothes until his shirt and pants were blood-soaked messes. In moments, Randy was a teenager again.

He fell to his knees in so much pain he couldn't even scream.

"And to think, this is just a small portion of the pain you've caused others," Kris remarked. "Imagine if I turned up the volume."

"No-no-no please don't...please," Randy blabbered.

"You have to choose, Dad," Kris said. The revolver appeared in his hand. "You can come with me." He looked at the portal in the tree's center. "Or you can end your own life."

"You know my choice," Randy answered.

"Yes," Kristopher replied, putting the gun to Randy's temple. "I knew you'd take the easy way out. Lucky for me you already tried and failed to kill yourself today, so come on, let's see what we've got behind door number two."

Randy howled as Kris lifted him over his head and threw him into the portal. Once it absorbed him, the doorway contracted, sucking the tree away with it.

"See you on the other side, Link," Kris said, fading away as well. "Make the most of the time you've got left."

Then he was gone.

EPILOGUE

One Year Later
Angola, LA

Lincoln Baker's life story lay between the pages of a scrapbook, thrown carelessly under the cot of his windowless Death Row cell. He hadn't looked at it since Moses brought it to him after the trial. He'd been too busy preparing to die. Lincoln had thought he was running out of firsts; however, the past twelve months had proven him wrong.

Lincoln made his way to where the tree had stood and found Karen Lafitte lying on the ground, with her eyes open and unseeing. He thought her dead until she blinked for the first time in minutes. Lincoln helped her over to where Brandon was just waking up. Coral remained unconscious.

Once the four of them were huddled together, the sun rose, casting a kaleidoscope of color across the hurricane-ravaged landscape formerly known as Lake City. Lincoln had seen plenty of sunrises in his life, but none even came close to rivaling the breathtaking beauty he witnessed the morning after Isaac's landing.

Lincoln spent a few days in a Baton Rouge hospital to heal his many wounds, once they were able to get out of the city.

The police escort helped.

Despite Brandon's protests, Lincoln had gone to the Lake City PD and unspooled a stunning confession of his kidnapping of Karen Lafitte and his direct role in the murders that ravaged the city. But no matter how much they bullied and badgered him, Lincoln wouldn't cop to the disappearance of Governor Lafitte, the destruction of the Lafitte estate, or offer an explanation for Coral Lafitte's vegetative state. The poor woman never recovered from the events of that night and had to be placed in assisted living.

All charges against Brandon were dropped.

The media was out of control.

Headlines like, *"The Monster Within the Monster,"* shocked the nation's collective consciousness. Countless stories were written about the flawed justice system. New legislation was proposed that would allow violent criminals seventeen and younger to be executed. The president expressed his sorrow for the victims of Hurricane Isaac in one breath, and condemned Lincoln Baker in the next. Karen was poked and prodded like a lab rat as her parents were upheld as tragic victims of a madman. Reporters embarrassed themselves trying to get the exclusive. Psychiatrists begged Lincoln to donate his brain to science so they could isolate the black insanity gene.

Through it all, Lincoln declined to comment and stoically awaited trial.

Another circus pitched its big top outside of the institution formerly known as the Louisiana State Penitentiary. Ninety-five percent of the prison population died during the storm. The warden disappeared, and with him went any explanation of this utter disregard for human life. For weeks afterwards, little to no news was reported regarding the mass deaths at Angola. Not until Jhonnette Deveaux and Moses Mouton emerged from the wreckage as two innocents, amazingly spared. It wasn't long before the powers that be tried to shut Jhonnette and Moses up. But the damage was already done.

Louisiana was in shambles.

With Randy Lafitte missing, opportunistic scavengers such as Bill Edwards vied for his post. The media cast Edwards as a hero, despite his shady past.

They were that desperate for leadership.

Polls taken a month after Hurricane Isaac indicated Edwards would be the frontrunner in the upcoming emergency gubernatorial election. But that all changed after Lincoln's trial.

Lincoln fasted and prayed from sun up, until sundown in preparation for the trial.

He marched calmly into the courtroom as uneasy murmurs rose from the peanut gallery. He didn't *look* like a crazed, murderous, criminal mastermind. The prosecution, armed with Lincoln's confession, assumed this would be an open and shut trial.

That all changed the moment Lincoln was asked to enter his plea. The headlines that evening said it all, *"Lincoln Baker: Not*

Guilty By Reason of Insanity?"

Politicians blustered, pundits raged, and late night TV personalities joked.

Then the defense began its case.

There had been more public memorials, eulogies, and declarations of Randy Lafitte's greatness and contributions than Lady Diana had after her untimely death. But there had been little to no examination of the facts. Lincoln's defense doled those facts out in deliberate and excruciating detail during the trial.

They told of a ruthless killer who'd eliminated everyone that ever got in his way, including his father Joseph, Walter Simmons, and far worse, his own son Kristopher. Even the atrocities at Angola were linked to him. Lafitte went from Gandhi to Hitler in the course of a few days testimony. Bill Edwards' tight association to Lafitte was the flame that exploded his political aspirations.

Before the defense rested, Lincoln asked to address the court.

"Your Honor," Lincoln began. "I would like to change my plea."

The judge frowned. "Mr. Baker, do not toy with my court. This is highly irregular. On what grounds are you changing your plea?"

"Well, Your Honor, it's true that I was on the insane side when I did all those terrible things. But the truth is...I've been insane a lot longer than that. I've been insane ever since I was separated from my birth mother. I was insane when I started banging when I was nine years old. I was insane when I killed all those people that day at Simmons Park. I was insane sitting on twenty-three hour lockdown with nothing to keep me company but my own insane life story—"

"Mr. Baker, if you have a point, please get to it. My patience is wearing thin."

Lincoln found Moses' eyes in the courtroom and gave him a subtle nod. "Yes sir, Your Honor. My point is…someone as crazy as me doesn't deserve to live. Even if I was pushed into this by Randy Lafitte. It doesn't excuse the life I've lived, and the lives I've taken. So, I'm changing my plea to guilty. Guilty of letting my past corrupt my future. Guilty of playing the victim while I victimized others— mostly my own people. Guilty of not forgiving anyone who ever hurt me. I stand here before you, guilty of all this and more. It's time for me to be the example I always should have been."

And that's all he would say until the day of his execution arrived.

After that speech, Lincoln thought they would have drug him into the street for an old-fashioned Louisiana lynching. But that didn't happen. It seemed it was nearly impossible to kill someone who *wanted* to die in this country.

He became everyone's pet cause.

Liberals lobbied for clemency. Right-wingers hired assassins. Christians elected him as the false prophet signaling the end-times. Satanists, for once, agreed.

Lincoln ordered a feast of crawfish, potatoes, and corn for his last meal. Everyone he cared about came to see him off. Moses, Brandon, Jhonnette, and even Karen Lafitte showed up.

They ate and talked.

Brandon and Karen spoke of starting college in a few weeks. Seeing them together gave Lincoln hope. Brandon had accepted a basketball scholarship at Florida A&M University in Tallahassee, Florida and Karen would be attending Florida State right up the street.

Jhonnette independently published Malcolm Wright's memoirs and started her own fictionalized book about the Curse of the Weeping Cypress, Walter Simmons' murder, the Simmons Park Massacre, Karen Lafitte's kidnapping, and the subsequent events. She called it, *One Blood.*

"But in my version," she said, choking up, "the hero goes free."

With only twenty minutes left, Jhonnette, Brandon, and Karen took turns hugging and kissing Lincoln goodbye.

"I wish we could have met under different circumstances," he said to Jhonnette. "You are the most beautiful woman I've ever met. You would have made me a better man."

With tears in her eyes, Jhonnette gave him one last squeeze and then left the room without looking back.

Lincoln turned to Brandon, his tears flowing freely now. "Little man, well, you ain't so little now. You are gonna be great. I've known it since I first laid eyes on you. But you got to let go of your anger. If you don't, you might end up...like me."

Brandon looked down at the ground.

"Look at me, Brandon."

Brandon complied.

"You know I love you, right?"

"I know," Brandon replied.

"Good. Now I want you to go out there and show the world what you're made of. I want you to go after your dreams and don't let nothing stop you, aight?"

"I will," Brandon replied through his sobs.

"You got a good woman here," Lincoln said, turning to Karen. "And you are her only family now."

Karen flinched.

"Don't let nothing ever separate ya'll. Not these ignorant bigots out here who don't understand what you got between you, not anybody. Can ya'll do that?"

They both nodded.

"Okay. I love ya'll."

Brandon hugged him fiercely and then let him go. Taking Karen's hand, they walked to the door.

Karen stopped and turned around. "Lincoln?"

"Yeah?"

"I want you to know that I don't hate you. None of this was your fault. Everything is gonna be alright now, okay?"

Lincoln nodded his thanks as they left the room.

After he collected himself, he looked at the only father he'd ever known. He was glad they had this time alone together, here at the end.

"Thanks for coming, Pop," he said quietly.

Moses nodded and patted his hand. They stared at each other from across the table.

"You know the thing I've been trying to figure out?" Lincoln asked, finally.

"What's that?" Moses replied.

Lincoln smiled. "What were you doing at Angola that day?"

Moses' smile faltered and he looked away.

"What? What is it?"

"It doesn't matter anymore, Son," Moses whispered.

"Oh, come on! They're getting ready to end me. Least you could do is be straight with me."

Moses stood up, knees popping, and ran his fingers through his salt and pepper afro.

"I'm sorry for yelling," Lincoln said. "Please sit back down. Please?"

Moses considered this and then his shoulders slumped in a gesture of defeat. He sat back down.

"Lincoln," he began. "What I'm going to tell you has no bearing on anything. I want you to know that."

"Okay, Pop," Lincoln replied uneasily.

"That day. I came that day to confront Panama...I mean Malcolm."

"Confront him about what?" Lincoln asked.

"Don't make me tell you, Son. You're better off not knowing, believe me."

"I want to know," Lincoln said, no longer slouching in his chair. Crawfish were burrowing deep in his gut.

"Okay. Here goes." He exhaled deeply. "Son, you know that Randy Lafitte killed Walter Simmons, right?"

"Of course."

"Well, that's only one side of the story."

Dear God.

Lincoln steeled himself. He was more afraid of what Moses was about to say than anything he'd ever faced in his life.

"You sure you want to hear this?"

Lincoln wasn't sure of anything anymore, but he motioned for Moses to go on.

"I was there that night. I went to talk to Walter about a sermon. When I got there, his office was on fire. Up on his floor, someone broke down the door from the inside. It was your mother. And someone else."

"Who?"

"Malcolm."

Lincoln's head was swimming. *Why hadn't Panama X ever told him this?*

"Juanita thought she was protecting you. She didn't even know the whole truth until later. Until she saw your face for the first time."

"What truth!" Lincoln screamed. A guard knocked on the door, signaling the end of their time.

Moses blurted out the rest.

"This is going to sound crazy, but somehow Malcolm took over Walter's body the day before he was murdered. He had sex with your mother as Walter and that moment decided everything else. The next day, Randy forced Walter's secretary to call your mother at gunpoint, threw Walter in the closet, and waited for Juanita to arrive. Juanita said that seeing you for the first time sparked a memory she'd repressed for years. A memory of what happened after she went into Walter's office. Before Malcolm broke her out."

"How do you know all this?" Lincoln asked.

"We found it with Amir's effects in a shoebox. There was a letter she'd written to Malcolm that she never mailed."

The guards opened the doors as Moses said, "She was raped, Lincoln. Randy raped her."

Lincoln had accepted that Randy was his father, and now he knew how it had happened. But he was still confused.

"What do you mean, Malcolm took over Walter Simmon's body?"

"I wouldn't believe it either if I hadn't seen it with my own eyes. But Malcolm was somehow able to insert himself into someone else's body temporarily. He took over Walter's body to be with Juanita."

Lincoln's mind was on fire. "Are you saying that either Randy or Malcolm was my father?"

Moses met his eyes. "Malcolm was deluded, Lincoln. Even if his laying with Juanita did impregnate her, you would still be Walter's child."

Lincoln processed Moses' words as the guards tried to cuff him. He struggled and the battering began. They held him down until they chained him. They held Moses back.

As they dragged him out of there, Moses yelled, "Lincoln! Son! This doesn't change anything! It doesn't take away anything you've done!"

Moses kept yelling, but Lincoln could barely hear him over his own truculent thoughts. His head swirled as the guards brought him into the injection center, a tiny room that became very cramped with the four men, gurney, and heart monitor currently crowding its space. They didn't waste any time strapping him onto the gurney. He was immediately relieved that his last wish had been honored.

The gallery seating before the room's only window was blessedly empty. Lincoln held no illusions he would die in peace, but at least he'd limited the number of people who would know how he went.

Didn't I make the right choice, Kris?

Lincoln knew that Kris couldn't communicate with him anymore, but over the past year he'd kept up an ongoing dialogue with the friend he'd be joining any minute now.

They affixed telemetry wires to his newly shaved torso. The executioner/physician entered as two of the three guards left, their duties done. He pressed a button and the heart-rate monitor came to life, conveying the news one bleep at a time that Lincoln lived, for now. The physician swabbed both of his arms, filling the room with the scent of rubbing alcohol.

Next, an I.V. was inserted into his right arm. The physician moved around the gurney to insert another into his left arm. Lincoln had read about the process of his death and knew that only one I.V. was necessary to carry out his execution. The other was reserved as a backup in case the primary line failed.

"Starting saline drip," the physician said to a man who'd just entered. Lincoln turned his head and laid his eyes on the new Warden, a hard-looking brown-skinned black man with narrow soul-piercing eyes and a mammoth face covered partially in unkempt black and grey whiskers.

"Proceed, Doctor."

Lincoln took his eyes off the Warden and focused back on Moses' revelation. Jhonnette had explicitly told him he was definitely Randy's son. Just like Isaac had been Luc Lafitte's illegitimate child. Still, hadn't Panama X always treated him like his son as well?

The saline flowed freely through his veins. Next, Lincoln would receive three sequential I.V. injections. The first would be sodium thiopental to render him temporarily unconscious. This would be followed by an injection of pancuronium to paralyze his skeletal and respiratory muscles, resulting in eventual death by asphyxiation. Finally, he would receive potassium chloride to stop his heart for good.

I need to know the truth.

This final uncertainty was a fate worse than anything awaiting him in the syringes.

"Administering sodium thiopental," the physician remarked in a tone similar to how Lincoln imagined he would tell his wife he was headed out for groceries.

"Thank you, Doctor," the Warden replied. "This is it, Lincoln. Do you have any last words?"

Panic descended over Lincoln and he blurted the first thing that came to him. "Looks are deceiving!"

He noted the Warden's perplexed expression as he simultaneously felt like something was dragging him into a deep dark hole. He tried to fight this sensation with the entirety of his being, but he was overmatched. Before he was swallowed by the void, his last conscious thought was a desperate plea for another chance.

"He's out," the physician stated.

"Good," the Warden replied. "Let's get this over with."

"Excuse me, Miss, you can't be in here!"

"You're very wrong about that," Jhonnette Deveaux replied before blowing a dark substance into the faces of the Warden and physician.

The doctor dropped the I.V. needle and collapsed.

Jhonnette unstrapped Lincoln, and then paused to sling an eye-patch through her hair and over her right eye.

Lincoln knew the darkness well. He'd lived in life's considerable shadow since birth. But he'd never experienced anything quite like the deep dark that swallowed him after that second injection. At first, there was nothing, and then he felt the blackness enclosing around and within him like a living, breathing organism determined to crush him with its oppressive weight.

For a long while, he fought against this beast until he heard faint beeps similar to Monday morning trash pick-ups back when he lived with Moses.

I'm never going to see Moses again. I'm not going to see what kind of man Brandon becomes.

These facts were unbearable. Lincoln burrowed out of the black hole like someone buried alive. He clawed at the dirty grime of his subconscious trying to find purpose. An indeterminable amount of time passed before he eventually pulled himself through the final layer of mental dirt. Until he felt the darkness release him.

Lincoln's body rushed forward from the back of his mind to full awareness. The first sensations of waking were of mingled pain and stiffness. He was having trouble breathing. And he wasn't alone.

Lincoln opened his eyes, just like he'd done in another hospital room long ago, and saw Jhonnette hovering over him. She was wearing an eye-patch like Panama X and smiled a brilliant smile at the sight of him.

"Welcome back to the realm of the living, Lincoln. I told you your story wasn't over. Consider yourself reborn."

ACKNOWLEDGEMENTS

Wow, so this is what it feels like to write an Acknowledgements section—alternately exhilarating and unnerving. Well, it took me nearly twelve years to get to these final words and I promise to make them count!

There's no way I can take sole credit for this novel, I've had far too much help from far too many collaborators to be that bold, or delusional.

The first seeds of the novel, originally titled Simmons Park, were planted when I read **Stephen King's** It, The Dark Tower series, and The Stand. The water on the seeds planted by Stephen King definitely came in the form of **Harper Lee's** To Kill a Mockingbird and **Richard Wright's** Native Son. Their powerful examinations of race from two wholly different perspectives showed me that great books had to do more than entertain, they had to educate as well. Bigger Thomas from Native Son was actually the beginning of Lincoln Baker. I imagined taking up where Wright had left off with Bigger and examining what Bigger would do with a second chance. **Anne Rice's** The Witching Hour was the sun shedding light into the darkest parts of my psyche. But the seeds didn't fully germinate until I discovered **Wilbur Smith's** The River God and **Tananarive Due's** work—most especially The Between, The Good House, and The Living Blood. One Blood would not exist in its current format without the master classes in fluid prose, setting, character development, pacing, and the importance of details given to me while reading these amazing works.

I began this process a true amateur who dared to start a novel after never having written anything longer than a poem. This book has had many incarnations and setbacks over the years. Every leap forward came as a result of seeking creativity beyond the rough caves of my imagination. As a young writer, it is important to invest time in learning about your craft. I still have the notes I took in that January Creative Writing Class at Florida A&M University during the 2000 Spring Semester. It was in this class that a writing exercise inspired the initial idea for the story.

I looked for inspiration in other writers, but also found it in the form of feedback from several key early readers:

Nekeisha B., you were the first person to ever invest precious time reading over my early drafts. Your words of encouragement kept me going in those hard early days.

Tony H., you challenged my initial premises and forced me to step up my game. I hope to follow in your footsteps and be as successful as you have been with *The Invisible Enemy: Black Fox* and *The Invisible Enemy II: Vendetta*.

Alicia S., you were so right! I'm four years late from our original publication timeline…thanks so much for all your support in the early years. You are one of the few people who were there at the very beginning of my writing career. I can't wait to hear what you think about the book.

Zakiya C-J, our mutual love of Stephen King and shared living experience in Brazil (and astrology – Cancers rule!) has created a great friendship. I remember nervously handing over pages to you and the feedback you gave me came at a crucial juncture.

I completed the first draft of the novel at that time titled *Bad Blood* in May 2006. Based on advice I'd taken to heart from Stephen King's On Writing, I printed out several copies of my book and sent them off to a few close friends for their thoughts:

Mike M., aka the one-man-book-club, you were the first person to complete my book, back when you were my boss. You read it in like 3 days, carrying an additional 8 pounds in your luggage. You correctly identified the fact that I'd written *Sunbird* (a novel by Wilbur Smith) when I should have written *The River God*. Can't wait to hear your thoughts on the final product inspired by your feedback.

Samantha T., I still remember sitting in my flat in Brazil and nearly tearing up when you said, "I love it." More beautiful words have never been expressed. Isn't it funny how parallel our lives have been over the years? I can't wait to reciprocate for you with *Seventeen Seasons*.

Julye A., you don't even read fiction and yet you took the time to read my book. Your enthusiasm has definitely kept me going in the tough editing moments since you finished. The "Big Joker" didn't make the final cut, but I hope you dig the book, nonetheless.

Aunt Sandra, your stewardship and advice has meant the world to me. Knowing I had someone within 2 degrees who had a book in bookstores (*Faradays Popcorn Factory*—check it out!) made me believe my dream was possible.

Ceallaigh P., you were there when I got to the end the second time around, and your laser sharp insights definitely contributed to the elevated level of the story—especially your thoughts on how badly I had written Juanita's pregnancy scene!

Courtney W., my last official roommate! Thanks for always being a welcome ear to bounce ideas off of. **Andrew M.**, aka Groo Man, Juanita Simmons crawls like an "awkward spider" thanks to your feedback! **Brad and Emily H.**, our many discussions on race over the years have been very enlightening. Thanks for always welcoming me into your home! **Jeremy C.**, the fact that I could impress you with some of the early chapters let me know I had something. **Tanisha L.**, I know you couldn't get through it, hopefully it will be better this time! **Steve P.**, my best friend since 1995, thanks for always being in my corner! **Canise J.**, I appreciated your willingness to read those pages and be a part of the beginning of TPC! **Fede, aka Rico**, our many conversations about life were so important. Thanks for being my brother, friend, and great early reader. **Lauren M.**, you came into my life at the perfect moment and immediately made a significant impact that extends far beyond writing!

No book would be possible without editing, the least glamorous, most grueling, and arguably most thankless task of book production. I have had the extreme fortune of having 6 outstanding editors over the years:

Michelle Chester, my first editor, you had no idea what you were signing up for after we met at the Black Writer's Reunion and Conference (BWRC), did you? Looking back on it now, would you ever again agree to content *and* copyedit a six-hundred page, one hundred eighty thousand word behemoth in 2 weeks? But you pulled it off, and in the process showed me how much work I still had left to do!

My sis, **Sameerah**! I could write a one hundred twenty-thousand word book using only the phrase THANK YOU and it still wouldn't accurately express how much I appreciate what you have done for me, unsolicited, to make this book a reality. You took it upon yourself to not only read, but edit the book TWICE! Your discipline and work ethic have always inspired me. I may be your older brother but I have learned a lot from watching you blossom over the course of our lives.

Ms. Anita Diggs, the manuscript editor, thank you for forcing me to address many serious issues with my manuscript, from character motivation to genre. Your feedback was a bitter pill to swallow, but like most medicine that tastes bad going down, it got the job done.

Stephanie Casher, aka KINDRED, meeting you changed my life. I had no idea back then just how pivotal you would prove to become – the official editor of *One Blood* (I'm sorry for putting you through hell twice!), my business partner with the Pantheon Collective, and my business conscience reminding me to slow down and smell the roses every now and again. I am so happy we have taken this independent publishing journey together. It goes without saying that your editing perfectionism, skill, and professionalism is unmatched. Authors, consider yourself exceptionally *blessed* if you ever get some of Stephanie Casher's magic red ink on your manuscript.

James W. Lewis, aka BigLew, J-Willy, Captain America, and TPC Leading Man, suffice it to say, I'm so happy you "stalked" Stephanie on Mondella's blog, haha. I am very appreciative of how our relationship has grown. You have taught me a ton about what it takes to be a successful author. Your hustle is unparalleled and your feedback as one of the final readers of *One Blood* was the icing on this bloody cake. Thank you for showing me the value of keeping things simple!

Author and Editor, Cateena Davis, put the final spit shine on *One Blood*, completing three lightning fast (but thorough) proofreads, and doing the final check that all my t's were crossed and i's were dotted. Thanks for your responsiveness, flexibility, availability, and help!

I also have to give a huge thank you to the entire **Gotham Writer's Workshop 2010 Spring Advanced Novel II writing class** led by **Diana Spechler,** author of *Who By Fire* and *Skinny*. **Terri, Kathryn, Sue, Mia, Sam, Patrizia, Todd, Frank, Elizabeth, and Nick**, thank you for all the feedback and challenges. Your collective fingerprints are all over the first 50 pages of this novel, which got considerably better as a result of your questioning. I can't wait to see the final incarnations of each of your projects as well!

Urbis.com was a huge resource to get real-time feedback from other writers on problem chapters.

The entire **Black on Black Rhyme family** and especially **Keith, Hazel, Shadow, Paul D., Ali, Salaam, and Brotha John – The Ancient Newcomer,** thanks for expanding my world and accepting me into this awesome collective! You showed me the power of collaboration and bringing the right group of people together at an early age!

Tia Ross, thank you for starting and maintaining the **Black Writer's Reunion and Conference**. Without you, The Pantheon Collective and our books *Sellout, When Love Isn't Enough, A Hard Man is Good to Find*, and *One Blood* might not exist.

Book Expo America Writer's Conference, thank you for providing a place for writers to up their I.Q. on the business of publishing. It was only through attending three of your conferences that I gained the confidence, and more importantly, the knowledge to get into independent publishing.

Literary agents who rejected my manuscript, thank you for forcing me to turn a lump of coal into a diamond. You knew I wasn't ready back when I thought I was, and you became the fuel for everything that has come since. I get it now, and respect your role, and more importantly, your process more than ever.

Book Cover Express: Cathi Stevenson – you took the image I've had in my head for years for the book cover and elevated it to another level. You were amazing to work with and I look forward to many future collaborations.

Multivision Productions: Rob, Edu, Ricky; Raven and Monica (makeup); Sheik (drums), and Danielle (actor) – it was amazing to see a scene from my head unfold on film. What a team! You all exceeded my expectations in every way. The book trailer you created was worth every penny!

Vanessa V., of Girls Gone Geek and Professional Illustrator David Benzal: I admit to being quite nervous about having virtual stranger bring my characters to life, but your recommendation weighed a ton Vanessa! And as soon as I saw David's vision for Randy Lafitte, I knew he was the right man for the job. Congrats again on the new addition to your family, David! You have an amazing gift and I hope these illustrations you did for *One Blood* bring you a lot of additional lucrative interest!

Of course I have to thank **my parents: Samuel and Sameerah, my older brothers: John, Patrick, and Kamau, my younger sister: Sameerah, my Aunt Janis, my niece, Kiarra, and my nephew, Hamilton.** Everything I am, I owe to all of you. To **my grandmother, Mabel Harris**, who passed away earlier this year at the blessed age of ninety-four, I wish you had lived to see this day, but I am grateful for the lifetime of lessons you bestowed upon me.

And last but not least, I have to thank **YOU**, for taking the time to read my debut novel and this rather lengthy acknowledgements section. Every writer claims to write for his/herself but at some point we have to get out of our own way and let the world have it. I know *One Blood* will be very safe in your hands and I look forward to many journeys to come. As always, Amazon reviews are greatly appreciated!

Qwantu Amaru
Jersey City, NJ
11/27/2011

Also Available from TPC Books